ABOUT THE AUTHOR

Dave Currey has over thirty years experience at the forefront of the environmental movement.

Pioneering undercover investigations as a co-founder of the Environmental Investigation Agency (EIA), he has sleuthed all over the world: posing as a businessman, tourist, photographer or bridegroom exposing criminal networks in Europe, Africa, Asia, North and South America.

Trained as a photographer, his campaign pictures have appeared in international magazines and newspapers including spreads in LIFE, The Sunday Times Magazine, The Daily Telegraph Magazine, and BBC Wildlife.

He has co-produced eleven award-winning television documentaries including the *Animal Detectives* series and co-written *To Save an Elephant* (Doubleday), a true story of infiltrating the international ivory trade. As EIA's executive director he has been a familiar face on television and in the press.

He is a recipient of the Albert Schweitzer Medal for "his work in protecting elephants and dolphins" and EIA was awarded the Global 500 Roll of Honour by UNEP for "outstanding contributions to the protection of the environment."

For ten years, with Indonesian and EIA colleagues, he has exposed the international timber Mafia, successfully forcing the violent, gritty reality on wood buyers and international decision makers, creating change. This provides the background for his first novel *Stripped*.

He lives in London and Ibiza with his civil partner, artist Gary Hodges, and their two dogs.

www.wild-photos.co.uk

THANKS

Writing a novel is a fairly lonely business, other than spending hours with the fictional characters dragging you off in another unexpected direction. But my partner Gary was always there, quietly placing a glass of red wine next to my laptop and responding to my quizzical gaze encouragingly with "it's after six!" I think some of my best ideas came after six.

Ibiza is a magical place to think. Our wonderful home in the Mediterranean island's pine-clad hills provided me with different outlooks to place my laptop and my mind. Our two dogs usually somewhere close.

It may sound a little too cosy, but home, family and friends have been my bedrock for years, providing the strength to work undercover in difficult and sometimes dangerous circumstances. It's not easy watching hundreds of whales being cut to death, smelling the carcasses of elephants mowed down with AK47s, or learning what you inevitably learn after thirty years in the environmental movement. Cosy is good.

My friends and colleagues at EIA and our Indonesian partner NGO Telapak know what I mean. Sharing experiences with them has maintained the hope in my life. Meeting other activists in Indonesia and other parts of the world reminds me how many extraordinarily motivated and brave people there are providing our world with a future.

My manuscript went through many drafts after helpful and critical comments from a group of readers: Ashlee Carter, Gill Christie, Nick Clayton, Felicity Dixon, Gary Hodges, Tom Kooning, Rula Lenska, Jack Murray and Annie Quigley. Thank you for your support and advice.

It was my mum and dad, Barbara and Allan, who gave me an empathy with nature. It hurts so much to watch its destruction. I know you would both understand the pain if you were still with us. But without pain it would be impossible to feel the intense joy of life. Thank you for giving me mine.

STRIPPED

Dave Currey

Wild Press
7 Marlborough Mews
London SW2 5TE

First published in paperback 2010

Dave Currey asserts the moral right to
be identified as the author of this work

© Dave Currey 2010
www.wild-photos.co.uk

A catalogue record of this book is
available from the British Library

ISBN: 978-0-9566671-1-3

Printed by Lightning Source
FSC CoC Certificate holder
Chain of custody (CoC) ensures the integrity of the
paper supply chain from responsibly managed forests

To Gary

You have been there for me through so
much of my life. You are quite simply
everything to me. Aren't we lucky? The
party goes on …

BACKGROUND

Stripped is set mainly in Indonesia, the world's fourth largest country by population – mostly Muslim. Its new democracy was hard fought for – former military dictator Suharto is believed to have allowed the genocide of a million Indonesians in his clampdown on communism in the 60s, supported by the west. He went on to rule for 30 years.

Its forests, of which up to 30% of Indonesians are directly dependent, are under serious threat. They still represent the most important forest resource in Asia, home to 10% of planet earth's biodiversity. Their destruction is fuelled by commercial exploitation eased by corruption, driven by demand for wood products and palm oil in Europe, the USA, China and Japan.

But to me, Indonesia is best defined by its diversity. The archipelago of over 17,000 islands stretches 5,200 kms across the equator from Sumatra, which neighbours Malaysia, to Papua, north of Australia. Its people come from vastly different ethnic backgrounds, from indigenous Dayaks in Borneo to the Sultans of Java. Despite systemic corruption they survive on patience, community and a wealth of humour.

Indonesia's cultural diversity leaves me with a general optimism for the human race.

PROLOGUE
Borneo

Koto didn't know why he felt so bad.

It had been a lovely day; he had even hustled up some extra work. His best friend was back in town and his motorbike was back on the road, so at least he could get into town again. His mother had sent a message to say all was well in the village.

He lay on his mattress listening to the rain drumming on the corrugated iron roof, staring at his guitar lying next to the door.

Why was he feeling as if his world had collapsed?

This was Koto's world: the wet tropical climate of Borneo, rain drenching everything almost every day. Children died of disease and mothers in child birth. Those able, worked hard, but rarely had any money to spare. Family and tribal allegiances were of paramount importance. Life was lived day by day, but optimism still overpowered its enemies, happiness survived.

There had been a lot of heartache for him in the last couple of years since his father died of malaria but he had come to accept that, as the only son, at 26, he had to think of his five sisters and mother. That was made more difficult by the tribal anger that had grown into real violence only a few years before. As a Dayak son he had seen some of the rampaging across a nearby town and even seen some of the heads of foreigners on stakes next to the church. But he hadn't been part of it.

The fighting had started over control of logging areas. One of the Madurese businessmen had started hauling huge logs into his compound without talking first to the village chief, Kardi. Normally this kind of anger would be quelled by careful negotiation and money, but on this occasion there was already a family scandal concerning Kardi's niece and the businessman. This cocktail of power and personalities had led to a Dayak gang defending its "honour" with *traditional* beheadings. When Kardi had been found floating in a log pond the next morning, the bloodshed had spread faster than the forest fires they had been plagued with these last few years.

Koto's village in the Indonesian province of Central Kalimantan was divided by greed. Some of the men just wanted to work on their land, breed fish in their fishponds, and care for their families. It was enough for them to lie with their wives and get their joy from being part of a community. But none of the villages were far from the buzz of chainsaws; the money to be made promised a new world.

Already Koto realised the price to pay for that promise was too high. When his village chief had sold out to the logging baron, new water channels were dug just outside his village to move the logs, stripped from the dense tropical forest. Within six months the fishponds dried up and the villagers now found it difficult to live off their land. More of the men left to join the logging gangs.

Koto was lucky. As a teenager he was sent to Palankaraya, the provincial capital, and studied in a Christian missionary school. He had learned *bahasa* Indonesia, the common language throughout his vast country, and English. This had given him some real opportunities to earn money from the occasional tourist. He had been taking small groups of foreigners into the forest for five years now, explaining Dayak culture and showing them crocodiles, birds and orang-utans.

A few drops of rain splat on Koto's guitar and he rolled off his mattress towards the door to rescue it. Sometimes he lay on his mattress holding the guitar like a lover, just rolling backwards and forwards to a slow sexual rhythm. But tonight he just moved it out of the way of the water leaking through the roof.

He didn't even feel like love.

The day had started well when he had paid off the last money he owed on his bike repair. Feeling freed from the sleepy town of Kumai, where he lived, he had driven the half hour to the city airport at Pangkalan Bun to see if any tourists had arrived on the morning plane. No luck today, but he had run into one of his very best friends, Murkha, arriving from Jakarta. Murkha and Koto had known each other for ten years having met at the missionary school.

It was Murkha who had helped Koto move out of his village into Kumai, providing a home for the first two months with him and his wife Setin. Within weeks Koto had made enough money to send back to his mother and after two months had been able to pay for his simple room with a mattress, but big enough for him and his guitar.

"Hey Koto" giggled Murkha when he saw him at the big table situated under a sign saying "bagage colect" in almost unintelligible red letters. Koto and Murkha had once decided they would like to get the job of correcting all the misspelled English in Borneo, but of course no-one would really care.

Murkha always giggled rather than laughed out loud, but that was because he always seemed to be mischievously happy, and now more than ever. Setin had given birth to their first child, a girl, only months earlier and Murkha joked that at last there was someone on the planet who would understand him!

"Hey Brother, there was no need to come and get me! What are you doing here?" Murkha said a little unconvincingly. Koto felt a slight pang of sadness, sensing an unusual reticence in his friend's voice.

"I was bored and my bike is working again" replied Koto holding his hands out to encourage Murkha's chubby arms to embrace him. They held each other longer than either of them had expected before heading off together to see Setin and the baby.

Their house, like many others, was simple with four rooms made from cheap local timber probably stolen from the nearby national park. Setin was waiting outside, under a flock of brightly painted wooden birds hanging from a metal bracket, erected by Murkha just before he left for Jakarta. Murkha hugged and kissed Setin and gave her three black coral bracelets, one for her, the baby and himself. They lovingly put each others bracelet on while Koto pretended to check the wheel of his motorbike.

Setin had prepared *nasi goreng* for breakfast and a huge pot of coffee before leaving the two men to sit and talk. Koto was really surprised as he sensed anger in Setin. It was aimed at Murkha, not him, but he had never felt this from her before. These thoughts quickly left him as Murkha started talking at him really fast.

"So I've been a naughty boy" spluttered Murkha. "I think maybe very very naughty."

"What are you talking about?" questioned Koto, wondering if Setin had caught Murkha with some other woman. But strangely, if this was so, Koto didn't really want to hear about it.

"You know the Vietnamese ship that's been loading with logs all week?" he asked. "Well, last week I took photos of it and the other one waiting offshore, and have given them to a friend of mine in Jakarta, a well connected friend. I don't think those ships will get to Vietnam!" he chortled.

Koto and Murkha had often talked about the logging and the timber baron. They despised what was happening to their land and their people. The millions of dollars made by the baron's family every month were being used to corrupt everyone in the province. The police and military were totally bought out, and even the Governor. There was little chance for anyone to stand up to that kind of wealth. Meanwhile, without planning or permit, the virgin tropical forest, that had provided both Koto's and Murkha's ancestors with their livelihoods for hundreds of years, was dying. They could both feel it.

Koto's response was to spend as much time in the forest as he could – especially with tourists, so he could explain to them the importance of every sound and smell to his culture. For Murkha the response was intelligent mischief. He had met up with some Indonesian environmental activists in Jakarta and been feeding them information. In turn they were using the information to get the government to act. But even this was difficult since the timber baron had also paid off politicians and Generals in Jakarta.

"I think the navy will seize the ships today" he boasted. "Just wait to see the reaction in town when everyone sees that he's not as powerful as everyone thinks!"

Koto had spent all day drinking coffee and smoking with Murkha and eventually Setin had joined them looking more relaxed. It had been one of those unexpected days, a meandering day with friends. It seemed that Murkha had even set up Koto with an English client who would be coming out in a few days.

He had left them once the rain started in the early evening and bought his dinner at the little street café just outside Kumai. There he had run into other young men, who he considered friends, and heard that there was a navy frigate just outside the bay. Some of

4

the fishermen had come back early because they always seemed to have to pay off men in military uniform and they weren't going to risk losing a night's catch. Koto had smiled knowingly to himself.

The rain was slowing down now and he could hear people moving around on the street outside. He pulled the guitar to his chest, hugged it as he thought of his village, his family and his father telling him stories as a child; stories of the animals in the forest.

A noisy 4x4 revved past his room, he heard a sudden thud on his door. Not a knock, a thud.

Koto shivered involuntarily, put his guitar to one side, went to his door and opened it. The darkness gave little away but looking down he instantly understood his anxiety and fear. Lying in the mud at his bare feet, only vaguely lit by his room lamp, was a chubby severed arm with a black coral bracelet around its wrist.

PART ONE: THE CHALLENGE

CHAPTER ONE
Bali – 10 days earlier

The beach was not quite what Matt had expected.

He'd envisaged white sands, palm trees and aquamarine blue sea gently lapping at the shoreline. He thought he would walk barefoot along the deserted beach as he gently chuckled at manic crabs running for cover. He dreamed of a rocky outcrop he easily scrambled over, to land alone, as if the first human invasion, on a tiny private cove where he would strip and lie naked. He would roll in the sand and bathe in the sea until all his confusions and fears had washed away. He would be rinsed totally clean so he could start fucking up his life all over again.

But Kuta beach in Bali is not like this. The sand is more grey than white from the thousands of dirty feet tramping over it every day. There are plenty of palm trees but they invariably mark the entrance to a restaurant, hotel or bar. Kuta attracts the surfers because of its raging sea. On a good day the surf hits three or four metres while even in the shallows you can be towed under. But most of the time the sea is just exhilarating.

Matt looked up the long, wide beach towards a water tower where flags were flying and a group of Australian lads were egging each other on to do some bungee jumping. *"What is it about Aussies and extreme sports?"* he thought, his only previous experience of Australians in Europe, Matt's turf. Now he was on theirs – Bali is to Australians what the Med is to northern Europeans: cheap, hot and comfortably familiar.

Anyone familiar with Indonesia will testify how un-Indonesian Bali actually is. This beach playground for ordinary Australians, and increasingly Europeans, lacks the austerity and piety of the world's largest Muslim nation and fourth largest country by population. Indonesia is vast, stretching from Aceh at the northern end of Sumatra which sits next to Malaysia, to Papua province on the island of New Guinea just north of Darwin in Australia. The Javanese who dominate Indonesia are as different to Papuans as the English are to Indians.

Bali is a little jewel. The kindness of the predominantly Hindu population is famous and the gentle nature of the island has survived, in recent times, the tourist invasion, which brought with it two bomb attacks. The first caused over 200 deaths, plunging the already poor population into dire poverty when the tourists deserted the island.

Matt was one of those travellers who wanted to give Bali his business. As a fairly widely travelled photographer he had been in difficult circumstances on many occasions. A beach holiday was not really his idea of a break but he had put it together very quickly and wanted to get as far away from London as possible. He was on the run, on the run from his girlfriend, or as he mused to himself, on the run from his ex-girlfriend, because there was no doubt about the finality of their parting.

"Mister, mister!" a middle aged woman in an official looking blue shirt was standing over him. "Massage mister. Good, very good mister."

"No thanks" he replied as politely as he could.

"Where you from mister? Australia?"

"No, England. London."

"English very nice mister. Massage very good."

"Maybe later, thanks" Matt responded apologetically. His first thought being that the woman was offering him sex, but when he looked up the beach he saw an army of middle aged women in blue shirts. "*Must be legit*" he thought to himself.

"When? One hour mister? I come in one hour" she insisted.

It was getting hot and Matt thought he would go to a restaurant for some lunch and to find some shade, so he started gathering his towel and small backpack.

"You back soon? Massage" the woman in the blue shirt shouted persistently.

"I'll be back soon" Matt lied, immediately feeling bad for leading the woman on. He had no intention of returning in this heat. She knew that and had already moved on up the beach to pester another first day, white tourist. Matt could already hear her saying "Where you from?"

So much for the solitude of a desert island, the space to think and the cleansing of the sea and sand. Matt decided he would have to think of Kuta in a different way – a more realistic way. Maybe this is where he could make some new friends, get drunk and party his stress away. Just maybe. But he wasn't too sure he was up to it.

He took that step from the deep sand onto the paved forecourt of the open restaurant, that step from the soft sand to the hard tourist enclave. He faltered on the concrete and felt as if everyone was watching his confidence shatter, as he confronted the smugness of tanned tourists, in their know-it-all second week.

"Pull yourself together" he thought. *"This is not like you Matt, chill man, chill."* He realised, at this moment, that the Matt he thought he was, had gone when Pauline left him after eight years. Now he was just Matt and he wasn't too sure who that was. But of course that was the purpose of getting away and finding himself. He could stay away from England as long as he liked, providing he could make some money somewhere. But for now he was OK. Just raw.

"Table for one mister?" a pretty young waitress asked abruptly as if ramming the obvious into his gut.

He sat facing inwards, suddenly realising that most of the other punters were now looking straight at him, as they had positioned themselves to people-watch the beach. Rather than change chairs, which would have required some remaining confidence, he hid his face in the large menu and stared at the vast choice of familiar food.

The girl returned with a pen and pad and stared at him expectantly, it was only at this point Matt realised he had focused on the words but the meaning was still lost to him. He concentrated harder until "fish 'n chips" actually conjured up battered cod on a plate with far too many greasy potato wedges. His eyes quickly darted down the list until they rested on *"gado gado"* and *"sate ayam"* – the safe Indonesian western specialities. His mind even managed to notice that at 10,000 rupiah, they were both very cheap and he had nothing to lose.

"Gado gado? Sate ayam?" The girl seemed to be reading his mind. But then he noticed that other than an exceptionally large young man in a rugby shirt eating sausage, bacon, eggs, chips and beans, everyone else had wooden sticks lying on their plates. A sure sign of tourist attempts at cultural sensitivity by choosing the *sate*. Or maybe it was just the best bet on the menu.

8

"Both please" Matt confirmed with a smile, unsure of whether it was cool to order both and this was going to be the right mix.

"*Nasi?*"

"Please" he responded, only because he didn't want to look stupid and the girl clearly assumed he would know what she meant.

"And an iced coffee please" he added, to appear chilled.

She moved away, exposing him to the sideways glances of other diners. Some of them appeared to look right through him. He noticed they were all in groups and he was the only solitary diner. It had been so long since he had been alone that he hadn't realised how unnatural he would feel. When he was alone ten years ago he had possessed a boyish cockiness common to many young guys in their early twenties. That *"look at me I'm young and invincible"* attitude of a strutting cockerel, unaware of all the weapons waiting to be fired at you. Unaware of the strangling hands. He was wounded now and loneliness really didn't feel so good.

"Where you from?" asked a girl on the table next to him.

"London. You?" replied Matt.

"Brisbane. I'm Lucy, this is Frag and Froo" she explained so fast that Matt had no idea what her friends were called, already struggling to remember if she had said Lucy or Juicy.

"Pleased to meet you. How long have you been in Bali?" he asked with what he felt was a balance between interest and the desperately lonely. Frag and Froo were looking at him. Frag, the guy, seemed very disinterested, but Froo had just eyed his crotch and was smiling at him in that "knowing" way. *"Knowing what?"* thought Matt.

"This is our second week" Froo purred. "And I'm certain it's going to be better than the first. Aren't you Lucy?"

"Yep. Certainly am Lou" she replied.

"OK it's Lou" thought Matt *"remember Lou and Lucy."*

Matt knew he was an attractive guy. He had been playing squash for four years and was definitely chat line *"fit and defined"*. His longish blond hair and blue eyes were northern European and his smile was a killer. He weighed in at a cool 75 kilos which for a 6 footer with his muscle definition was slim. He saw himself as European which is how he knew he weighed a metric 75 kilos, but had a lingering British feel to himself which liked the ability to dive back into his insular shell when he wanted – hence the six feet. At least that's what Pauline used to say. On a good day he could play his looks better than most, but he had to believe it to play it. Today he felt alone and unsure of himself.

"Why don't you join us" cooed Lucy. Matt noticed Frag frown at the suggestion and felt used.

"No thanks. I'm just chilling. I don't want to be in the way."

"It's cool" cut in Frag rather too quickly.

"Shut up Brad!" sneered Lou without even looking at him "why don't you go and play bungee with your mates, mate."

Matt's food arrived just in time for him to concentrate on something else. First the mixed vegetable or *gado gado* and then the chicken *sate*. He was just digging in when a huge plate of rice arrived. "*Oh great*" he thought, "*I'll end up looking like the fat geezer in the rugby shirt.*"

"I think this is yours" offered a young, casually well-dressed Indonesian man. "It was given to me by mistake." Matt took the iced coffee from him thankfully, more for saving him momentarily from Lucy Lou. Brad was getting up to leave now and with any luck Lucy Lou would go with him. There was an argument over the bill between Lucy and Lou because Lou had apparently eaten most of Lucy's ice cream sundae.

"May I join you? My name is Ardi" he offered as he sat down without waiting for a reply. He was wearing well fitting jeans, a white T-shirt and his jet black hair was cut quite fashionably long. His face was bright and optimistic with a faint touch of mischief displayed by his cheek dimples and the up curl of his smiling mouth. This was a young man with an identity, but Matt wasn't immediately sure whose.

"I'm Matt. Would you like a drink?"

"I'm fine thanks. Please tell me to go away if I'm interrupting something, but to be honest it looked as if you needed help." He paused and added "you've got beautiful blond hair. You don't mind me complimenting you I hope?" He paused before smiling and adding "I love blond hair."

Matt felt totally off guard and involuntarily flashed his killer smile back at Ardi. "*Oh shit*" he thought "*this is what got me into this emotional mess in the first place.*"

"No I can't stay. I've got someone to see" explained Ardi. "But I'll be at *Club Komodo* tonight if you're interested to meet again. I'd like to learn all about you Matt." He stood, put his hands together, politely bowed before turning and walked away.

Matt could see that the table next to him was now empty and the three Aussies had already left, while he had been mesmerised by Ardi's face and every word.

After eating, he walked back to the beach, felt strangely refreshed and a little freer than when he had left it. He knew he was still very uptight but somehow believed he was less alone. There was definitely a future, whatever it may bring.

"Mister mister! You late mister. You said an hour!" the woman in the blue shirt scolded Matt. "No problem, OK. Good massage. *Bagus* mister. You like now?"

"I like now" repeated Matt as he lay on the sand. "It's definitely time to chill so let's get started. I've got a long way to go."

CHAPTER TWO
Bali

Nusa Dua is as un-Balinese as Bali is un-Indonesian. Situated south of Denpasar, Bali's capital, Nusa Dua is a peninsular that has been divided up for the rich. Here the Bali Sheraton and Grand Hyatt Hotel gardens occupy more land than many villages. This is the zone of upper end tourism, where the hotels provide Jacuzzis the size of pools and "ethnic" dancers by the bar after dark. The gardens are constantly tended by workers, dressed in the branded colours of the hotel chain, instructed to spray and poison the mosquitoes, rats and snakes that would normally inhabit the hedgerows.

The hotels of Nusa Dua also provide conference facilities and security for the region's political and business elite – a perfect setting to discuss unsavoury issues such as human rights abuses, environmental destruction and poverty.

Bambang Santoso was already wondering why his precious time was being wasted in side meeting after side meeting. He understood that timber theft was an environmental disaster but felt this would be better dealt with by his Minister of Environment or Forestry. Why the Coordinating Minister for Politics and Security should be dragged in to this debate he was unclear, but the President had insisted. Bambang suspected it was because the regional Vice-President of the World Bank was taking it seriously and his government was after more low interest loans. He picked at the king prawns on his plate while some girl from a small non governmental organisation (NGO) explained to him how her village was being threatened by some timber baron. He tried to look concerned.

"The local police are all paid off by the baron and arrest anyone who stands up to him" she was explaining, "and we need your help Minister to bring this matter up with the Chief of National Police."

Bambang smiled at the girl who was clearly very nervous. He was struck by her beautiful, innocent face; her eyes had the brightness of youth and her expression seemed to expect so much of him. He decided to encourage her to explain more about the timber baron, partly because he was aware of a much older austere woman, probably the girl's boss, pacing around the dining table with no empty seat to occupy, and partly because he enjoyed looking at her sweet face ranting naïve idealism. "What's the name of the timber trader?" he asked.

"Abdullah Aziz" she replied quickly. "He's based in Pangkalan Bun in Central Kalimantan but lives mainly in Singapore now where he keeps his money" she explained. "He and his family virtually own the area, yet he started as a poor man. We are very frightened Minister. This is not just about losing our forest, it is about corruption and the destruction of law and order, it is about handing our precious country over to the Mafia" she pushed home her point acutely aware that time was not on her side.

"That's a serious accusation young lady" Bambang replied brightly. He liked this girl and knew that her description of this man's wealth and Singapore bank accounts was a familiar story. Singapore's wealthy regional status, untested extradition treaty with Indonesia, and lack of money laundering laws, made it home to many thousands of extremely rich Indonesians whose money came from illegal activities. "What did you say your name is?"

She handed him her card "Rita Purnama sir. I'm from YHB, an NGO called *Yayasan Hutan Bagus* based in Jakarta."

"Please send me a briefing on your accusations and I'll make sure this matter is raised with the Chief of National Police as you ask" he responded. He pushed his chair back to signal that the conversation was now over and three officials stood before he was able to get out of his chair. He was aware that the pacing woman was now directly behind him, no doubt ready to pounce, so he rather pompously lied "I must go now to phone the President on some important matters of state."

He and his officials rapidly left the dining area before Rita realised what he had said. She looked at her untouched plate of food in front of her and at the now vacant chairs and saw Debi, her boss, sitting down next to her. "You should have introduced me to him" she reprimanded Rita, "didn't you see me standing there?"

Debi Sudarto was fighting for the forest when Rita was only a child. She had seen Debi on television before she had met her in the flesh and to Rita, Debi represented a unique type of female

13

activist who had grown out of the New Order regime of dictator President Suharto. For over thirty years opposition to Suharto was barely possible, but somehow over the last decade of his regime which had ended in 1998, a new breed of environmentalist had emerged. Since Suharto's fall from power the new emerging democracy was giving activists like Debi opportunities to voice the issues publicly for the first time.

"He offered to talk to the Chief of National Police" explained Rita excitedly, "and appeared interested in the issue." Debi was unimpressed and very agitated. She saw her standing in these issues so high that she was not used to being snubbed, even by a senior minister. "He wants a brief on the subject" added Rita.

"OK let's find Sam and get the brief to him this evening" ordered Debi "did you get the contact details of his Secretary General?"

"He just left too quickly" Rita said apologetically. She was beginning to feel a strange mixture of anger and foolishness: anger at Debi for putting her down without listening and foolish for not getting the contact details, although she was certain that Debi knew how to get the briefing to the minister. She was saved from having to explain any of the conversation by the arrival of Sam Galingging, her friend and work colleague.

"From where I was standing it looked like Bambang fancied you!" he blurted out before even looking at Debi. His face was beaming proudly as he put his arms around Rita. Sam was, like Rita, in his mid twenties and had been to university in his home town of Medan. His parents were shopkeepers who were so proud of him they gave a street party to celebrate his graduation. His family was Batak, the fiercely proud, mainly Christian people, of north Sumatra.

"Don't be silly" blushed Rita, "it was just that I was so persuasive" she joked.

"I saw his eyes lusting after you" Sam continued, kissing Rita playfully on the cheek to see if he could get her to blush even more.

It was clear Debi wasn't seeing the humour. "I've got a meeting with a Kompas newspaper journalist tonight, so let's cut out the chit chat and get to work. I would like to get to sleep before two for a change" she quipped.

The others were sad that Debi always seemed so serious, but imagined it had to do with her past during the New Order regime, the terrible loss of her husband and baby daughter. The story they had heard was that one night the army had visited her house when she had been in the Netherlands at a conference. Nobody seemed to know the details, but her husband and child were found drowned in a small lake not far from their home. The police had said he was drunk and it looked like a terrible accident, but nobody believed them. Debi had suffered enormous loss and hardship until she had established YHB in 1996 which had focused her anger on her work and unfortunately, sometimes on her work mates.

Rita picked up her bag and suggested they all went up to her room to adapt a briefing for the minister which she would try to deliver personally over breakfast. Sam followed obediently and Debi said she would join them soon. As they walked across reception to their wing of the hotel they were unaware of a small official looking man, turning his back on them as they passed, to dial the house phone.

"Hello" the phone was answered.

"The girl talked to Santoso directly."

"OK, stay where you are and let me know when they emerge again." The man put his phone down, lifted a Kent cigarette from his ashtray and drew hard on it. He breathed out the smoke slowly as his eyes gazed out of the window to the gardens below, where a man was spraying the plants. "I had hoped it would never come to this" he murmured to himself as he purposely stubbed out the cigarette and lifted the phone to dial a number in Pangkalan Bun.

CHAPTER THREE
Bali

The entrance to *Club Komodo* feels a little bit like the entrance to a Hollywood party without the valet parking and, in fact, without the cars. Instead, motorbikes are everywhere, revving their noisy engines, young girls wearing small black helmets getting off the back of their proud boyfriends' bikes. Palm trees surround the small sandy entrance and the beach stretches out in both directions with the sea pounding the shoreline at least 100 metres away.

Matt paid his motorbike taxi driver and wandered through the mild chaos to a wooden arch where people were queuing to get in. As he stood under the Club Komodo "CK" logo, not unlike that of the New York fashion house, two young Indonesian guys stood in front of him. They checked him out before paying, disappearing into the crowd. Matt had no idea what to expect and had been in two minds whether to come out tonight, but the guide book described the club as if it was part of the history of Bali in party mode with a "mixed" crowd and he felt he might as well give it a try. After all he was on his own now with a mission to chill.

Inside, the party was already in full swing with a mixture of Indonesians and foreign tourists, although Matt realised that inside was actually outside because *Club Komodo* is an open-air club with a pool, large dance floor, live DJs and ample room to cruise. He strolled around the dance floor keeping to the swimming pool side and arrived at the long bar at the back and exchanged his entrance ticket for a cold beer. "*Not bad*" he thought, "*entrance and a drink for 25,000 rupiah*" which he mentally calculated to be around £1.50.

The music was what Matt called happy house, bright sunny house music which keeps you dancing without stopping or thinking for hours. Groups of Australians were on the dance floor, many of the guys in beach shorts and baggy t shirts, the girls wearing matching tops with short skirts and new trainers. The Indonesians were definitely smarter but still casual, usually wearing clothes that showed off their physiques more than the tourists. It was clear that there were all kinds of people here tonight from tourists to businessmen and local lovers to boys and girls for sale. As in all places where wealth mixes with poverty *Club Komodo* was

16

packed with preconceptions and misconceptions, the players and the played. But it was also full of people just out for their own kind of fun.

The bar was no place to stay unless you sat on a bar stool. It was one of those areas you find in all crowded clubs where, no matter where you stand, you find yourself in a major thoroughfare within minutes. Fed up with being pushed around all the time he finished his beer, ordered another and took it with him to stand by the pool.

It didn't look as if the pool was ever used and it didn't look too clean. But around it, on the side next to the dance floor, groups of people were standing, talking and watching. There were five or six groups of foreign tourists with one young man pretty wasted already, dozens of locals and Indonesians standing in small groups pointing and laughing at the crowd. Amongst the locals were a handful of young men standing alone looking around, one of them staring at Matt who was feeling very self conscious, beginning to think he would have been better to catch up on some sleep in his hotel.

He looked away from the young man's stare and moved around the dance floor until he was on the other side under the DJ box. This was also an area where people were standing, but in much smaller groups and alone. The music was too loud here to be able to talk and most of the clubbers were moving to the music even if not actually dancing. He felt more comfortably anonymous here and started to lose some of his angst as the music and beer kicked in.

This was the first time he had been out on his own for years. Pauline had never really been into clubbing, but had insisted on accompanying him on those few occasions he had gone out with friends. He had always enjoyed dancing wildly with anyone up for it, but on reflection, had often been corralled into the space occupied by other guys, ironically by Pauline's accusing eyes. Every time he smiled at another girl. *"Pushed into the arms of a man by my girlfriend!"* he thought, more confused than ever.

The dance floor was respectably busy but certainly not at full capacity, still plenty of room to move around the periphery. The large area on the far side of the pool was almost completely deserted although a lone barman was standing behind a small bar talking to a pretty, tanned western girl. An Indonesian couple were dancing together right in front of Matt, the man smiling very romantically at his girlfriend and just behind them three Aussie lads were dancing with three local girls.

"Where you from?" asked a stunningly beautiful young Indonesian girl in a hugging aquamarine dress. Matt could see her bright eyes reflecting the flashing lights as she shone a huge wide open smile at him.

"England" he replied without any attempt at returning her invitation.

It was at times like this that Matt hated the huge wealth gap you inevitably experience when visiting developing countries. There was rarely any real opportunity to casually meet people on equal terms whether you wanted to or not. It was a wealthy person's luxury to trust, knowing that whatever you lost you could afford it. But the local half of the union may be trying to be genuinely friendly with no ulterior motive – in which case they were bound to be offended by the misinterpretation of their hospitality, or they may be manipulatively putting a deal together that they desperately needed. Either way it was such infertile ground for real, equal and stimulating relationships.

The beautiful girl recognised the snub immediately and moved away and that's when Matt felt like an absolute bastard. In these circumstances it was always too late when you recognised the genuine friendliness of a stranger and Matt was perfectly aware that had this girl been a hooker she would not have given up so easily. *"My first night out in Bali and I'm already being rude to the locals"* thought Matt helplessly. *"And she was gorgeous."*

He wasn't sure he wanted to stay here much longer, but before he left, he desperately needed a piss. Just to the left of the bar he first visited, were some crowded steps with a sign over them, clearly stating this was the way to the toilets.

He made his way carefully through the growing crowd, up the steps, down the other side to a large area behind the bar with people hanging around smoking and talking. This looked like the service area, where people emerged from their sweaty jobs for just enough time to smoke a cigarette, while happy holidaymakers brushed past them for only a second on their way to relieve themselves of the free-flowing beer.

He was in the toilet for less than a minute and came out feeling he still had some partying left in him. A good looking, muscular local guy asked him if he wanted a cigarette and although Matt had stopped smoking seven years ago when Pauline had given him an ultimatum, felt obliged to say "yes please, thanks." The man handed him a cigarette and pulled out a lighter. "You want girl, mister?" he whispered. "I can get you the best girl for the night or the week. Best price mister."

Matt coughed as he inhaled the first drag, but still had time to surprise himself with his answer "No girl thanks, you got any ecstasy?"

The muscular lad turned away quickly and pointed to another young guy with long hair in a ponytail sitting on the steps between the toilets and the dance floor. "Take pill and come back to me for girl, OK?" he insisted.

Matt wandered over to the guy on the step who was already talking to an American tourist. He wasn't sure he wanted to ask for E again but the American looked relaxed which gave him some confidence. He knew that drugs are common in Bali but if you get caught up in a drug bust you can be in very serious trouble. The Indonesian authorities have many foreign nationals in jail for drug offences and if you are proven to have been dealing or smuggling drugs, the death sentence is actively encouraged.

"Hi" said Matt to the American. "Alright?"

"Hi. Guess you're after what I'm after" he replied. "Just don't pay more than 100,000, that's all. These guys are getting greedy."

The Indonesian man with the pony tail smiled and sighed. He wasn't going anywhere and neither were his clients. He knew that. "Two hundred" he offered.

"Man! You've got to be kidding me" complained the American.

"For two" said Matt who had plenty of worldly experience in bartering.

"Three hundred for two" said ponytail turning his attention to Matt.

"Three hundred for three" Matt replied with an air of finality.

Ponytail looked around nervously as if he had suddenly realised they were talking about drugs, "it's not worth it" he complained.

"Three for three" repeated Matt.

After being directed to the toilets Matt closed his deal, giving one to the American for 100,000 rupiah and keeping the other two for himself. He went back to the bar alone, bought another beer which he used to wash one pill down his throat. Before he swallowed he felt that nauseous feeling you get from the taste of the pill, confirming he'd just bought the genuine article.

He already felt different. By taking a pill he had dispelled any idea of going back to his lonely hotel room, committing himself to a few hours of partying at least. The second pill in his pocket was there just in case.

He walked back to his former position below the DJ box and watched the dancers really going for the music. It was anthem time and the mixed group of tourists and locals in front of him were dancing the universal language of waving their arms, then punching the air as the music reached its crescendo. The party had clearly been kick-started helpfully by ponytail and his colleagues and was likely to go for hours.

He thought he'd have another look around before the pill kicked in and moved over towards the pool where it was now quite difficult to move. People were even dancing on the other side; he could see the lone barman busily serving his customers as eagerly as he had been talking to the tanned girl an hour earlier. The famed Bali friendliness was easy to feel, even in this club, and Matt sensed he had definitely come to the right place to get away from Pauline. People here were so lovely and open. Everyone was smiling, now he could actually feel the music affecting his mood, bringing him up, launching him on an adventure.

Experience warned him the pill had kicked in.

"There you are Matt, I've been looking for you!" It was Ardi, the young guy from the restaurant and the reason Matt had come to *Club Komodo*. He looked so beautiful and sexy, Matt felt relieved and happy that Ardi had found him, rescued him from so many uncertainties, so many strangers. He was like an old lost friend.

"Ardi" he shouted, flashing the wide smile that usually ended in trouble. "You're late!"

CHAPTER FOUR
Jakarta

Bambang Santoso's office wasn't deliberately designed to make you feel uncomfortable, but that was the inevitable reaction when you first entered. His desk empty, except for a notepad and pen, a laptop computer and five gold framed photographs of his wife and four daughters. Behind his large leather chair on the wall were the obligatory photographs of the President and Vice-President of the Republic of Indonesia. But, had they not been obligatory for a government office, Bambang would have hung them anyway.

In the middle of this huge room were four large black leather sofas facing an imposing carved teak coffee-table and the walls were lined with hardwood bookcases full of books in Javanese, Indonesian, English, Dutch and Arabic. The space around the sofas was four times the size of the area occupied by them, and it was the effect of scale that put most visitors off balance. The office was in the corner of the building on the twelfth floor, with views from windows on two sides, overlooking Jakarta's bustling noisy traffic.

The Coordinating Minister for Politics and Security was a strange mixture of strict arrogance and fastidiousness, yet with an endless capacity for love. He had been promoted to a two star General when he was only fifty two, but after his wife's death from cancer he had retired from the army just three years later and spent months with his daughters reminiscing and honouring his wife. Now at sixty three, despite a lack of hard ambition, he was one of the steadiest and most powerful political characters in Southeast Asia reporting directly to the President. He believed he received his strength from Allah, his President, his four daughters, and his wife in no particular order, and other than these bastions of support, he trusted nobody.

His army career had spanned the entire New Order regime of President Suharto, and he knew he was tainted by the excesses of the era, but he had remained loyal to his country and the direction it was taking at the time. He regularly reminded foreign visitors to Indonesia that, although the world prefers to remember the alleged torture and disappearances of Suharto's opponents, the accusations of untold wealth stolen from the nation and secreted away in foreign bank accounts of Suharto himself, they forget that Indonesia grew in stature during this time. They forget that Suharto killed communists and was befriended by America and they forget that he fed his people, at least until the Southeast Asian economic collapse and the last year of his Presidency.

It was clear to Bambang that despite his nationalistic tendencies to keep Indonesia together, he had no idea how any government could achieve it.

Indonesia is the world's fourth largest country by population, just a little smaller than the United States. Its majority Muslim population is known as largely moderate, a Southeast Asian tolerant interpretation of Islam acknowledging other religious faiths. He loved his country but the upheavals since Suharto had troubled his ordered mind. How could a country this size prevent the extremists from bombing night-clubs or beheading children while they are walking home from school? How could he, in his ministerial role, counter the organised Islamic militia that want an area encompassing southern Thailand, Malaysia, the southern Philippines and Indonesia under *Sharia* law?

If there was anything that Bambang couldn't forgive Suharto for, it was the endemic corruption that had held his elite together, because this was the strongest legacy his government now had to deal with. It was so bad that sometimes he just wanted to fire every civil servant and start again. Corruption was at the centre of every major struggle that Indonesia faced: economic recovery, military reform, poverty, illegal resource stripping, and terrorism. He knew that he couldn't trust the military or the police and neither could the ordinary Indonesian citizen. The courts were so corrupt that a recent survey of high court judges had revealed that most believed it was alright to accept presents from the accused, as long as it was after the case had been decided!

Bambang reached into his brief case and pulled out the dossier he had been given in Bali four days earlier by that pretty young lady from an NGO. It contained testimony, photographs, and showed military owned barges piled high with logs leaving Central Kalimantan allegedly heading for Malaysia despite a log export ban imposed by his government last year. The timber, it claimed, had been logged in Tanjung Puting National Park by teams paid by Abdullah Aziz, the local timber baron. It claimed he was making twenty to thirty million US dollars from this illegal business every year.

A heavy sigh came from Bambang as he read the statistics of vanishing species and the descriptions of Dayak holy areas being desecrated. What was it that the young lady had said? Something like *"it's not just about the forest, it is about corruption and law and order, it is about handing our country over to the Mafia."* Yes, he remembered that last line because underlining her nervous presentation there was a very real profound sense of sadness. And he had felt ashamed at that moment as if it was one of his daughters asking him *"daddy, why have you given everything away to those bad people?"*

He buzzed his secretary who entered immediately through a door at the far end and walked across the room towards Bambang. Neither of the men could see the absurdity of this long walk, which must have taken thirty seconds in each direction, probably ten to twenty times a day. Time and motion efficiency experts would be pulling their hair out in frustration at the time wasted, every day, by one of the busiest men in Indonesia.

"Copy this and get it to the Sec Gen. I want to see him in my office in ten minutes" he ordered. The secretary turned and walked back towards the door without saying a word and by the time he had left the room Bambang was already on the phone to the Forestry Minister.

"Will I see you at the mosque tonight?" he asked in a manner that was clearly a summons. "I have something I need to discuss with you. I know I looked fed up in Bali, but I think I understand why the President insisted I was there and I'd like to chew a few thoughts over with you. Good. I'll see you then." He needed to know if the Forestry Minister was one of the "bad people" and his best chance would be face to face in the mosque. They were both devout Muslims which made their local mosque the most obvious place to meet.

The door opened and his secretary said the Secretary General of his Ministry, the chief civil servant, was waiting outside. Secretary General Widodo had come with the job and Bambang wasn't sure whether he wanted to keep him, after all this was a key, very senior position with enormous power and responsibility. He would prefer to have one of his own men in that role, but he had to admit that Widodo had already proven to be invaluable support and he didn't really have anyone else he could immediately think of to replace him. He walked out of his office to welcome Widodo and nodded at his secretary to arrange coffee.

"Ah, good, please come in" he greeted Widodo. "I see you have the dossier."

As Widodo entered a waft of strong cologne accompanied this short, slightly plump lifelong civil servant. His immaculate uniform was complemented by a neatly fashioned moustache.

"Yes, but I've only just looked at the first page Minister" Widodo apologised. "Is this the dossier you mentioned when we were in Bali?"

"Yes. Have you heard of this man? Abdullah Aziz?"

"Yes Minister, there have been various accusations made before I believe. But nothing substantiated."

"Is he a crook?"

"I believe he has been very generous to your party Minister. I would suggest you talk to your party chairman about him. He has built mosques in Central Kalimantan and visited Mecca last year on a Haj. I believe he is a good man." He paused to judge Santoso's reaction, but his boss had a blank expression. Almost cold. "These NGOs are getting a bit full of themselves nowadays because the media always want their story and there don't really seem to be any checks on them anymore."

"You're saying the NGO is making this up?" Bambang asked.

"The link to *Pak* Aziz is unproven Minister. There is no doubt that trees are being stolen but not on this scale and not by *Pak* Aziz. These environmentalists are not what they first seem to be."

Bambang thought of the girl he had met in Bali and his instincts clearly told him she was exactly what she first seemed to be: a caring, sweet young lady with a mission to save her home. Was Widodo just echoing the conservative thoughts of a life in a Suharto administration, who believed that NGOs were only worthwhile if they represented his ideas?

"Have you met Abdullah Aziz?" Bambang asked, already rather surprised how quickly Widodo was dismissing these serious claims.

"No Minister, I've just heard about him."

"And what have you heard?"

"There's been quite a lot written about him in the press and his name is often linked to the timber business" Widodo explained. "But those that know him say it is just a consequence of his success as a businessman that competitors set up NGOs to try and hurt his business."

"And what is his business then if it's not timber?" asked Bambang.

"I really don't know Minister. I can ask for a dossier to be put together if you like."

"No don't bother, I'm meeting the Forestry Minister later, I'll ask him" Bambang said dismissively.

"Oh" said Widodo looking strangely uncomfortable. "Do you want me to come with you?"

"No" replied Bambang curtly. He'd had enough of this conversation and was disturbed by the vigorous defence of Aziz by his Secretary General, a man he said he had only heard of, didn't know what his business was if not timber and claimed was funding his political party.

His secretary entered the room with coffee but Bambang waived him away.

Nothing more to discuss.

CHAPTER FIVE
Jakarta

The Forestry Ministry is based in the centre of Jakarta in a vast complex called *Manggala Wanabakti*. To an outsider the market stalls in the building would seem out of place, but when they had walked the faceless corridors of the ministry past the bowling alley, the gym, the pool, the travel agency, the restaurants and the wedding shop, they would either have given up on any rational explanation or simply accepted *Manggala*, as it is known, for what it is.

As befitting a Forestry Ministry, it is surrounded by grass and ancient trees, with a huge metal tree sculpture proudly greeting visitors outside the main entrance. The modern sculpture can be seen from many parts of the building and countless ministry workers and visitors have commented that, with the state of Indonesia's forests, this metal sculpture may well be the last tree standing.

Forestry used to be known as a cash cow ministry, providing money to powerful individuals and political groupings. There is no doubt that huge sums of money in brown envelopes still walked the corridors of *Manggala*, but at the top was a new regime headed by Mohammed Probowo, a Minister who was trying to root out corruption and prevent the wholesale theft of Indonesia's forests. He and his team had already received many threats from Generals and politicians alike, and he had learned to be cautious.

His black bullet proof Lexus pulled up outside the Ministry and he walked quickly down the steps past his officials who were outside having a cigarette. They straightened up when they saw him, less as a formality but more like naughty school boys caught smoking behind the shed, even though he walked past them at least twice a day. The government's no smoking policy in public places was very unpopular. His driver greeted him cheerily, waited for him to strap himself into the back seat before speeding off around the building and out on to the two lane road outside *Manggala*.

The more senior Coordinating Minister for Politics and Security put his hands in the safety of his police escort. His black bullet proof Mercedes was guarded by two motorbike outriders to the front and two behind. In addition to this a second car with bodyguards and intelligence agents was directly behind him. Despite the sirens and flashing lights, it had often occurred to Bambang that his vehicle rarely moved faster than any other; on one occasion he had noticed his driver cut up a filthy blue taxi, only to see it edge past ten minutes later on an inside lane! He took little notice of any of this anymore, preferring to call one of his daughters on his way home or go through the papers for his next meeting.

The journey home was only twenty minutes or so, although on a bad day, or on Friday, when Jakarta traffic gridlocked, you really believed that you may never get home. Even with his outriders and flashing blue lights, a gridlock is a gridlock. Home in Jakarta was a lovely four bed-roomed villa in a compound for government ministers, where security was higher and all the drivers and servants could be checked by intelligence agents. Bambang had little faith in the agents who had already allowed a journalist from the opposition's daily newspaper to be hired as his gardener, causing embarrassing leaks from his house.

When he drove past the Forestry Minister's house he noticed that his car was not outside, yet evening prayers were in less than half an hour. Bambang had heard conflicting reports about Probo, as he was known. There were those who regarded him as a moderniser, someone who didn't just support reform but was addicted to it. He was said to be a workaholic but affable, his best attributes being his flair for life and sense of humour. Those that disliked him said he was opportunistic, untalented and making a complete mess of the timber industry. It was a fact that many sawmills had closed since Probo took over the ministry, but then they were said to be operating on illegal logs and without licenses. In fact as Bambang understood, the mills weren't even Probo's responsibility because the licenses were issued by the Ministry of Trade & Industry. But the timber supply was.

On balance, when Bambang had met Probo in Cabinet meetings and heard him speak, he had liked him. Young, energetic, he seemed to speak as if his every thought was to help the President and, of course therefore, the country. He was looking forward to tonight's private meeting and hoped Probo wouldn't keep him waiting. He knew that his own obsession with punctuality was a curse in a country where people had little concept of time and Jakarta's transport system gave no chance of actually guessing when you may arrive. But obsessed he was, and angry he would become, if Probo was late.

The Forestry Minister's Lexus edged its way through the Jakarta rush hour with less noise and fuss than the Coordinating Minister's security convoy, hardly causing heads to turn, yet moving just as quickly. As it slowed to pay at a toll booth on the slip road to the overpass, a truck pulled out behind it, gushing black diesel fumes into the surrounding crawl of traffic. The three lanes were moving at a slow but steady pace and regular commuters knew that in one or two kilometres the traffic thinned out enough to gain some real speed.

The shining black limousine moved into the middle lane, its driver anticipating the clearer road ahead, and with a roar of its engine, accompanied by a black cloud, the truck pulled out into the fast lane alongside. Probo's driver gave the truck driver a disapproving look, mainly because of his limo status, not really bothered as he knew the road would be quieter soon. A few minutes later, with a purr, the Lexus pulled comfortably ahead of the bullying truck although a motorbike had matched its speed on the inside lane and was level with the Minister's door.

The bike rider pulled out a small gun and fired directly at the inside front tyre of the limousine before rapidly slowing and moving into the middle lane behind. The Lexus spun towards the inside lane but the driver skilfully gained control and was straightening up when the truck, now alongside in the outside lane, rammed mercilessly into the Lexus pushing it at speed into, and through, the crash barrier. It flew off the overpass; rolled and landed on its roof on a stationary taxi in traffic thirty metres below.

CHAPTER SIX
Bali

It had been easy, at first, for Matt to put aside the fantasies of white virgin beaches and petulant sand crabs, as long as the freshness of discovery of Ardi's body and mind remained.

They had shared hours of drug fuelled uninhibited sex on the first day, exploring the sensitive areas of each others bodies in minute detail, laughing and playfully embracing each other as if the day would never end. Matt's firm body looked whiter than ever against Ardi's brown and sun tanned skin. Ardi had an infectious laugh and flashed his white teeth so brightly that Matt wondered if they actually glowed and lit up his mouth. Ardi's body was much smaller than Matt's but beautifully toned and smooth.

Matt had bought four more pills from ponytail before leaving *Club Komodo* and this kept the two of them going all day with increased sensitivity and a sense of love, partly driven by the drug. He had turned the hotel cleaning staff away at around two so they could play without interruption, only calling for room service to bring beer, water and a plate of rice for Ardi. It seemed that even ecstasy couldn't quell Ardi's need for *nasi*. He even got a bit angry when Matt playfully dipped a finger in the bowl. Sweat dripping from his tired but exhilarated body, Matt smiled as Ardi ate, realising how relaxed his companion was about any kind of sex. But nobody messed with his rice!

By the end of the day when Ardi said he must go, the drugs convinced Matt he had fallen in love. The laughter, the tenderness, and in some funny kind of way, the mild anger, somehow made the relationship real. Both of them had revelled in each others bodies with a total lack of inhibition, taking photos with Ardi's camera phone, laughing and playing. Matt felt that in some ways he knew Ardi better than he knew Pauline after so many years.

When Matt awoke the next morning he felt flat and lonely. The sweat and cum stained sheets were wrapped around him, the dirty glasses and empty rice bowl had already attracted flies. Cigarette ends were stubbed out in used cigarette packets and he had a dry and slightly sore throat.

"Stupid bastard" he said out loud as he reached for his first cigarette of the day. He walked into the bathroom and stared at himself in the mirror until the cigarette was finished. He looked totally and proudly fucked: that kind of worn out look you can only get from drugs and sex; when your body is glowing in its tiredness. His face had two nights of stubble obscuring some of its lines, but a red love bite glowed from the skin covering his Adam's apple.

His body looked good but there were strap marks on his arse, shafing around his ankles and dried cum in his pubic hair. He was unsure whether to be worried by his debauchery or turned on by the clear display of love making his body now offered. He shook his head, jumped in the shower, emerging with a towel around him to his dirty room and the sound of knocking at his door.

"Clean mister?" asked an eager girl staring at Matt's naked chest and wet straggly blond hair.

Matt's first thought was that this scene was very weird. If he hadn't just had a shower would the girl have said "dirty mister?" Then his confused brain clicked back into place and he ushered her into his room to clean up the mess.

After an afternoon on the beach, he returned to his room to find Ardi sitting outside the door with a small backpack.

"Hey Ardi!" he exclaimed rather over-enthusiastically, but he was genuinely pleased and relieved to see Ardi back again.

"You on your own?" he asked cheekily but with a firmness that puzzled Matt.

"As far as I know!" Matt joked "unless that woman from the beach followed me for her tip."

"What woman?"

"I'm kidding" Matt responded as he unlocked his door. "Come on in."

That night they went to the infamous _Q Bar_ and sat upstairs in the lounge area drinking ice cold gin and tonics, watching throngs of gay men strolling past looking back at them. They moved downstairs to the dance floor after midnight and had another drink, ending up at the outside bar. Ardi seemed to know a lot of the local guys and some of the westerners, but every time Matt commented on some cute guy, Ardi frowned at him.

An hour or so later they crossed the road to *Kudos*, another gay-owned bar with go go dancers, where a famous local DJ was playing. Matt and Ardi were both already a little drunk so they hung on to their entrance tickets which could be exchanged for a drink at the bar and headed straight for the dance floor. It was already heaving with a mixed crowd similar to that of *Club Komodo*. After about ten minutes Matt went to the bar with both their tickets, leaving Ardi dancing with two local guys.

"Two gin tonic please" Matt said as he unconsciously picked up one of the local language characteristics of no plurals. He looked around at the sea of bodies partying this night away with no worries about work in the morning, just the short walk to the beach, lunch and splashing around in the surf. His drinks arrived and he turned to find Ardi directly in front of him checking out the men either side of Matt with suspicion.

"You took a long time" he complained as he accepted his drink with a pout.

Sex was short but good that night and Ardi left after his bowl of rice and fried chicken for breakfast.

During the next few days Matt enjoyed his days on the beach catching up with some reading, massage and washing away his past in the waves. On Ardi's advice he bought himself a Telkomsel pay-as-you-go sim card for his mobile phone so that he had a local number. This made him feel as if he was going to stay in Indonesia for a while and helped him feel more at home.

At night Ardi accompanied him to different restaurants, three or four bars and always ended up at *Kudos* around two. Ardi became increasingly possessive of Matt, even shouting at one guy who provocatively cupped Matt's right bicep in his hand as he brushed past at *Q Bar*. Matt protested to Ardi, telling him to chill, but this only made him angrier. He stormed out in a move that eerily reminded Matt of Pauline's display of anger at a London dinner party when she had found out about Matt's indiscretion with a guy. "*Pauline had good reason to be really pissed off*" thought Matt, "*but Ardi?*"

He had been in Bali for a week now and was able to step confidently from the sand to the pavement in front of the lunch restaurants, sit facing the sea and order what he really wanted without feeling the slightest bit conspicuous. In fact he had a sexy spring in his step, freely flashed his smile, which was already brighter due to his golden tan, and enjoyed chatting to anyone who was feeling sociable. There was only really one thing bugging him. Ardi.

He had begun to realise he knew nothing about Ardi and whenever he asked even simple questions like "what's your job?" he never got a real response. The nights were getting repetitive with such a small "scene" available and now that Matt was feeling better about himself he was increasingly bothered by Ardi's unfounded jealousy: unfounded because Ardi didn't let Matt out of his sight except during the day. And even then he quizzed him every evening about who he had met and what he had done.

Even more disturbing was the feeling that he was missing out and that Ardi wasn't as cute as he had first thought. In fact, if he really thought hard about it, which he was now doing while lying on the sand, Ardi had rapidly become his jealous and demanding boyfriend shielding him from spontaneity and excitement.

Matt was beginning to feel very sad and concerned about Pauline, realising he was missing her terribly even though he knew he could never go back. He was unsure whether this holiday, if that's what it was, was a good idea. His feelings for her were horribly confused by the gay direction his life had willingly taken this last week – perhaps as a counterbalance to all those years with Pauline. Although he knew he was attracted to women as well, his eyes and dick had been exclusively focused on men, for the first time in his life. It was so easy. Perhaps that was not such a good thing?

He was tiring of Kuta, thinking he should head off around the island, visit temples and hang out on a deserted beach. Or perhaps he should go home to London, pick up on some work and hang out in bars near Pauline's Brixton flat. After all, it used to be his flat and he was well known in the area.

Maybe one night Pauline would hear he was around, rush to be with him and beg for the past to be forgotten. *Who was he kidding?* She had made the finality of their parting crystal clear in her last tirade "if I ever see you again. Ever. Again in my life. I'll toast your genitals in a Breville's sandwich maker." She had paused as the venom had dripped from her lower lip. "Fuck off!" Not a lot of room for reconciliation really. It seemed so real and premeditated that she had even decided the brand of the toaster.

His phone rang and he knew it must be Ardi because he was the only person who called him. He had sent messages to friends in England giving them his number, but it was unlikely that any would bother calling a mobile in Indonesia just to see how the surf was in Bali. It seems to be a common trait of all those people living in cold and wet countries that anyone enjoying themselves in the sun had to be viewed as a traitorous and contemptible show off. This was a view made worse by the invention of the camera phone which actively encourages holiday makers to tease and torment friends and work colleagues back home with pictures of them enjoying themselves in the sun, therefore reinforcing the existing contempt.

"Hi, it's Matt" he answered rather unnecessarily. Ardi asked him where he was and wanted to know what time and where to meet him. "I'd like to go somewhere different tonight, not back to *Q* and *Kudos*. I'll call you back with an idea. OK?" suggested Matt and hung up before he could get a response. He had heard of a reggae bar in Legian just along the beach somewhere over towards *Club Komodo*, very near the bars that got blown up in the October 2002 bomb attack.

He stood up, picked his towel off the sand and shook it vigorously. An Australian guy was laying a few metres away with a surf board next to him and Matt decided to ask him if he knew of this bar. He strolled over and noticed the guy was watching him already.

"How's it going?" greeted Matt.

"How are you?" responded the Aussie.

"I just wondered if you could help me?"

The Australian smiled and looked directly at Matt's crutch. "Sure I can" he responded.

"No" spluttered Matt. "I'm trying to find out the name of a reggae bar round here somewhere. Have you got any idea what it's called?"

"*Apache*. It's over in Legian. Not a bad place, but I thought you would be going to *Q* tonight, I've seen you there."

"Thought I'd try something different" Matt responded. The Australian smiled again.

"How different?" he asked.

"Thanks. See you around" Matt finished the banter and turned away feeling a bit tired of the ease of it all. He'd only been free for a week and only had sex with one guy, but literally dozens had already made it clear that a quick fuck would be a good idea. "*My God*" he thought rather prudishly, "*doesn't anyone date anymore?*" before realising that, had he spoken out loud, he would have sounded like a character in *Will and Grace*.

He called Ardi and arranged to meet at *Apache* at nine.

It takes a small leap of the imagination to see Indonesians singing and playing reggae, some adorned in the Rastafarian colours of green, gold and red. But it is not really any stranger than Americans singing Italian opera or Britons singing California rock. At least in Bali there are many similarities to Jamaica with its laid back atmosphere, sun, sand, palm trees and of course, weed. Apache is just down the road from the 2002 Bali bomb memorial where two bars, Paddy's and Sari Club, were blown up by a suicide bomber and a separate car bomb. The street is lined with shops, bars and restaurants and is one of the popular night areas for tourists.

Matt was there before Ardi, he sat down near the very quiet dance floor and ordered a cold beer. Pulling a packet of Marlboro from a pocket in his jeans he realised he had forgotten his lighter. Next to him there were two Indonesians leaning back in their chairs talking to each other. They looked like lovers but their conversation was very animated and seemed to be about politics.

The girl, Matt thought, must be in her mid twenties and the guy looked a bit younger. She was very pretty with optimistic eyes and soft, silky, black hair cut fashionably short. Confidently dressed in tight jeans and a light blouse, she revealed enough of her figure to impress any wandering eyes, but the strongest immediate impression was of her animation and enthusiasm.

He stood up and went over to ask for a light.

"Sure, no problem" the man responded and pulled out his lighter from a pocket in his shorts. "You here alone?"

"I'm waiting for a friend" Matt replied "and I don't want to interrupt you, you seem to be having a really animated chat!"

"We're always like this" the guy responded, turning to beam at his companion, "especially when we've been working together. What's your name and where are you from?"

"Matt. I'm from England."

"Hi Matt, I'm Sam and this is my best friend and work colleague Rita. Please join us until your friend arrives."

CHAPTER SEVEN
Jakarta

Bambang Santoso showered and changed before walking to the mosque from his house in the compound. He enjoyed strolling down the road with two bodyguards just behind, it gave a sense of entourage which befitted his rank. But even Bambang could feel sadness in the fact that such security was necessary in this new democracy, where his sense of duty was not good enough for others to believe him, or theirs good enough for him to trust.

The call for prayers was probably his most familiar sound, something he had heard since the day he was born. His family were good Muslims and sent him to boarding school to learn Arabic and read the Koran. His home life was loving and supportive rather than austere; his religion was as much a part of his life as the sun and the moon. He removed his shoes and entered the mosque without anyone approaching him, lobbying him, or even staring at him. Everyone knew this was a time for yourself and your God and any other worldly business must wait until after prayers. Bambang kneeled and prayed as an ordinary citizen of God's world. The responsibilities of life that often tormented him during the day were gone as his knees hit the mat; he lowered his whole body in reverence to Allah, his mind drifting to his beloved wife and his wonderful daughters. He imagined them all together at breakfast laughing and joking and he shared a secret proud smile with his wife across the breakfast table. Cancer may have physically taken her from him but he could always be with her in the mosque.

As he emerged an hour later his happiness was quickly replaced by the anger of an important man snubbed. Three or four people approached to talk but he made it clear he had no intention of hanging around today after prayers. He smiled and nodded but motioned to his bodyguards that he was walking straight home and anyway it looked as if it might start to rain. *"Whatever the Forestry Minister is like, the evidence suggests he is arrogant, rude and unpunctual"* thought Bambang as he strode back home in half the time it had taken to walk to the mosque.

36

"Oh good you're back" said his youngest daughter, the only one still living with him. "The Forestry Minister called and apologised for not coming to the mosque tonight. He says he'll be here in a few minutes. He sounded very agitated on the phone."

He grunted slightly as he looked away from her fixed stare.

"Dad, go easy on him, apparently there's been an accident."

"How well his family knew his obsession with time-keeping" he thought. As she smiled lovingly he saw a white Honda Civic with blacked-out windows pull up to the security post by his house. It was ushered into his compound, Probo stepped out from the car to be met by an astonished Bambang, who didn't drive himself and didn't expect any other cabinet members to either. Although on reflection he realised that this was hardly likely.

"I'm so sorry to keep you waiting sir" Probo apologised profusely. "I was called to an accident to identify my driver's body. Apparently my official car was hit by a truck on the toll-way overpass at Kuningan and was pushed over the edge. It's a terrible tragedy and my driver's wife is about to have her first child." His voice broke slightly. "To be honest sir, I'm quite shaken."

Bambang's anger dissolved as fast as it had risen and he awkwardly put his arm around Probo, ushering him into the house. "That's awful" he said rather inadequately. "But where were you at the time?"

Probo explained that he preferred to drive himself, feeling safer with the anonymity. His driver always dropped him in an underground car park attached to a shopping mall not far from *Manggala Wanabakti* where he kept his own car, this Honda Civic. His driver continued to Probo's house to complete the security deception. "I'm afraid I don't trust many people nowadays, especially since the threats are now being made to my home phone." Again, hardly detectable, a slight break in his voice. "My wife is getting increasingly scared."

Bambang was taken aback. One of his ministers was receiving threats at his home in this compound and this was the first he had heard about it. Probo was being given a glass of water by his daughter and seemed to be calming down a little. Why on earth hadn't he told him about the threats since this was a matter of importance for the entire cabinet? He was, after all the Coordinating Minister for Politics and *Security*!

He sat down opposite Probo and looked at this man in his 40s. Well educated and determined, that was all certain. But to keep such a security risk from him was a real breach of common sense.

"Who are the threats coming from?" asked Bambang.

"It's quite difficult to tie them down directly sir" replied Probo. "But they started to come after I had asked for a dossier on a particular timber baron last month" he continued. "I had calls from two Generals and one Member of Parliament warning me off, which I ignored: then after my staff started talking to the police and gathering information, the threats started to become quite sinister, but anonymous."

"And why wasn't I informed?" asked Bambang directly.

Probo looked anxious as if he thought he may have talked too much already. He scratched his head awkwardly and asked if he may have another glass of water to buy himself time. When Bambang's daughter had left the room he explained "I'm sorry sir, but this has been a very stressful time for me. I didn't really want to involve you in all of this."

Bambang looked puzzled so Probo continued. "I did tell your Secretary General and he promised to let you know. But I was very uncomfortable about the threats and I really couldn't tell Widodo that they had started after my interest in the timber baron."

"Why on earth not?" asked Bambang totally confused. As far as he was concerned one of his ministers was being threatened and there may even have been an attempt on his life tonight. Widodo hadn't told him anything about this and he'd certainly be talking to him in the morning.

"Well, it was Widodo who had introduced me to the timber baron in the first place, suggesting we should talk about mutual interests in forest conservation."

"Had he been helpful?"

"It had been a complete waste of time. He wanted to buy me out. This man's Mafia."

Bambang paused, looked out of his window as the rain started to fall before turning back to look directly at Probo. "And his name?"

Probo's face, which had been rather flushed, visibly whitened. "You know sir, I don't think I had realised how scared I was until you asked me his name. And now I'm thinking of my driver's wife who I must go and see tonight."

"Well?" asked Bambang again.

"Abdullah Aziz" said Probo in quick response. "And he owns Central Kalimantan."

CHAPTER EIGHT
Bali

A small reggae band was playing the other side of the deserted dance floor. The strange mix of Native American iconography and Jamaican reggae roots emphasised the conflicting cultures that attracted Australian, Indonesian, Japanese, British and other European clients to *Apache*; almost kitsch, but somehow achieving a friendly diversity, it was early and the party was yet to begin. A waiter came as soon as Matt joined his new acquaintances and he offered them a drink.

"Yes, two beers please" Rita replied.

"So, what makes you so animated? I've spent the last week watching people chilling, smiling and dancing, but not really talking!" questioned Matt.

"We've just been in a long conference" Sam explained, "to try and get the government to stop all the illegal logging in our country." Encouraged by Matt's attention he continued "it hurts us to our soul to see what is happening. Rita is from Borneo and her family are Dayak. They live in the forest, depend on it, and their ancestors are buried in the forest."

"Whoa!" interrupted Matt, "you really are animated aren't you? I respect your concerns but do you think you can really do anything about it?" He reached for his drink and took a sip as Sam stared back at him a little crestfallen. Sam was clean shaven with a square jaw and a slightly flattened nose that made him look really handsome, although Matt was certain he wouldn't take the compliment. His black hair was cut short and in different surroundings he would have looked as if he might be a policeman or in the military: but in *Apache* his loose white shirt and shorts blended with the other customers.

"I'm sorry" said Rita sensing Sam's discomfort. "You're on holiday trying to get away from your hectic life and we're bringing all these troubles into the conversation. You're right, let's relax and enjoy the music." She looked towards the band playing to an empty dance floor.

"No, please don't get me wrong" complained Matt, "I'm really interested, but this probably isn't the best place to talk."

"We were talking fine" quipped Sam.

Realising he'd upset his company Matt tried to engage them in further conversation. "I'm a photographer and am thinking of travelling a bit in the region. Is it safe to go to Borneo?"

"In most areas its fine if you are just travelling" responded Rita, equally uncomfortable, "it's just if you get in the way it becomes dangerous. My sister lives in the south of Borneo in Central Kalimantan, near a national park called Tanjung Puting. Have you heard of it? It's very famous for its orang-utans."

Matt had to admit that he knew very little about Indonesia having only decided to come to Bali two days before travelling. He was about to apologise when Ardi appeared, scowled at Sam and ignored Rita.

"I've been looking for you" Ardi complained, looking directly at Matt as if nobody else existed.

"Hi, Ardi this is Sam and Rita" Matt attempted to make amends.

"Thank you for the drink" interrupted Sam. "I think your friend needs your full attention."

Matt felt very uncomfortable and wished he had talked a bit more before Ardi had arrived. At that moment the waiter came, asked Matt if they would like another drink. Already tired of Ardi's tantrums and his continued attempts to segregate him from all other Indonesians, he replied "three beers please and whatever Ardi wants."

"Nothing for me" he replied "I have to see a friend. I'll call you later Matt."

Ardi turned, said something to the waiter before walking to the side of the bar, along the pathway out to the street. The waiter looked uncomfortable, turned away and walked to the bar just as the band ended a number. A few people applauded.

"I'm really sorry for that" apologised Matt. "It's been brewing for a few days and just came out after I had rudely dismissed your concerns and work. I'm really sorry."

"That's alright" responded Rita, although Sam, whose eyes were following a few tourists onto the dance floor, still looked as if his crest needed considerable lifting.

"You know, you guys are the first people I've met since I arrived that are interested in something other than sun, sea and sex" persevered Matt. "I would really like you to accept my apology so we can enjoy a beer together and carry on with the conversation."

Rita nodded supportively.

Matt smiled and continued "Sam, please accept my apology and tell me something about your work."

It was clear Sam wasn't accepting Matt's apology as easily as Rita. The beer arrived giving him a small break to reconsider his position. "So, please tell me why you come to Bali" he asked "and why these young men look at you, and run around after you?"

Touché.

The band stopped playing and the dancers returned to their chairs.

"OK Sam" Matt replied slowly, giving himself time to consider his response. He didn't know these people, yet he was being asked a very direct and, possibly difficult question, by a good-looking young man with a passion to save the world. There was absolutely no need to respond, but somehow Matt felt he wanted to at least give it a try and see if this would be accepted or rejected. "I'm English and therefore perceived by most people here as rich, although in my country I'm not rich at all. I'm also interested in both guys and girls but, since my first night here have been enjoying the gay scene and spending my nights with Ardi, who you just met."

He paused to judge the reaction so far; seeing blank faces he decided to continue. "Ardi has rapidly become very jealous of my every move and it is beginning to piss me off. And yes, it is true that young men are running around looking at me and, you know what? I'm loving it!" He was talking really fast. "I had completely lost my confidence when I flew out here having split from my girlfriend. The boys from Bali have made me feel special."

Sam looked into his beer unsure how to respond to this extraordinary and unexpected candour from a complete stranger. As if having waited for Matt to finish his confession, the band started up again on a familiar Bob Marley number.

Rita raised her glass. "Refreshing honesty" she said kindly, turning to smile at Sam. "There are a lot of gay men in Bali and they come from all over Indonesia to escape the prejudice of their families and friends. It is very hard for gay men in Indonesia you know, you must not think it is all like Bali."

Matt looked at this beautiful and comfortable young woman who was moving the conversation along intelligently.

"If you live in Jakarta or Surabaya it may be alright," she continued, "but most communities don't even talk about homosexuality, just as they prefer to ignore the rights of women or the crimes of former regimes. Our society has learned to avoid uncomfortable subjects. Give us time though, there's a wonderful opportunity now for Indonesia to confront itself."

"I hadn't realised it was so difficult" said Matt appreciatively "and although I've been around gay men all week, Rita you are the first person to explain this to me."

"I'm not surprised" she laughed "you don't discuss politics in gay bars! You know, in my culture, Dayak culture, we only see sex as something that creates babies. So, for us, if a husband sleeps with another woman, this is wrong. It destabilises the community and causes real problems. But if he sleeps with another man, that is not really sex."

Matt raised his eyebrows and beamed at Rita.

"I'm not saying that Dayak men are all having sex with each other, because they're not, but I'm trying to explain a different view of the world." She smiled back at Matt and then turned to Sam before saying "now what's up with you?"

Sam had been listening to Rita but looked away again as Rita and Matt sipped beer from their glasses. He had already finished his and had no fall back position. He noticed the Bob Marley song had helped fill the dance floor and concentrated on a couple dancing not far from their table.

Rita pushed him again. "Come on Sam, you like to talk. What's up?"

Sam looked up and stared at Rita as if he had been betrayed. "Why are you trying to embarrass me Rita?"

"I don't remember seeing you like this before Sam" replied Rita quietly.

"It's OK" interrupted Matt "it's my fault for being so dismissive of your work and your efforts to protect your home. I'm really sorry."

Sam's face softened and he reached out to hold Rita's hand. "I'm sorry I reacted so childishly, but I found Matt's friend offensive." He lowered his head and looked into Rita's eyes with a sad expression on his face. His eyes were watery with emotion. She placed her other hand over his as he turned to Matt.

Without any awkwardness there was a long pause, a rare moment even between friends, but the precise moment that Matt realised he wanted to know Rita and Sam and their life better: the moment he felt warm again after weeks of emotional loneliness. He stared at these two new friends, sensing a deep bond between the two of them, something he doubted they even knew.

Sam felt the moment as well and smiled at Rita. Speaking more to her than Matt he opened up and explained "Matt's friend told the waiter I was working the bar as a rent boy and should be thrown out of *Apache*. I don't think the waiter believed him but it was obvious that they know each other." He paused, looked down in a lost puppy-dog way and asked "I don't look gay do I?"

Now it was Matt's turn to try and repair the damage caused by Ardi's brief appearance. "Oh shit, I'm really sorry Sam. I had no idea he said that. He was jealous of you because you're a young, good looking guy. Please don't worry about the gay thing. Look, do you think I look gay?"

"Not really."

"Being gay is not about what you look like Sam!" he replied fixing his eyes on Sam's. "It's true that many people try to fit stereotypes, but there are far more who are just ordinary or extraordinary people getting on with their lives." He paused, thinking carefully about his next remark. "If you're asking if you are cute then the answer is definitely yes, but I think Rita would agree with me on that!"

Rita smiled and then, as if caught off guard, blushed a little and responded "Sam's not cute! Oh my god! No way!" She paused. "He's Sam."

Matt smiled conspiratorially at Rita. The bar had filled even more and the reggae band had pumped out a few classics – enough to keep the dance floor lively.

"Now I'd be really interested to hear about this national park you were talking about if you don't mind changing the subject" suggested Matt. "Would I be able to visit it and what would the photography be like?"

On safer ground Sam and Rita explained the park was one of the world's most famous places for orang-utan which translates from Indonesian as "man of the forest", *orang hutan*. They told him this was true swamp, fantastically rich in biodiversity and one of the most important parks in Indonesia. Rita spoke proudly of the wildlife and plants and explained that Tanjung Puting was so inhospitable that Dayak tribes had never lived on this land, but lived all around it. Her sister Setin lived in the local town and had just had a baby with her husband Murkha who was coming to Jakarta tomorrow. "I fly back in the morning to meet him" she explained.

Matt was making up his mind to try and get to this swamp, partly to shoot potentially valuable photographs, but equally to escape the boys of Bali. "How would I get into the park?" he asked.

"That's easy!" replied Rita. "We're planning to go there soon. Give us your phone number and we can take you to meet Murkha's friend who takes foreigners around the park. He lives in Kumai, the last village before the park."

Sam looked less enthusiastic, but swapped his number with Matt, and uttered a friendly but guarded warning. "I'm OK with you coming with us to Borneo if you really want to. But please remember how we feel about the criminal destruction of the forest."

"I respect that Sam."

"Not just Rita's community but communities all over Indonesia. I'm Batak from Sumatra, we're warriors, and even though you're just looking for some photos, I'm there to fight with proof of what is really going on. Don't think you will be able to avoid all that. In the end you may even understand that it's not about whether we can really change things. It's quite simply a matter of survival."

45

They swapped their mobile phone numbers.

Matt was already feeling that something newly indescribable had just entered his life.

CHAPTER NINE
Jakarta

Jakarta is a dirty and frustrating city. It is heavily polluted and its occasional opulence looks backwards rather than forwards. Its few impressive skyscrapers offer a false sense of modern financial order which is impossible to find even in the corridors of power. The real taste of the city is better expressed by the dozens of its citizens hanging onto the outside of every diesel bus, blowing out that kind of black smoke that a movie props designer would find difficult to artificially reproduce.

The city is criss-crossed by toll roads designed to take the fast traffic but, nowadays, is overburdened by the sheer volume of cars and trucks that on the worst days appear as if they will never ever move even a single metre, ever again.

It is easy as a visitor to only see these toll roads, skyscrapers and the hotel bars, but the real Jakarta lies between and under these modern symbols of wealth and international comfort. Tiny lanes and small roads lined by houses and businesses cover vast areas of modern Jakarta with stalls and street restaurants, offering ordinary residents an affordable means to survive. It was in one of these streets that the world headquarters of *Yayasan Hutan Bagus* was housed. Loosely translated as the *Good Forest Organisation*, YHB occupied a small house with four rooms, one toilet and one *mandy* or shower.

Debi Sudarto was presiding over a meeting in the small garden around an old teak table. Also there were Rita, Sam and Murkha who had just arrived from his home in Pangkalan Bun in Central Kalimantan. Murkha was fortunate to have been educated at a Christian missionary school and learned *bahasa* Indonesia and English before graduating. This had given him opportunities to train to be a teacher and he was currently teaching in a school near his home. His wife Setin was Rita's sister.

"Whatever you do, don't tell Setin I came to see you!" giggled Murkha with an air of seriousness.

"Why on earth not?" asked Rita.

Murkha knocked a cigarette from his packet and lit it slowly. He sucked so hard that his features were momentarily completely obscured by smoke and he thoughtfully responded from the dramatic smokescreen he had created "she's scared. And she's right. She's always right, Rita. God I love your sister she's so always right!"

They all fell silent although Sam had just started opening a paper-wrapped snack which always accompanies meetings in Indonesia. The crinkling of the paper focused Sam's thoughts, partly through the inappropriateness of the sound, on what Murkha was alluding to.

"This guy's dangerous. We have a new baby. Setin is trying to protect us from the bad things around us by backing away. But I feel differently and it scares her." He stopped for a moment to take a long drag on his cigarette. "I feel that with our new baby I want to think ahead. I want to make sure that she has a home that's worth living in. This corrupt town that we now live in will never provide what I want for my daughter unless we can fight the awful greed, the violence and the immorality" Murkha said straight faced. Then, to their surprise he giggled "almost sounds as if I'm moral and brave, doesn't it?" he added.

"You never fooled me" replied Rita smiling "remember I've known you longer than even Setin."

Sam decided it was alright now to eat his snack without breaking the mood. Debi took control and asked Murkha to tell them what information he had for them.

"OK. You're always to the point Debi, but you're right. Women! Setin is always right and you too. You know we men think we are in control of everything but that's a bad joke. You lot are much better at life than we are."

"Yes Murkha, I'm glad you've figured that out" Debi replied somewhat impatiently without humour. "Now what have you got?"

Murkha explained there were two Vietnamese ships in Pangkalan Bun, one of which was loading logs stolen from the national park. Everyone knew they were there and everyone knew the logs were owned by Abdullah Aziz, but no one was prepared to fight him. Murkha wanted YHB to help get this information to the government as a test of whether they would act to fight the timber baron.

"What are the names of the two ships?" asked Debi."

"Na Trang II and something like Hanoisset" he replied. "But their names have been painted out and they're flying Indonesian flags as they load the logs. They are the biggest ships in town and really shouldn't be difficult for any law enforcement officers to find" he chuckled adding "except of course for the police and military in Pangkalan Bun."

"How long have we got?" asked Sam.

"Na Trang II has been loading for four days already and I would guess it will be fully loaded in two or three day's time. Then I would expect the other ship to move into the berth and start loading, but we can't be sure. Of course, if it isn't there to load, what is it there for? So, probably about ten days before the second ship is loaded, but the Na Trang II may sail as soon as it is fully loaded in two or three days time."

"How do you know the logs are owned by Aziz?" questioned Rita. "Are the boats carrying paperwork that will implicate him?"

"I don't know" replied Murkha. "But everyone in town just knows! This is no secret. The local police and military are protecting the ships from anyone snooping around and they only do this for Abdullah Aziz."

"And you are happy for me to take this intelligence to the government?" asked Debi. "It could be dangerous for you Murkha."

"Yes, but if the government ask the local police to follow up this information then they won't find anything. This will have to involve the national police or military and it will be very difficult to keep this quiet from the local authorities."

"I really don't know how the government will deal with this without implicating Generals, the Governor and probably senior government officials, but that's their problem not mine" Debi stated matter-of-factly.

Murkha laughed out loud. "Sometimes it takes a thief to catch a thief!"

*

Mohammed Probowo knew his political life would not last very long but he was determined to make the most of his position while he had some power. He had a good feeling about his neighbour and senior cabinet colleague the Coordinating Minister for Politics and Security, although he found him a little pompous and unusually naïve. How could a man that had risen to his rank in the army, taken one of the most influential jobs in government, be naïve? Probo was pondering this question when he was informed that Debi had arrived and was being ushered into his study on the ground floor of his house. He went to greet her.

"Welcome Debi" he stated with his arms stretched out in a generous gesture. He had known Debi for fifteen years and had been a close friend of her husband. He would always have time for her and knew more about her past than most of her daily colleagues. There had been a time after her husband's and child's deaths when he had been her closest male friend, but she had become so bitter, he had slowly backed away.

She had called him on his mobile phone just before he had left his office and he had arranged to meet her at his home because he thought it would be safer.

"Minister" Debi lowered her gaze in deference to his government position. "Thank you for seeing me at such short notice."

"Please Debi, sit down." Probo felt uncomfortable with the formality of her greeting but recognised that formality gave him a status he would otherwise not achieve.

"I'll be swift Minister. Your time is valuable and I don't have much to say but what I do have is a test of your government's will or ability to fight the timber mafia in our country."

She passed on the information Murkha had given her earlier without revealing his name. Probo knew that her information would be accurate without pushing for the credentials of her source, who they both knew would be safer anonymous.

"You realise that if I am able to act on this information it will send signals across the country that may be difficult to resist?" he asked.

"We both understand the difficulty of our tasks" she replied softly, looking compassionately at this old friend with the weight of the world on his shoulders. "I'm so sorry to hear of your driver's murder Probo" she added. "You realise it was supposed to be you, don't you? You know you've gone so far now that you only have two alternate paths to follow."

"Two?" Probo asked quizzically.

"Yes" she answered emphatically, but grinning slightly. "You can take hundreds of thousands of dollars from the timber thieves" she paused smiling at him "and move to Singapore."

"And the second?"

"Fight to win. Please be careful Probo, choose your political comrades carefully because they are the most unpredictable."

"Thank you Debi" Probo smiled as she turned and walked out of the study towards her waiting car.

As she was driven out of the Forestry Minister's compound she noticed a security guard watching her curiously before making a call on his phone. She dialled Probo's number quickly and he answered immediately.

"Outside, the security guard with the fat stomach. Get your men to grab his phone and find out who he just talked to Probo. Our lives may depend on it."

Further up the street she asked her driver to pull over and watched as Probo's security men pulled an unwilling guard back into Probo's compound.

"Good luck Probo, Allah be with you" she whispered under her breath.

CHAPTER TEN
Borneo

There really are few reasons why anyone would fly to Pangkalan Bun. The first would be to return home if you live in the vicinity of this southern part of the Indonesian province of Central Kalimantan on the island of Borneo. If not a local, you may have come to do business, which probably means you deal in timber, gold or oil palm. If none of this applies, you are likely to be a tourist travelling to Tanjung Puting National Park which is currently being ravaged by timber and gold thieves and illegal encroachment by oil palm estates. The flight is so early that you are made to suffer even before you arrive, unless you are one of those annoyingly cheerful "morning people."

Murkha was one of them. He was returning home slightly troubled, yet peculiarly elated after his visit to Jakarta. He knew that sharing his information could cause him problems but he had followed his heart, set something in motion and only had to wait to find out which direction that motion would take. His mind had been buzzing ever since he boarded the commercial flight across the Java Sea to his wife and baby. What if the authorities really do act on his information? What will they do and who will do it? Will they arrest Abdullah Aziz? Would Aziz realise he had been the one to pass on the information? Where could they run to? Would YHB offer his family protection somewhere in Jakarta? Then he realised his imagination was running away with itself, after all Aziz was so powerful that there was nobody in government capable of confronting him, so why had he taken such a risk? But he was doing it for his daughter and her future and although his wife Setin didn't understand, she would soon see that this was the only way forward. He chuckled to himself when he thought of Setin holding his baby daughter and how they would both be so pleased to see him after his mysterious visit to Java.

He bounced off the aircraft into the humid hot air that hit him like a familiar and welcoming friend. His rotund figure strutted with slightly exaggerated pride as he entered the small airport and walked with his overnight bag towards the table where passengers' luggage was piled up for collection. He saw Koto, one of his oldest friends and his "brother" from school, who was standing near the red "bagage colect" sign and to his surprise he sensed a pang of suspicion rather than joy.

"Hey Koto!" he shouted feeling an overwhelming sadness and fear as he called out to his friend. Why was Koto at the airport and how did he know he was arriving today? Even Setin had no idea he would be back so soon. Was he being watched by his oldest friend?

"Hey Brother, there was no need to come and get me! What are you doing here?" he tried to add without any sense of accusation, but he knew Koto had already felt the distrust. He lit up a cigarette ignoring the new signs announcing the airport's "no smoking" policy dreamt up, presumed Murkha, by some silly little bureaucrat trying to make this tin-pot airport feel as if it fitted into the disturbing international trend to control all pleasure. He suddenly felt awful and even their long hug had an uncomfortable parting.

They quickly shook off this negative greeting without truly understanding its cause. Koto explained his bike was repaired and he had driven out to the airport on the off chance of picking up some tourists. This explanation was enough for Murkha and as Koto drove him home on the back of his motorbike the coolness of the rushing air blew away the bad feeling. Murkha marvelled at how extraordinary it was that the rushing air on a bike or the feeling of water splashing through your hair in the morning *mandy* can wash away fears, suspicions and cleanse your emotions. Once again Koto could hear Murkha's familiar giggle behind him and he smiled to himself as they approached Murkha's home and family.

The homecoming was muted. Murkha thought it was because of Koto's presence but Setin had lightened up when he had given her the black coral bracelet and shown her the tiny one for their baby and the one he now wore around his wrist. The day had passed very differently to the one he had dreamed of on the plane, but at last, when Koto had gone, he held Setin in his arms while their daughter slept peacefully.

"You know my love" romanticised Murkha "it's moments like this that give me hope. The future looks so sad, but to feel your body against mine, breathing in unison with our baby beside us, is really all I could hope for." He put his arm alongside that of his wife and his daughter; their new black coral bracelets looked as if they had always been with them, three bracelets lined up together like a family. After a silent pause he broke the moment by reaching for and lighting a cigarette. Setin moved away from his embrace, looked at him and shook her head. Outside it started to rain.

"What have you done?" she asked quietly.

"What do you mean?" he replied rather surprised by her response to his emotional outpouring.

"You only talk to me like that when you know I'll be angry with you for something."

Murkha smiled and held her again in his arms, slowly explaining his visit to Jakarta, the information he had passed on about the Vietnamese ships loading logs in Pangkalan Bun. She was quiet. Encouraged by her silence he explained how excited he was that the ships might be seized. "This is a moment Setin, a moment when we can help our people fight the corruption of Aziz and his crooks. We can build a better life for our family and our friends."

He looked down at his wife and saw streams of tears pouring down her cheeks; she took in an enormous breath and pushed herself away from him. As she let the breath out the sound wavered and her face contorted into anger, no longer tranquil and no longer safely quiet. In fact she shrieked so loud that their baby woke, started to cry and Murkha felt a terrifying sense that he had been very bad indeed. This almost childlike emotion welled up so deeply inside him that tears started to stream down his face in a way he had never experienced before.

He grabbed her and pulled her close and they both cried uncontrollably in each others arms. In these seconds Murkha understood Setin's fear and realised everything she was feeling: the risk of his actions affected his family and not just himself, but wasn't that why he had done it in the first place? She saw a life without him and without support, a child who wouldn't remember her father and a family that would forever blame him for letting them all down.

The moment was so intense that neither needed to speak and, when the metallic green Mitsubishi Pajero 4x4 pulled up outside their door, they were frozen in recognition of what was unfolding in their lives. Murkha was first to recover as his adrenalin rushed to the rescue of his family. He pushed Setin to the back of the room where she picked up their baby and held her protectively in her arms. Murkha was in front of her with his arms out stretched, as if it made a protective shield, but three men wearing scarves over their faces had already entered the room. The tallest had a gun in his hand and told Murkha to come quietly and his family would be alright. Setin screamed and started to shout out "No don't take him!" repeatedly but Murkha simply walked out of the door with the men and got into their vehicle without turning back.

He was in the back of the Mitsubishi Pajero with one of the men on either side. The man with the gun sat in the front passenger seat next to a driver. They pulled out onto the road slowly and carefully, Murkha noticed that the driver even switched on his indicator before pulling out, like any polite and considered driver, and there were precious few of them. They didn't ask him anything or blindfold him, in fact they had acted with little aggression, although Murkha put up no resistance. It was dark outside; looking ahead Murkha could see through the rain in the headlights that they were heading out of town past his school. The sight of the building reminded him that his students would be returning to the class with their latest assignment: hopes for the future written on one page and their fears written opposite. It was part of a school strategy to get the children to think about their world. He wondered if he would live to hear their hopes and fears now he had so many himself.

None of the men spoke to him and, although he knew many people from the area, he had no idea who they were except he thought they may be Javanese. They all wore scarves over their faces but he could see the eyes of the man on his right in the rear view mirror. They were young and dark but didn't appear to show any particular emotion. Maybe he could see a little fear.

They turned off the road but he couldn't see anything through the rain to give him a bearing. It was certainly on the stretch between Pangkalan Bun and Kumai and not far from the truck wash where trucks were driven onto a wooden bridge over a river and washed down by hand. Murkha used to go to the truck wash as a teenager with his friends to listen to stories told by the drivers.

He had accepted his first cigarette from a truck driver and used it to burn leaches between his toes.

The Pajero bumped along for a few kilometres as Murkha thought of Setin and his daughter. The abductors had said his family would be safe and he thought they were probably telling the truth. His stupidity had brought such danger to his family that he wondered what could possibly have possessed him to be so foolhardy: probably his ego, his belief that he could change the world. He had always been transfixed by the knowledge that so many huge changes had been carried out by small groups of people. He had loved reading of Dayak leaders, capable of calling up the powers of the forest and everything that lived in it, but he now felt inadequate, realising that his actions assumed he mattered. At this moment he really didn't believe he mattered at all, as long as his family would be safe.

The driver slowed down, turned the Pajero around in a circle and Murkha could see through the pounding rain in the headlights they were in a forest clearing less than fifty metres across. The vehicle stopped and the driver turned off the engine. The man on his left got out of the vehicle and beckoned him to follow. The driver and the tall man with the gun came around and Murkha noticed the young man who had appeared a little afraid had opened the heavy door at the back of the vehicle. He couldn't see what he was getting out but heard the unmistakeable sound of steel against steel.

"Come with me" ushered the tall man with the gun. Murkha followed him into the darkness and could hear the others behind him. "Stop here and take your clothes off" he ordered. Now Murkha was very afraid, but, without even questioning the order, he removed his shirt and then his jeans and sandals. Absurdly he felt slightly ashamed of his body, plump and neglected. "All your clothes" repeated the tall man. Murkha pulled his underpants down and put them on top of the rest of his clothes. It was at this moment he realised he was going to die.

The pile of clothes recalled stories he had read in the newspaper about missing people whose clothes were found on a beach neatly folded; but no sign of the owner.

"Lie flat on the ground on your back with your arms and legs out in a star position" the tall man ordered softly. Murkha simply obeyed and once on the ground he closed his eyes. He could sense the four men taking up positions around him. "For Allah" shouted the men together and Murkha felt a pain in his arms and legs. He heard the men walking away and opened his eyes to see each man with one of his limbs in one hand and a machete in the other.

Mercifully he blanked out and was dead in minutes.

CHAPTER ELEVEN
Borneo

The rain had suddenly turned red. It was beating against mud and splashing off the macabre horror of the severed arm. Some of the bouncing rain drops were lit weakly by the naked light shining out from Koto's room, sparkling in pink, as if they had been to a party and hadn't realised there had been a death. Like loved-up dancers, oblivious of the dead reveller under their feet, the guy who misjudged his cocktail of pills and powder and gave his heart one thump too many.

Koto stared and kneeled in front of the limb before his mind understood the real consequences of what he was seeing. Once that recognition arrived, he retched and heaved like a dog which has deliberately eaten grass; his body, bent double, rocked backwards and forwards over what was left of his old friend.

He was unaware of anything or anybody else, but his neighbour had come out of her house with her baby in her arms and walked over to see what was wrong. On seeing the limb she had shrieked repeatedly and, holding her child, rushed back through her front door, slamming it behind her. A man on the other side of the road had pulled off his t shirt, walked out into the rain and crossed the road to see what the commotion was all about. Within minutes a small crowd was staring at Koto rocking backwards and forwards in front of the limb, as if it was an altar. If it hadn't been raining, the crowd would have been even larger. One thing stood out and they had all commented on it - the black coral bracelet still worn on the wrist.

Similar scenes were being played out in Pangkalan Bun near the police station, outside the head teacher's house and in Murkha and Setin's bathroom. Murkha's left leg had been thrown out of the Pajero onto a porch outside the teacher's house, his right at the police station's picket fence and his left arm had gone straight through an open window into the bathroom of his own house, where Setin was already being sedated by her doctor, with two friends in attendance. The shock of recognising that the projectile was a limb was bad enough, but for Setin and Koto the realisation that they were Murkha's limbs was unbearable.

58

Koto slowly started to cry as he felt his youth pass out of him like a spirit leaving a corpse. His crying was slow and level, only changing its tone because of his rocking body movement. He remained unaware of the crowd around him but started to feel Murkha's presence in a way that built and forced itself into his heart. He suddenly stopped rocking, looked down at the chubby arm, smiled, picked it up off the ground, holding it close to his bare chest like a child. Only then did he see the others staring down at him, he held the limb even tighter like a frightened mother protecting her baby from a violent mob. When he was sure the threat was no more, Koto stood, carried Murkha's arm into his room and shut the door.

The head teacher had no idea what the severed leg was doing on his porch or whose it was. His reaction was to tell his wife to stay in the house and to call the police. The reply from the police station had taken him aback, as the policeman on the other end of the phone had simply said "oh, you've got one too then" and asked for his address. He was later to realise that the limb was there to warn him against teaching the children the importance of the national park on their doorstep. It seemed that his teaching had angered one of the grand parents of little Nanang Aziz.

The police were equally confused by the leg thrown up against their picket fence. It was already a very difficult night for them because of the presence of officers from the national police office in Jakarta and rumours of naval activities at the mouth of the bay outside Kumai. Something was definitely not right and the chief of police in Pangkalan Bun had already been on the phone to his superior in the capital, Palankaraya, and to local dignitary Abdullah Aziz's son, Hazim. The latter had not been at home, his mother saying he was on a business trip in Singapore, a story that the chief of police found difficult to believe since he'd had lunch with him earlier in the day and Singapore had never been mentioned.

If it had been Murkha's intention to stir up his local town, he had, at least in part, been very successful. The tactics of the assassination squad had created maximum fear and it was days before it became common knowledge whose limbs had been delivered and to whom. Most people would never dare ask "why?" other than link the murder to the other unusual activities of the night: the arrest of two large Vietnamese vessels and their crew, the boats having been chartered by Abdullah Aziz.

The navy had blocked the bay with two warships under direct command of the Admiral of the Western Fleet, a fellow college graduate of Bambang Santoso's. Fourteen inflatable Zodiacs had been launched from the ships in a show of force and determination unprecedented, aimed at sending a message to the illegal loggers and their boss. Unaware of the message being sent back to them by the assassination squad at the exact time that they were boarding the Vietnamese ships, the naval contingent had successfully cooperated with national police from Jakarta who had simultaneously neutralised the local police chief and his officers.

A battle was being fought with both sides unaware of each others activities and both sides believing they had scored a major victory.

Jakarta

Probo was still in his office at the Ministry of Forestry waiting to hear from the navy. He was reading through a file that had been compiled on the activities, investments and contacts of Abdullah Aziz. It was incredible that this man had stolen at least three million dollars worth of timber from the national park every month for the last six years. His sawmills had been built on the banks of the river near the park and small villages of thousands of workers had grown around them. He had bought a shipping company, two small local banks, a leisure centre in Balikpapan in East Kalimantan, a town that exploded with oil money when rigs were built off the coast. He was rumoured to own the *Regency*, a five star hotel in Singapore and probably had many other unknown foreign investments.

On a sheet of blue paper were typed the affiliations Aziz had with influential people in Southeast Asia and it was this sheet that particularly interested and concerned Probo. He recognised most of the names as Indonesian businessmen, politicians and high ranked military officers but he hadn't expected to see the respect that Aziz had bought in the Muslim community in the Philippines, Malaysia and all over Java and Sulawesi. Some of this was explained by his generous donations to Muslim organisations and his construction of five mosques in Kalimantan and two in Sulawesi. But most worrying to Probo was his strong interest in East Javanese *pesantrans*, or Muslim boarding schools. It appeared that he had given two million dollars each year for the last three years to a religious leader, Imam Bakti, in Solo, East Java for community work with the poor. The information had come from a respected religious scholar and politician who claimed that Aziz had accompanied this cleric on the *Haj* pilgrimage to Mecca the previous year.

The revelations on this blue sheet of paper sent shivers through Probo's body and he looked up from his desk at the large empty room around him. His secretary had already gone home; from experience Probo was certain virtually all of his Ministry staff had left the building at five o'clock. He could hear traffic noise outside and the sound of cicadas in the old trees in the Ministry grounds, but no hint of any human activity in the Ministry itself. The night watchmen and his new driver would be outside somewhere, but he felt totally alone in the sprawling maze of offices that make up *Manggala Wanabakti*.

Was Aziz really a religious man? It would appear so, especially since he had visited Mecca last year, built mosques and donated huge sums of money to help the poor. How did he reconcile all this with his pillage of the park and blatant bribery of officials? Did he believe that God was merciful to such corrupt and violent men? The modern world around Probo confused and angered him as his thoughts moved on to Bambang Santoso and his naval friend. Could he really trust Bambang? Surely a man of his rank and influence had only got to that position by bending the rules and owing the rich and powerful too much to be truly honest to himself, his country and his God?

A door slammed further up the corridor and Probo's thoughts were interrupted by the steady sound of approaching footsteps. Another door opened and closed, the footsteps continued to make their way towards his office. Probo looked around his room at the table light shining brightly on the coffee table next to the sofa where guests were seated for meetings, wondering if he should extinguish the light and hide from the intruder. He was about to

61

get up out of his chair when he suddenly felt ridiculous for hiding from an unknown person in *his* Ministry. He was the boss and no one would dare threaten him on his own turf. He was a minister in the Government of the Republic of Indonesia and had the full power of his President, his Cabinet position and the law. When he thought of "the law" he realised he was fooling himself with his momentary sense of self-importance, the law didn't protect you from the kind of power he was up against. He shivered involuntarily.

Half way along the wall of his office was a door that went straight out to the corridor. At the far end of his office another door led into the forward waiting area where, during the day, his secretary had a desk and ushered guests in to see him. He heard the footsteps stop outside the door onto the corridor and someone tried to turn the handle. The door was locked. Whoever it was moved on towards his forward waiting room and Probo got up from his chair, dashed across the huge room, opened the door into the waiting room and stood confronted by a night watchman.

"Oh I'm sorry sir" bumbled the startled employee. "I hadn't realised there was anyone in the building sir."

Probo, sweating very noticeably, stepped back through the doorway to regain his composure. "That's alright, I'm just finishing off some work before going home" he explained unnecessarily. Behind him on his desk at the other end of his office his mobile phone started to ring. He turned and shut the door to his office behind him, leaving the night watchman in his waiting area bewildered by his behaviour. It would be unusual for these men, moving in such vastly different social circles, to even exchange glances, no matter actually talk to each other. Probo had appeared as if he was up to no good and had been caught out unexpected.

As he walked across his room towards his phone he heard the call for prayers from his local mosque, the familiar sound of the Imam calling the faithful towards the mosque with his waling song amplified through a tinny public address system. Nevertheless the sound reassured Probo, bringing him back to the present with a comforting and helping hand. As he reached for his phone the ringing stopped and the mobile diverted to voicemail. Probo tidied away the file on Aziz and put it in his briefcase for reading later at home before calling his voicemail, expecting it to be his daughter chastising him for being late home for dinner again.

The recording was broken, as if the call had come from a very long way away. A rather disembodied voice was just possible to encipher, as it asked Probo a simple question, before qualifying the reason for asking.

"Are you praying brother? This is a call for prayer. Your faithful voicemail asks you to pray for the soul of the giggling informer, the man who can be in four places at the same time, yet laughs no more."

CHAPTER TWELVE
Borneo

Rita and Sam picked up their bags from the table under the sign "bagage colect" without speaking and stepped out into the pouring rain to find a taxi. The drive from Pangkalan Bun airport seemed too familiar to Rita to make any sense; men and women on motorbikes wearing black poncho style rain coats, the potholed road passing the same *warang* street restaurants and the same rows of simple wooden houses. Life could not just go on as normal in this tin pot town with its tyrant carrying on business as usual; it defied any order to life and questioned the purpose of any rules of any kind. Rita was angry. She hadn't cried since she had heard of Murkha's murder, driving through the rain in the damp heat hadn't brought her any closer to breaking open her feelings and spilling her heart all over those around her.

Debi had been stoic of course. Murkha's murder was shocking but just a reminder of the forces we were all up against. *"That's fine for her to say"* thought Rita *"she hasn't just lost her beautiful brother-in-law and friend."*

Sam had come, as much to be with his friend Rita, as to represent YHB, although Debi had insisted he "got to the bottom" of what had happened. He felt hollow. The excitement of the knowledge of a naval blockade before it happened had been replaced by a sense of helplessness. He realised his sense of importance at being privy to sensitive military and government information had been stupid and unrealistic. He had talked to enough people, about the war that was being waged in the forest, to have known better – it wasn't that easy. He had just hoped that Debi's government contact had been powerful enough to hit back. Even though there had been an unprecedented military action against Aziz, it was impossible for Sam to see its significance, at this moment, beyond the death of gentle Murkha.

Their taxi drew up outside the house; they paused before getting out in the rain and facing the house. They knocked on the door, standing under the flock of brightly painted wooden birds moving erratically in the rain. There was no answer, so they knocked again, hearing movement inside but feeling unable to enter uninvited.

Rita looked at Sam for a reaction, but he shrugged his shoulders as confused as she was, but as they looked at each other the door flung open and Setin shouted uncontrollably as she punched at Rita's face and body in a vicious rage.

"You used him" she screamed. "He trusted you and you used him, I hate you!"

Sam moved between them taking some of the blows on his own face. He was shocked at Setin's strength; it was as if she was possessed. Rita burst into tears and dropped to the ground submissively as Setin kicked her in the chest. "I hate you" she repeated with less conviction than before, doubling up and collapsing next to Rita on the ground in a puddle, tears pouring down her cheeks from her red and swollen eyes. They sobbed together.

Sam moved away from the house and strolled slowly down the road to give them some time alone. As he got out of range of the sisters' grief he started to cry himself, his tears washed away by the rain. He hadn't expected their arrival to be met with such raw anger; it was only now he started to feel a depth of responsibility he had never experienced before. He noticed a few people watching him from outside their houses and wondered if they understood what had happened to Murkha or why. He wondered if they understood how Murkha had fought for his community, only to be, literally, cut down at his first battle. He wondered if they held him responsible. He wondered if they cared.

He reached for his cigarettes.

A bare-chested, skinny, elderly Dayak man in cheap blue trousers and flip flops crossed the road and walked confidently up to Sam, offering him a light in a friendly warm gesture, cupping his hand to shield the flame from the rain. Sam breathed in deeply and looked into the man's eyes before lifting his cigarette to accept the kindness. As the tip burned red he inhaled the smoke, looked again at the man's eyes and saw a gentle wisdom, built over six decades, staring back at him.

"Courage is always worthwhile young friend" the man crisply and unequivocally stated, smiling. "Violence is a last and hopeless resort and your dead friend has shown us the inevitability of recovery. Please thank your friend for me." He turned and walked along the street towards Murkha's house, briefly stopping outside and respectfully placing the palms of his hands together, bowing his head at the painted birds before moving on, his trousers clinging to his undernourished legs in the driving rain.

PART TWO: MEN OF THE FOREST

CHAPTER THIRTEEN
Singapore

Singapore's *Regency* hotel had seen better days, before Abdullah Aziz bought it outright from his Chinese Singaporean golfing companion, to help him get out of "rather a pickle." Something to do with a Filipino maid, a baby and a substantial stash of cocaine, but Aziz hadn't asked; in Singapore you never mentioned drugs. He had been looking for property investment in this island city state he now considered his second home, and what could be better than one of the island's five star hotels. He paid considerably less than it was worth, but the cash had been just what his friend was looking for. It was important to help rich friends when they needed you; you just might need them one day.

Aziz had refurbished the hotel to the highest standards new money could buy. Jacuzzis in all the rooms, marble throughout the gigantic entrance hall and gold chandeliers dripping from all the public areas. The ground floor atrium, although part of the original hotel, after modernisation, had become its most famous feature. He had opened a new Lebanese restaurant to complement the famous Chinese Dim Sum restaurant patronised by wealthy Chinese families on Sundays. A nightclub had been fashioned out of the basement reminiscent of shadowy Middle Eastern bars; Filipino singers, sheiks dressed in white peering out of darkened corners like ghosts, a bottle of Chivas Regal on their private table.

The hotel was near the financial district attracting Chinese, Middle Eastern and wealthy western business clients as well as a splattering of tourists when the Orchard Road hotels were overbooked. His managing director had successfully negotiated a contract with two airlines based in the Middle East and their crew always stayed in the economy rooms, while their executives enjoyed the splendour of the upper floors of the 26 storey building. The top floor had been divided into penthouse suites, each enjoying views across the island from at least two aspects.

The south facing side of the top floor was a temple to the Singaporean dollar and used mainly by Aziz and his personal guests. Its eastern corner boasted a bedroom fit for a king and at least three queens. Adjoining was a bathroom with a sunken bath which had steps leading into its foaming waters, electronic curtains, video projection and its own staff of three young girls. One was always on duty.

The western corner was a private lounge with an open bar to relax in at sunset. It was perfect to close a deal with a business partner, no hotel staff present to witness the identity of the guests, although Aziz often brought his own barman with him, a young Indonesian man he completely trusted. After sunset the area could be converted, by touch of a button, into a dining area or a theatre with the best electronic gadgetry Singapore could offer. Along the south side of the Penthouse were offices, a private health spa and gym, and other bedrooms and lounges which could be opened up to each other.

Singapore gave Aziz the comfortable knowledge that he was close to home as well as his money. This small island state has surpassed the social critics of the 80s, when it was common to joke about the absurd fines for stubbing out a cigarette in the street or being refused entry for having long hair; now Singapore's music clubs boast some of the best visiting DJs in the world, while its fashionable classes spend their ample money on luxuries that many in the west could never afford. Its financial district drives much of the business in Southeast Asia, between the region and the west, and banks its profits. But the core wealth in Singapore remains its trade, with ever growing container ports and the world's largest cargo ships and oil tankers passing through the Malacca Straits between Indonesian Sumatra and Malaysia, heading to and from Singapore.

Singapore's success has been through geographical luck, political and financial stealth and forward looking policies. At this moment the government, authoritarian in so many ways, is trying to open its island to the rest of the world by offering unrivalled shopping, the best airline and airport in the world and a social scene that provides comfort for a few days while the guest is in transit. Its main threat is the booming economy of China and its historical competition with Malaysia. By far the largest neighbour, Indonesia provides its resources and, in return, Singapore provides safe haven for Indonesia's biggest crooks. If a newly negotiated extradition treaty between the two countries was ever successfully implemented, first class seats on flights out of Singapore would be fully booked for weeks.

Abdullah Aziz sat back in the huge white leather sofa facing the western skies as the orange sun hovered above the horizon. His small bespectacled clean shaven figure, wearing an Armani suit but bulging in all the wrong places, held a presence more by failing to fit-in than by confidence, yet he dominated the room. It was if the only explanation for his presence could be money, and buckets of money at that. He smiled in the knowledge that, in this hotel, he was king.

He had dismissed his Indonesian barman to make way for his next visitor; even trusted servants didn't need to know all your secrets. He had known Aman Widodo for many years and his promotion to Secretary General to the Coordinating Minister of Politics and Security had made him a valuable ally, but Aziz was dismayed he had received no warning of the raid on the Vietnamese ships carrying his timber. He owed him an explanation.

Widodo entered the penthouse and quietly called out *"Pak Aziz?"*

"Over here Aman" the relaxed voice of Aziz welcomed him. "Come and join me in a sun-downer." Aziz stood up, strolled over to the bar, poured two gin and tonics and placed one on a glass coffee table next to a white armchair before sitting back on the sofa with the other.

Widodo, dressed in patterned trousers and a cashmere sweater more suited to a golf course than a lounge, came over and sat down in the chair, pulling a packet of Kent from his pocket. "Would you care for a cigarette?" he asked, more to gain permission to smoke than out of friendliness.

"So how have you been Aman? It must be three or four months since you last visited me at the *Regency*."

"Extremely busy I'm afraid, the minister is proving to be quite a handful." He lit his cigarette and sank back in the chair with his gin and tonic in his other hand.

"I gathered that. My contacts tell me he is the reason the navy were in Pangkalan Bun last week. You do realise that the timber on those two ships is worth millions of dollars to me, don't you Aman?"

Widodo shifted a little in his chair.

"You see I was rather surprised to learn about the raids from my son Hazim rather than in advance from you."

A confidently handsome young man appeared behind the bar. Tall and dark, he was dressed in a well fitted white designer suit with a pair of sunglasses pushed up on his head. Narrowly trimmed sideburns fashionably joined his moustache to completely frame his mouth. "Hello *Pak* Widodo, how very good to see you again." Hazim smiled at their guest and raised a glass.

"Ah, Hazim, I'm glad you have joined us. I was just asking Widodo why he gave me no warning about the navy raid last week."

The sunset over, the wall lights automatically came on to compensate for the loss of the sun and both father and son were silent, waiting to hear from their important guest. Widodo took another hit from his cigarette before shifting again, increasingly uncomfortable in his chair. He had known the reason for the summons to the *Regency* but felt extremely unhappy the way Aziz had cornered him with his appalling spoilt and thuggish son. He had known Hazim since he was a small boy and even then he was cruel and unpleasant. Aziz should have seen him alone. Their relationship went back so many years, yet he now realised he had never really liked this man, whose wealth had increased his power and influence over him. Widodo had to admit he had become Aziz's paid lackey.

"I'm sorry *Pak* Aziz, but I had no previous knowledge of the raid. This was organised by Probowo, the Forestry Minister, with Bambang Santoso's support. But it seems that Santoso didn't trust me enough to bring me in on the plans." Widodo paused but his audience remained silent. "Santoso asked me about you a couple of weeks ago and I assured him that you were not the criminal that the newspapers and some NGOs describe you as. In fact I warned him that you donated heavily to his party."

"I see" responded Aziz.

"He seemed unimpressed by my defence of your activities and became dismissive of me. This was the first time I had ever felt this from him and nothing has been the same since this conversation."

Aziz nodded at his son Hazim who came and sat next to his father with his drink before speaking. "Please forgive my candour *Pak* Widodo, but that's a load of fucking bullshit now isn't it?" Hazim was uncannily calm and his father just stared at Widodo.

"You knew that Probowo was up to something and you knew that Santoso was talking with him, yet you failed to find out from anyone what this was about." He put his drink on the table, turned towards his father and nodded reverentially before standing and taking three steps to tower over Widodo. "I knew about the informer days before he was executed, so how come our government insider knows nothing about the fucking navy?"

Widodo shivered at the reference to the murder and stood defiantly, but Hazim pushed him back in his seat.

"I won't be talked to like this *Pak* Aziz" he complained turning to look at the older man "when I've helped you and your family for years without any questioning of my loyalty."

"Oh don't be so shocked Aman" Aziz replied calmly. "I pay you ten thousand dollars a month for your loyalty and you've done very well all these years out of our special relationship. I don't doubt your concern about my little problem and I don't doubt your willingness to put things right. We're friends after all, aren't we?"

"I certainly thought so Abdullah" he replied shakily.

"So you go off with Hazim to explain to him how you are going to get my boats back and we'll all be happy families all over again" Aziz stated cheerily. In contrast to the tone in his voice he dismissed Widodo with a wave of his hand before standing and walking over to the window to inspect the Singaporean skyline.

Hazim led a trembling Widodo out of the room. Smiling from diamond studded ear to diamond studded ear, Hazim could feel his dick pushing against his silk boxers. Power peppered with the threat of violence always aroused him like this. He had never forgotten Widodo ratting on him when he had caught him cutting his right arm with a razor blade. The childhood resentment he felt towards this old man only added to the joy of now being 23 years old, rich, handsome and ruthless.

CHAPTER FOURTEEN
Singapore

Colin Grady had been in the timber business for 25 years, first working for a major flooring distributor but, for the last five years, becoming his own boss. He liked the feeling of working for himself but had found it wasn't necessarily the quickest way to get rich. Despite knowing the business back to front he had found it quite difficult to make decent profits importing tropical hardwood for his growing portfolio of clients, although he had felt more confident in the last twelve months since he had set up a supply deal with one of Britain's larger retailers of quality timber products.

The last year had been difficult for other reasons. The business was changing and Colin realised he only had a few years to cash in on his lifetime knowledge and contacts. Governments, spurred on by greenies, were beginning to change the way he and his colleagues did business, blaming them for buying "stolen" wood and throwing the responsibility of proving the legality of their supplies onto the importers. He considered this extremely unfair, putting the blame of the lawlessness and corruption in hardwood supply countries such as the Congo, Brazil and Indonesia onto poor old Colin Grady from St Albans, England. Ridiculous really. How could he be blamed, as long as he assured the appropriate paperwork accompanied each shipment?

OK, he had known for years that most of the paperwork was forged or bought by bribing forestry officials, customs officers and police. But that is business. New rules were coming in, even new legislation in the European Union – trust those bloody foreign bureaucrats to find a way to line their own pockets with "consultancies" for "scoping reports" – and now his own timber association was even buying into it. It seemed as if they would all have to start paying for inspectors, forgery-proof bar-coding, and blacklists of unreliable traders. That would ruin him and hand everything over to the big boys who would no doubt be sitting on government committees and drinking in expensive wine bars with the same greenies that put him out of business.

At 57, having worked all his life, Colin felt he deserved to be more secure. His wife, Mary, constantly fretted over his business venture. He knew that, having brought up their three children, she had hoped to enjoy the later years of their life with a safe pension and a more relaxed lifestyle. Instead of this, Colin was more nervous than he had ever been, his foreign trips were less predictable than before, and she had just found out he had re-mortgaged their home to keep his company afloat. Her fears fuelled his anxiety and he was guiltily pleased to be away from her for a few days to concentrate on making good money. She just didn't understand the timber business.

The *Regency* was much posher than he was used to, but he could hardly have refused his host since he was hoping to get into a regular business relationship with him. However, he was a little worried he might have to pay for his room himself, even though he had been invited to stay by Mr Aziz. He had been to Singapore many times before to do business with traders, many of whom had already moved on to deal in other commodities. It was a safe haven from the dodgy and dirty mill towns in Indonesia where he had found himself holed up more times than he cared to remember. So he had been pleasantly surprised to be invited to Singapore to do business with an Indonesian timber supplier.

He had been told to take the South elevator to the Penthouse at eight. Another first for Colin: he had heard about Penthouse parties but had never been invited. He was sure that tonight would be just a meeting with Mr Aziz, but nonetheless felt special when he pressed the top button simply marked with a "P". At first the lift failed to move, but after a few seconds the doors closed and he was very swiftly catapulted upwards towards the twenty sixth floor. The lift slowed and stopped for a moment before the doors opened and Colin was welcomed by a casually dressed young man with a glass of champagne in his hand, which he promptly offered to Colin.

"Please come with me Mr Grady, my father is very pleased you have come all this way to visit him" said Hazim, now wearing black Italian chinos with a dark green t-shirt hugging his young muscular frame. His command of English was impressive, having studied in Kuala Lumpur.

Colin shifted his briefcase from his right hand into his left so he could hold the champagne flute politely. "Thank you, you're very kind." Leading the way Hazim smiled to himself, this silly Englishman was so out of his depth, his father would soon be able to see if he was genuine or one of those imperialist environmentalists trying to put his family out of business.

"Ah, Mr Grady, welcome to Singapore and welcome to the *Regency*" Aziz quietly greeted Colin outside a small office. "Thank you for travelling so far to talk, this is the way I like to do business." Aziz glanced at the briefcase as he smiled and caught his son's eye without Colin even noticing. "Please, leave your briefcase and come and relax in the lounge, my chef is preparing an Indonesian speciality in your honour." Colin looked at Hazim who offered to take the briefcase from him with a smile.

They moved into the lounge while Hazim held back and moved calmly into the office. He put the briefcase on the desk, spun it round to face him, pressed the latches on either side and slowly opened the case to reveal a small notebook, a couple of brochures, a packet of mints, name cards, a credit card and assorted pens. There were no hidden cameras or recording devices. Mr Grady was probably a timber businessman as his website had suggested and was probably genuinely here to do business with his father. Hazim was a little disappointed; his run-in with Widodo had been loud and threatening, but non-violent. A part of him had wanted Grady to be an environmentalist. He left the case on the desk and moved on to the lounge.

His father was giving Grady the family history: the poor parents, how he had worked every daylight hour and made friends with the military. Now he owned huge sawmills and timber processing factories with an endless supply of timber. Some described him as Mafia, but that was jealousy fed by his competitors. He was an honest businessman who had worked hard, encouraged his family and prayed to God.

"Do you have family Mr Grady?" asked Aziz.

"Please, call me Colin" he replied. "I have three children who have all grown up, my two sons are in university and my daughter has already married. My wife and I are very proud of them all. I've been in the timber business for twenty five years, working for myself the last five."

"Ah, you are also a hard-working self-made man, I can see, Colin" Aziz responded appropriately. "I have a daughter in Borneo who has made me a grandfather. Hazim here is my only son, but he has decided to work with me in this business. He's my right hand man."

Hazim smiled at his father and nodded gently in confirmation that the briefcase was clean.

"Let's talk business, shall we, so that afterwards we can relax and dine" offered Aziz.

Sitting in the same chair in which Widodo had so recently been threatened, Colin Grady talked about his supply needs for the clients he had built up over the last few years. He was surprised to hear the range of timber species and products on offer by Aziz. The dried and treated sawn timber was of great interest, as were the mouldings made to order in his factory in the forest in Central Kalimantan. He was shown pictures, given prices and offered preferential terms if his orders were regular over a number of years.

"I like my clients to also be my friends" Aziz smiled as Hazim refilled Colin's champagne glass.

"I'm pleased to hear that Mr Aziz" Colin responded. "I like to be upfront about business and know where we all stand before signing contracts and taking delivery. To be frank Mr Aziz, one of the reasons I came all this way to talk is because I need products that are not easy to come by nowadays."

Hazim, smiling politely, exchanged glances with his father.

"And I need them to be accompanied by all the appropriate documents to satisfy my clients of their legality, and in some cases the sustainability of the logging operations from which the timber came. This has become very important in my business."

"I fully understand" responded Aziz. "You've come to the right man. I like you Colin, upfront."

Aziz stood and walked to the window overlooking the Singaporean skyline. He spoke slowly "I can offer you most of the species and products you would expect. If necessary we can ship via Malaysia or China and the country of origin can be stated on the paperwork as you please. Documentation is no problem, Colin, you don't get to my position without counting the most influential people as your friends."

He turned to look directly at Grady and continued "your business is safe in my hands because I will offer you what you need, not what you have to scrape around to find: and at fair prices. I want your business to succeed because then you will always remain my client." He paused and smiled. "And friend."

They raised their glasses in recognition of the beginning of a fruitful relationship. Colin was feeling the effect of two glasses of champagne on an empty stomach, but believed he had hit a jackpot. He became aware of lounge music playing quietly in the background, and realised that a substantial and beautifully decorated dining table had appeared in front of the glass window a little further along from where Aziz was now standing, overlooking Singapore's twinkling lights. A very beautiful young lady in a tight fitting black dress sat down next to Hazim on the white leather sofa and suggested that they all eat.

Hazim stood with the girl and introduced her to Colin as his host, Michelle. She must have been about twenty four, probably eastern European, with a figure that a 57 year old businessman from St Albans could only dream of embracing. She was tall, sophisticated, and stunningly beautiful. Colin understood she was there to make him feel good but was unsure how far that actually went. He had always been faithful to Mary and had no intention of changing any of that tonight, but then he'd never felt so important before.

The meal was spectacular, washed down with the finest wine Colin had ever experienced. Michelle talked to them all, surprising Colin with her knowledge of the timber industry, and he became increasingly relaxed in the company of his new friends.

"You must come to see our factories before going home" suggested Aziz kindly. Colin had always known he must see their operation before signing any deals, but had been unsure how to approach this subject amid the generosity already shown by Mr Aziz.

"Hazim will arrange everything, you'll be in Pangkalan Bun in two days time and my private speedboat will take you upriver to my sawmills and factories. Then we'll get down to the serious business of contracts and payments before you fly home to your patient wife" Aziz smiled, glanced at Michelle, and stood. "And I'm afraid to say I must now go and see my patient wife" he laughed. "She's at home waiting for me. It was a great pleasure meeting you Colin. Next time you come so far you must bring your wife with you."

Colin had assumed Aziz lived in this penthouse suite, but, when he had gone Hazim and Michelle explained he had a beautiful villa on the shore where he spent most of his time with his fourth wife. Hazim poured brandy for them all and changed the music to a faster thumping beat which made Colin feel quite old, but flattered that his two young hosts assumed he would enjoy it. After a second brandy he was beginning to understand the energy of the music and felt quite rejuvenated.

Hazim had been talking enthusiastically about his father's status in Kalimantan, mentioned his charity work with Muslim boarding schools and his Mosque building programme. Michelle had interrupted a few times to add detail and embellish the admiration.

"He's always been a good Muslim and visited Mecca last year with Haj Imam Bakti, a leader of righteous people." Hazim lowered his head in respect, his mood seeming to change from the smiling party animal he had appeared to be for the last half hour, since his father had left, to a solemn youth. He stood, announced he must go to prepare Colin's flights and itinerary. "Michelle, please show Colin around, I'm sure he'd love to see the Penthouse living quarters." With that he left the room without even looking at Colin.

"You must forgive Hazim" explained Michelle, "he's deeply religious and often finds business and pleasure difficult to resolve. Now let me show you around."

Colin was staggered by the opulence of all the bedrooms and adjoining lounges, and the fantastic views across Singapore. Michelle had rushed ahead, telling him to make his way to the eastern wing where she would meet him, but to his surprise the gigantic bedroom that straddled the southeast corner of the hotel was deserted when he entered. On the wall he recognised paintings by French impressionists and assumed they were prints or copies, but he wasn't sure. Next to the huge bed were dark carved wooden elephants and at the base of the bed a very long dark wooden trunk. The bedclothes were crisply clean and a green silk bedspread comfortably displayed the contours of the sheets below. The lush green curtains were drawn, a bottle of *Dom Perignon* sat in an ice bucket next to the bed on a tray held up by a small wooden carved peasant figure. Next to the ice bucket was his briefcase.

Colin crossed the room to a carved wooden door, pushed it open to see the bathroom with two huge video screens showing sweepingly energetic landscapes shot from helicopters or spacecraft and heard accompanying chill out music, playing quietly in the unforgiving hard acoustics of the marble emporium, built to display wealth and privilege. Appearing in front of him through the steam, Michelle, naked, glided towards him up the steps from the sunken bath, her skin soaked in oils and her smile the most welcoming he had ever experienced. She grabbed his right hand, placed it on her left breast and drew him closer in an embrace. They kissed and Colin's thoughts of his wife, Mary, were left behind in another world: the suburban world of work, graft and failure.

He was on a run of success, he could feel it, and Michelle graciously removed his jacket, then his tie and shirt before chastising him for teasing her, walking back down the steps into the bath. He stripped and failed to notice his own sagging tits, flat arse and beer paunch: tonight Colin Grady was the Emperor of Siam, the Sultan of East Java, King of Malacca. He followed Michelle into the steamy bath, feeling her tongue touch his dick before he could even see her. His hands reached down to her head with affection and he lowered himself into the bath to kiss her. She soaped his body, told him he was beautiful, and lowered herself onto him so gently that Colin sighed louder than Michelle as he reached up to run his hands over her perfect oily breasts.

He spent the night licking her body as if it was his spiritual temple, going down on her when he sensed she needed his expertise, the kind of sexual satisfaction only an older experienced man can provide. He believed in himself and knew from her delight and pleasure that she believed in him too. It was so extraordinarily and immediately right to remember what an attractive man he still was, and he was incredibly thankful to Michelle for reminding him of the obvious truth.

He came inside her again with a loving sigh, before withdrawing and rolling onto the green silk bedspread. His dick lay hard on his stomach with only the light from the table lamps catching its dampness and defining its shape by the reflection of the light.

Above the lamp, the wonder of the latest low-light miniature digital technology recorded every orgasm, every spoken compliment, and every bit of flab on Colin's neglected body. In a room not far away Hazim bent forward, his chinos around his ankles, laughed at the pathetic little Englishman on the video monitor.

"Insurance" he muttered to nobody in particular, although the two naked girls licking his balls wondered if he was talking to them.

CHAPTER FIFTEEN
Borneo

Matt was ready for an adventure after two weeks in the relative safety of Bali. He had spent a few days on the northern beaches, partly to avoid Ardi, which he realised was not the kind of vacation he had expected. A quick call to Rita had confirmed she had secured a guide for him in Borneo. It was time to move on.

He had only seen Ardi once since his night in the *Apache* when he had met Rita and Sam. Ardi had been confrontational and demanding so he had let him shout and complain without really caring. It was this lack of interest that had helped him see the pointlessness of this relationship. It had been good at the beginning; actually it had been great, but that was down to the novelty, the drugs and the sex. Who was Matt kidding? It was all about the sex. Ardi's behaviour the last few days in the bars, on the phone and his totally inexcusable attack on Sam had left Matt realising it was best to get out of this one as soon as possible. So he had told him it was over and to his surprise Ardi had just walked away.

As the daily commercial flight from Semarang landed Matt could see how much of a backwater Pangkalan Bun really was, and when he stepped from the plane the humidity hit him like the sauna rush from water on burning coals. This tiny municipal city is on a river near the southern coast of Borneo, itself the jungle of our fantasies, the impenetrable backdrop to a youthful David Attenborough, the third largest island in the world.

He walked from the plane to the airport building, and inside, an overweight Englishman ahead of him from First Class was being approached by a young man in a white t-shirt, with bright but troubled eyes. He could see a younger, well dressed man, with bodyguards approaching them so decided to look for his bag rather than move into this situation. Matt had a strong sense for trouble and it had saved him considerable strife on many occasions. Although he had no idea what this was about, and to him they were complete strangers, he could feel a tension growing between these two young men.

Sure enough, the man with the bodyguards had shouted something angrily at the other guy; the Englishman had looked surprised but relieved and had been escorted outside by the bodyguards. Matt was collecting his backpack when he saw the bodyguards return, nod at a policeman standing nearby, and move towards the man in the white t-shirt, pushing him up against the wall. When they walked away he was slumped on the ground bent double, coughing and spluttering, with blood running from his nose. Next to him on the floor was a small sign with black letters spelling out "Mr Matt".

Koto felt a strange feeling of relief after this attack, as if it helped assuage some of the guilt he was experiencing after his close friend's death. The last few days had been difficult after he was pulled from his home and questioned at the police station for six hours. The police found him lying on his back on his mattress hugging Murkha's arm, which was resting on his bare chest. He was covered in blood from head to toe as if he had rubbed it all over himself. They had asked him what he knew about Murkha's activities, who he knew, who he must have upset. The questioning seemed to Koto to be accusatory and he felt that the police knew far more about the killing than he did himself. He hadn't told them about Murkha's visit to Jakarta and he withheld information about Murkha's involvement in the seizure of the Vietnamese ships. He knew he couldn't trust the police. Now, befitting for Murkha's close friend, he had been attacked by the hired thugs of his killer.

Matt strolled over to the young man on the airport floor. "Are you here to meet me?" he questioned with a whimsical curl to his mouth, not quite his full pick-up smile but, under the circumstances still slightly outrageous. The young man brushed his hand across his bloody nose and his bright troubled eyes stared up at Matt, only just remembering he had been at the airport to meet an Englishman. He realised he'd picked the wrong one, but considering the scarcity of foreigners in Pangkalan Bun, could be forgiven for his mistake, although apparently not by Hazim.

"Um, Mr Matt?" Koto managed to say before coughing repeatedly and doubling over again. His longish scruffy black hair had fallen across his face and when he looked up he was shaken but defiant. "I'm really sorry sir; I hope you forgive me for my condition. *Saya Koto*. I think it must have been a case of mistaken identity" Koto stated as if reading from a Sherlock Holmes story.

"Not me guv!" said Matt laughing and not believing a word of it. He was pleasantly surprised at himself for so easily accepting the situation.

"*Apa?* Um, what?" responded Koto confused.

"Don't worry, let's get out of here" Matt said offering his hand to Koto and pulling him to his feet.

They found a taxi that took them to the police station for Matt to register with the authorities, and then to the small town of Kumai where Koto lived. It was here Matt bought supplies for themselves and the crew of the *klotok*, a small boat with a large cabin and an incredibly noisy diesel engine that would take them upriver into Tanjung Puting National Park. Koto explained they should pay park fees, but the park office had been burned down a few months earlier by a crowd of loggers. He said they could pay at a ranger post in the park.

Kumai is a one street town with houses and small shops offering a range of simple supplies from rice to beer. It only took about half an hour for them to buy the supplies and Matt could see that Koto led him to three shops when they could have got everything in the first. It was because of Matt's experience of travelling that he understood this was how Koto remained popular in town, sharing out his good fortune at being able to talk with foreigners.

Behind the shops were wooden jetties with wooden huts built over them, washing hanging out on blue nylon lines. The air carried a strong salty smell laced with fish and rotting flesh. Along the jetties were large white wooden boats loading with planks of wood, their crews carrying out their daily business: washing, cooking, painting, and smoking. Leaning over the back of one of these *Sulawesi* sailing ships was a small boy oblivious to the rest of the world, tattered shorts around his ankles, having his morning crap.

Further along to the right were three brightly painted green and red speedboats with powerful outboard engines slung up out of the water; on the jetty beyond them a bigger yellow speedboat with two Mercury 75s gave a sense of urgency and unseen wealth to this otherwise gentle and slow paced community. It was difficult to imagine anything could be so important as to need such speed in this steamy and indifferent floating wooden maze.

Beyond the jetties was a wide expanse of water narrowing to the left but opening out to the sea on the right: the Java Sea according to the map Matt had looked at before embarking on this journey. Somewhere on the opposite side of Kumai Bay was the mouth of the Sekonyer River, which would take them into the western and northern parts of the Park, where wild orang-utans lived in the treetops and gibbons called out while hanging from branches by their absurdly long arms. Matt looked across the bay for a clue as to where the river started, but from Kumai it just looked like a continuous bank about two kilometres across the water.

The peace was broken by a very loud clattering, an engine firing up and the repetitive sound of metal bluntly hitting metal. It was like a chronically badly tuned engine with its tappets screaming for attention. Just after the sound started he got a waft of diesel fumes as if to confirm a mechanical sickness.

"That is our boat *Bukit Tiga* testing its engines" explained Koto. "It is the biggest *klotok* in Kumai and very comfortable."

"Bucket what?" replied Matt smiling uncontrollably at the situation he found himself in; he was really pleased to be out of Bali starting out on this new journey. Koto seemed a total mess, the boat was clearly unfit for hire and he had already been bitten to pieces by Kumai's resident mosquitoes that probably carried malaria. It appeared local politics put his guide on a hit list and he knew he had just been badly overcharged for his supplies: all ingredients for a genuine unpredictable adventure. Thanks to Rita and Sam he had escaped from adoration by dozens of men and women, relaxing massage, sun, sea and sand. His smile burst into open laughter. It was just what he needed.

"*Bukit Tiga*" Koto stated coolly, perturbed by Matt's behaviour. "It means *Three Hills* in *bahasa* Indonesia and is called that because the skipper comes from an area north called *Three Hills*." There was a pause as Koto confirmed Matt was listening. "Because there are three hills" he added rather unnecessarily. Koto looked serious; the matted blood in his hair, blood stains around the neck of his white t-shirt gave him a slight air of menace.

"I apologise" spluttered Matt, desperately trying to match Koto's seriousness. "But do you think the boat is safe? That engine sounds pretty rough."

"Oh they all sound like that, it's a very fine boat Mr Matt, Koto would only use the best."

Matt laughed again and suggested they went to get a coffee before setting out on their adventure. He realised it might be important to get to know his guide a bit better and it was still very early. The day had not started that well and a bit of bonding never did any harm. Koto led him to his motorbike which was parked to the side of his room. They drove to a small café just outside Kumai where Koto seemed to know most of the men hanging around smoking.

Inside, the café looked like so many small restaurants found across Indonesia. An upright red fridge with a glass door contained juices and a few fizzy drinks, including beer and cola. Eight large tables were positioned in the room with a cluster of sauces on each of them next to a glass jar containing large crispy wafers. A door led to the kitchen from which the clunking of pans could be heard. Each table had three or four resident flies, the only ones that resisted the cleaning of the plastic table cloths and the regular use of fly spray.

Koto ordered two coffees from a young girl who smiled sweetly at him, two men came and spoke in Indonesian and offered him a cigarette. "Mr Matt, do you smoke?" he asked.

"In Indonesia I smoke" Matt replied pulling his own Marlboro Lights out of his bag. He'd been offered the local *Kretek* cigarettes in Bali and the clove flavour had made him retch, so to avoid refusing and upsetting the locals, he politely offered his Marlboros to Koto and his two friends first.

They accepted with delight and one of the friends, a big man with very long hair growing right down his back, responded with "wank yu" in an attempt to speak English. Koto shared a glance and a smile with Matt explaining to his friends in Indonesian what he had mistakenly said, before they all shared the same joke and laughed out loud.

Two thick hot black coffees arrived in glass mugs; Koto piled four large teaspoons of sugar into his and offered the spoon to

Matt. "Thank you" Matt replied in exaggerated English and they all repeated after him "Thank you" before bursting out in laughter again. For Matt, this was the kind of comradeship he had missed in Bali, where, by his own choosing, his encounters with guys had always had a sexual tension. In this small café in Kumai he was simply having a laugh with some strangers and it felt really good.

After a while Koto insisted Matt should go to the boat and meet the captain, so they drove the bike back to Koto's small room and walked onto the jetty where the *Bukit Tiga* was still hammering out its engine noise. To Matt it already sounded normal. He couldn't hear anything but the engine and realised his journey was not going to be very peaceful. He walked the gangplank onto the vessel and looked back towards Koto who had gone back to the road to collect a box of supplies.

Koto was on the ground, next to the box with broken beer bottles around him, as if he had dropped one of the crates. But the look on his face was not one of foolish clumsiness, it was one of fear. He saw Koto drop his head and start to cry as he rushed back down the gangplank to see if he could help. By the time he reached the scene Koto was lifting his head, breathing in deeply to recompose himself in front of his client.

"I am sorry Mr Matt, I broke three bottles" apologised Koto staring up with a look that pleaded with Matt to ask no questions. Matt squatted down next to him, pulled out his pack of cigarettes. Koto smiled appreciatively, took one from the packet and accepted a light. He sucked the smoke deeply into his lungs and smiled, pretending everything was normal. Matt noticed as he glanced back at a metallic green 4x4 as it sped past; his brown face visibly whitening, revealing the mask of a man desperately trying to control his emotions.

CHAPTER SIXTEEN
Borneo

Sitting on the roof of *Bukit Tiga,* slowly moving across the bay, Matt felt the cool air on his face and the emotional change from Bali to something new. He had already warmed to Koto, this tall young Dayak man with dark, wide, bright eyes and shaggy, long black hair. Koto's flattened nose gave the impression of impishness, but his smile and demeanour revealed a young man more confident with himself than the last three hours would indicate.

The captain was no older than Matt and his mate barely nineteen; they seemed pleasant enough and spoke a few words of English. Since they had left the jetty in Kumai the privilege of the moment had hit home to Matt, the foreigner with his own guide, boat and crew, travelling into a forest so extraordinary it had been chosen to be protected for future generations. The friendly banter in the café had given him a momentary feeling of belonging, but sitting on top of this boat with the others all down below, reminded him of the gap that his culture and relative wealth carved out when travelling in many wild places.

He reached for his camera bag, removed one of his Nikons from a padded pocket and loaded a roll of Kodachrome from his lead-lined bag. He always carried his film in lead because he passed through so many security devices in airports and hotels that he had once shot three rolls of film in Ghana only to find they had been totally fogged. It had cost him another two days to replace the shots; in his business there was little point spending money on travelling if you couldn't protect your film. He had decided to shoot film on this trip because he guessed he may not be close enough to power supplies to recharge a digital camera and download the images. Besides, film offered him a warmth and tonal range he preferred and although he would have to wait to see the results, without carrying a laptop computer, digital results were limited to the tiny screen on the camera.

He opened the back of his camera, loaded the film and wound it on three shots before reaching inside another pocket for one of his lenses. He was going through the daily routine of a photographer, caring for his cameras, cleaning the lenses and feeling the balance of the equipment in his hand, when Koto joined him on the roof. He noticed he had washed his face, cleaned the blood from his hair and removed his blood and beer stained white t-shirt, revealing a lightly muscled hairless chest with a bold wisp of dark hair below his belly button, pointing down into his shorts which were perched on a tiny waist. Matt pulled his thoughts away from Koto's body and looked at his face. He seemed more relaxed but was squinting slightly in the sun.

"You can move back under that wooden shelter" Koto advised while pointing at a dirty hardboard roof resting on a small wooden frame towards the back of the boat. "You'll find it gets too hot to stay in the sun. We can spend time in the bay before heading up river because Skipper says he saw a dolphin here this morning. Would you like to see dolphin?"

"That would be great," Matt replied simply and looked out over the water, "you're the guide!"

It occurred to him it was unlikely any well-respected dolphin would be hanging around this bay near a boat as noisy as the *Bukit* and that this was probably a routine by his guide and crew to raise the expectancy for the trip. It was alright by him though, sitting up on top of the boat he was absorbing a different atmosphere, slowly working his way into this adventure. He knew so little of what was going to be ahead of him. Was it far to the Park? How long would he be staying there, what would he eat and where would he sleep? Would he really see an orang-utan? He almost stopped Koto from going down below again to ask him all these questions, but decided it was better to let everything just happen, it would be more fun. He was sure he was in good hands.

Playing along with the moment he eagerly scanned the water for any sign of a fin. He had seen dolphins on many occasions, usually riding the bow of a boat or just passing by an idyllic island beach in Thailand. He had read stories in newspapers of dolphins rescuing people from sharks when their boat capsized, and knew that the bond people felt with dolphins was extremely strong. The rather bleak dark water stretching across the bay did not seem the best environment for a marine dolphin and he was sure that there were no river dolphins in this part of the world. The chance of a dolphin bow riding the *Bukit* was so unlikely, not just because of the hammering noise, but it really didn't go fast enough to create any bow wave!

Once they were in the middle of the bay he looked back towards Kumai, along the coast either side of the town. Further along the banks to the right he could see two sawmills with tugboats moored on jetties outside, and to the left a huge metal barge loaded high with logs. He put a long lens on his camera and knocked off a few shots of the barge. Through the telephoto lens he could see two tugboats alongside and men high up on the upper logs pulling on ropes. He had never seen such a huge barge, staggered that so many hundreds of logs could be stacked so high without it capsizing.

He turned to look at the other side of the bay realising it was dotted with sawmills and small boats. One of these looked like *Bukit* but was towing two hundred metres of logs tied together, floating behind the vessel. It was making painfully slow progress but like *Bukit* gave the impression of being a solidly reliable work horse: except for the noise that is. Behind the boats there seemed to be little habitation other than near the saw-mills, but somewhere behind all this lay the wild forest of Tanjung Puting National Park.

"Over there" shouted Koto. Matt hadn't even noticed him come onto the roof. The noise of the *klotok* removed any chance to use the sense of sound. "Quick, a dolphin, over there!" he was pointing back towards Kumai.

It took a couple of minutes before Matt saw the dolphin slowly making its way through the bay. It was probably about three or four metres long, a huge animal, and when it casually broke the surface he could see its long beak. Its dark fin stood out clearly and he saw a small spray of water as it blew air out of its blow hole. Everything suddenly went very quiet as Skipper turned off the engines and they could hear the blow the next time the dolphin surfaced. Skipper and Matey, as they had been introduced, had joined them on the roof and Matt was encouraged by their enthusiasm.

"Bottlenose dolphin" explained Koto. "We get them in the bay quite often, they're after fish. But this is a big one, certainly male."

The boat gently bobbed silently in the water and the next time the dolphin surfaced it was only about ten metres from the bow, and they could see its head clearly enough to notice scars above its left eye. Skipper was talking to Koto quietly, but even without understanding the language, it was obvious he recognised the dolphin.

"He knows him," Koto explained. "He calls him Scarface. According to Skipper, this dolphin hasn't been seen around here for two years."

Matt took a few shots, but knew from experience that dolphin photos rarely look good from the surface, unless the animals are bow riding a boat and you can get directly above them. This was a great start to his trip and he was already impressed by Koto and his crew. They all watched the dolphin take its time to swim well out of their range before firing up the engines and getting on their way.

Skipper smiled for the first time at Matt and he returned the polite recognition of a shared interest in dolphins. Skipper was a short man with receding short hair, hidden by a baseball cap most of the day, revealing a real vanity. His dark moustache and bushy eyebrows framed a face that suggested a serious and responsible man. Almost the complete opposite except for his height, little Matey was a sexy lad wearing nothing but a tiny pair of shorts. His black hair was cropped so short that it was little more than a dark shadow over his tight featured young face. He smiled a huge beam that almost split his face in two and he kept glancing at Matt inquisitively. On command from Skipper, he nimbly dropped over the edge of the roof to see what he could do for his boss.

The boat turned and headed towards the opposite bank. The saw-mills were becoming even clearer as they turned again and sailed towards the open sea keeping the bank on their left. Through his biggest lens Matt could make out huge rafts of logs floating in the water all along the bank and he remembered Sam's sad words about the destruction of Rita's home. It was difficult to believe these logs came illegally from the Park as they had claimed, it was all so open.

Twenty minutes later he could see the mouth of the Sekonyer River coming up on their left, the boat slowly turned through the slightly turbulent water created as the river ran into the bay. Matt had already moved back under the hardboard sun shade as he felt the sun starting to burn his fair skin, despite already being tanned and his liberal application of protective sun cream. Ahead of him, upriver, he could see a bank of clouds suggesting afternoon rain. He had read in a guide book that it rains most days in the forests of Kalimantan and had prepared for this by buying an expensive waterproof poncho in Bali.

As they moved into the river it narrowed to about two hundred metres across, and the *klotok* now felt like the most appropriate mode of travel: it was slow and steady and in the calm waters of this protected river, it was smooth. After ten minutes the banks on both sides were lined with low, but fabulously full nipa palms, lushly green and branching out over the river, their stems submerged. These plants grow on the edges of mangrove and despite their palms growing up to 9 metres in length; they have no trunk and are supported by underground stems and a massive root system. A wall of them gave the impression of a vast impenetrable forest beyond the river, but it was impossible to tell. Judging by the floating logs, Matt wondered if the palms obscured a horrible truth of clear-cut devastation. Sam's words had echoed in his head on many occasions in the last week and he wondered, warmly, if he would ever see Sam again.

Koto appeared, cheerily offering hot coffee to break his pensive mood. "Beautiful, ya?" he asked beaming, placing the coffee on the deck.

"Yes, it's wonderful. But can I ask you about the logging Koto?" Matt was unsure if this would be crossing a line with his guide and didn't want to compromise their developing relationship. To his surprise Koto sat down beside him and raised his head to look at Matt, tears forming in the corner of his eyes. He brushed them away in a gesture that reminded Matt of the incident at the airport that same morning when he had brushed the blood from his nose. Had he only met Koto hours earlier?

"I feel as if I've walked into something so intense, it's almost rude and too personal to ask you about it" offered Matt, "but Rita and Sam said things to me about this forest that I can't forget."

Koto smiled and nodded his head, but was unable to prevent a flood of tears streaming down his cheeks. This time he didn't even try to brush them aside, but breathed in deeply and let out a cry so loud, that it pierced through the hammering noise of *Bukit*, and set a large flock of small birds on the palms to flight. Skipper and Matey appeared on the roof within seconds, but seeing Koto sitting cross-legged, chest expanded disproportionately, face soaked in tears, looking proud and in profound pain, they nodded knowingly and retreated to the main deck.

Matt stared in shock at this tough young man's pain. He realised his shallow understanding of the personal nature of the forest to Koto was totally inadequate. He had no idea what this Dayak son was feeling or what he could do to lessen the pain, but he felt an overwhelming bonding with Koto, not sexual in the least, but spiritual. Had anyone asked Matt about spiritual bonding earlier that day he would have flippantly cracked a joke to avoid answering and showing his ignorance. But at this moment, facing Koto's pain, he just knew. He offered his hand to Koto, who took it greedily, holding it firmly until the glaze in his eyes had disappeared and he was breathing normally again, his bare chest deflated to normal size.

"It's killing me" Koto whispered in Matt's ear. "The logging is killing me."

CHAPTER SEVENTEEN
Borneo

It had been a hot and tiring day, but Colin Grady was more than satisfied with what he had seen. He was already looking at the third of Aziz's processing factories and Hazim told him there were two more, further upriver. This one, the biggest he had seen and the size of three aircraft hangers, had its own workforce living in wooden huts attached to the factory. It was very impressive, not so much for the quality of product, but its shear size. The entire complex was carved out of the forest on the river bank, and the only access was by river.

"We can provide you with any size of dowels, frames, tongue and groove. You name it and it's yours" boasted Hazim, still looking refreshed in a light, loose fitting grey suit and shining Italian shoes.

At the front of the factory on the river, three or four hundred logs floated, waiting to be hauled to the giant saw operated by a small man dressed only in shorts. The smell was that of freshly sawn wood, slightly burned by the friction of the saw. Behind him were stacked planks at least three metres high on dozens of rows of racks. In a separate area towards the back a range of mechanical saws were adjusted to shape the finished product. Five drying kilns were active behind the covered factory, drying the timber to given specifications.

"This is all ramin" explained Hazim, referring to the species of tree being worked in the factory. "This entire factory specialises in ramin."

This was music to Colin's ears. Ramin had already been banned for export from Indonesia even though it was only here that large mature ramin trees remained. Through an international convention, trade in the species had come under scrutiny and was becoming scarcer and scarcer to source. It's hard, yet easily fashioned texture, made it perfect for shaping into picture frames, dowels and other mouldings. The last stands of this tree were to be found in the peat forests of Kalimantan and Sumatra, and the last big trees in areas previously unexploited: protected areas such as Tanjung Puting National Park.

"So how would I be able to import ramin from this factory?" asked Colin.

"We provide you with all the paperwork and can ship it to you in Europe via China, stating the raw material came from Malaysia. It's not complicated and, given the high value of ramin, not expensive" Hazim explained. "We would advise you to import through a Mediterranean port where they tend to ask less questions, but rest assured, the paperwork will be totally correct."

Colin knew enough to realise this was all completely plausible. The timber trade, although under pressure at the moment, was still totally unregulated. Only species like ramin had any degree of scrutiny and that would only be cursory. The paperwork would keep his big client happy and he would be the biggest importer of ramin to Europe. "How much can you supply?" he asked greedily.

"At the moment there is no shortage of supply" replied Hazim "so if you were a regular client I could offer you ten thousand cubic metres every couple of months. We only sell processed product, but you can set up your own quality control here in the factory. The equipment is state of the art; we bought it from Sarawak in Malaysia only last year."

"That's sixty thousand cubic metres a year? You can guarantee that?"

"Look Colin" Hazim sighed. "If you offer a good price I could double that, but the supply won't be for much longer. My guess is that even we will start to run out of supply in two years. So, if you want to do business, now is the time."

Colin quickly calculated in his head the kind of figures they were looking at. He had no idea what they charged for finished product, but would expect to pay at least seven hundred dollars per cubic metre. Even at the lower supply level of sixty thousand cubic metres he could see his profit being millions of dollars. This was his reason for quitting his previous job and going it alone, to make big money quickly so that he could retire, and although he realised that this entire Aziz operation was technically illegal, it seemed to him that in this neck of the woods, Aziz was the law.

"I don't think there's any need to go further upriver Hazim, thank you" stated Colin confidently. "I've seen enough and am ready to do business."

Hazim grinned and nodded at Colin. This greedy fat Englishman was just what they had been looking for. The Chinese market was very difficult for them and his father did not like relying on the Chinese timber traders as much as he did. With a European importer they would get premium prices and be able to reduce their reliance on Chinese deals. He would tie Grady down to a first deal and then start to ratchet up the costs from then on. They would all make money, but if Grady got too greedy he would be easy to deal with. One large seizure of his shipment and the stupid little man would be financially destroyed. One large blow-up of his disgusting body with Michelle and he would be emotionally destroyed.

"It will be a pleasure doing business with you Colin" Hazim looked into Colin's eyes, smiled and offered his hand to seal the deal.

The ride back to Pangkalan Bun in the company speedboat seemed much quicker than the outward journey. They travelled in silence since it was too difficult to talk over the revving engines, and they were met by two Mitsubishi Pajeros on the jetty. Hazim acknowledged a young but solemn looking tall man wearing Islamic dress, a rap around skirt with a long white embroidered shirt, and exchanged a few words with him. There was something in the eyes of the stranger that disturbed Colin but he couldn't quite make out what it was. Something indicated his complete disinterest in Colin, much more than indifference, yet he smiled at him disingenuously.

Colin was taken to the *Sungai Arut Hotel* where he had a room, and Hazim promised to pick him up in a couple of hours to discuss the terms of their first business deal.

The *Sungai Arut Hotel* is the watering hole for the timber business in Pangkalan Bun. Its rooms are very average but the air conditioning usually works properly and the staff provides at least a minimal level of service. Borneo has bugs that can compete with any other tropical part of the world, as befits an area with outstanding biodiversity and three such creatures the size of golf balls, but with wings, had decided that Colin's room offered them sanctuary. Colin was of a different opinion.

While the staff "sorted out" Colin's room, he went downstairs to the restaurant, a neon lit basement with plastic tablecloths and a strong smell of tobacco. Five men were talking around one table smoking and drinking Coke, but other than them, the place was deserted. Colin sat alone waiting to be served, feeling very obviously out of place, staring at a leaflet on Tanjung Puting National Park he had picked up at reception. The men lowered their voices when he sat down and it was impossible for Colin to hear their conversation until one of them came over to talk to him.

"Where are you from?" a middle aged man with a thick moustache asked.

"Europe" responded Colin warily.

"England?" asked the man, probing for more information. "I'm from Sabah in Malaysia" he offered.

"Yes, England" replied Colin realising that the man was just being friendly.

"You alone? Maybe you would like to join us? It's not much fun in this town if you're alone."

Colin was inquisitive and decided it could do no harm to talk with some strangers for a short while, at least until his room was sprayed, and accepted the invitation to join them; after all it didn't look likely that anyone would serve him. The conversation was focused on a horrible murder that had apparently occurred in this town only a week earlier; something about a torso still being missing. The man murdered was a local Dayak schoolteacher and the men were discussing the fear that this could cause riots and Dayak revenge killings if it wasn't dealt with properly.

"Everyone is scared" said one man in very good English. The men were all from Malaysia and Hong Kong and seemed to know Pangkalan Bun quite well through their businesses.

"But there's no chance of the killing being investigated openly" stated one of the two Chinese men from Hong Kong "we all know that!"

"It's only been a few years since the Dayaks in Sampit rampaged through the Province" continued the same Chinese timber businessman. "I didn't come to Central Kalimantan at all during that period, it was too dangerous." He turned towards Colin and said "I lost a lot of money. You know over four hundred people died, many of them beheaded by gangs of Dayak youths. It was timber that started the killing that time and it will be timber that'll do it again."

Colin was a bit disturbed by the discussion because he had read about the beheadings at the time. These killings had been portrayed as a small dispute that had got out of hand, and of course, journalists had described the beheadings as if they were cannibal instincts re-emerging. He was interested to know why these men connected the riots to the timber industry. So he asked.

"Everything around here is connected to timber" replied the Malaysian man with the thick moustache. "This town is almost totally built on timber. That's what we're all doing here. The only other reason to come here would be to go to the national park, what's left of it. The police and army are friends of the timber baron. There are very few people around here who would dare stand up to him."

"Or his psychopathic son" added one of the Chinese men.

The men went silent and Colin noticed two of them look around to make sure nobody was listening.

"Don't pay any attention to all this nonsense" interrupted the other Chinese man, as if suddenly realising they knew nothing about Colin and it wasn't wise to talk in front of strangers.

The receptionist appeared, gestured to Colin that his room was now ready and Colin made a polite exit. He wanted to get showered and change his clothes before meeting up with Hazim to negotiate the deal. The conversation had disturbed him but he was still buzzing with the realisation that this relationship could make him a very rich man. He pulled out a calculator from his briefcase and played around with a few figures. He wanted ramin and could shift large quantities of mixed sawn timber.

An earlier conversation with Hazim had revealed that his father had strong and powerful connections in Papua, the Indonesian half of the island of New Guinea. This was the last wild source of large quantities of timber and all the big players had started shifting logs out of there. Fortunately for business, there was general unrest in Papua which provided excellent opportunities for deals with the military and plenty of money was still to be made. Colin knew he could build up some business in solid wood flooring and return to Indonesia with other orders for merbau timber, a local valuable Papuan species, within weeks. He was in the land of opportunity with one of the best and most powerful opportunists in the business.

His room phone rang and the receptionist told him a car had arrived to pick him up. His clean white shirt was peppered with huge rain drops as he ran the short distance from the hotel to the car. Minutes later he was in a small, dingy office in the centre of town talking quantities, prices, terms and delivery times with Hazim. He had been firm and managed to bring Hazim's first unit price offer down by twenty percent, which reminded Colin that he really was one of the best European timber buyers in the business. He was feeling confident and although Hazim had, at first, seemed disappointed by the negotiation; he was invited to join him to "have a bit of fun."

Hazim drove them both back towards the river jetty in driving rain and tooted his horn three times. The Islamic dressed stranger came out of a small building and jumped in the other Pajero, the two cars drove out of town with Hazim leading the way. They both turned off the road up a dirt track until they reached a small wooden shack built on stilts over a small pond. The water looked filthy even with the rain completely disfiguring the surface and Colin guessed it would be best not to get bitten by mosquitoes around here. He kept quiet, feeling strangely elated by the deal and proud to be driven and entertained by Hazim. He remembered the calm and suave evening in the *Regency* and how polite and generous Hazim had been. He felt safe, but also a bit guilty.

He was told to stay in the vehicle as Hazim and the tall stranger climbed up the steps to a door in the wooden hut and went inside. Colin waited for about ten minutes hearing nothing but the rain pounding on the roof of the car. Hazim had switched off the engine, the damp heat had penetrated the air conditioning of the car and he was beginning to sweat. He saw a flash of light as the hut door opened, Hazim and his accomplice came out, each with a young girl in tow. Colin thought they looked as if they were being treated rather roughly although it was difficult to see through the rain. They moved down the steps towards the cars, a woman appeared in the doorway and started to scream at them waving her

98

arms around and waling uncontrollably. Colin couldn't see or hear properly and couldn't understand what she was shouting anyway.

"Sorry to be so long" apologised Hazim as he opened a back door of the car and the two girls climbed into the back seats silently. The oldest looked about sixteen and she was holding on protectively to a girl who looked no older than twelve. "Their father didn't seem to understand the seriousness of his debt to my father and it took longer than I had expected."

The stranger, who seemed to have got his long embroidered shirt badly messed up in the house, nodded at Hazim and ran over to the other car. Hazim got into the driving seat, his shirt sleeves now rolled up as if he meant business and switched on the headlights. It really was a filthy night, the rain was torrential, it was very difficult to see further than the beams of light from the Pajero, but as the car turned, Colin thought he could see someone lying in the water at the edge of the pond under the hut.

"OK, let's go to *Mandi's*, it's not far from here and we can all get a private room and a bottle of whisky!" suggested Hazim.

Colin glanced at his host, his young sweaty face gleaming with confidence. He could see his left arm was covered by a series of long scars and as the headlights of the other Pajero shone through the splattered windscreen a menacingly large black scar stood out from Hazim's right wrist.

He turned quickly away towards the girls. They were both dressed in jeans and t-shirts, the youngest was crying and she reminded him of his own daughter the day she had come home in the rain to find her cat dead in the road, hit by a car. Her sister, because that's who Colin assumed the older girl was, had a blank face resigned to the ways of the world, but was clinging onto the young girl so tightly it was as if she would fall away forever if she let go.

"I can't believe the nerve of their father" stated Hazim casually. "He stole a speedboat from us to tow logs to another saw-mill and yet thought he could get away with it!"

Disturbed by the sight of the young girls, Colin realised that Hazim's idea of "fun" was way outside his own sensibilities and it was time to make his excuses and get back to his hotel. He feigned a stomach pain and, although he was sure Hazim didn't believe him, was dropped off at the *Sungai Arut Hotel* at his request.

As he looked back from reception he saw the young Muslim pulling the older girl out of Hazim's car and dragging her to his own. She sat next to him in the front seat, but as he followed Hazim out of the driveway there was no sign of her sitting up in her seat. But the face of the stranger, behind the steering wheel, was staring straight ahead with that same disturbing look in his eyes he had seen earlier.

Colin now recognised it as hate.

CHAPTER EIGHTEEN
Borneo

The Sekonyer River is one of four major rivers that penetrate the peat swamp and freshwater forest of the biosphere reserve known as Tanjung Puting National Park, before emptying through the mangroves into the Java Sea. It separates the north western part of the Park from a few tiny villages and illegal gold mines on its western bank. Although both banks appear lush from the river, landsat images show the virtual de-nudification of the western bank. Tributaries of the Sekonyer penetrate deeper into the forest and the park.

Bukit Tiga slowly and surely made its way up the river, past huge nipa palms and mangrove forest towards a village on its left bank at Tanjung Harapan. At this point the river is less than fifty metres across and human habitation was first apparent to Matt when he saw three separate dug-out canoes hugging the western bank. As the *klotok* passed, the fishermen turned their canoes to minimise the affect of the wash, which gently buffeted the sides before they turned again and carried on upriver. Most waved at the *klotok* crew and smiled at the visitor sitting on the top deck. Although Tanjung Puting gets few visitors, considering its beauty and uniqueness, it is off the beaten track enough to attract visitors who like adventure. The fishermen saw visitors most days, and their families had started to sell handicrafts to them from the village.

On the other bank was a small jetty, with a speedboat alongside, and *Bukit* motored over, backed up and was tied securely on the other side. Matt was unsure what their schedule was to be, but was content to put himself in the hands of his young Dayak guide.

"This is where the government vet lives" explained Koto. "She has sick baby orang-utans and it's a good place to stop, talk and eat."

They jumped off the boat on to the jetty, Matt carrying one of his cameras and a couple of lenses. A few simple buildings in a clearing came into view and Matt could see three people sitting on the steps of the furthest hut. Koto went ahead and told Matt to follow. Walking behind him, he could see that, although tall for an Indonesian, Koto was still shorter than him but his stride was long.

He had put on a green t-shirt and changed from his jeans into shorts and was walking ahead, clearly in charge. As they approached the group on the stairs Matt recognised the crew cut of Sam, looking even less official than in the *Apache* reggae bar, in just a pair of shorts. Next to him was Rita, wearing jeans and a t-shirt, her hair no longer framing her face but pushed back and dishevelled.

Matt smiled warmly and out of the corner of his vision he noticed Koto watching him closely. "I had no idea I was going to see you guys today!" he exclaimed excitedly.

"Hi Matt" replied Rita rather solemnly. Matt looked at her face and was stunned at the change in her: it was as if her light had gone out. "Didn't Koto tell you we would be here?"

Matt turned to look at Koto who was lighting up a cigarette and grinning back at him. "No, he didn't" he replied.

Sam looked at Matt for the first time, nodded in recognition before standing and walking over to speak with Koto.

"This is Dr Adnan, she's the vet here" explained Rita. "She's been filling us in on the latest information about the Park." The doctor nodded at Matt.

"So, what's been going on?" asked Matt feeling as if he had gate-crashed a secret meeting.

"Just work, you know" lied Rita. "You must see the baby orangutans. Is that OK doctor?"

The doctor and Rita stood and asked Matt to follow them towards one of the other buildings, leaving Sam and Koto talking and smoking together, sitting cross-legged on the ground. It was now extremely hot and humid and a relief to stop under a small tree in the shade. Both the women were looking directly at him, neither smiling, when Matt sensed a movement just above his head and looked up. Hanging from a branch were two tiny baby orangutans clinging tightly, their huge black eyes staring inquisitively at their visitor, their bodies browner than Matt had expected and virtually naked. Bright orange hair had only sparsely formed on their heads, arms and legs and each of them was the size of a small human baby.

"Wow!" gasped Matt displaying an involuntary smile.

The babies were watching him, he moved slowly around so he was facing them. They were hanging by tiny hands and feet, perfectly formed and agile. They moved slowly, their large light coloured eyelids emphasising the darkness of their eyes. They were cute but not joyful, and as Matt reached out towards them, the baby on the right held out its arm and closed its hand around the forefinger of Matt's right hand. It held on tight and Matt looked over towards Rita for advice.

"They always cling on" said the doctor "these two are so young they constantly need milk and without a mother they suck on anything. I'll get a bottle for you to offer to them." She walked away leaving Rita and Matt alone.

"Thanks" said Matt with the baby orang-utan still hanging on. The other was now reaching out at Matt's hand as well. "I'm so glad I left Bali and came out here. I've only been in Kalimantan since this morning, but the river, the forest, and Koto have already brought a new feeling of nature to me; something my time in Bali ignored. We even saw a dolphin."

Rita smiled for the first time and came over to help Matt get free from the two very needy orang-utans. "These two were brought in three days ago" she explained. "Dr Adnan doesn't think they've got much chance of survival. No one knows what happened to their mother." They both looked at the tiny bundles of life, clinging on to this strange visitor, unaware of the dangers they would face if they survived this early part of their life. "Has Koto been good?"

"He's great" replied Matt. "He seems to be in some kind of trouble though and I have no idea what it's about."

Rita looked worried as Matt explained the attack at the airport and the incident at the jetty in Kumai. "It looks a bit as if trouble follows him around" chuckled Matt unaware of Rita's deep concern, "but I'm sure he's a great guide."

The vet brought a bottle of milk with a rubber teat on the end, just like a baby's bottle, and left as quickly as she had come. Matt turned back to the two baby orang-utans and watched as the one on the right eagerly took the bottle in its mouth and started to suck gently. The other laid its foot along the bottle and pushed it away, as if trying to stop its companion from enjoying the milk. After a

103

few minutes Matt managed to remove the bottle from the baby's mouth, move it over to the second orang-utan who reached out for it, and guide it towards its mouth.

After the feeding it was time for some photographs and Matt easily shot a roll of film on these two babies hanging helplessly in the tree. It was good to get back to shooting some pictures. He was very happy with the ease he was able to frame beautiful portraits of the obligingly photogenic babies.

"Let's go and find the others" suggested Rita after a while, and Matt obediently followed her back towards the boat where Koto and Sam were sitting with Skipper and Matey, smoking and drinking coffee under the wooden shade on the outside deck. On seeing Matt, Skipper and Matey stood and slipped over the side into the cabin and Koto stood to leave.

"Please don't go" pleaded Matt. "Look, I know I'm paying for the boat and your services, but that's because I can. I really don't want to be treated like a boss, I just want to have a good time, so, Koto, please stay and smoke with us."

Sam spoke to Matt for the first time "Koto's a great guide and he really is close to this forest. His ancestors wash through its rivers and his soul is linked to every smell, sound and sight in Tanjung Puting. Dayak men are capable of extraordinary powers when they're on their land, just like Batak warriors in Sumatra. You're very lucky to be travelling with Koto."

"I can see that already" replied Matt looking at Koto to judge his reaction. He was pensively staring at the cigarette in his hand.

Sam and Rita exchanged glances before Rita sat down and gestured to Matt to do the same.

"I'm afraid we have to tell you something, Matt" she said quietly. "I'm only telling you this because it will explain many things, and you still have an opportunity to back out. It's only fair that you know."

It was Matt's turn to look worried.

"Last week my brother-in-law was murdered for providing information on logging to the authorities." She waited to see if Matt wanted her to go on. He was staring at her and nodded gently. "He was also Koto's best friend and another Dayak son. The threats to Koto are real and, by travelling with him, the loggers may believe you are a journalist or from a foreign organisation interested in exposing the logging. You may also be at risk."

"How much of a risk?" asked Matt.

"If you are on holiday just wanting to take a few photos, we think you should get a new guide" answered Sam.

"And if I'm interested in the logging and Koto's story?"

"You must understand that your life may be at risk" added Rita.

Matt's reason for coming to Borneo was becoming clearer to him. He had known he would never be a tourist; just there for a photo of an orang-utan, and then home. He had known he wanted to understand what lay at the heart of his new found friends' fight to save the forest. But he hadn't realised that he may be risking his life.

He looked at Rita, her solemn pretty face looking straight back at him; her simple courage, warning him to go away while she was under threat herself. He noticed Sam was looking at Rita, worried for her safety and scared for his own, but knowing he must be there for her. And then there was Koto, young, proud, and really quite fragile. But there was something else to Koto that Matt had never experienced before, something primal that he wanted to understand.

"I'm not just a tourist" Matt replied to Rita. "I'm a long way from my country escaping my own life and looking for something new. I want to see wild orang-utans, smell and hear the forest. I would be privileged to do that with a Dayak guide" he looked over to Koto. "If I can take some photos to help your campaign then I will. I'm not promising that I'm going to end up in a bar in Bali ranting on about trees, but this feels good right now. I feel as if I'm in very safe hands."

There was further discussion about the risks, but nobody referred again to Murkha's death nor explained to Matt the manner of his murder; they didn't think it was wise or necessary. Together, they ate rice and fried eggs, before Rita and Sam left to allow Koto and Matt to carry on further up river. As *Bukit* pulled out from the jetty it started to rain a little, Matt put on his wet-weather poncho, but before the vet's station was out of sight they saw Rita and

Sam's speedboat pull out into the river and with a roar of its outboard, head in the opposite direction towards Kumai.

Matt had surprised himself at how easy it had been to make his decision to carry on, and looking ahead at the peacefulness of the slow flowing river, he wondered if they weren't all just a little bit paranoid about the threats. After an hour, as if to emphasise the calmness ahead, a pair of large black birds with heavy bills crossed the river ahead of them, their wings beating slowly in the rain.

"Hornbills" stated Koto. "We're in the forest now."

CHAPTER NINETEEN
Jakarta

Widodo had never liked ports. He had grown up in Surabaya where the Eastern fleet of the Indonesian navy was based and had seen the fighting, drinking and whoring that accompanied it. The merchant fleet was even worse, and as a boy he had been clipped round the ear by smelly, filthy sailors whom he considered the lowest of the low. He preferred the land: it seemed to offer more certainty and could be organised with rules and regulations.

Tanjung Priok port in Jakarta was no different, although as Secretary General he had a status that ensured he received a little respect. He sat in an ante room outside a very senior naval officer's temporary office. Next to him sat the Deputy Chief of the National Police, waiting patiently with him for their naval counterpart to arrive for a meeting. Widodo felt extremely uncomfortable, the white tips of three Kent cigarettes already sat in the ashtray on the coffee table in front of him. After shaking hands with the policeman and exchanging a few banal pleasantries, it was clear to both of them they inhabited different worlds. Without speaking, they adopted an amicable silence to pass the time, with Widodo reading a newspaper, while the policeman stared ahead as if in a trance.

"I can't wait much longer" said the policeman to nobody in particular, although Widodo was the only other person in the room. The General had a twisted, unkind face, with thick eyebrows and a black moustache, which, given his age, was probably artificially blackened. He wore his uniform badly with the lower buttons on his shirt missing so it stretched out, revealing his slightly yellowed undershirt. "Do you have a proposition to resolve the stalemate over these Vietnamese ships, Secretary General?" he asked directly.

"I'd rather talk to you both at the same time, General" Widodo replied, feeling very unsure about opening the discussion with the police while the navy still had jurisdiction over the timber. "I'm sure the Vice-Admiral will be here soon."

As if on command, the door opened, and a young man in white uniform came in and ushered them into the temporary office. The

Vice-Admiral, a tall fit man in his fifties, was sitting behind a heavy desk in the small room with two chairs facing him and an old air conditioning unit providing an uncomfortably loud background noise. As they entered, he stood, moving around the desk to shake each man's hand. "Welcome to Tanjung Priok gentlemen" he said loudly with a grin on his face as he gestured for them both to sit down. They were offered coffee before he broke the silence and took command with a report on the current situation.

"We have the two Vietnamese ships at anchor in the port and the timber is still on board" he explained. "Both the ships and the valuable cargo are currently under naval arrest."

"We would like the cargo brought ashore as soon as possible so that we can pursue our investigations" stated the policeman without even glancing at Widodo.

"All in good time General" replied the Vice-Admiral. "I understood that we were here today to seek solutions beneficial to us all, not to make demands. Is that right Secretary General?"

Widodo was grateful to the Vice-Admiral for fending off this rather unpleasant policeman. That was the trouble with the police, everyone knew they were corrupt from top to bottom and they made very little effort to hide it. This matter required some caution and Widodo wasn't at all sure if this particular policeman was capable of subtlety. He was certain the chief of police and the Admiral of the fleet were aware of this meeting, and that these two slightly less senior negotiators mistakenly believed he was there representing his minister. He had to reinforce that illusion if he had any chance of success.

"Yes, thank you Vice-Admiral" Widodo replied, faking confidence. "It is very important to each of our offices that we come to some kind of agreement as soon as possible. The Vietnamese Embassy has been demanding the release of the ships and the crew and, of course, the timber is extremely valuable."

"Our estimate is around ten million US dollars. The *Na Trang II* has 25,000 cubic metres of mixed logs on board and the *Hanoi VII*, although only partly loaded, about 10,000" reported the Vice-Admiral. "That's a lot of timber. The bill of lading documents make it clear the timber is owned by a company run by Abdullah

Aziz, a notorious timber baron based in Central Kalimantan where the ships were seized."

Widodo shifted nervously in his seat and his discomfort was noticed by the Vice-Admiral who looked directly at him. "Do you know Aziz?" he asked Widodo. The policeman turned to look at him as well.

"It seems that the cargo should be discharged as soon as possible" Widodo stated without answering the question "and my office expects the case to be in the hands of the national police within twenty four hours. Of course we understand the inconvenience of this to you, Vice-Admiral, and would suggest that the ships remain under the jurisdiction of the navy until the case comes to trial. We are confident the port fees, and other expenses the ship owners will pay before release, will compensate the navy sufficiently." Widodo knew it would be easier to pay off the police for the logs and the sooner they were brought ashore the better.

"The navy expects to maintain jurisdiction for the time being" replied the Vice-Admiral, who, from Widodo's discomfort, was pretty sure that the old rascal was looking after Aziz's interests more than his minister's. Santoso's honesty was as well known as the timber baron's dishonesty. The navy knew that as long as they held the ships and the cargo, they were in a strong bargaining position, and the Vice-Admiral enjoyed bringing these two self-important men to his tiny temporary office and letting them know who was in charge. "Would you like to see the ships?" he asked.

Widodo was furious but kept his anger concealed. He knew that Santoso's contacts in the navy were very good, but had believed that the Western fleet was outside his sphere of influence. Now he was less certain. Clearly the Vice-Admiral had no intention of releasing the cargo until a deal had been thrashed out and it seemed that today was just a fishing trip. They had all played their first hand, but there were no real winners, and at this moment in time the navy held the bargaining advantage. This was going to be more difficult than he had imagined.

Outside, a minibus ferried the dignitaries to a small naval launch and out to the anchored Vietnamese ships. Widodo, on seeing the size of these vessels, realised for the first time what he was up against. From the water he could see that these were huge cargo ships, and the scale of the plunder of the forests came into focus for him for the first time. In the same way that the police failed to bother to hide their greed, so Aziz was flaunting his theft. The naval launch motored slowly around both ships before going alongside *Na Trang II* to where a rope ladder hung over the side of the ship. The distance from the small launch to the deck of *Na Trang II* was so high that Widodo was uncertain if he had the strength to climb it, but when the General explained he had to get back to his office and had no need to see the logs, Widodo stepped out onto the ladder and started climbing.

The Vice-Admiral joined him on deck as the policeman was motored back to the minibus. "Didn't look like he had the stamina!" joked the Vice-Admiral as Widodo laughed with him at the policeman's expense. "OK, follow me."

The view of Tanjung Priok port from the *Na Trang II* was impressive. Alongside the quay were three steely grey warships displaying their guns proudly, with each cannon covered in black protective tarpaulins, leaving no doubt as to the purpose of the vessels. Although old and outdated in international terms, they still provided a vital protection to Indonesia's shipping which passed through the most pirated seas in the world.

As they walked along the deck to the bridge, Widodo had to pass hundreds of logs, although as he now saw them: tree trunks stripped of their branches piled on top of each other. Most parts of the ship had logs piled high, and it wasn't until he looked down, across the vast ship from the bridge at the stern, he could see thousands more stacked in the open hold which stretched out in front of him. The modern illuminated instruments of the ship's navigation systems gave a bizarre hi-tech sense of the industrial scale of Aziz's operations. This was something Widodo could understand: it was ordered and controlled and the logs were neatly stacked. This was clearly a massive, professional business involving officials from every government department involved with shipping, forestry and trade. The fact that these ships had been seized was unsurprising: what was difficult to understand was how ships like this could ever get away with such enormous theft.

"Extraordinary isn't it" declared the Vice-Admiral, as if reading Widodo's thoughts. They both stared at the booty and shook their heads. "I'm not clear what your interest is in this *Pak* Widodo?" he asked directly.

This was the moment that Widodo had been waiting for. Now they had got rid of the policeman, the Vice-Admiral was asking him directly what he wanted. The navy held the advantage and he had to lay his cards on the table now or precious time would be wasted. Widodo was under enormous pressure; Hazim was in Jakarta waiting to hear from him and if he couldn't assure him everything was under control, he feared for his family. The sexually violent language used by Hazim to describe his wife, his daughter and his two sons, had haunted him ever since he had flown home from Singapore. He knew how violent Aziz's son could be, even slashing himself in frustrated anger when a child.

"Timber theft is an international crime" Widodo started. "In this case we are dealing with a friendly government and an extremely wealthy and powerful citizen. It is very important that this case is dealt with swiftly and cautiously."

"So what do you want?"

"As I explained, we believe the cargo should be released to the national police for due process."

"You mean so that Aziz can get his timber back? You know that the police will release the cargo once they've been paid off" the Vice-Admiral confronted Widodo.

They both looked around at the three military police guards on the bridge, started to walk out and down the steps. As they strolled along the deck towards the ship's bow they gazed at the cargo and realised that, what they were looking at, was a snapshot of what was happening to their country; it was being sold out. For a split second Widodo felt remorse, but realising the value of the timber, this was rapidly replaced by fear.

When they were on the bow they looked over the port towards *Hanoi VII* which looked almost the same as the ship they were currently standing on.

"You know Vice-Admiral" explained Widodo philosophically, "we don't get to choose all our friends, nor all our enemies. We're both old enough to know that we're survivors, and we've only achieved that by bending the rules." Widodo paused and looked into the face of this navy officer. He could see he understood what

111

he was saying, so he felt emboldened and went on "and this is one of those times. Aziz has given enormous donations to my Minister's political party." He paused. "I think you understand."

The Vice-Admiral was resting his arms on the railing looking out over the port. "I understand" he replied nodding, "but what's in this for me?" As he finished his question, his mobile phone rang; he reached into his pocket to answer it, turning slightly away from Widodo. "Yes sir, he's with me now. I think we are beginning to understand each other. Yes I'm sure we'll get what we want."

Widodo assumed this was the Admiral checking in on the meeting, and from the telephone conversation, felt that the negotiations were going as well as he could expect. He would have to talk to Hazim to see what could be offered, but felt sure they could come to an agreement. He was relieved that he had been direct with the Vice-Admiral. It had saved time and would get Hazim off his back.

When the Vice-Admiral had finished his call he smiled, led Widodo back to the ladder and they climbed down into a launch. They made their way back without talking. Widodo's car came to meet him and the two men shook hands. "I'll be in touch" assured Widodo.

"Yes, let me know what you can do for us" replied the Vice-Admiral, adding "but *Pak* Widodo, please don't leave it too long. We'd like to get this business cleaned up in a matter of days."

"Suits me fine" thought the Secretary General.

CHAPTER TWENTY
Borneo

The first night on the *klotok*, tied alongside a small jetty, *was* more comfortable than Matt had expected. He was provided with a foam mat, and the similarity this insulation had to his name provided laughter and speculation to his companions as to how many people had slept on "Matt". He played along happily and the rain, beating on the upper deck, soon felt like a soothing friend in the cosy, dry interior of *Bukit Tiga*. A small mosquito net was hung from a metal hook on the roof above him and, lying under a thin blanket, he was asleep in minutes.

In the morning he recognised the loud chattering of some animals playing on the upper deck of the boat with Matey shouting at them to go away. Then he smelt coffee. Opening his eyes he could see Skipper and Koto crouched near him silently drinking and smoking their first cigarette of the day. It was sunny outside; the bright contrast of the light off the water momentarily blinded him until Matey dropped off the upper deck, slid through the side, and settled on the deck next to the rest of them, casting a shadow over Matt for which he was grateful.

"*Kopi?*" asked Koto pulling the mosquito net aside and holding out a glass with steaming thick sweet coffee in it. "*Selamat pagi*" he offered warmly.

"Morning" responded Matt monosyllabically. "Sorry, you won't get much out of me for a few minutes." He lit up a Marlboro Light, slightly surprised at how easily he had returned to cigarettes, and took a sip of coffee as his three hosts watched. He sat up, folded the blanket and put it to one side. The animals, which he now recognised as macaques, leaped back onto the upper deck. Matey jumped to his feet, swung back up, shouting and shooing.

Outside it was warming up slowly but the damp air still carried a chill, prompting Matt to notice that Koto was wearing a grey hooded sweatshirt and jeans. They were worn in a way that suggested they were new and making a statement, but to Matt, Koto could have fitted in very well hanging out at any British shopping centre. Sucking hard on his cigarette, he considered the bizarre juxtaposition of Koto the hoodie at Brent Cross, with the sounds of Matey shouting at lippy macaques; he hoped it was all part of the brain waking up and dealing with the unfamiliar.

Slightly self consciously, wearing only his Calvin Klein underpants, he tried to stand up but hit his head on the roof. "Shit" he cursed quietly, but loud enough to get a chuckling response from both Skipper and Koto. "I'm going up top to breathe the forest air" he explained unnecessarily.

"Breakfast will be up soon" offered Koto feeling a bit guilty for laughing at Matt's discomfort. "It's still cold up there, take the blanket" he said, picking it up and passing it over to a thankful Matt who clambered through the open window and hoisted himself up on the top deck.

Across from him, crouching on his haunches, Matey acknowledged Matt with a smile as he conspicuously, and curiously, looked at his near naked body from head to toe. Matt blushed and swung the blanket over his shoulders, brushed his blond hair from his face, saying rather awkwardly "it's a bit cold up here, isn't it?" Matey smiled again, looking Matt in the eyes and tucking his left arm under his t-shirt, raising it to rub his chest, in what was to Matt, a provocative display; but even Matt realised this was just a young man's tactile, innocent response to the morning; not him. Or was it? To his embarrassment, as if to tease him even further, Matey pushed himself upright and slipped back over the side with a final glance and grin at the bulge under Matt's underpants.

Two macaques immediately appeared, realising their enemy had retreated and not reckoning Matt would be much opposition. They took up a crouching position close to where Matey had just been positioned and stared at Matt's morning hard-on.

"Shoo, shoo, fuck off!" shouted Matt angrily. It was one thing feeling uncomfortable when the crew were watching him, but monkeys? The macaques, as if reciprocating disinterest, didn't blink. The one on the left spat and scratched his balls.

Jumping off the boat onto the jetty, Matt walked twenty metres before pissing against a tree, relieving himself not only of the tea last night, but also of the embarrassment this morning. The sounds of the forest seemed so loud that he imagined every creature must be huge, and, as if to corroborate his theory, a massive glistening black and electric blue butterfly flapped and struggled to keep aloft as its wings dried out in the early sun. He looked up the path that led into the forest and saw the shards of yellow morning light penetrating the dense forest canopy. On the ground, at every point where the sun lit the wet rotting leaves, a small mist appeared, rising like smoke up the light rays. The forest was enduring its first warming of the day.

Turning back to look at the *klotok* he noticed the macaques were now behind him on the path picking up bits of forest debris, inspecting it, and putting it back on the ground. Just next to the boat on the jetty a tiny infant macaque had become unattached from its mother, sitting, looking at the same black and electric blue butterfly he had admired moments earlier. It tried to jump at the airborne game, but was picked up from the wooden plank by its mother and held close to her chest, where it settled without complaint to suckle. "Breakfast" thought Matt as he made his way back to the boat.

"*Nasi*" offered Koto apologetically as he held out a wooden bowl full of boiled rice. "This is the best we can do this morning, although I tried to persuade Matey to fry eggs. But he said you were strong and would be OK on rice. Do you know what he means?"

"No idea" Matt responded. "But rice is fine. How about more coffee?"

"Yes, coming." Koto paused and looked seriously at Matt. "Are you OK Mr Matt? I realise this journey is very strange for you. Not only is everything different – the food, the boat, the forest. But you also got to deal with the threat, and, um… with me… I'm sorry."

"Let's have an adventure, Koto" responded Matt gently. "You're great, and I'm very happy to be in the forest with a Dayak warrior. For me, it's a privilege, not a problem." He deliberately smiled his killer smile and Koto's face lit up so brightly that when the huge butterfly flapped between them, he was certain he could see the detail in the wings more clearly.

The eggs never materialised, Matt stayed on the upper deck as the boat started its clanking engine, pulled out into the river and headed steadily deeper into the forest. The morning chill slowly lifted, the bright sunlight creating a sense of a Disney cruise. From his comfortable position he saw, to the left, sitting on a branch, a large black and white kingfisher dive into the river as they passed by, almost at the same level as the branch. On the right, egrets lined the muddy river bank, silently pointing their long black bills at the water. Matt sat, great white explorer, camera around his neck. The "staff" down below.

After about half an hour Koto joined him on the upper deck with a pair of binoculars, pointing ahead at the right bank of the river. About two thirds up the trees Matt could make out some monkeys sitting on branches near each other. As they got closer Koto passed him the binoculars so he could see them more clearly.

"Proboscis monkeys" stated Koto. "One of nine species of primate found in this Park. This is one of the strangest monkeys in the world – look at its long nose." Sure enough, it had a long pink nose hanging off its face, but for Matt it was its eyes that attracted him. The monkeys were watching the boat with the same curious look that Matey had displayed earlier when watching Matt's embarrassment. Their eyes were darting from the boat to their hands, which were picking fruits from the tree. Then they were looking at each other, always alert.

"We call them Dutch monkeys" said Koto smiling at Matt. Realising that Matt didn't understand the reason for the name he explained "the early white visitors to Borneo were the Dutch colonialists. To us, white people have really long noses. At least compared to mine" he laughed as he touched his nose and further flattened it against his face.

Matt smiled back. "So you think I look like that?" he asked pointing at the monkeys.

"Not at all" replied Koto with a deadpan face and pausing for obvious effect. "I like monkeys, they're beautiful!" They both laughed out loud enough to disturb the proboscis monkeys' feeding. A large male stood on his branch, called to his family with a honking sound and slowly led the way by leaping to a dead branch close to the water. They were even easier to see now and Matt and Koto froze while Matt reached for his camera. The boat had already tied up on an overhanging branch on the opposite bank, the engine switched off. In the welcome silence they could hear the monkeys moving in the branches with the sound of the vast forest behind. They stared at each other across the river.

Matt shot a roll of film, zooming in on those noses, not flattered by Koto's remarks but certain now that he could never be mistaken for a monkey. Their hands and feet were incredible as they held onto the branches and picked fruit without wavering, their tails playing an equally important role in steadying their bodies. Their faces revealed permanent caution. This is what touched and surprised him the most, their constant state of awareness, their unwavering alertness. They were conscious of danger every moment of their lives. This was no Disney cruise, this really was the wild.

Koto tapped Matt on his shoulder and pointed below the branch to the muddy bank. Matt focussed his telephoto lens so that he could see what it was: the same colour as the mud, a small crocodile-like animal with a long toothy, slightly cartoon-like but supercilious jaw, crouched on the mud. It didn't move and for a while Matt guessed it was a bizarre fossil that Koto always showed his clients. But moments later, just as one of the young proboscis monkeys splashed the sparkling sunlit river water with its tail, the creature slipped silently into the water. Only its pop-up eyes and identikit nostrils, balanced on the end of its long jaw, were visible, both breaking the surface of the water for a few moments, until it disappeared completely.

"Gharial" said Koto quietly, slightly reverentially.

In the quiet Matt was able to hear another sound, more familiar but less welcome: the high pitched wine of a mosquito making its way from his blood, past his ear, to try and find another landing point. The experienced traveller knows only too well that, once you've heard a mosquito, it is already too late. Their tiny proboscis, not comical and pink like the monkey's, but pointed and refined for its purpose, has already injected its blood thinning compounds to enable it to feed on your blood. The sound is enough to anger a grown man in an air-conditioned hotel room, or create a rapid emergency response as the western traveller slaps their face or legs uncontrollably. This tiny hunter is rarely alone and often carries weapons far greater than the initial irritation caused by the bite.

Malaria, the best known disease carried by these insects comes in four different types. In Borneo it is not uncommon to suffer from more than one at the same time and if one of them is "hemorrhagic" then you probably die. This land is so unexplored that scientists still discover insects and reptiles unrecorded by science. But if you get down to it, the diseases, parasites, and viruses that inhabit this vast island are hardly even known. Only the Dayak medicine men have some answers, and usually these are guesswork based on pulling the bad, hot, feverish energy from the body.

Being bitten by a mosquito in the forest during the day is probably fairly safe. The really bad malaria carrying mosquitoes get you at dusk and dawn and anytime you wander around at night. If you live in a city in Indonesia it may be a different daytime species of mosquito that passes on dengue fever, again in four different models, the worst being "hemorrhagic" and deadly. Hemorrhagic really just means that your body gives up and your organs bleed until you die, especially your brain.

"Let's move again" said Koto, also being eaten by the mosquitoes. "I don't like being stranded in the still warmth of the river."

He smiled weakly at Matt who, wondering why Koto had moved them on so quickly, noticed he had removed the hooded sweatshirt and jeans and was only wearing a pair of shorts. He was a million miles from Brent Cross shopping centre now, a young man smelling the air, sensing the sounds of the forest, looking the part of the Dayak guide leading them into a land better known to his ancestors.

CHAPTER TWENTY ONE
Jakarta

Debi was unsure whether she wanted to have dinner with Probo. It had been a long time since they had met socially and he was now married with children. She felt it would be better to keep her relationship with him professional, let each of them stick to their role. But he had sounded very concerned on the phone and said he needed to talk to someone he trusted. They had known each other for fifteen years; he had been a good friend to her husband, and after his disappearance, to her.

Friendship was something Debi had shied away from more recently, but Probo came from a happier time, when she had opened her heart to her friends; he probably knew her better than most. She wondered why he had chosen the restaurant at the Hyatt, although she acknowledged it was conspicuous and public places offered protection.

The Grand Hyatt Hotel occupies prime Jakarta space. It couldn't be more central. Attached to the Plaza Indonesia shopping mall, it overlooks the "circle", Jakarta's most famous huge traffic roundabout with a massive fountain display in its centre. At least, that's in good times. The fountain rarely displayed after the students were shot in 1998 or in the following weeks, after the Chinese Indonesians fled the country when their part of town, known as Glodok, was invaded by brutal militarised rapists and arsonists. The water seems to act as a litmus test on the health of Indonesia or at least on the city's read on its health. In recent years the circle has become the centre for demonstrations, and it is rare to drive past without seeing placards and banners complaining about something, in this newly found freedom to protest.

On the opposite corner of the circle is the Mandarin Oriental, another five star hotel but smaller, less American and more personal. No escalators here. This is the favourite hangout for foreign correspondents and diplomats, dining or drinking in *Zigolinis*, the Italian restaurant on the first floor. Next door, the razor wire identifies the vulnerable British Embassy, and around the corner, the *Deutch* building, home to the offices of the BBC, Al

Jazeera, Reuters, Associated Press and dozens of foreign press. Other embassies, restaurants and expat bars punctuate the area.

Perhaps more important is the ugly dilapidated structure on the corner next to the Hyatt. This was the first western style hotel built in the days of Indonesia's first President, Sukarno. It is the western hotel featured in *"The Year of Living Dangerously"*, made into a film starring a young Mel Gibson as a rookie reporter in Jakarta at the time of the coup which removed Sukarno, replacing him with General Suharto, who would rule Indonesia for the next thirty years. In recent years Hotel Indonesia has failed to attract the same class of visitor, completely outsmarted by most of the other hotels in central Jakarta. But it still maintained its arrogance. It was latterly best known as an overpriced tourist hotel and, for the locals, for its swimming pool. Open to the public and a place to show off, young men and women would swim, play tennis, and generally display their assets to anyone who was interested; in some cases, to anyone who would pay. That is, until it closed, zoned for some undefined protection. But, already the new flashy shopping mall and expensive apartments built around it are threatening its relevance even as an historic relic.

Debi was dropped off by taxi at the new neon lit entertainment centre attached to Plaza Indonesia, by mistake. This was unfamiliar territory to her. The cinemas, bowling alley, restaurants, shops and designer clad Jakartans were not part of her normal day. She would probably have felt more comfortable picking her way through the rubble that lines the corridors of Hotel Indonesia, rummaging through the sad memories of her past. But fifteen minutes later, having experienced more of middle class Jakartan life than she had in the previous year, she arrived at the Grand Hyatt through double doors that join it to Plaza Indonesia. She made her way upstairs to the steak and seafood restaurant.

"I'm meeting Minister Probowo" she explained to the maitre'di and was led to a table overlooking the Jakarta cityscape. Probo was already there and rose to welcome her to his table. She was wearing a stylish long blue evening dress last worn with her husband. She had no idea what had possessed her to dress up like this, but when Probo stood and came around to pull out her chair, she couldn't help but feel an overwhelming sense of betrayal to her husband and child.

"I'm so sorry I'm late Minister" she apologised.

"I'm pleased you came, Debi. You look wonderful and I thank you for trusting me." He put out his hand. Debi felt a heartfelt welcome she hadn't experienced for years. She believed him, he was here to talk, he needed her help. Probo returned to his chair and smiled a warm inclusive greeting, without any threat of intrusion.

Conversation started cautiously: the responsibility of being a minister, his wife, her NGO, how could they have guessed what they'd be doing so many years earlier. Then they talked about her husband and child, but Debi changed the subject abruptly.

"So, did you trace the number your security guard called?" she asked.

Probo smiled sadly. "OK Debi, I realise you're still very lost. I had hoped you could find a way to move on, it's what he would have wanted."

Debi had a flash of her husband's face smiling at her, making her feel safe. She was lost, she realised that, but she liked being that way. She knew better than anyone else how YHB had become a means to avoid her personal failures. She also knew better than anyone that she had turned into a cold, sometimes unkind, driven woman with an enemy to unleash her anger on. But she wasn't about to open herself up to an old friend as if she was in need of therapy. She still had her husband with her when she needed him and she wasn't going to share him with a therapist.

"Let's order, shall we?" she insisted. She looked at her menu, was troubled by the prices: grilled fish cost the same as most peoples' weekly wage and, although she was sure Probo would pay, felt uncomfortable with the opulence. Probo seemed aware of her discomfort.

"I invited you here because I believe it to be safe" he explained. "My job puts me in a very difficult position and being seen with you in public like this is the best for both of us. It also demonstrates there is no impropriety."

Debi nodded and looked down again at her menu.

"The security guard revealed very little" he explained, answering her question. "The number didn't answer when we tried it on a number of occasions. But it was marked in his phone as *HA*. We asked him who this was and he said it was his friend who was repairing his motorcycle, but we got no further with him. I asked to see him on his next shift but he's disappeared, he never came back to work."

"You realise that *HA* is probably Haj Abdullah don't you?"

"Of course I've considered this" he responded uncomfortably quickly "and I am sure that the call was connected to *Pak* Aziz, but I would be very surprised to find my security guard dealing directly with him. No, I think it's someone else, but the number is now dead. It was a pre-paid hand phone number and can't be traced. But he had called that number every night for over two weeks, including the days before my driver was forced off the road. Before that, nothing."

"That corresponds with the attempt on your life and the murder of Rita's brother-in-law. I'm sure it's all linked to your investigation of Aziz and the seizure of the Vietnamese ships"

"So, that unfortunate soul killed in Pangkalan Bun was Rita's family and your source? I feared that was the case. I feel awful. They were mutilating him at the same time as the navy boarded those ships." Probo paused and offered Debi a drink which she declined. Probo was drinking water. "You know they called me that night and left a message on my voicemail. I didn't really understand what it meant but, even then, I feared someone had died."

Debi looked at Probo's face, and for the first time that night, realised that this man was carrying more than he could handle. She knew what that meant and put her hand across the table to rest it on his hand. Probo withdrew, startled by her move, but looking into her eyes saw that he had over-reacted.

"Relax Probo" said Debi gently. "You can't take all these terrible acts as your responsibility, you know? You're fighting with your own arsenal as best you can. Murkha knew what he was doing but I'm ashamed to say that we all underestimated the level of greed that Aziz is protecting."

They ordered fish. When it arrived Debi encouraged Probo to talk about his wife and family to remove any guilt on his part for meeting a single woman for dinner. He warmed up and spoke of his wife, a university lecturer, with great pride. But he was frightened. It was alright to rationalise, take precautions, and seek support from the security services, but he knew the reality was that he, or his family, could be hurt with relative ease.

They ate their food before Probo moved onto his reason for dinner.

"I wanted to talk to you about Aziz" he commented rather obviously. When he noticed the confusion on Debi's face, he explained. "I'm getting very frightened the more I know about this man. I want to pass my thoughts by you to get some feedback; I don't know who else to talk to. You must promise me that you won't repeat any of this to anyone."

"If you've got information on Aziz you must let me get it out" she replied.

"No!" Probo responded rather too loudly. He stopped and looked around to see if he had attracted any attention, but in this restaurant the tables were far apart and you were barely conscious of other diners, other than their background noise.

"OK, please don't worry" said Debi rather surprised "I'm sorry, you can trust me. Nothing you say will be repeated to another soul without your permission. I give you my word." She was taken aback by the intensity of Probo's fear and regretted trying to push him; it was clear he was already under too much strain. She looked into his face and smiled caringly at him with warmth she hadn't felt for years; two old friends conspiratorially needing each other.

"What do you know of the *Laksar Jihad*?" he asked without further explanation.

It was Debi's turn to be surprised by this simple question. "Probably as much as most Indonesians, what I've read in the newspapers."

Laksar Jihad had been an Islamic militia group numbering, probably, many thousands of Indonesians, armed and trained, some say, by factions of the military. It had been reported that they were at the heart of the religious clashes, between Muslims and Christians in Central Sulawesi and the Malukus in eastern

Indonesia, which had started in 1999 after Suharto's fall, resulting in thousands of deaths. Famously, after the bombing of two bars in Bali in 2002 killing over two hundred, including mostly foreigners, *Laksar Jihad's* website disappeared and they claimed to have disbanded.

"What do you think happens to thousands of trained and armed Islamic extremists?" he asked.

"I don't suppose they went back to the paddy fields. What are you saying? How is Aziz linked to Islamic militia?"

"I really don't know. But his generous donations to build mosques and support a particular *pesantran* in East Java bother me more than I can explain. I know he's protected in very high places and we've recently learned of his ability to be violent. But you don't just get violent; you need the apparatus for his kind of protection and reach. So I started wondering if his huge investment in his faith was a part of his protection or just plain altruism. I asked God in prayer and I've got a really empty feeling."

Debi was aghast. Minutes earlier she had been pondering how to outwit a crime boss and now she was being presented with an enemy far more dangerous and unknown. "Let's look at this rationally" she stated rather pompously and Probo looked her straight in the eyes waiting for the next observation. "All we know is that Aziz pays money to some Muslim boarding school and has built mosques. In most peoples' minds that is rather good isn't it? What links him to the *Laksar Jihad* or any other militia? What do you know?"

"That's it. I don't have the evidence, but I do have a very strong and growing suspicion. This is why I need your feedback. I've been turning this around in my head for days now and I always come to the same frightening conclusion. I'm hoping you will be able to deconstruct my logic. But I must repeat, you mustn't repeat this to anyone."

Debi promised again.

Probo explained that Aziz's generosity had started three years ago after an east Javanese religious leader had visited him in Pangkalan Bun. This man was known to have strong sympathies with violent jihad and was criticised by mainstream Indonesian Muslim leaders for failing to criticise the Bali bomb tragedy in

2002. Aziz had given him six million dollars in the last three years in addition to building mosques and supporting *pesantrans*. The money was said to be for community work with the poor, but Probo had searched and found no record of any programme run by this man. But since he had met Aziz he had been living in Malaysia, making regular trips to Mindanao in the southern Philippines where Muslim fighters are waging war for a Southeast Asian Islamic state.

Debi looked at Probo, for the first time realising how alone he must feel. "This is only circumstantial you know."

Probo smiled. "I know. But there's more."

Three years ago Aziz had cleared an area of forest on the border of Tanjung Puting National Park and planted oil palms, the highly profitable cash crop that was spreading across the region like a plague. This was perfectly understandable, although illegal; but nonetheless a sensible way of laundering his money within Borneo. What was strange was not the plantation, but the communications technology he had installed at the oil palm headquarters. It was so unusual that both the Indonesian intelligence and the Americans had been alerted. A high powered transmitter had been listened into by intelligence but the messages were so well encoded they had failed to understand the purpose of the communications. Although the Americans had been very interested for a while, a report by a senior US intelligence officer put their minds at ease. That officer now owns 2% of the shares in "Sawit Trading", a Singapore company owned by Aziz.

"So what makes you think this is *Laksar Jihad?*" asked Debi.

"People from *Laksar Jihad*" corrected Probo. "I'm not suggesting the organisation is still active, but some of its trained militia are bound to be still operating. After all, they're trained soldiers with weapons and a vision – their own Islamic state covering the southern Philippines, Indonesia and Malaysia, under *Sharia* law. They're not all going to just give that up, throw their weapons away and grow rice, are they?"

"I still don't get it. Why?"

"Three years ago Aziz came under repeated accusations of running a timber mafia operation" said Probo. "You know because you were part of the lobby against him. At that time he moved to

Singapore, bought the *Regency* and settled into life out there handing his Borneo operation over to his son, Hazim. This I think is *HA*. At the same time attacks on his opponents began. Not crowd violence as might be expected, but assassinations. Rita's brother-in-law was almost ritually murdered, cold-bloodedly, for a purpose beyond timber profit. I believe it was a calculated warning carried out by trained militia. My driver was killed in Jakarta; an attack almost certainly aimed at me, a minister. This is more than business, it's an attack on society designed to build up fear."

"But surely you don't think he's funding militia for anything other than his own protection and business interests?"

"I just don't know Debi. I just don't know. But I do feel as if I'm being watched every moment of the day. I've moved my family out of the house and started to take extra precautions."

Debi stared at him over the table, suddenly conscious of all the people eating and moving around the restaurant. She started considering the threat, relieved to know that Rita and Sam were heading for the relative safety of Singapore, although they were looking for Aziz's business connections on this island state.

"I understand why you're so frightened" responded Debi. "And I'm afraid to say that your logic makes too much sense."

Probo pondered her words for a moment and nodded slowly. He seemed to have aged five years over dinner, Debi felt completely overdressed for this occasion. She was distressed by what she had heard, but it eerily started to put Aziz's untouchable status into a different context, one that she had not considered before.

"I have some friends working on human rights issues that may be able to shed some light on your hypothesis if you'll allow me to sound them out. Of course I won't mention Aziz, Kalimantan or you."

Probo smiled and nodded his head, grateful for the support. A problem shared …

"You must be careful too" Probo warned. "Under no circumstances should you or any of your team go back to Tanjung Puting."

Debi stared at Probo, raising her hand to her mouth with a slightly audible intake of breath.

126

CHAPTER TWENTY TWO
Borneo

The Sekonyer River's dark brown water meanders through the forest, as wide as an Olympic pool, every bend offering the chance of a surprise ahead. The trees on the river banks seem to grow from the black mud, reaching straight for the sky, yet taking their turn in the layers of vegetation, providing a depth to the sounds that emanate from the darkness beyond. Hornbills, egrets, kingfishers and mosquitoes, all have a place in the dense, wet greenery; their presence promising a chance to see something more: perhaps a gibbon or an orang-utan.

Lost in his thoughts, Matt sat on the upper deck with Koto watching the river ahead, sharing his Marlboros. He felt more comfortable in this place than he had anywhere since leaving London, despite it being more alien to him than anywhere he had known. It was partly his company, but largely the knowledge that somewhere out there in this forest, clouded leopards hunted for their survival, orang-utans swung from tree to tree and sloth bears, one of the more ferocious animals in the forest, secretly stared down from a high branch vantage point. The forest didn't just look intact, it sounded and smelt complete.

Bukit moved upstream, the floating vegetation brushing past its hull without concern. Skipper knew this river, its currents and its dangers. As they took a wide sweep on a bend, they saw another *klotok* heading towards them very slowly. At first it wasn't obvious what was ahead, but as they approached it became clear it was towing logs, strapped together and pulled by ropes. *Bukit* slowed its engines and as they came alongside, Matey, on the bow, shouted out very loudly to the other crew. After a brief exchange he turned, smiling at Koto, giving him a thumbs-up.

"Have you got some money?" Koto asked Matt. On receiving two hundred thousand rupiah he went forward and talked to a young man on the other boat, counting out one hundred and fifty thousand and handing it over. Matey, grinning wildly, moved below.

Koto returned to Matt and gave him back fifty thousand. "Twelve bottles of beer for tonight" he explained. "Matey's getting it on board."

After a few minutes the engines clattered to life, they sluggishly pulled ahead and drifted towards the opposite bank before heading upstream again. Matt pulled out his camera and photographed the other *klotok* and the logs being towed, but was shocked at the length of this log raft. Two minutes later, still moving forward, the logs were continuing to pass on his left, yet he could only just see the end of the raft. A small boy with an older man was crouching barefoot on the big floating logs at the back, checking that everything was holding together. From his position above them, Matt shot off some more film of the pair, dressed only in dirty shorts, staring up at him with wide eyes, as he focused on their inquisitive faces. It struck him that, despite these people being in charge of a log raft at least five metres wide and two or three hundred metres long, in a protected national park, they looked as if it was all in a day's work.

"Ramin" said Koto quietly. "They take other trees as well, but ramin is the main one, it's the most valuable."

"But it's so open" exclaimed Matt with incredulity. "If the authorities wanted to stop this it would be so easy. How long before that raft reaches the bay?"

"It'll go as far as possible today and arrive in the bay tonight. They're not afraid of authority, only competitors or angry locals. There is opposition to this, but we have little power. These boatmen make more money towing logs for the timber boss than waiting for another tourist." Koto went quiet.

They sat next to each other for at least half an hour without speaking as the forest passed by. It was getting warm and Matt pulled his t-shirt off to catch a bit of sun. He reached into his bag to pull out his sun cream, starting to squeeze it onto his hand when Koto stood up quickly and ran forward to shout at Skipper. The engine hiccupped to a halt.

Koto returned to Matt's side and pointed, without speaking, to the right bank. At first Matt couldn't see what he was pointing at, but after a while saw that a branch, set back a bit from the river bank, was swaying back and forth. Lower down on the branch, mainly hidden by foliage, a large orange shape was lounging around, staring straight at them.

"Oh shit" exclaimed Matt, realising he was looking at his first wild orang-utan. He quickly slapped the sun cream onto his chest, without rubbing it in, then rubbed his greasy hand over his leg in an attempt to clean his hand. The orang-utan dropped a little lower on the tree, now almost completely obscured by the leaves on surrounding trees and bushes. Frantically Matt wiped his hand over his shorts to try and dry it before picking up his camera. He felt stupid at being so unprepared and, by the time he had focused on the animal, it had moved so he could only see a fraction of its body.

Matey and Skipper had come onto the upper deck to see the orang-utan. Although they often saw them at the rehabilitation centre further upriver, a truly wild sighting like this was special. *Bukit* had been tied to an overhanging branch on the opposite bank about fifty metres from the red ape.

The orang-utan was watching them carefully but seemed unafraid of their presence. It was a young male, living alone in the canopy of this vast forest, searching for fruits and leaves and enjoying the dry warmth of this sunny morning. The forest is drenched in rain so much of the time that moments like this seem to provide a short reprieve, even to the orang-utans.

Matt took a couple of shots to remind him of the moment, but knew that the pictures themselves were hopeless, just a glimpse of orange fur amongst leaves. But maybe they were a more honest representation of these highly endangered animals than the cute close-ups he had shot of the baby orphans the day before.

Koto had gone below with Skipper and the engines started up again. Matey, standing next to Matt, reached over and put his hand on Matt's chest, rubbing the sun cream. He giggled and looked at Matt's face seeking approval, then rubbed his greasy hand over his own face showing a broad smile. Although confused, Matt looked back with a friendly grin. Taking this as encouragement Matey reached down and rubbed his greasy hand over Matt's right leg and then roughly wiped his hand on Matt's shorts pushing hard on his already responding crutch, always staring at his face.

Matt stepped back suddenly and a slightly alarmed Matey scampered to the bow of the boat unable to understand whether he was in trouble or not. His concern was put at rest when Koto appeared on the deck and Matt, although looking slightly awkward, made no attempt to complain. Matey smiled at Matt and swung over the side to the lower deck.

"Not a great sighting" Koto apologised, "but it's good to see truly wild orang-utan. You look as if you're in quite a state there. Why don't you get those greasy shorts off and I'll ask Matey to wash them for you."

Matt changed and Koto brought him some soap and water to clean the grease from his hands. He sat on the upper deck alone, washing in a bowl, as *Bukit* continued upriver for a few minutes before slowing and starting to turn. Koto appeared on deck.

"You can see the black water" he enthused.

Looking ahead there was a clear delineation between the dark brown water of the main Sekonyer river and the pitch black water ahead on a narrower tributary. *Bukit* ploughed into the black water and Matt's adventure felt even more intense now that the river banks were much closer. This part of the river was wide enough for two *klotok* to slowly pass, but not much more. On his right he saw a kingfisher on a branch. Not the first, but now that the river was so narrow, definitely the closest. It perched quietly as the boat approached, but flew before the bow came alongside. Instead of passing by the wildlife on the river, here they were flushing it out.

Matt moved to the bow and sat next to Koto who seemed more relaxed now they had left the main river. He wanted Matt to understand the beauty of this forest. The black water was the colour of a healthy peat swamp forest river. The colour was from tiny vegetative particles, a natural nutritious soup draining from the peat and winding its way through, and contributing to, the ecosystem.

Koto explained that this right tributary, known as the Sekonyer *Kanan*, feeds into the main Sekonyer which is brown. The lighter colour is because it has been polluted by mercury from the process of illegal gold mining, and by river traffic and logging; decades earlier the entire area was black water, brackish beyond the fork they had just taken. Even though this area was designated a

Biosphere Reserve and a National Park, it had already been violated.

"The extremely rare dragon fish lives in the black water" enthused Koto. "In other parts of Kalimantan, this was the favourite water for Dayaks to bathe in. It contains the spirit of the forest. If you saw a change in the black water you knew that the forest was being defiled. Somewhere, something was wrong."

Matt looked ahead. The blackness of the water and lack of surface current gave a mirror quality to the river, reflecting the overhanging branches and the river banks with a clarity he had never seen before. His camera worked overtime. It was as if, whenever he thought he had never been to such a wild and remote area, he was thrust forward just a little further. He really did sense something different, but wasn't sure it was as comfortable as he might have hoped. Koto sitting next to him gave a reassuring smile as he attempted to build up the enthusiasm for the forest he needed so badly. The atmosphere between them was raw. They both moved slowly forward on the boat, wondering what lay ahead.

The engines slowed down as they entered an area where the forest opened and a watery, swampy lake appeared occasionally where the river bank disappeared. On the right on the muddy, dark bank between two openings to the lake, a huge mud coloured estuarine crocodile lay silent and still. Its jaws alone must have been well over a metre in length, and its thick fat body was so huge that both Koto and Matt could only stare. As the *klotok* invaded its space, it clumsily pulled its head from the mud, swinging its body around towards the water. Straightening itself up, facing the opposite bank it slipped into the river, hardly disturbing the mirrored surface. It would resurface to rest quietly once the *klotok* had passed, waiting for a careless sambal deer, wild pig or macaque to stumble towards its jaws. It only had to wait.

"Wow!" exhaled Matt prompting a wide smile from Koto. "I wouldn't like to come across that on my own."

"A policeman was eaten last month further upriver" Koto replied. "He was swimming in the river to cool off. We all do it, you have no chance if a crocodile grabs you, they easily sense your movements in the water and pull you under to drown. Some say they store your body on the river bed for later. I don't know."

Matt shivered audibly and smiled at Koto. But Koto didn't seem to notice. He was just facing ahead with a determined expression. His black hair fell over his eyes and his hands were rested on his knees as he sat upright on the bow.

"It's always like this" he said with the wisdom of a man much older. "If you enter a land in which you don't belong, you don't stand a chance. It's simple; it's just not your world."

Rita was beginning to unwind for the first time since hearing of her brother-in-law's death. Setin, her sister, Murkha's widow, had moved to Jakarta with her baby to escape Pangkalan Bun. She was safe enough in Rita's small apartment and Rita's friends were fussing around the little girl. But Rita had discovered rather brutally that she had become used to her own life, her privacy. Even though she had grown up very close to Setin, being around her and the baby was difficult. So when Debi had asked Sam to go to Singapore to find where Aziz lived and investigate his business connections, Rita had, rather too quickly, suggested she went with him.

The *Asialite Hotel*, on Orchard Street, is a favourite with western tourists. It is conveniently situated near the main shopping district, not too expensive, and quite well equipped with television and internet in all the rooms. Rita and Sam were unfazed by the prospect of sharing a twin bedded double room; they were used to cutting costs. Given the circumstances of their research, it also made them feel a little safer. They were surprised to find that they had been given a suite with two rooms, two televisions, a massage chair, but one double bed.

"I'll sleep on the sofa" offered Sam gallantly. Rita just nodded and smiled.

They had booked for three days but had no real idea how long their work would keep them on this island state. Rita had been to Singapore earlier in the year to represent YHB at a conference, but it was Sam's first trip, and more significantly, his first time out of Indonesia. He was nervous and excited at the same time. But most of all, he was thrilled to be with his friend Rita.

"You're not far from home!" joked Rita.

Singapore is very close to the Indonesian island of Sumatra where Sam's family lived and he was born. But Medan, his home city, has none of the order of Singapore. The traffic in Medan jumps lights that probably don't work anyway, and the buses belch out black fumes. Pavements are cracked, pedestrians remaining

133

constantly aware of not falling through the holes revealed by missing paving stones.

Medan is a large city of diversity, but not yet understanding the beauty of that diversity. It is still a city at war: on Christmas day in 2000 bombs ripped through Christian churches in the city; there still exists distrust between the local Batak people, who are predominantly Christian, and the Muslims from neighbouring provinces. Medan has taken a huge influx of Acehnese since the appalling tsunami on Boxing Day in 2004 killed two hundred thousand people from that province alone. Another essential part of Medan's diversity is the Chinese Indonesians with strong links across the Malacca Straits to Malaysia and Singapore. Sam, an indigenous Batak, had grown up in a happy, but simple, home with his family in the Chinese district. His parents owned one of the few Batak clothes shops in the city.

Unlike its neighbour, Singapore is clean, modern and ordered. Too ordered for many, but the casual tourist in transit from Europe to Australia, hardly goes beyond some of the best shopping in the world and candlelit dinners. Behind the glitz of Singapore is a repression of flamboyant cultures, but not a wholesale rejection. Singapore is a bit like a grey bureaucrat, secretly reminiscing the chaos and trying to reinvent it in his ordered way.

Sam left Rita at the hotel to go and check Aziz's business interests through company records. Singapore offers sophisticated systems to search the files and it took him thirty minutes to identify three Singapore companies with Aziz as the major shareholder. The first was the 'Borneo Trading Company' described as an import-export company. The second was 'Regency Holdings' which seemed to be the company behind his hotel interests, and the third was 'Sawit Trading', his palm oil company. Even better, the Singapore address given for Aziz looked like a house address: Sam thought he might have found Aziz's home.

He was so pleased with himself that, on his way back to the hotel, he decided to call into the *Regency* and take a few photographs. Most guests at this hotel arrived by car or taxi, but Sam had walked from the MRT underground station, arriving on foot. The long sweeping drive leading up to the covered entrance was lined both sides by flowering tropical plants which shone out in the bright sunlight. At one point he had to move out into the road to avoid automatic water sprinklers that were adding to the already uncomfortable humidity. Sam took some photographs of the driveway, the flowers and the imposing hotel reaching towards the blue sky and reflecting the cityscape in its glass. To him it represented a statement of arrogance and he could see no beauty in it. But he knew too much and disliked the owner so much that he could not be objective. The driveway, the scent and colour of the tropical flowers were a simple introduction to the opulence that the *Regency* achieved, not only with its architecture and location, but by its slavish service to its guests.

As he approached the glass covered entrance, he felt his first pang of concern. It hadn't occurred to him that he would sense any danger entering a hotel, but he was completely out of his own comfort zone. His jeans and t-shirt blended with the casual wear of many of the wealthy guests, but his tiny backpack was out of place and he self consciously moved like a street boy when he set foot on the cold marble of the reception hall. His eyes darted towards the teak desks at reception, with uniformed staff smiling at their seated clients, and then over to a raised carpeted area with large leather sofas. He had lost any courage to even lift his camera to take a photograph.

He walked towards a pair of fully mature date palms, marking a wide walkway towards the rear of the foyer, and shivered. Most of the guests would have been dropped off from their air conditioned cars and assisted directly into the cool hotel environment, but he felt a chill as the air cooled the sweat on his face; he brushed his forehead with the back of his hand. Beyond the palms he found a crazy paved pathway which passed over a small bridge, out towards an atrium. A uniformed man approached him.

"Can I help you, sir?"

Sam was socially scared.

"Um, yes. Yes please" he spurted out.

"Would you like a table? Is it just you, sir?"

Two men, probably Indonesians, were just leaving a table in front of him and for no rational reason Sam decided he wanted their table.

"Yes, I'd like to sit there."

The usher led him towards the table, quickly removing his tip and the glasses left by the two men. Still gathering their small bags, the Indonesian men stared at Sam. They were dressed in long, cool white embroidered shirts often worn by Muslims on Fridays in Medan and, although no older than him, they had cold and pious faces. The taller of the two, with hair cropped as closely as Sam's, seemed to look straight through him, but the other glanced nervously around the atrium. Having checked the other customers, he reached down to pick up his bag before leaving with his companion. In Sam's heightened state of nervousness he thought he had met a fellow fish out of water.

He sat down, asked for an iced coffee, but had no idea what this would cost him, hoping it would be within his budget for dinner. He was determined to take at least one photograph inside the hotel, if for no other reason than to prove to Rita where he had been, but when he pulled his camera from his bag the lens and viewfinder were completely covered in mist. The glass had condensed the humidity on entering the air conditioned hotel. He would have to wait.

Two teenage blonde girls came over the bridge towards him and quickened their pace when they saw him. He thought they were probably American or Scottish, judging by their casual clothes he associated with characters in TV imports like *Smallville* and *Highlander*. They moved further into the atrium to a table already occupied by a couple, probably their parents. They both looked back towards him and giggled which encouraged the adults to turn and look at him as well.

Sam was pulling out a guide to Singapore from his backpack when his iced coffee arrived.

"Are you staying with us, sir" the young Chinese waiter with fashionably cut jet black hair asked politely.

"No, just visiting." The waiter smiled and moved away.

According to the guide book, the *Regency* was one of the most exclusive hotels in Singapore. It provided a comfort, some said, beyond that of the famous Raffles Hotel or any of the international hotel brands. Catering for an international clientele it was much favoured by Middle Eastern clients and wealthy Americans. Its facilities were exceptional, including a banquet hall for over eight hundred guests and an eighteen hole golf course. This hotel was where business deals were agreed in the most personal surroundings offered to visitors of Singapore. Or so the book said.

He looked around at the huge atrium with water running through it, bridges and ponds covered with flowering lilies and an extraordinary array of lush tropical plants. In amongst all this, intricately carved wooden benches provided cosy privacy for a drink, and solid wood tables offered diners an outdoor experience without the discomfort of the heat. The walls that surrounded this massive area were completely covered in vegetation hanging from a height of at least thirty metres, except for one side which had water plunging from the same height into a pool. The guide book insisted that the atrium was worth a visit all on its own.

The camera lens was still misted up but Sam felt much more confident now he had been given a reason to be there. The irony of nature being destroyed in Kalimantan so that it could be recreated for the wealthy in Singapore had not passed Sam by. He had already decided to bring Rita here and he could take a picture next time. He motioned to the Chinese waiter for his bill, paid and made his way back to the reception. Throwing caution to the wind he went outside and jumped into a taxi.

The lobby at the *Asialite* had appeared quite spacious to Sam when he had checked in, but now, twenty minutes after sipping iced coffee in the *Regency*, is seemed cheap and pokey. He saw Rita sitting in the lounge area to the right of reception and he went over to join her.

"Ah Sam" she exclaimed quite loudly. "Here you are."

He noticed that two men were sitting opposite her and felt immediately protective, but this was replaced by mild shock when he saw they were the same two Indonesians he had seen at the *Regency*. They turned to look at him and stood abruptly.

"Sam, come and meet these two men from Solo" but Rita was already too late because they had both walked briskly away without bothering with any pleasantries.

"That's weird" she commented as Sam sat down in one of the vacated chairs. "They were very friendly before you arrived, in fact too friendly. I heard them speaking Indonesian, they looked really handsome and I started talking with them. But the taller one freaked me out a bit with his intensive stare. The other one looked a little nervous."

"Probably realised they had no chance with you when I arrived and just decided to leave" said Sam unconvincingly. He was not a great believer in coincidence. "I saw them earlier and thought they looked a bit over zealous."

"You're not kidding" replied Rita. "The nervous one kept touching himself. The other one was saying something about not being on God's earth for long and wanting to make the most of it. He was eyeing up my tits!"

Sam blushed and quickly changed the subject.

In room 721 the tall young man was packing his bag. He didn't believe in coincidences either and they were getting out of Singapore tonight to Johor Baru, across the bridge to Malaysia. That Batak had smelt of bad sweat in the *Regency* and the Dayak girl deserved no better.

The nervous young Muslim, instead of scolding himself for his lechery, was in the bathroom taking practical steps to prevent a repeat of the risk they had just taken. Although forbidden, he thought today's masturbation could be argued to be in the line of duty.

CHAPTER TWENTY FOUR
Borneo

It was getting really hot on the river but at least a small breeze came with the forward motion. The last few kilometres had given Matt the impression of chugging closer and closer to something unknown, something usually out of reach, even unreachable. Besides the feeling, he had no idea where this journey was heading or whether he expected anything out of it. It was easy to let his mind wander as this slow boat ploughed through the black water of the Sekonyer *Kanan*.

He had no doubts about leaving Bali. It now seemed almost surreal: his nights with Ardi, the 24/7 urgency to have fun, the escapist interlude he never planned. Why had his libido taken over the second he had boarded the plane from England? It was as if, after eight years with Pauline, he had rushed to make up for lost time. But that was his choice he realised. *"I'm not transferring any blame on dear Pauline"* he thought, *"it was me who fucked up."*

The banks drew closer the further upriver they sailed and when the river suddenly opened up, the change was highlighted by the slowing of *Bukit* as it turned to reverse alongside a wooden jetty. The change in engine noise focused him back on the forest; the slowing boat reduced the breeze enough for him to feel the sweat dripping from his brow, his t-shirt clammy against his skin. A small speedboat was moored out in the water, an anchor holding it in position not far from the opposite bank. Two wooden jetties led to a group of wooden huts and paths cut out of the dense damp forest. *Bukit's* engine stopped, the humid air almost audibly penetrated the silence.

Matt gathered his camera equipment and prepared himself for going ashore. He couldn't find his mosquito repellent and was putting a bottle of water in his small back pack, hardly aware of Koto climbing onto the upper deck and standing next to him. He only responded when Koto warned him with a serious look on his face "we're being watched."

Matt froze. He looked around and back to Koto who was still staring at him. With a slight movement of his eyes and head Koto indicated that Matt should turn around, which he did very slowly.

He couldn't see anything but Koto was still staring at him intensely. "Open your senses" he whispered.

Focusing his mind on Koto's command, Matt dismissed his preparation for photography and smelt the citronella of his mosquito repellent behind him. Three metres away, sitting in the shade at the back of the boat was an orang-utan, her head slightly tipped to one side with a gentle suggestion of curiosity. Her dark brown eyes stared directly at him, but in her hands she turned the green and white repellent stick he had bought in *Boots* on Brixton High Street just weeks earlier. It was as if she was considering whether the smell was appropriate or if its owner was welcome. He looked back towards Koto who was grinning so much it seemed likely he would burst into laughter.

Matt cautiously dropped to a sitting position and, as if moving in slow motion, picked up his camera, to shoot a few pictures of her face, in particular her eyes which seemed to have an unfathomable depth as mysterious and dark as the black water. He didn't see her as almost human, but himself as almost wild, a realisation which gave him an even greater appreciation of Koto who he could sense quietly sitting behind him, still smiling. In her hands, with their exquisitely formed four fingers and a thumb covered with orange hairs, she had already removed the cap, turning the repellent stick, occasionally lifting it towards her nose and squinting without any sense of comedy. She was in control.

Hiding behind his lens Matt unwittingly focused on the pictures rather than the experience, even shooting a sequence of her rolling the repellent stick around in her hands. He had already envisaged the expensive advertising campaign using the pictures with the simple copy *"Don't believe us, ask the experts."* He wanted to improve the light but realised she wasn't going to move and sit in the baking sun voluntarily. He changed lenses, fired off a roll of film, sat back and stared at her.

"When you've finished with Betty, you must take pictures of Julia and her baby" said Koto knowingly as Matt turned to look at him. "What do you think Julia? It's a bit quiet and serious here isn't it?" Koto took the remains of a banana from Julia's hand and put it in his mouth.

Matt gasped at Koto who was sharing a small ripe brown banana with a female orang-utan leaning up against him with a tiny baby clinging to her chest. She slowly took her eyes off the banana skin as Matt turned to look at her. It was his turn to grin, but in a less controlled way than any of them and he burst into full belly laughter. Betty started to bang the repellent stick on the wooden deck when she realised she had lost Matt's undivided attention.

"OK now, it's time to go ashore" Koto stated as he gently pushed Julia away from him and gestured to Betty and Matt. "If Skipper sees them up here he'll start to shout. Last time we were here they threw a tourist's hat in the water and Matey had to dive in to get it."

Matt stood and followed Koto down below, before jumping onto the jetty. The orang-utans reluctantly followed by swinging over the side of *Bukit*, but with an air of obvious nonchalance. They were making it clear they were not following these visitors, just checking them out.

"Welcome to Camp Leakey" offered a young man in a green ranger's uniform who had emerged from one of the huts closest to the jetty. He had a broad smile and greeted Koto with a warm hug before shooing the orang-utans towards the huts. "They get too interested in the food on the *klotok*" he explained "so we try and keep them off the boats."

They all moved into the camp and Matt paid his park fees before he was shown a small exhibition in one of the huts closest to the jetty. It explained much about orang-utans, Camp Leakey and other fauna and flora found in Tanjung Puting National Park. While Koto led Matt around explaining what had happened to his home, the ranger went off to get a receipt and make coffee.

Camp Leakey is named after the renowned Anglo-Kenyan archaeologist and anthropologist, Louis Leakey, best known for early primate fossil discoveries. Leakey had taken an interest in the great apes and chosen three young women to study them. Probably the most famous was Dian Fossey whose work and murder were immortalised in the Hollywood blockbuster "Gorillas in the Mist." A second, Jane Goodall, still lectures around the world having devoted her life to chimpanzees and the conservation of all great apes and their habitat. Possibly the least known is Birute Galdikas, a naturalised Canadian who has lived with and studied orang-utans for over thirty five years in Tanjung Puting. Camp Leakey is her field study area where scientists and enthusiasts have lived, studied and wondered about orang-utans, their behaviour and survival. It is here that she and another scientist, Dr Gary Shapiro, used sign language to communicate with their orange cousins.

The threats to orang-utans were so great that Dr Galdikas, a passionate and sensitive woman, inevitably started to try to prevent their demise. Adult orang-utans, driven from the forest by logging and fires, were being killed all over Borneo, sometimes to protect crops but often to seize the youngsters that clung to them, to sell as pets. Young orang-utans could be bought in markets in cities in Borneo and Sumatra, where they also occur in the wild, as well as Jakarta and other Javan cities. They were sold to wealthy Indonesians or transported to South Korea, Taiwan, Japan and Thailand.

The trade in youngsters was most evident during the appalling forest fires that swept Kalimantan in 1997 and 1998. The fires came about as a result of companies and farmers burning to clear the land. They also, at that time, coincided with President Suharto's disastrous "million hectare rice project." A huge part of Kalimantan was destroyed in the bizarre, misguided Presidential belief that this acidic peat swamp could be converted to rice paddies to help feed the Indonesian people. Although, in reality, the companies and Suharto cronies were far more interested in lucrative contracts to cut trees, build canals and "neutralise" the acidity with tonnes of chemicals dumped into this delicate ecosystem.

Suharto's government also moved people into this area from Java and other islands in his "transmigration" scheme to potentially lessen the burden on over populated areas, often building resentment from the local population as the migrants also faced appalling poverty when their crops failed. Rapidly the "million hectares" earmarked for this project represented a dying regime, a bad idea going up in smoke, literally. Dayak villagers, having already suffered theft of their forest resources by Suharto cronies, were suddenly no longer able to drink their water or bathe in the black water without erupting in skin rashes from the chemical pollution. Everyone was left to find a way to survive.

Stories about orang-utans caught in fires were common at this time. Unable to swim, orang-utans out-ran the fires as far as the river banks, but when the raging inferno finally caught up with them they could be seen hanging from the top of the last tree standing until the fire consumed them as well. The vast tracts of blackened land, disease and starvation provided a warning for the future. But even today land is cleared illegally by fire and huge cities in Sumatra, Malaysia and Singapore are consumed by the choking haze that they create.

The orphans of trade, logging and fire became Dr Galdikas's mission. Local people and officials brought these hapless youngsters to her from all over Kalimantan and she provided what she could, releasing many of them back into the wild. Some, already used to the company of humans, stayed near the camp and socialised with people. Others made their way into the forest and brought up their own truly wild families.

But as the years progressed, the wild diminished. After Suharto came a new threat: illegal logging on a commercial scale. Even the national parks of Indonesia were no longer safe, and as the timber barons built up their wealth, the corrupt military, police and forest officials gained greater power. The battles were not just to find land for orphaned orang-utans, but to prevent officials from re-drawing boundaries of parks, to stand up to physical threats and to try and stay sane as the world around Dr Galdikas, and hundreds of brave activists, became smaller, dirtier and crueller. Tanjung Puting became a symbol of forest destruction. Yet despite enormous national and international attention, the chainsaws continued to slash at its increasingly weakened ecosystem, and the log rafts made their daily journey to the greedy outside world.

Matt sat on the steps of the exhibition hut in Camp Leakey absorbing all that Koto explained and saw another orang-utan approaching. In the tree above the hut opposite, a gibbon was hanging by its cartoon-like long spidery arms. Butterflies were flitting around in the sunlit greenery as if the energy of the sun alone made them happy and the dense, heavily humid smell of mid-day was almost overwhelming. He brushed tears from his eyes at the sheer beauty of this orange ape staring at him as she approached, a gesture that was noticed by Koto.

"Are you OK?"

"I think I opened my senses" Matt responded in a whisper without looking at his companion. "But I'm not sure I can stand it."

They sat in silence as the orang-utan came closer and reached out to touch Matt's camera. She was gentle and inquisitive as she slowly looked up at Matt's face and his long blond hair. No longer interested in the camera, her hand ran itself from the top of his head through his hair as she watched intently. Tears ran down his face, but the orang-utan continued stroking his hair, and after repeating this movement a few times, she brushed his cheeks with the back of her hairy hand, dabbing his tears away. Appearing satisfied with this contact, she sat down in front of him, seemed to recognise he had stopped crying, put her hands in front of her, and stared.

Koto, in a similar gesture, crouching next to Matt, raised his hand and wiped one last tear from Matt's cheek and smiled.

CHAPTER TWENTY FIVE
Jakarta

Aman Widodo started his working life in the government telecommunications company at the age of seventeen. His first job in the civil service, in 1975, had been as an assistant to the director of television in the Ministry of Information and he had rapidly increased his rank and influence by joining the Golkar Party of President Suharto and never questioning orders. He had lived a comfortable family life raising three children with his wife, the daughter of a Golkar senior politician. His daughter and eldest son had both married and lived in Jakarta, but his youngest son who was now twenty one, lived with him and his wife.

Widodo prided himself in his political agility, keeping his Golkar membership, attending the mosque preferred by other Party members and avoiding scandal. On two occasions he had been obliged to provide evidence against colleagues who had been less cautious than himself, but he considered that to be their failing, not his. His devotion to the government had not passed unnoticed and he had risen rapidly through the ranks.

Tired of the games he had been forced to play for thirty years he was looking forward to retirement, but they were beginning to catch up on him. Aziz's patronage was his most serious immediate problem but he also felt exposed by the uncertainty of modern politics. It had been easier in the days of single party rule, you knew where you stood. Now, politicians seemed to believe they should comment on everything and the media lapped it up. It left a tired Widodo even keener to get out. It was Aziz's monthly payments and other smaller contributions that would provide him with this escape, but now even that was threatened; he was caught between Aziz and his immediate boss, Santoso. Two incredibly powerful men.

He decided to spend a quiet evening with his wife before calling Hazim to negotiate the deal with the navy. Although this kind of arrangement had been common place throughout his career, this was the first time his instincts scared him enough to keep a written account of each day's activities and relevant records in a strong box in his bank. Only he and his lawyer had access. Aziz had been

145

very generous over the last ten years and, in truth, he hadn't really been required to get him out of any trouble in all that time. But he had been a crucial conduit to Jakarta's political circle. It was through Widodo that Aziz had donated considerable funds to his minister's political party, and it was through him that Aziz had built his political contact list. He felt Aziz had already got his money's worth.

As he climbed out of his official car outside his front door, he saw the back end of a black Mercedes parked around the side, and felt a sickening feeling in his stomach. His wife came out and warned him they had a guest, a good-looking young man who said he was the son of Pak Aziz. He was in the garden with their son, Mohammed. Widodo, on hearing this, hurried into the house, through the large living room and out onto the veranda.

"Ah, Pak Widodo, how lovely to see you sir" greeted a casually dressed Hazim, standing. "I was just inviting Mo out on the town with me tonight. It seems you keep him under lock and key and he's never been to any of Jakarta's best night spots!"

"It's not quite like that" laughed Widodo's son, too obviously the son of a civil servant despite being dressed in jeans and a t-shirt. His small round face was puckered with an attempt at a beard and he already showed signs of a small paunch.

"It's not like that at all!" stated Widodo rather too loudly. His wife, sensing trouble, interrupted to offer Hazim coffee, which he declined. "Let's walk in the garden" suggested Widodo slightly more calmly, exchanging knowing glances with his wife. As they stepped off the veranda he noticed, with relief, her ushering Mohammed into the safety of the house.

Hazim, dropping his pretence, was straight to the point. "Where is our timber *Pak* Widodo? I know you haven't forgotten your friends."

"No I haven't" replied Widodo with more confidence than he actually felt. He explained his meeting with the Vice-Admiral and his plan to have the timber released into the hands of the police. "It's only a matter of price."

"I'm not interested in how much you have to pay, just get the timber into the hands of the police by tomorrow and we will consider your friendship intact."

Widodo, wondering if he had heard this arrogant young bully accurately was about to respond when Hazim pulled a photo from his back pocket, forced it into his right hand and closed his fingers around it. Widodo opened his hand instinctively, the snapshot uncurled to reveal a bloody mound lying on the ground. The sandaled feet of someone in blue jeans were at the top, giving the picture a sense of scale and perspective.

"We have nothing more to say to each other *Pak* Widodo. Call me when our shipment is released. You can keep the picture, I've got another. I'm very keen on photography." Hazim chuckled as he walked to the left of the house where his Mercedes was parked, stepped into the back and was driven away.

This was very bad indeed. Widodo had no doubt that he was holding a photograph of the remains of the informant murdered in Pangkalan Bun and no doubt what this meant. Perhaps of more concern was the refusal to negotiate and pay, but to leave the payment up to him. Widodo was not a rich man, although the monthly gifts from Aziz had built up over the last few years. But to pay off the navy was likely to clean him out completely. He expected it to cost at least one hundred thousand dollars, and possibly even more.

"Are you alright?" asked his wife quietly. She had come out into the garden when she heard Hazim's car pull away. "What's that in your hand?"

"It's nothing" he replied crunching it up in his palm again. "I have to make a call and go out later, things to sort out." He looked at her and could tell that she knew something very bad had just happened. "Don't let Mohammed out of the house until I say so" he added, reinforcing her fear.

Widodo had to think fast. Hazim had only given him a day to sort out this awful mess and, although he knew they still needed him, he knew that Hazim was a violent psychopath who would take pleasure in hurting him. It was too late to appeal to *Pak* Aziz who appeared to have washed his hands of their relationship, passing on the resolution of this problem to his son. He must call the Vice-Admiral and negotiate as low a sum of money as possible to release the timber into the hands of the police. He'd start at forty thousand and hope to get away with fifty. As he was thinking, he was still trying to find a way out of this to avoid spending his own money. If it went above a hundred thousand he would have nothing. Nothing. After all these years. Maybe he could appeal to *Pak* Aziz once this ugly business was over. He could still introduce him to some important people. He picked up his mobile phone and called the Vice-Admiral arranging to meet him at Tanjung Priok port at ten. Just three hours before he would have a better sense of what was possible. At least it was moving fast.

It was a dark wet night in Jakarta. Widodo's driver took a direct route up *Jalan* Sudirman, *Jalan* Thamrin and then through the Chinese part of town. A "gentlemen's club" lit in neon on his left, scores of taxis outside the *Club Gila*, a seedy looking building unknown to Widodo. *"Probably some rat infested night club frequented by the likes of Hazim"* he thought. The rain was pounding on the road in front of them and he told his driver to be careful. It would be ridiculous to die in a traffic accident on his way to a meeting to prevent death by psychopath! They moved onto a toll road, started to move a little faster, arriving at the port a few minutes early.

Entering the same ante room, he realised it had only been a day since he was last there, but it seemed as if so much had happened. The same young sailor asked him to take a seat. The Vice-Admiral had phoned to say he was on his way. He pulled a Kent out of his pocket and lit up.

The big question was really how many people expected a slice of the payment? It was obviously very worrying that the Vice-Admiral had already estimated the value of the timber at ten million dollars. Forty thousand would sound totally inadequate. Maybe he should try to offer the Vice-Admiral something on the side to get him to agree. Although, last time he had received a call, almost certainly from his boss, the Admiral. So it seemed likely that he would call him again this time to confirm the deal. He could use the Coordinating Minister's name to pull rank – that might save some money. He would have to see what the Vice-Admiral had to say. He had seemed like a reasonable, pragmatic man.

"Ah, Secretary General" called out the Vice-Admiral as he entered the ante room from outside, pulling off a rain coat. "Thank you for calling me so quickly. I hope we can sort out this business tonight between the two of us. Please come into my office."

Widodo stubbed out his cigarette and followed him into the small office, the air conditioning unit still gasping for life. The Vice-Admiral went back to talk briefly to the young sailor, returned and sat opposite him.

"Now, let's get down to business shall we?"

"Thank you for seeing me so rapidly" started Widodo politely. "I'm pleased we both recognise the importance of resolving this problem as quickly as possible. My Minister will be most grateful."

"Yes, yes. What do you want and what do you have to offer Secretary General? It's late, it's pouring with rain outside, my wife is furious at me for coming out so late. So let's cut out the crap, shall we?"

"If you wish" responded Widodo rather surprised at the blunt attitude of the Vice-Admiral. "My Minister wants this incident to be over tomorrow. He wants the timber released to the police so that, as you said yesterday, they will release it to its owner for their own price. For reasons that need not concern you, the faster this is done, the better it will be for our country." He thought this was quite a good line, playing the *"we know better"* and patriot card.

The Vice-Admiral said nothing.

"We realise the considerable time and effort the navy has put into this case. Especially you Vice-Admiral" Widodo smiled. "We would suggest a payment of fifty thousand dollars to cover out of pocket expenses for the navy and an additional ten thousand for yourself." He really couldn't suggest forty thousand, it just felt completely wrong.

The Vice-Admiral laughed out loud. He stood and said "you've wasted my time Secretary General. I'm disappointed. You know the value of this cargo and yet you insult your country's armed forces this way."

"I have no intention of insulting you" Widodo bartered. "Did you have a figure in mind?"

"Nothing less than ten per cent" he replied coldly, staring straight at Widodo who recoiled in shock. There was no way he could come up with a million. That would involve selling his house, his shares in businesses and calling in favours all over Jakarta. He would be ruined. He would have to talk to *Pak* Aziz.

"My Minister will be very concerned at the demands you make Vice-Admiral. It may be worth you reflecting on the fact that the Minister of Defence shares the same party as my Minister."

The Vice-Admiral had already lifted his mobile phone and dialled. "I think you need to come in now and deal with him directly" he said quite openly.

Widodo was confused. Was the Admiral outside? That would make it very difficult because he'd want to deal directly with his Minister, Santoso, and of course this was impossible because he knew nothing of this deal.

"I'm sorry Secretary General, but you've insulted us long enough" said the Vice-Admiral very quietly. "Please stay where you are." He left the room.

This was not going well at all. It was undoubtedly because of the low offer, thought Widodo. The navy were as greedy as everyone else and ten per cent was probably the going rate. But he had no way of pulling that off quickly, even if he agreed to it. He'd have to sell property, meet dozens of people. The deadline set by Hazim had just made it far too difficult. He realised he still had the grizzly photograph in his pocket. He was backed into a corner and for the first time recognised he might not escape with his life.

After five minutes alone Widodo wondered if he should just get up and leave. After all, he was Secretary General to one of the most important men in Indonesia. He was powerful himself and this might just be the moment to use that power. He stood to leave, not sure what he should do, but as he rose from his chair, the door opened.

He recognised the Admiral immediately and stepped aside to let him walk quietly past. But the second person to enter the room came as a shock. He looked furious, his face contorted with anger. Three armed sailors entered, closed the door and stood guard.

His mind started spinning as he sat back in his chair. Towering over him, looking as if he was out for the kill was the Coordinating Minister for Politics and Security, his boss, Bambang Santoso.

CHAPTER TWENTY SIX
Borneo

He looked around cautiously, taking in the scene in front of him. Two men sat on the steps of the hut at the edge of the forest clearing. Two young females, one with a baby, were lying in the shade to the left of the men. A gibbon was quietly sitting in the fork of the main branch of a tree near the river, so far unaware of his presence. The heavy afternoon air was hot, but there was rain on its way which would cool him down before evening. Slowly, he stepped forward into the open.

The gibbon started to call out in alarm, although most would suspect this was gratuitous noise rather than a real expression of fear. Koto, hearing the commotion, looked up and saw the huge male orang-utan emerging from the undergrowth. His size and colour distinguishing him as the dominant male, moving with a cumbersome gait slowly forwards, his brown beady eyes, shifting from left to right, his small muddy nose audibly sniffing the scene. His fur was a dark brown rather than orange, and large dark brown, hairless cheek flaps surrounded his bored looking face. Once in the open, this forest giant lowered his body onto the ground, plonking his head on the dirt. And stared.

Dominant male orang-utans have a presence about them that immediately demands respect. They differ from their female companions in size, temperament, colour and habits. This male was known to Koto and had come to see who had arrived on the *klotok*, although he neither appeared interested nor concerned. He just was. He just was, well, dominant.

Adult male orang-utans are solitary except when mating and look as if that might be the main thing on their minds much of the time, if they can be bothered. Wild orang-utans build nests in the tree canopy every night, moving on, following the nuts and berries they feed on every day. They rarely touch the ground, swinging from branches to move through the forest, avoiding dangerous animals, such as wild pigs, which can cause serious damage if they charge. Rehabilitated orang-utans sometimes prefer to hang around humans, walking as much as swinging, accepting food at feeding areas provided within the park.

"Wow!" gasped Matt when he first spotted the big male.

"Be quiet and don't make any sudden moves" advised Koto. "He's OK and used to tourists, but he's strong enough to snap you in half if he feels like it."

Matt raised his camera and zoomed in on the deep set brown eyes looking directly at him. His senses were taking a beating since the female orang-utan had wiped away his tear. His mood was pensive. *"How does a male orang-utan feel?"* he thought. It's not as if he would sit around with other male orang-utans discussing fatherhood, what it was like to be male. He had to make it up himself, perhaps instinctively. Nature had made him bigger than all the rest, so it made some sense that he was just a dominant, sometimes violent control freak. Matt lay on the ground resting his camera at the same level as the orang-utan's face about six metres from him. They continued to stare at each other silently.

Was this why some men lashed out, because they were lonely and simply instinctively male? Built bigger, bored, feeling the pressure of being the bread winner, while others experienced the relief of uncertainty and could talk themselves into being more sensitive, less aggressive and share responsibilities with their partners.

Does a male orang-utan ever wipe away a tear?

He seemed so different to the females. They were curious, gentle and exuded a wisdom you could almost touch, but his brute dominance seemed to obscure any idea that he had sensibilities or could experience passion. Did he ever seek the company of other males or were his hormones too charged to give him this opportunity, like a macho pet dog protecting his turf. Matt's mind wandered as he tried to equate raw instinct with the choices he had personally faced; he was too messed up to understand anything clearly. He looked deep into those dark brown eyes and saw never ending loneliness.

"Does he live alone?" he asked, slowly pulling himself up off the ground. He kept an eye on the big male, brushed the dirt from his shorts and sat back on the steps next to Koto.

"You're never alone in the forest" Koto replied.

"Are you sure?"

Matt felt the uncomfortable bites of mosquitoes on the back of both his legs as if to remind him that not all companions are welcome. He reached into his bag for the repellent stick before remembering he had left it in the hands of Betty. Looking over towards her he saw the stick lying on the ground near her feet. She seemed disinterested in it now and was holding her head high, sniffing the air with her companions, looking slightly supercilious. She had already decided this newcomer was nothing to get excited about. When she saw him approaching her however, she decided the stick was worth coveting a little longer, moving forward to pick it up before he arrived.

Koto laughed out loud and Matt retreated to the steps. "Betty!" stated Koto firmly as he removed a small banana from his bag. This did the trick and Betty came over to negotiate the exchange, refusing to let go of the stick until the fruit was handed over, like a cold-war spy exchange. She reluctantly gave up the stick and retreated with her prize.

The two men collected some food and water from *Bukit* and sat under a tree to eat lunch. The heat and humidity had reached the point when moving was exhausting and they were content to eat, drink and rest for a while. Clouds had moved in and the bright light had already been replaced by a claustrophobic flat mood, a rumbling could be heard in the distance warning of rain. Koto took advantage of this sultry moment and closed his eyes while Matt, conscious that everything here was new to him, forced himself to walk around the camp photographing flowers, leaves, lines of ants, and of course the orang-utans. He was careful not to get any closer to the large dominant male, assuming correctly that he had already set his own parameters.

After a while, even his rooky enthusiasm was overcome by the turgid heat. He settled down next to Koto under the tree staring at his guide, sleeping quietly, and wondered how much of his passion for his home dominated normal life. He had already witnessed some pain felt by Koto, but Rita's warning went some way towards explaining the rather extreme circumstances of his journey: Koto's best friend had been murdered and he had been threatened. Looking at his sleeping face he could recognise the slightly puffy, tell-tale skin of tiredness under his eyes, with his jet black hair clinging to his damp neck. This was a man experiencing an emotional rollercoaster that he, despite his own turmoil, had not even boarded.

The afternoon heat persuaded him to relax and close his eyes next to Koto, only to be woken ten minutes later by the ranger. "We're going to the feeding place now" he explained.

Koto sat up, yawned and held his head in his hands, pushing it both ways until his neck cracked twice, sniffed loudly, and stood, stretching out his arms. "I'll get water and then we can hike to the feeding station."

The walk took them out of the camp, along a trail, which in some places involved balancing on narrow branches laid over wet, swampy ground. Betty, Julia and her baby followed at a distance, but there was no sign of the large male. The ranger led the group carrying a large bucket filled with fruit, occasionally calling out with a whooping sound, to alert any orang-utans out there in the forest that it was time for free food.

After about twenty minutes they arrived at a small clearing with two trees lying on the forest floor, a discarded plastic bucket and a raised platform built above the ground. Another ranger was already there with a very large container of fruit. It was quite dark, the dense vegetation cutting out much of the light, which was already dulled by the thick black clouds that had gathered. The first ranger continued whooping.

Three adult orang-utans appeared high in the forest canopy and cautiously approached. Matt realised that behind him Betty had climbed up a tree and was hanging by her arms from two branches. She kept puckering her lips as she concentrated on her approaching companions. The first drop of rain started a slow downpour which fell through the tall trees, moving leaves and puncturing the air with its irregular sound. The orang-utans were more interested in the fruit which the ranger had started to pass out.

Matt shot off a roll of film on Julia with her baby clinging to her breast. She had positioned herself in a tree behind him to look as endearing as possible. In the rain he carefully moved around her to make the most of the little light available, focusing on the baby's eyes and the nearby pink nipple of his mother. The baby, with

154

wisps of orange hair comically topping an otherwise bald head, stared inquisitively at Matt who looked up from his camera. In the foliage opposite, on the edge of the clearing, the large dominant male was standing, watching the proceedings. He had pulled some large leaves from a plant and was balancing them on his head to protect his face from the rain. His huge dark frame, with one orange furry arm holding the leaf umbrella in place and the other across his chest, undermined any ability to take him seriously, although Matt was sure he should not be under-estimated. Anyway, no matter how ridiculous this male looked, he was the driest one there!

The mosquitoes started to annoy Matt who had liberally applied the repellent stick. It was clear that any romantic notion of tropical rainforest was well off the mark. The oppressive heat, rain, biting insects, disease and swamp were not somewhere to survive easily and the way these amazing animals had adapted to live here was fascinating. After a while the rain stopped and a ray of sun penetrated the canopy shining on Julia's baby. A buzzing sound could be heard in the distance.

"Cicadas?" he asked.

"Chainsaws" replied the ranger. "Loggers. They have a camp in the forest a few kilometres from here and we can sometimes hear them. They've been getting closer and I'm afraid that we might have to move out of Camp Leakey."

Matt turned to look at Koto who nodded. "The guys here are frightened. I don't think Camp Leakey will be abandoned, but the forest is being seriously damaged."

They trekked back through the dripping forest to the camp and boarded *Bukit* for some water. Matey and Skipper were swimming in the river and Koto suggested it would be a good idea for them to cool off before they moved on. Matt stripped to his CKs and lowered himself into the cool and strangely nutrient thick water alongside the *klotok*. It was impossible to see his hands ahead of him as he swam. "Isn't this a bit dangerous?" he asked Koto as they swam out into the river together.

Koto laughed and dived under, disappearing completely for at least thirty seconds, slightly freaking Matt. When he surfaced he said "I see no danger. In fact I see nothing!" He turned and started to swim back to the boat. "We hope that the big crocodiles stay away from the Camp, but it's not always like that. When the policeman was killed recently he was swimming across the river on his own. I think the more of us are in the water the better." He paused. "It feels good doesn't it?"

Matt had to agree that it felt wonderful and cool, but his mind couldn't help but think of those underwater film shots of tasty limbs splashing in the water, waiting to be ripped from their owner. He was relieved to climb onto the boat behind Koto. They both went onto the upper deck and sat on the side. Betty, Julia and her baby had come to watch, standing on the jetty; Betty had worked up white foam on her arm from soap she had taken from Matey who was sitting on the jetty watching her with some irritation.

When they had dried, Skipper started the engines. *Bukit* pulled out of Camp Leakey, headed further upriver for fifteen minutes before stopping and tying up alongside another jetty, where they were planning to spend the night. The river here was narrow, not much more than ten metres across and to Skipper's surprise a speedboat was already tied alongside the jetty, but there was nobody to be seen. A trail led from the jetty into the forest but there were no buildings and no sign of life. Matey chopped an onion, threw oil in a pan and started to prepare their evening meal.

Matt organised his camera equipment, cleaning the lenses, placing the exposed films in a separate bag and writing down his location and shots in a small notebook. He sat back, listening to the sounds of the forest as this background noise increased, the cooler and darker it became. This was something so different to temperate environments. Here, the night-time sounds were much louder, as if every living creature waited for the darkness before coming out to play.

Koto joined him on the upper deck with two cold bottles of beer. "I've offered beer to Skipper and Matey, I hope that is alright?"

Matt smiled, nodded, accepted the cold beer and looked into the forest with a true sense of privilege. The day had surpassed any he could remember, his emotions were enhanced, his company safe, undemanding, his surroundings new and exciting. The orang-

156

utans he had met had left a lasting memory, albeit it slightly disturbing.

"Those chainsaws" he asked, "is the forest really going to disappear? Is Julia's baby going to have nowhere to live?"

Koto looked at the speedboat on the other side of the jetty and up the trail that led into the forest. Three men were coming towards them, one of them carrying a gun. "Ask them" he said simply.

The men stepped onto the jetty and spoke to Skipper for a few minutes before stepping back and getting into the speedboat. The man with the gun sat at the front and stared briefly at Matt and Koto without acknowledging them. The speedboat pulled gently out into the river, revved its engine and sped off downstream, towards Kumai Bay, creating an unnecessary wake which rocked *Bukit* and provoked a short cry of protest from Skipper.

This unpleasant encounter was soon forgotten when Matey served up rice, fried vegetables and sate sauce washed down with cold beer. The four of them ate together, enjoying a comradeship that had so far been missing, the different roles forgotten as these four men shared beer, cigarettes and laughter. Koto translated when necessary, but after food Skipper brought a pack of cards on deck and they played poker for Matt's cigarettes. The bottles of beer were large and they soon started to feel a bit drunk. Matey became very giggly, staring and laughing at Matt, and after a while Koto commented that Matey was intrigued by Matt's long blonde hair. It seemed that he wanted to know if all Matt's hair was the same colour.

Matt was taken aback by Matey and Koto's unabashed questioning, realising that his own sense of embarrassment was different to theirs, although he was sure their forthright questioning was fuelled by the beer. Standing to get closer to the naked bulb hanging on the upper deck, Matt lowered his jeans enough to prove he was truly blond. Matey and Koto were in fits of laughter; Skipper took another drag on his cigarette and smiled. It was obvious, without translation, that the shouting that accompanied their laughter was daring him to pull his jeans down. Even in this slightly drunken haze it seemed amusing to Matt that the equivalent to a pub crawl "get your cocks out lads!" was happening in this peaceful jungle thousands of kilometres around the globe. He pointed at Matey and Koto and shook his head, laughing with them.

Matey suddenly jumped up and pulled his shorts around his ankles, but the revelry was abruptly ended by Skipper's intervention, one short comment aimed at Matey. He pulled his shorts up, sat down, lit a cigarette and didn't utter another word.

They played cards for another ten minutes but the spontaneity had already gone and when Skipper stood to go to bed, Matey obediently followed.

"Oops" said Matt quietly, "did we go too far? Is Skipper offended?"

Koto grinned and shook his head. "Jealous" he replied without further explanation.

CHAPTER TWENTY SEVEN
Singapore

Sam had woken with a cricked neck, his boxers twisted around his waist. Rita was already up; he could hear the shower running in the bathroom connected to the bedroom where, no doubt, she had slept comfortably. He had tossed and turned all night thinking about Aziz, although the reason he had slept badly was because he was so cold. The air conditioning control seemed to be unresponsive. He rolled off the sofa, stood, strolled over to the window, the bright daylight creeping in between the curtains. Singapore was already buzzing, people on the street below, buses and cars winding themselves around the hotel.

"*Selamat pagi*" greeted Rita as she poked her head around the bedroom door, carefully hiding the rest of her body from Sam. They were good friends, soul mates even, but they both respected each others' modesty.

"Yeah" responded Sam less enthusiastically, but when he saw her face he couldn't resist a broad smile.

"Debi sent an SMS with the phone number of the informant" she stated, trying to start the day with a positive lead. Debi had been contacted anonymously by a trader based in Singapore, who, for some reason, was prepared to talk about Abdullah Aziz. "I'll give him a call and set up a meeting. You shower" she suggested rather bossily.

Abdullah Aziz had already been up for three hours. Always an early riser, he believed he made his best decisions before mid-day. His wife had gone out with friends and, other than the servants, he was alone. He was feeling anxious about the two cargo ships seized by the Indonesian navy but felt fortunate to have such a loyal and resourceful son to support him. There had been some concern, when he had married for the fourth time, that Hazim would refuse to accept his current wife, but the lad had shown considerable maturity by accepting that his own mother was well provided for in Pangkalan Bun. Now that he was running the mill business in Kalimantan he probably saw more of his mother than he had for years. It was certainly better now he had given Hazim more responsibility and his own life had improved since he had bought the *Regency* and moved to Singapore.

It was almost as if he had been reborn. His younger wife had enormous energy for social networking which had already paid off in Singapore. She instinctively knew who to invite for dinner or offer a suite in the *Regency*. Many of their new friends were interesting and powerful and Abdullah was surprised how easy it was to become popular on this island state. Of course, being a billionaire helped. She had said she was having lunch with the American Ambassador's wife and a few friends. He chuckled.

An hour later his black Lexus pulled up outside the *Regency* just as Rita and Sam stepped out of a taxi.

"Look, quickly, over there" whispered Sam. Rita immediately recognised Aziz and felt an urge to run over and scream at him, but Sam anticipated her rage and held firmly onto her arm. "Be calm" he said quietly, "this isn't the time." He pointed his camera at waist height and shot a few pictures of Aziz entering the hotel.

Aziz, flanked by bodyguards, walked to the right and entered a small private lift. Sam and Rita were ushered through double doors into the foyer and he led her past the date palms into the atrium. He was disappointed at her disinterest, hoping she might be stunned by its opulence as much he had been. She was still obsessed by Aziz.

"Look at that waterfall" he said in an attempt to enthuse, but she didn't even try to smile.

They sat at a table near where the family had sat the day before, but today the atrium was completely empty; they were the only customers. Sam wiped the misted screen on the back of his digital camera and was relieved to see that Aziz's face was clearly to be seen in one of his photos. Not a bad start to the day. It would take a while before he could take more photos now they were in the air conditioned atmosphere.

"Got him" he said to Rita, who was beginning to take in her surroundings.

"Let's see."

She smiled for the first time that morning, realising that this chance encounter had already been useful. They both understood the campaign advantage offered by photographs of the target going about their dirty business. As far as they were concerned, Aziz entering his Singapore hotel, bought with the blood of Indonesians, was a minor coup. The waiter left two menus in front of them.

"Well done Sam" she said gently and put her hand on his. "I'm sorry I lost it, but I guess his involvement in Murkha's death is too raw for me."

She saw immediately in Sam's face that he understood. He was a true friend and they had worked together long enough to recognise each other's feelings without question. He was sitting, his face warmly expressing how much he cared for her and for a brief moment, for the first time, she saw lust in his sexy brown eyes. Diving back into the safety of work she withdrew her hand and suggested they just had coffee.

"It's too expensive for lunch" she uttered unnecessarily "so we'd better eat somewhere else before meeting Debi's contact at two."

During coffee they both looked around at the extraordinary building, mature plants growing out of concrete, dainty bridges and sparkling streams. They were close enough to the waterfall to see that the pool under it was stocked with carp. A large electric blue butterfly fluttered past. They talked about the wealth required to own such a place and the horror behind such beauty. When they finished their coffee, they asked the waiter to take a picture of them on Sam's camera, before taking pictures themselves of the waterfall, tables and the hanging plants.

Twenty six floors above, Abdullah Aziz had summoned Michelle for a relaxing massage, which she always performed with absolute professionalism. Dressed in a white tunic she had mixed essential oils to ensure he felt calm and pampered. He often confided in her in much the same way women will talk to their hairdressers, he was sure her discretion was guaranteed by the salary he provided. The only thing on his mind today seemed to be the two ships seized by the navy.

"I'm so lucky to have Hazim picking up these difficult issues for me" he casually stated. "He's become so adept at resolving problems. I really don't know how he does it. It used to cost me a lot more in the old days."

161

Michelle moved her firm hands to his lower back and swung her thumbs over the points in the middle of his buttocks and pushed hard. The relief and energy was remarkable and Aziz let out a short sigh. "I do worry sometimes" he went on "that Hazim might be using violence too often and too easily."

Michelle pushed again saying nothing. *"Silly old fool has no idea how powerful Hazim is becoming"* she thought, certain she'd allied herself to the up and coming star in the Aziz family.

"Violence has a nasty habit of catching up with you" he added pensively.

Rita and Sam had eaten lunch and already found the contact's address, who wanted to be known as Nate. It was an anonymous and soul-less office building near the airport and Nate's suite was on the third floor. They knocked, entered and were surprised at the orange painted room with orange and white furniture. The blinds were dark green, the same colour as the suit being worn by the only occupant, a short Chinese man in his late thirties sitting behind a white desk. He smiled and waved them in.

"Come in!" he called out brightly as he stood to greet them. "I have been expecting you." His eagerness baffled Sam who felt very awkward in this bizarre office but Rita had warmed to him immediately. "You look perfect in your beautiful top" he gushed at Rita "although I'm afraid it is very difficult to blend in my office! I had no idea it would make people feel so alien, but I'm told it's too *imposing*. Oh dear, oh dear, poor boy, you do look sullen!"

Rita laughed and looked over at Sam who was already certain that this coquettish man in a green suit was of no use to their enquiries. He was saddened by the laugh as much as the comment.

They were offered fruit tea and ushered over to a large white leather sofa under the window. Nate sat in a white-painted rocking chair.

"Debi informed us you had contacted her regarding our campaign to protect Tanjung Puting National Park" introduced Rita rather unnecessarily, more to start the conversation than to provide information.

Nate smiled and looked at Sam. "She's the one wearing the trousers around here, isn't she honey?" he rubbed salt into the wound.

"Do you have information on Abdullah Aziz?" Sam asked abruptly.

"My, oh my! Not just a pretty face then" cooed Nate. "Lemon or Camomile?"

"Lemon please" responded Rita, giving Sam a very stern look. "Have you worked with Mr Aziz?"

"Yes, I've known him for a few years here in Singapore. Now young man, would you prefer coffee?"

Sam, reeling from Rita's stare, realised he had been unwise to dismiss Nate so rapidly; he knew Aziz and could offer a new insight. "Are you in the timber business?" he asked, looking around the office for any tell-tale signs of shipping, retail or trade magazines.

"Oh no! Coffee it is then" he said moving over to the kettle which had just boiled. "I do like strong silent boys."

They both realised they had to wait until Nate had provided them with drinks before he was prepared to talk so Rita made a few complementary comments about the décor. Sam looked around, feeling completely out of place.

"Now, there you are." Nate gave them each a drink and settled on the rocking chair, a camomile tea in his hand. "I bet you're dying to know how I can help you" he enthused.

He went on to explain he was in *entertainment logistics*, an expression that neither of them understood. It turned out he organised parties: the venues, entertainers, food, decoration, drinks, and sometimes even the guests. "Yes, some of my clients don't have any friends, you see, so I lend them some of mine!"

Sam was beginning to see the funny side of this meeting and had started exchanging smiles with Rita who was loving every minute of it.

"Now, what do you want to know?" he paused, not expecting a response. "Aziz owns the *Regency* and I've thrown a few parties for him in his penthouse suite. I've even organised parties in his hotel for others, but I don't imagine that would interest you, although I could tell you a thing or two about ... no, perhaps not." He focused back on the issue at hand: "I read about the terrible things he does and thought I might be able to help."

"Who comes to his parties?" asked Rita.

"Mainly friends of his wife. He lets her get on with organising his social life. But I provided him with an Indonesian waiter two years ago who now runs his private bar in the penthouse. Nice boy. Straight."

"Maybe we could meet him" suggested Sam.

"No, I don't think he'll help you, but he talks to me quite a lot. He's poured drinks for Indonesian ministers, politicians, the police chief, actresses, all kinds. I could give you a list if that helps."

"Why?" asked Rita. "Why would you do that?"

"To help, of course!"

Rita stood up, to both Sam and Nate's surprise. "I'm sorry, but I don't think you can be of any help" she said moving towards the door. Sam, confused but loyal, followed.

Nate turned in the rocking chair to look at her. "Alright young lady, I understand. But it's not that easy you see" he stammered a little. "Please sit down. I'll tell you anything I can to help you." They sat back on the sofa.

"I need to understand why you would help us. Aziz is dangerous, so why would you take a risk?" she explained.

He stared at her as if he was deciding whether she was worth it. "I will help you because I hate Aziz and his family, his son, they're scum." Tears started to stream down his face as he sobbed. Rita felt she had opened a Pandora's Box and regretted her theatrics. Nate was crying uncontrollably, his chest heaving as he tried to catch his breath. They waited for him to calm down.

"Oh deary me! It's his son, you see."

"It's alright. Take your time" Rita tried to get him to focus.

"He ruined my life you see."

More tears.

"He killed my Jamie."

Sam looked at Rita and she noticed he had a tear in his eye. She loved Sam for his heart, one of the purest she had ever encountered. They both moved over to hug Nate, this camp party animal; a stranger only minutes earlier. Yet they realised he was deeply wounded and shared a loss at least as great as theirs. He opened himself to their kind embrace.

Through his sobbing he told them he had always known he was different, but not really blossomed as a gay man until he had

164

started partying in Kuala Lumpur at weekends. Many revellers travelled the few hours to KL for weekend parties, preferring to let their hair down away from home. It was then he realised Singapore needed its own parties, its own identity. In just a few years he had become well known on the party scene, where, despite draconian laws against gay men, being gay was considered cool. It was at this time he had met Jamie, a twenty something son of an English banker.

They had lived together, blissfully happy, for nine years. Then they met Hazim, just two years ago. At first Nate had been charmed by Hazim's good looks and money, but it was his cruelty that had attracted Jamie. Nate had always known of Jamie's masochistic interests, but until he had met Hazim he had never met a true sadist. The details of Jamie's demise were cloudy, but while Nate was in London, Jamie had died during a weekend party from a cocktail of drugs and alcohol. The truth was obscured by Singapore's squeaky clean image and Jamie's father's stature. But Nate had been allowed to say goodbye to his lover in the Singapore morgue: the young man's body was covered in welts from whip lashings and his right nipple had been cut off. The assistant coroner had told Nate he had been gang raped.

Sam and Rita moved back to the sofa and watched as this eccentric little man in his dark green suit, with mustered dignity, wiped his eyes and looked straight into Rita's face, took a very deep breath and said "now, how can we get the bastards?"

They left his office three hours later with pages of information about Aziz, his wife and Hazim. Most of it seemed to be of little use other than painting a useful picture of the family, but one piece of information stuck in their minds. Last year Nate had organised a party in the penthouse at the *Regency* for Hazim and a "special guest". He had chosen the night because his father was in Hong Kong on business and he had exclusive use of the penthouse. Nate had provided a DJ, girls, and partygoers that included a reliable coke dealer. The party had lasted through the next day and Hazim and his guest had become close allies, according to some of the guests. It had been interesting that the word "allies" had been used rather than "friends", especially since the man in question was

Imam Bakti, the pious Indonesian cleric rumoured to be associated with violent jihad.

They talked through the information over dinner before returning to their hotel. It had been an emotional day and they both felt exhausted. Sam stripped down to his boxers and collapsed on the sofa before remembering how cold he had been the night before. He gently knocked on the bedroom door "is there a spare blanket in there, Rita?"

The door opened and Sam, surprised to see Rita topless, jumped back in embarrassment. Rita smiled, reached out, pulled him towards her and without any further thought he kissed her lovingly, she responded enthusiastically dragging him towards the bed.

Friends, work colleagues. They understood this, but neither of them had ever consciously thought they might be lovers. Their passion exploded as they both caught up for lost time. Sam licked her neck gently before his tongue moved down to her breasts. She writhed with pleasure as he concentrated on her right nipple, and as she sighed she pushed her hands into his boxers.

"I think I've always loved you Sam Galingging" Rita whispered, "but today I realised how much I wanted to be with you."

His smile was so reassuring that Rita only realised he had lowered her panties when she felt his tongue penetrate her for the first time. He pulled back quickly and looked up at Rita, tentatively, for permission. She beamed back at him, glowing. "Wow" he gasped enthusiastically, plunging in for a second time.

CHAPTER TWENTY EIGHT
Borneo

They all slept a little late and Matt's first recognition of morning was a splash outside as Matey took an early plunge. He lay still under his blanket until the urge for his first cigarette forced him to rise. The others had already taken advantage of their newly acquired cigarette stashes from last night's poker game. He joined them for a mug of coffee.

The atmosphere was calm and rested; he was pleased that Skipper's discomfort the night before had not spoiled the morning. The sun was already quite high and there was warmth outside he had not felt on previous mornings. The boat, tied up alongside the jetty, felt so safe and familiar to him now, even though it had only been a few days since he left Bali. The crew had become companions, and he dared to feel that Koto had become a friend.

He pulled some shorts on over his CKs, grabbed a camera and climbed onto the jetty. The morning rays of sunlight penetrated the forest canopy in places and he wandered a few hundred metres along the path, framing shots of spider webs in shards of light, backlit red bark, and looking back towards *Bukit*, the crew preparing for the day. He felt more comfortable now than he had for months, yet he realised he was deep in the wild where clouded leopards still pounced on their prey for survival. The sounds, the smells, were all new, but comforting because they belonged. He was exhilarated.

He heard his name called from the boat and guessed that breakfast was ready. They were so far upriver he wondered if *Bukit* could travel much further without running aground, so he thought he might suggest to Koto they take a walk in the forest, although he was aware that forest paths were few and far between. This one seemed to be quite well trodden, perhaps because it led to a loggers' camp. He turned back towards the boat and saw three men walking slowly towards him and it wasn't until they were close he recognised them from the night before. The first smiled as he passed but the second, the man who had the gun the night before, said something to him in Indonesian which he could only guess from his look was an unfriendly comment. The third laughed, somewhat unnervingly.

Matt walked briskly back to the boat. A new cup of coffee, rice and fried eggs awaited him.

"You saw the loggers?" asked Koto. "They are not friendly."

Matt nodded. "Where have they been?"

"Kumai. We think of it being two days, but by speedboat it's only a few hours. They were carrying wages."

They finished their breakfast in silence before Matt suggested walking in the forest. Koto explained that there were no trails in Tanjung Puting, except those made by loggers or scientists. The *klotok* was unable to travel further upriver because it grew narrower and shallower, so they would return to Camp Leakey and take a trail from there.

"I'll show you some of the plants my people use for medicine" Koto offered. "But first, I'll ask Skipper to start the engine so we can swim and wash without risk of being eaten. The noise keeps the crocodiles away."

Matt returned to the upper deck, carefully packed his cameras and lenses leaving one on top for quick access. When he heard the engines start up he looked over the side and saw Koto with a bar of soap jump naked into the river. Removing his clothes, he followed.

"We're OK as long as we don't go too far from the boat" Koto shouted over the noise of the engines as he swam out into the middle of the river. "Make sure you don't drift downriver."

Matt could see the loggers' green and red speedboat was moored alongside the jetty opposite *Bukit*. He was uncertain about his safety and kept close to Koto as they treaded water and shared the soap. It was difficult to imagine they could actually get clean in this black water, but it felt good to wash thoroughly after a few days on the road.

Without warning they were thrown together by a wave, created by a large yellow speedboat that seemed to have come from nowhere. The soap slipped out of Matt's hands and sunk to the river bottom.

"Shit" he exclaimed.

Koto was paying no attention to Matt, his eyes fixed on the yellow speedboat which turned and went alongside *Bukit*. It was the same one they had spotted in Kumai with two huge Mercury 75s on the back. They saw two men carrying guns leap onto *Bukit* and after some shouting they saw Skipper and Matey being ordered to move the boat at gunpoint. The *klotok* slowly backed out of its berth into the river towards them, forcing them to swim a little upstream, and then changed gear to move forward, chugging towards Camp Leakey. They watched as their companions stared helplessly at them from the wheel, Matey struggling in the arms of one of his captives before being hit over the head by the butt of an AK47 and falling to the deck.

The yellow speedboat, its engines still running, backed out into the river and cautiously came alongside Koto and Matt who were still treading water. A tall young man, wearing a scarf across his face, leaned over and offered an arm to pull Matt out of the water. He was hoisted into the speed boat and Koto followed. Another man, also young and wearing a scarf was driving the boat.

Matt, alarmed at seeing *Bukit*, his home, heading downstream with all his possessions on board, replaced his fear with anger.

"What the hell do you think you're doing?" he demanded. "Take us back to our boat immediately." He realised he sounded like an angry tourist who had been told the rest of the tour was cancelled. But this was clearly more serious and both he and Koto were very conscious of how exposed they felt sitting in this huge speedboat, dripping, naked. The two young men seemed unperturbed and didn't reply.

Koto spoke softly in Indonesian but they ignored him as well.

The speedboat turned and started to move slowly upriver, the power of its engines understated as they set off at a gentle cruise. Matt looked around and saw the two men had brought water, binoculars, a map, and rain ponchos. There was little else in the boat other than the AK47s each man had slung over his shoulder. Their scarves were in fact more like Arab head-dresses and the scene more closely resembled a terrorist kidnapping than Matt preferred to believe.

"What the fuck are you doing? Where are we going?"

Still no reply.

The driver was manoeuvring the boat very carefully, avoiding debris in the river and overhanging branches. The speedboat was large for this part of the river and on two occasions they had to switch off the engines to unravel vegetation from the propeller of the right engine. Matt and Koto were made to sit on the bow which made them feel even more exposed, and it gave them no opportunity to surprise either of their captors. The tall young man sat closest to them on the left of the speedboat with his AK47, his expression difficult to determine under the scarf, but there seemed to be a slight smile on his lips. He was watching the banks of the river as if he was looking for something in particular.

"These are the men that followed us to Kumai" whispered Koto, "the men who probably killed my friend. If they are, then they're going to kill us."

Matt was silent. He had been warned by Rita that Koto could be a liability and he may be mistaken by the loggers for a western activist. She had been very specific, yet he had ignored the warning and put his faith in a Dayak guide he had only known for hours. He remembered how shocked he was at the revelations by Rita, Sam and Koto, but he also remembered the warmth he felt for this young Dayak man, preferring to see him as a warrior leading him into his ancestral lands. Once again his romantic fantasy had led him astray, because sitting next to Koto now, both of them naked, he could only feel fear. It had all been part of a big adventure, yet now it seemed like a colossal error of judgement.

"Who do you think we are?" he asked loudly, looking straight into the eyes of the tall young man.

"We know who you are" he replied in excellent English staring directly at Matt as he spoke.

"I think there must be a mistake. I'm just a tourist with a guide enjoying this national park."

The driver had slowed the engine so he could hear what Matt was saying, but seemed unimpressed by this simple statement. The engines revved and they moved forward at a faster pace.

"Look. What is it you want? Is it money? I can get money?"

The taller young man laughed out loud. "That's all you westerners think we want, isn't it? Look at you! Frightened,

170

stripped, sitting with your Dayak friend. What could I possibly want from you?"

They stared at each other for longer than necessary, but without any further conversation. The boat had started to make quite a wake and the river banks were battered as they passed by. It seemed as if the men knew where they were heading.

Matt looked at Koto, was confused by the look on his face. He didn't seem ready to jump these kidnappers if the moment presented itself, which was the only thing on Matt's mind. Koto looked as if he had already passed on to another place, his face had widened slightly, and his nostrils were dilating as they deeply sniffed the air. He was smiling broadly.

The speedboat slowed as they turned a sharp bend into a small lake. They stopped for a moment as the two men talked in an unfamiliar language, *probably Arabic* thought Matt, the engines ticking over quietly, waiting. The driver pointed over Matt and Koto's heads and put the speedboat into a very slow gear. They edged forward, the tall man looking ahead through his binoculars and guiding the driver. Matt watched the driver carefully, realising that while the other man was looking through binoculars it may offer them an opportunity to attack. But he was looking straight at him, grinning, holding his AK47, pointing it directly at his face.

Matt turned to see where they were heading, but Koto had already guessed their fate. "When we hit the water do exactly what I say, calmly, without question" he said as he laid his hand on Matt's arm. "If you do this we will live." Confused, Matt looked around and back to the two men hiding behind their scarves. Then he saw it: a huge crocodile, five metres long basking on the right bank of this small lake, watching the speedboat approach.

The tall man stood and moved forward in the boat. "Over you go, Dayak. Join your schoolteacher friend." He prodded Koto with the gun who fell over the side into the river no further than twenty metres from the huge crocodile. It pushed its massive body forward until it slipped into the water, disappearing under the black water.

The entire scene was so alien to Matt that he was slow to realise these men not only intended to kill them, but to pass off their deaths as a result of a crocodile attack. He stood and screamed.

171

"You next" shouted the tall young man without emotion, prodding Matt with the AK47. He bent down, grabbed Matt's feet to put him off balance and tossed him over the side. Without any hesitation, the speedboat immediately turned, revved slightly and headed downstream, disappearing around the sharp bend as it headed back to Kumai, its occupants confident of another successful mission. The assassins, cold and professional, knew this particular animal had already proven its appetite for human flesh.

Underwater, Matt felt something grabbing his leg, holding him down. At first, because of delayed fear he imagined it was the crocodile, but the adrenalin rushing through his body focused his mind: the "something" was Koto, preventing him from surfacing while the speedboat moved away, out of sight. He realised his friend was calm, moving slowly and deliberately.

The black water was so dense he could only just see Koto's hand grasping his leg, beyond there was no visibility. He could feel tiny particles of vegetation on his face as they passed in the current, indicating the fairly rapid flow, but his lungs were already craving for air. His mind raced, as if there was so little time to bring absurdly irrelevant ideas together. He recognised there would be no point bringing diving tours to Tanjung Puting, that crocodiles can be extremely large, and that the sound "duh dum" associated with sharks could aptly be used for crocodiles as well. He really needed air urgently.

As he broke the surface he heard Koto whisper clear orders: "float on your back, try not to move, hold my hand and touch your foot against mine. We must be huge."

Thankful for the brief explanation, Matt lay as motionless as possible on his back, grateful for Koto's reassuring touch, trying not to sink. It took a few attempts, his limbs dangerously gangling below water, to master a calm floating position, but once his body was straightened out he lay on the surface feeling the current take them slowly away from the bank where the crocodile had rested just moments earlier. His floating body, attached by the left hand and foot to Koto, created an animal far larger than their adversary's usual prey.

Matt felt the river pass over his intensely sensitive skin which was warmed by a charge of energy up his arm and leg, flowing

172

from Koto's body. He stared at the stormy sky and felt an extraordinary total surrender to his friend, something he had never before given to another person: he had nothing to do, nothing to worry about. He was safely encompassed in a warm river of fire that he could feel moving over every part of his body, a realisation only interrupted by a sharp, but brief change of current pass coldly over his back before the warmth returned.

He had no idea how long he floated with Koto, probably only minutes, but it could just as easily have been hours. He only felt the mud beneath him when Koto let go of his hand and quietly suggested they climb onto the river bank. Looking up he saw the wide smile of his Dayak guide beaming at him. He scrambled onto dry land before looking back across the open water where he could see the crocodile had already climbed back onto the mud on the opposite bank.

"Did you feel it beneath us?" asked Koto prompting Matt to realise that the change of current he had experienced had been this gigantic carnivore checking out its lunch. "I think we have an adventure, Mr Matt" spoke Koto quietly as he stood. "You wanted to walk in the forest today and you will get your wish. I think maybe we walk for many days!"

Matt looked at Koto who seemed to have grown taller. His wet hair was clinging to his neck, brown muddy water dripping from its ends and painting lines down the contours of his chest onto his belly. His friend was naked, yet seemed to have gained some new strength that he, also naked, would need to survive this "adventure". He felt the muddy water dripping from his own hair.

"Ugh. Your hair is as brown as mine!" howled Koto. "If you don't mind me saying, Mr Matt, you look like shit!"

As if on cue, Matt started to shiver, bent double and threw up his breakfast.

PART THREE: ANCESTORS AWAKENED

CHAPTER TWENTY NINE
London

Pauline's work days seemed to be longer than ever, each story she worked on more tedious and irrelevant than the last. The one she had just finished had been about a young Brixton dope-head who swallowed a large chunk of hash, thinking it was the rest of his *munchies* chocolate cake. He had woken on three consecutive days with the increasingly alarming realisation he was still very, very stoned.

On the third day, firmly hidden away behind a locked door, he had decided to worship a particularly dirty, brown patterned candle that had sat on his floor for three years, next to his carved wooden dope box. After staring at it for a couple of hours he had, with gargantuan fortitude, stood up, found a box of matches and, placing his hands together in prayer for two minutes, eventually lit it. Four hours later, with him still staring at it, it had ignited his discarded clothes and set fire to his room. The unfortunate firemen who had rescued him had been viciously maligned by the extremely fortunate young man for "invading his place of worship."

She stared across the "news" room of the *Greater London Gazette*, a paper struggling for its identity since it had been purchased by a huge publishing house and twinned with a national daily. Only twelve months earlier her workplace would have been buzzing with gossip, steaming coffee and smoking ashtrays, but since the new anti-smoking legislation most of her colleagues were constantly out "on a story". She had never smoked and had managed to keep her life relatively smoke-free, avoiding bars and men that believed a way to her heart was through itchy eyes and foul smelling clothes. Such a hardened critic of tobacco, it had come as a shock when she realised the removal of cigarettes had seriously affected her life. Work was no fun, friends had shunned her attempts at fun-filled weekend escapes in the green English countryside, and she felt more alone than she could have imagined. The pages in her diary were packed with appointments and

174

reminders, but at the bottom of the right hand page, Saturday and Sunday were either empty or pencilled in with "clean flat" or "visit mum & dad".

"I will not be a sad fucker" she thought so loudly that she wondered if she had actually spoken the words. She looked around to make sure there had been no recognition of her mantra by anyone in the room. The new girl from Sri Lanka was studiously checking through her weekly agenda, the young lad who was their erroneously named "runner", which was so far from describing his energy levels that Pauline secretly believed he was from the same family as the dope-head in her story, had his feet up on the photocopier. Above each work-station a TV monitor flickered to bring the latest breaking stories. Not that anyone really cared. It seemed unlikely that Al Qaeda was going to focus its worldly anger on the mum who had raised £4,000 for cancer relief by "walking on water" ("waterskiing" to the rest of us). Pauline wondered if her cynicism was a result of her work, or the other way around.

It's difficult for such a barren environment to "go silent" but, without any doubt, that is what suddenly happened in Pauline's world. There was no loud chatter to quieten, nor any furiously busy rush to quell, but the entire room kind of stopped. Except that is for the TV monitors. Staring out at every workstation from the screens was a ridiculously tanned English man, smiling, almost mocking, eminently important as the ticker underneath revealed: *"kidnapped, believed lost in the Borneo jungle."* White, blond, handsome, yet lost. Matt. Her two-timing, man-fucking, ex.

She was transfixed, staring wide-eyed at the screen in front of her, still seeing it as some kind of cruel test. It wasn't until the ticker flashed up the words *"Brixton man ..."* that she realised Matt had shoe-horned his way back into her life, her professional life. Cheap trick. This was now a *local* story.

She turned up the volume on her monitor as an Asian woman was answering questions live from a press conference in Jakarta. *"Matt Johnson and Koto, his local Tanjung Puting National Park guide, were taken from their tourist boat at gunpoint and driven off in a speedboat. That was yesterday and we have no idea what has happened to them. It has to be said though, that Koto was a good friend of a local schoolteacher who was horribly murdered recently and he had been threatened by the same people believed responsible for that assassination, thugs hired by timber tycoon Abdullah Aziz."* The woman speaking was identified as Debi Sudarto, executive director of YHB.

Photographs of Matt and Koto gazing happily at the camera came on the screen followed by pictures of orang-utans. *"These pictures were taken by Mr Johnson just before his abduction. The next picture may give some clue to the reason for his disappearance."* A picture of the log raft Matt had shot on the Sekonyer River came on the screen and the woman continued *"this is just a small example of the illegal plunder of this priceless region promoted by the timber baron."*

Pauline turned to see her editor leaning over her. "That's your Matt, isn't it?" he asked.

"Not mine!" she responded rather too abruptly.

"Yeah, but that's Matt. I'd recognise his ugly smirk anywhere" he persisted. "I've already briefed our publishing group's stringer in Asia; check out the earliest flights to Jakarta Pauline. I'm serious. I want you out there to work with him. This is too good a story to miss. Girlfriend searching for the truth, handsome Brixton lad lost in jungle, wild animals, criminals. We can syndicate this around the world."

"But I left him two weeks ago" she complained. "He's not my boyfriend."

"OK. Ex-girlfriend wants to make up. I don't care Pauline. We could run on this for weeks and all the TV networks are already gearing up for death watch. Sorry."

Pauline stared at him in horror. *Death watch.* For the first time in weeks she smelt Matt's sweat after squash and touched his face. It was ice cold.

"Economy. No big budget, you check with me on all expenditures." He turned and walked away leaving her staring at the screen that now had a picture of the guide sharing a banana with an orang-utan holding its baby in its arms. *"Cute lad"* she thought. *"You're such a fucker Matt."*

*

Colin Grady had just got home from a good day talking up new orders from his clients. He had parked his BMW 335i convertible on the drive in front of their St Alban's house to remind him to take Mary out for a drive to a country pub for dinner. That's what he told himself anyway. It was much more to do with showing off his recent success to anyone who could see. What was the point of hiding his new £40,000 car behind garage doors?

"I've booked our flights, honey" he said as he entered the house. "You'll be in Singapore for two weeks. It'll give you plenty of time to shop and, if you want, you can nip up to Kuala Lumpur for a few days while I'm in Indonesia." She wasn't in the kitchen as he had expected so he climbed the stairs to check out the spare room where Mary had recently started to spend a lot of time on the computer. Sure enough, she was staring at the screen. He had told her many times to rest for a few minutes every hour or she would start to get all kinds of problems, but she had discovered free internet phone calls and sometimes spent more than an hour just talking to one of their children and seeing their grandchildren on the webcam.

"Did you hear me? I've booked the flights."

Mary turned towards him and he knew instantly that something was wrong. Her expensively coiffured hair was badly ruffled and her eyes looked tired, as if she had been crying.

"Might not be going now" she said in a staccato voice. "You probably don't know this, dear, because you've been busy selling forests to your pals, but your great rich business pal has been accused of killing a good looking English lad. It's all over the television and the web."

Colin took a few moments to judge his wife's outburst. She seemed angry with him yet everything had seemed to be going so well. What was she talking about? What business pal?

She pulled up a web page on BBC online which faithfully reported the Jakarta press conference. "Abdullah Aziz. That's his name isn't it?" she paused, waiting for some response, but Colin just looked confused. "I should have known that making all this money came at a terrible cost." She moved her cursor over to a link to YHB's website which had a photograph of Aziz, log rafts, factories and testimonials from local Dayak people accusing him of destroying their ancestral land.

"What has got into you?" Colin asked quietly, slightly exasperated by his wife's anger and accusations. She wanted him to do well so she could have a peaceful time and he was taking her with him on his next trip, not without some personal concern. Yet here she was reading some greeny's website as if it was the only portal to the truth. He raised his voice slightly. "My god woman, what are you thinking? That I would deal with someone raping the forest and killing English tourists? It's not a request I would make very often with you, but loyalty and trust wouldn't go amiss."

She turned and looked him in the face. Maybe he was right; maybe she was jumping to conclusions and being too judgmental. But it had been difficult for her to believe Colin was capable of making his business successful. She lost unconditional trust in him when she learned he had re-mortgaged their home without telling her. She knew she was angry with him, but this did look rather serious, his supplier being accused of murder on international television news.

"But how do you know you can trust this Aziz?" she asked in a more reasonable tone.

"If you get off your high, uninformed horse, you'll get to judge that yourself in a week" he shouted, throwing the air tickets on the computer table, storming out of the room.

As he slammed the front door and climbed into his car, he hesitated before turning the ignition. Of course she was right really, how did he know he could trust Aziz?

The smell of new leather brought him back to his senses, he slid a new dance CD into the player; just a little something to remind him of his night with the beautiful Michelle. Mary didn't even know he had started to listen to dance music when driving alone to business meetings, she hadn't noticed the youthful spring in his step. Colin was no longer certain he wanted to share the rest of his life with this woman in the safe, but boring house in St Alban's. He had embarked on a new life without her even noticing the change in him, but she seemed content to look at old photos and play grandmother.

His BMW pulled out of the neatly landscaped cul-de-sac and slowed to a stop. The hard top folded back, he drove onto a wider street and pushed his foot hard on the accelerator. He didn't know what he felt at the moment, but he was sure he didn't want to sit in a picture-postcard country pub all night with an untrusting, boring, nagging, disloyal, old, yes old, wife. There was more to Colin Grady than retirement. He turned the music up, felt the air rush past him and headed for London.

CHAPTER THIRTY
Jakarta

Aman Widodo, Secretary General, waited in his tiny, hot, damp cell. He had been driven, handcuffed, to naval military police headquarters in Jakarta, humiliatingly stripped to his underpants and thrown into this cockroach infested three metre square soulless space. Lying awake all night, he kept wondering where he had gone wrong, how he could have avoided this mess. His Minister had called him a traitor and dismissed him like insignificant scum. Just before daybreak he even considered suicide, but the ordered, rational civil servant in him resurfaced to argue that he had no idea what lay ahead: there would be plenty of time to kill himself sometime in the future.

Rice and murky water was pushed through a hatch in the door of the cell, but he just stared at the two bowls. Already the odour of his own urine, in a bucket in the corner, permeated his sense of smell, causing him to feel sick at the thought of food. He was dying for a cigarette.

As if to command, his door was flung open and a young military policeman entered, carrying his clothes, phone and cigarettes. "Put these on" he said without emotion, placing everything on the bed, giving the prisoner his first hope all night; but before leaving he looked down at Widodo's underpants, slightly soiled and yellow, and couldn't resist a sneer. "One night, and you're already a disgrace, old man. You won't last a week." Widodo, horrified by the insubordination, nonetheless thought he was probably right.

Left alone, Widodo reached into his jacket pocket for his cigarettes and lighter. They were there, but as he put them on the bed he felt a sense of panic and checked all his jacket and trouser pockets twice. The mobile phone was there, but nothing else. How stupid had he been? Taking that grisly photo of the torso that Hazim had given him to a meeting with the navy! He checked his pockets again, but it had gone.

*

The bluebird taxi was waiting outside Widodo's house at one in the morning, just as Hazim Aziz had promised. His mother had been asleep for hours and Mohammed quietly slipped away, feeling a strong charge from his disobedience. What was his mother thinking, telling her twenty one year old son not to leave the house? Outrageous!

He had never been to *Club Gila*, but had heard the stories of wild weekend parties when the club remained open from Friday until Monday morning. Mohammed's common sense told him that most of the stories of wild sex, drugs and non-stop dance music were exaggerated. It was just one of those things that boys lied about, like the size of their penises, but he was hoping that, like most good lies, they were based on an element of truth. He was expecting a good night, although in all honesty, he wasn't quite sure whether he had ever had one. Hanging out with Hazim, handsome, rich and sophisticated, would be a new and exciting experience.

Like many young Indonesian Muslims, Mohammed was used to simple pleasures, not the complicated world of alcohol and drugs. An evening with young friends drinking *Seven Up* at the shopping mall had brought many moments of laughter and joviality into his life. His wildest parties were held around Ramadan when his family and friends broke the daylight fast and spent hours at night time, eating, talking and laughing. It is safe to say that as Mohammed entered *Club Gila*, he was going into an alien world.

Set on the main drag through the Chinese area of Glodok, *Club Gila*, meaning *crazy club*, worked hard to deserve its name. To a visitor it seems surprising that such a club would exist in the world's largest Muslim country. But those that remember the wonderfully seedy *Tanamur*, more of an institution in Jakarta than democracy, now closed after thirty years of welcoming transsexuals, gays, straights, Indonesians, westerners, greens, yellows and browns, will realise that Jakarta has always found a way of accommodating diversity. *Tanamur's* demise is partly due to a proliferation of hotel clubs and a growing middle class, but *Club Gila* has pushed the barriers further and further beyond legality. The newspapers may be full of stories of police raids one day, but the next you'll be offered ecstasy pills with your first beer. It's not difficult to figure out that raids only occur when someone in authority is not being paid enough.

In your right mind you would turn away before entering the building. The shouting, dealing and general cacophony in the steamy heat outside should be warning enough, but once you've entered the air conditioned building you are shunted along to the lift that opens to different pleasures at every floor. On the fourth floor, the one Mohammed had been told to head for, you are led through a short line to pay the two or three dollars entrance (including your first drink, drugs extra) before stepping out onto a huge theatre like dance floor with thousands of revellers, pumping sound, attitude and sweat. Around the edges people hang in the shadows and the further back the darker it becomes, not just devoid of light.

Above the dance floor, the DJ, the toilets - all memorable experiences - are private rooms overlooking the masses. Having uttered the magic words "Hazim's friend" at the entrance, this is where Mohammed Widodo was led. A dark corridor snaked around the "dress circle", occasional people leaning against the wall, and as is usual with "occasional people", they stared as Mohammed passed. Deep in the darkness, towards the end of the corridor, his guide knocked on a door and he was ushered inside.

The private room, furnished in dark wood and comfortable scarlet chill-out cushions, had its own bar, private bathroom and optional sound system which had been overridden by the music being energetically blasted to thousands of revellers who could be seen below through a huge glass window. A large square glass-topped teak coffee table was at the centre of the room.

"Mo! I thought you weren't coming!" effused a welcoming and sociable Hazim. He grabbed Mohammed by his arm, pulled him closer in a manly embrace, like lost friends reuniting. "These are my close friends in Jakarta, and I am so happy you can meet them."

Inclined on the cushions were two beautiful women in their twenties, smiling warmly, almost hungrily, at Mohammed as he entered the room. His badly groomed attempt at a beard on his undefined, flabby, young frame was a contrast to Hazim and another male guest, a youth, probably only fifteen, wearing a bright red t-shirt with tight jeans. Mohammed noticed he was barefoot and had a smile that competed with the welcome glaze of the women sitting next to him.

"Would you like a drink Mo?" shouted Hazim above the loud music, as he poured a gin and tonic, which Mohammed took willingly as he sat between the women.

Both moved to talk to him, both wearing revealing tight tops and blue jeans, coming so close that he felt their breath more clearly than he heard the sound. His legs were already moving to the repetitive beat of the dance music and the energy in the room surpassed anything he had ever felt before. The women, he noticed, had also removed their shoes and were now pulling their legs up on to the cushions, one of them encouraging him to do the same. Hazim smiled widely at him, a kind of buddy smile, male bonding. It was all new to him, who, without really thinking about it, had just decided to let go: to go for it, whatever that was. This was his moment to forget his religious teaching, the strict piety of his mother and father, and find out about Mo, the man.

Hazim, he noticed, was more casually dressed than he had been at his house. A simple black tank top hugged his sculptured youthful, powerful body, and expensive embroidered jeans hugged his muscled arse. Mohammed was surprised that he had noticed this, but he was already feeling so horny, attracted to everyone in the room. One of the girls gently put her hand on the side of his head and turned it until her mouth was over his, her lips lubricating his, her hands stroking his inner thigh. He held the kiss for a while until he felt uncomfortable.

"Hazim, thank you for the invitation" he said clumsily. Hazim looked over at him bemused, taking a long drag on a cigarette. The girl asserted her grip on his head and pulled it around again. It was time, Mohammed thought, to either leave or let go. The MDMA that, unknown to him laced his gin and tonic, had already determined his journey; his tongue reached out between his lips, greedily diving for the girl's mouth. She sucked him inside.

The dance music resonated with his energy and he felt at home; more at home than ever before, for the first time enjoying the repetitive sound driving his body's rhythm, pumping his blood, pushing his soul towards another person. As he came to terms with such a powerful new experience, the girl on his other side had already come to terms with his jeans, edging them lower, pulling his underpants with them; revealing his circumcised virgin penis, wavering in anticipation. Mo was in full embrace with the kisser and the sensation of being given a blow job was too much. As her thick ruby lips closed around the head, he lurched forward in ecstasy, unknown to him, unusually, ejaculating so quickly under the influence of a drug so aptly named.

*

Bambang Santoso had deliberately chosen the orchid room in his private club. He hadn't risen to his position without wile and creativity, and he knew that this was a moment to exercise extreme caution. On the face of it, Widodo was a corrupt official who deserved no mercy, but in reality he was an influential man with contacts throughout the elite. Having caught him totally compromised could be used to an advantage if he could determine his use to him. This forestry business was very worrying and his President had deliberately pushed him to use his influence to support the Forestry Minister in his fight against crime in Borneo.

Aman Widodo however was completely confused by the beauty of the furniture, the curtains, the flowers and the courtesy of the staff. Just moments earlier he had been in his cell. He felt dirty: his jacket was crumpled badly, his breath tasted of smoke and he had been without sleep for twenty eight hours. He viewed himself with a disdain which echoed that of the young sailor less than an hour earlier. As he was ordered to sit in an armchair opposite the Coordinating Minister for Politics and Security, he felt his soiled underpants stick to his groin.

"Coffee?" asked Bambang Santoso.

"Thank you, sir" replied Widodo, becoming more nervous with every kindness. He took the cup offered him, welcoming the first sip as eagerly as an addict reaches for their next fix. He knew that Santoso was watching his every move, but he had lost his composure, which always reflected his dignity.

"I want you to explain your relationship with Aziz, in detail, without leaving anything out" stated Santoso. "Who you

184

introduced him to, how much he paid you, what his business empire looks like and what he has asked you to do. I want to know if he has anything to do with the disappearance of this English tourist in Central Kalimantan. Everything."

The next hour was a relatively candid confession of monthly payments made to politicians and military chiefs on behalf of Aziz, bribes, introductions, and favours. Missing was self incriminating knowledge of violence and gross subversion of the law, including a denial of anything to do with the missing tourist. He spoke of a fifteen year relationship with Aziz, his enormous growing wealth, influence and support. With genuine affection he told of Aziz's generosity, his support in building mosques and his financial contributions to Imam Bakti's foundation, although he admitted to knowing nothing of what it actually did.

Santoso had listened intently, taken notes and gently encouraged him to continue. When it appeared that Widodo had finished, he asked quietly "and what do you think I should do with you, Secretary General? You speak of deception, lies and disloyalty, although it is a story that is, sadly, in our country too familiar."

"I can be your servant, sir" replied Widodo bowing his head in shame.

There was a long pause as the Coordinating Minister wrote a few bullet points in his leather bound note book before looking up. His eyes were piercing and fiery, no longer accommodating and kind.

"There is a very strong stench in this room, Secretary General" he said angrily. "You betray me, then, when it suits you, you turn on Aziz. I can never trust you, I know that, but I will use you for my own devices until I no longer need you. You have become my obedient servant, prepared to do what he is told, any time of the day. You will help me destroy Aziz, clean up the forest and bring down my enemies. If you betray me again, you and your family will be finished."

Widodo was utterly shocked at the venom by which his boss spat out these awful words. He would have to play along and deal with the consequences as they arose, but he also knew that Hazim, who he had left out of his confession, would not give up easily.

Just as he thought he had a little room for manoeuvre he saw Santoso turning a screwed up photograph in his right hand.

"You have no idea what I could do to you. But first I want a strategy to bring down Aziz. I have a feeling that the good Imam may be a key." He stared at the picture before putting it in his pocket, shaking his head, standing and walking out of the room.

*

The second gin, tonic and MDMA gave Mo a sense of confidence and sexual prowess he could never have guessed at. The girl who had blown him removed his trousers and passed them over to Hazim who appeared to be laughing; probably in a manly, camaraderie way, he thought. The girl removed her top and her beautiful, perfectly formed breasts were just too tempting to ignore, so he licked each one ravenously, yet his mouth was strangely dry. He asked for another drink. The girl on his other side was now completely naked, and she gently coerced him to remove his t-shirt so he would be naked as well, then she placed his left hand on her right breast. He squeezed it clumsily; she withdrew and exchanged a few words with Hazim.

"Come on Mo, you're so cute and wild. I've never been with such a man" she cooed. Behind her on the coffee table Hazim was chopping five fat lines of white powder and she watched greedily. Mo was being encouraged to sit up and join in the coke ritual being played out in front of him. He really had no idea what was going on, but had already stopped fighting his conscience, and was one of the gang. Hazim pulled out a silver straw and snorted the first line. Mo, without questioning, copied his host, followed by the others.

Minutes later he felt a rush of heat slam his head and one of the girls held his naked body gently, helping him lie on his back. As she kissed him affectionately, keeping him sensually preoccupied, the young boy, now naked, proudly displaying an erect cock, bent over Mo's flaccid penis and put it in his mouth. He expertly worked it hard in seconds, all the time Mo being unaware it was the boy. Once it was hard, he stared up at Hazim's video camera with child-like wide eyes as the other girl held Mo's hand over the boy's head, forcing him down, grimacing for the camera. Hazim nodded and the boy withdrew, dressed and left the room.

"Hey, Mo. How are you feeling?" asked Hazim. "Do you feel like dancing?"

Mo smiled, took another line of coke on offer, swigged his drink, dressed and was accompanied out of the room by one of the girls. They went down to the dance floor, close to the speakers at the stage end of the club. The music was pounding and although Mo was feeling really wonderful in the crowd, he was beginning to lose his balance. The girl helped him around the back of the stage to the toilets where dozens of men were hanging around the entrance, a few standing at urinals. Mo found an empty cubicle, locked himself inside, dropped his trousers, sat on the toilet and passed out. Fifteen minutes later the door was smashed down and an armed, uniformed policeman pulled the sad looking, slightly overweight, young man outside, his trousers around his ankles.

"Turn out your pockets" barked an older policeman over the pumping music.

Mo, confused, looked down at his trousers and pulled them up. "I'm with Hazim" he said conspiratorially."

The policeman seemed unimpressed. "Empty your pockets."

Mo obediently reached down and pulled out a wad of hundred thousand rupiah notes from his left pocket. He swayed, put a hand out to steady himself as he stared at the money. "I don't have that much money" he slurred weakly, "not mine!" He smiled at the policeman but this man was unkind and would never understand such a beautiful emotion. Gaining balance, he reached into his other pocket and found a small plastic bag containing thirty small white pills and six tiny packets closed by wire twists. "I don't know what these are" he said honestly before collapsing to the ground.

*

The Secretary General's car had been waiting outside Santoso's club; Widodo acknowledged the driver and told him to take him home. The last twenty four hours had completely changed the direction of his life and he was very unsure how to deal with the new threats he was facing. He still felt fuzzy from the emotions that had hijacked him in the cell.

First and foremost, he had to contact Hazim today and offer him something, but it was not clear what that could possibly be; the photograph of the grisly scene in Pangkalan Bun was now in Santoso's hands, but that made it no less of a threat from Hazim. He had to think quickly or his new found freedom would get him killed. He had to bring Hazim into the deal with Santoso or he risked his life, and even more important, the lives of his family.

The official car pulled up outside his house and he climbed from the backseat with as much dignity he could muster in the circumstances. His wife came rushing out to greet him, fear clearly showing on her fixed smiling face.

"You didn't call" she complained.

"I'll explain everything, but I need to shower and get some rest for a couple of hours" he replied giving her little room for relief. She knew something bad had happened but understood so little of his affairs she couldn't even guess the reason for his dishevelled appearance and gaunt, tired looking eyes. The phone was ringing and they both turned to enter the house. He grabbed it impatiently.

"Yes." His wife watched as he stood motionless listening to a voice on the phone. His body remained upright but his face seemed to dive for the ground, tears pouring from his eyes. She hadn't seen him cry since his father's funeral eight years earlier. She moved over, touched his arm and felt a tremble passing through his body as he turned towards her, putting the handset back in its cradle, providing time to compose himself.

"It's Mohammed" he stated evenly. But his eyes, itchy from lack of sleep, flickered and narrowed in a way his wife had never seen before. "I told you to keep him in your sight woman!" he screamed. "All you had to do was protect your son! You stupid, fucking lazy bitch!"

She was confused and hurt.

"Now he's been arrested for supplying drugs."

She collapsed to the floor in horror. Widodo, in tears added cruelly "and it's all your fucking fault."

CHAPTER THIRTY ONE
Borneo

The circle on the water's surface below would have appeared beautiful yesterday, but at this moment it accelerated Matt's sense of fear – a seemingly minor threat, but now it was going to rain. He could never have imagined the awful new experiences he had already been through, one on top of the other; each without an adequate personal response. He remembered Koto's comment yesterday - was it only yesterday? *"If you enter a land in which you don't belong, you don't stand a chance."* As he walked he had started to repeat out loud "you don't stand a chance…"

They had decided to move northeast along the river, away from Camp Leakey and river traffic. Their attackers believed them to be dead and it was clear that this was probably their only advantage. Koto advised that they should walk around the small lake and find a narrow stretch on the river to cross. He knew of an abandoned logging camp where he hoped they might find a few useful implements to help them on their journey as well as shelter for the night: his plan was to head east towards the Seruyan River to seek help in a Dayak village. His mother and sisters still lived in the area and he was confident they would both be safe there.

It took Matt five minutes to realise that even walking in this dense forest was exhausting. First there was the heat and humidity which are easily manageable when you're carrying water, but they were not only without water, they had nothing to carry it in anyway. Secondly, and most worrying, was the lack of any clothes or footwear. There were no trails to follow; they had to move from one muddy bank to another, balancing on tree roots and crawling over fallen trees, pushing the branches out of their way with their bare hands. The first hundred metres had taken over an hour and they had crawled to the river bank to scoop the black water up in their hands to cool off and drink. Since then they had staggered for another four or five hours, hardly speaking. Matt's repetitive whisper had become increasingly desperate as he counted the wounds on his now bloody feet; it was almost impossible to put any weight on his right foot since he had trodden on a thorn which had not only cut him badly, but had since caused his heal to swell to almost twice its normal size.

Now, crossing the river, crawling slowly along a fallen tree trunk that straddled the river, the raindrop simply gave him an additional threat to fear. The thunder had rumbled for over an hour, but the rain was now falling, slowly at first. Matt collapsed, lying on his front on the tree trunk, gazing at the splashes in the river below and feeling the warm drops all over his body. His voice crackled as he whispered for the hundredth time "I don't stand a chance" breaking into louder sobbing. Ahead of him, Koto had crossed the river and was looking back at this man, broken by the forest within hours, his filthy naked body covered in cuts, lying over the tree shaking in fear surrounded by mosquitoes. "You must try and stand, Mr Matt" he pleaded, but it was obvious to him that his English client had already lost his will to survive.

Koto was finding it tough but knew they had travelled in the most difficult terrain; following the river meant they were navigating small inlets and huge root systems all the time. Once they were across the river, he thought he remembered a trail to the logging camp. He had a goal: to reach the camp and hopefully find a knife and some form of shelter and clothing. He dreamed there may be some discarded flip flops around the camp. His feet were also torn.

The rain was tipping down. He pushed his wet, dark hair from his face and headed back along the tree trunk towards Matt's prostrate body. "Please try and stand" he shouted through the noise of the rain, looking at the lacerations over the back of Matt's legs, the water drops bathing the wounds. Matt was under a small branch that grew from the trunk where Koto was standing. As he stared at his broken companion, he saw a small green and yellow snake curling around that branch, making its way towards Matt's bleeding buttocks. Without thinking he stepped forward, grabbed Matt's shoulders and pushed him off the tree trunk into the river, jumping in beside him.

At first he couldn't see Matt, but then he heard his name being cried out and turned to see him swimming towards him. "Koto, what the fuck …" the splashing rain curtailed the sound of Matt's anger as he reached for him and they both swam to the shore,

Koto dragging himself onto the riverbank, Matt pulling himself up and landing on top of him. Matt's body, once again collapsed into a dead weight, crushed some of the air out of Koto's lungs as he tried to explain "there was a snake, you had to move, it's alright Mr Matt."

Matt, hearing the explanation and finding himself lying naked on top of Koto, smiled weakly for the first time in hours. "Thanks" he exhaled as he lifted himself a little and rolled over to lie on his back next to his friend. He looked over, saw Koto's scratched body being pounded by the rain and this kind young man smiling back. "OK" he said "how far is it to this logging camp?"

Koto, relieved by Matt's change of mood, stood and looked around for signs of a trail. Realising that any delay could easily cause Matt to give up, he chose a direction and marched into the undergrowth cheerily, shouting out "come on Mr Matt, this is the way." Matt wearily got to his feet, slowly limping after him, checking out the thick undergrowth with disbelief. But the river had refreshed him and it seemed as if they should at least give Koto's plan one more chance.

They scrambled over another small inlet choked with organic debris, continually lacerating their legs, hardly noticing any pain. Koto climbed out towards the tree trunk they had unceremoniously leapt from moments earlier; stood gazing around before kneeling on the ground, looking into the dense forest. The rain was heavy now and Koto's long hair hung down in front of his face, a constant stream of water running down its length towards the ground. His eyes were bright and alert and, as he looked around, his hair swung heavily onto his shoulders, as the whites of his eyes darted from the ground to the seemingly impenetrable forest interior.

When Matt caught up, he looked back along the tree trunk to the point where he had collapsed, then back to the route Koto was gazing along. He could see knife marks on a small tree a few metres ahead. "This is the trail" declared Koto happily. "The camp won't be far from the river."

Initial optimism was brutally dashed when they found themselves standing near a third knife mark on a tree, surrounded by undergrowth. "There's no path here" Matt complained, looking more forlorn than ever. His upright, confident gait replaced by a cowed, wounded and submissive figure soaked by the rain, one leg slightly raised from the ground to avoid applying pressure to his wounded foot. He leaned against the tree with the knife mark and bowed his head.

Koto had not given up. Knife marks do not just appear in a tree; it was clear that someone had been here before. He glanced at Matt's body, every part in decline, and wondered if a bad forest spirit had entered his soul and broken it. The previously proud blond hair had taken on a soiled wetness. He could see Matt's lips moving, but could hear nothing other than the rain on the leaves and the branches that seemed to close in around them. Mosquitoes were lingering between his legs, out of the rain, and one had even landed on his frightened, shrivelled scrotum. Koto determinedly grabbed Matt's hand and pulled him behind him, through huge green leaves growing from the forest floor into a large dark puddle into which the rain was pounding mercilessly. From either side of the puddle a rudimentary path broke through the undergrowth.

"That's it! Mr Matt, the trail!" He pulled him unwillingly to the right, following a route between the trees, tripping on exposed roots, hungrily seeking assurance they were nearing the camp. The path became well defined and when they saw roughly cut branches laid across a ditch, they both became convinced that their abject misery may soon be alleviated. Matt stopped whispering his chant.

A few minutes later the pathway entered a small clearing no more than ten metres across, scattered with tree stumps and decaying vegetation. Matt found one of the larger stumps, squatted down on it while Koto carefully moved around the camp to see what it offered. He crouched, picking at the ground before standing and moving on, slowly examining this potential treasure chest. Matt, although relieved they had reached their first destination, felt an intense terror creeping up on him when he saw this rough, deserted, flattened clearing. It was difficult to imagine how this would help them survive.

He cradled his head in his hands, staring at the rain water running over his naked body, forming a puddle where it ran off the end of his penis. He watched, mesmerised by the water, until it stopped flowing and only the occasional drip fell from his creased foreskin, plunging into the water below. He could hear the pounding of his heart, slowing now he had stopped moving, although he had no recollection of hearing it for the last six hours. A bird called. He felt a warm, kind hand on his back, rubbing his shoulders, bringing him cigarettes, coffee and offering crisp, clean white sheets.

"Matt!" he looked up to see Koto. "Please, you must stay awake. We are OK, there is shelter here." The sun broke through the clouds and shone behind Koto's face which was wide and hopeful, yet displayed a deeply furrowed brow. "We must rest here tonight and decide what to do in the morning." He helped Matt stand, leading him to the other side of the clearing where there was a raised platform made from roughly cut planks of wood, with a crudely constructed wooden roof covered in large leaves. It was leaking badly but Koto had already collected new leaves to fill the gaps. The sun was warming the raised area and steam had started to cloud the rays. "Sit on this, I'll put leaves over the hole" reassured Koto. "It will be dark in two hours."

The planks seemed familiarly comforting, as if the chainsaw that a man had crudely used to shape them was a vital human link. A dark stain in the centre of the two by two metre platform no doubt had a story behind it; the notches in the upright pole may have represented a primitive calendar. For someone, this small, wild clearing had provided sanctuary, and for that, Matt was reassured. Lying down, he examined his wretched body, scratched all over; he found a particularly painful cut under his right arm. It was still full of blood and he thought this had probably occurred when he had been pulled out of the fallen tree trunk to avoid the snake. His hands were covered in mud but he could feel an aching wound from a thorn in his right palm.

As he inspected his stomach he found it was speckled with blood, although he could not find any particular injury. His genitals were brown with mud and a twig protruded from his pubic hair. He could see black specks on his testicles but assumed they were mud. His legs were grazed, cut with deep lacerations around both ankles, the right foot being severely swollen across the heel with a throbbing wound, painful to the touch. His toes were speckled

193

with black particles. He was overwhelmed by the bombardment his body had suffered in the last few hours.

Across the clearing Koto was collecting more huge leaves from a low growing plant, tearing the stems roughly and shaking the rainwater from them before piling them on top of each other. Next to the big pile there was a small collection of dark green leaves. He was chanting something as he worked, sometimes stopping and kneeling next to his harvest, touching each pile with his forehead. The sun seemed to be refuelling him, just as it had reawakened insects and butterflies that now flew in its rays. The clearing had taken on a different identity since the rain had stopped, offering something very small, but known. Within this camp were the two men, a shelter, and now, new leaves to make them safer. Koto's ritual a few metres away, whatever it meant, signified something human and steeped in tradition. It gave substance to their existence. Something which Matt had lost in the last few hours.

"Help me, please" called out Koto as he dragged a few huge leaves towards the shelter. Matt hobbled over and carried the rest, placing the dark green leaves on top of the others.

"What are these for?" he asked.

"Sleep" answered Koto, somewhat cryptically. "We have plenty of rain water to drink from the empty can, at least for tonight. Do you want to go back to the river to wash?"

Matt said he did not want to leave the clearing ever again, except by helicopter, which he thought was amusing under the circumstances. But Koto frowned and expressed concern, not realising this was a wishful joke. "We cannot let anyone know we are alive until we control the situation" he replied seriously. He dropped a mango in front of Matt and smiled. "We can live in the forest, it is OK. Please Mr Matt, get up on the platform and I inspect you."

Matt did as he was told, unsure what this was all about, but excited by the ripeness of the mango in his hand. He bit into the fruit hungrily, surprised at its sweetness. Koto was staring at his back, running his hand gently down his arms before raising them and picking something out of his armpit roughly.

"What's that?"

"Nothing to worry about. Best to get them out now though. Please turn around and stand." Matt did as he was told. Koto rested a hand on the back of his thigh and pushing, slightly parted his legs. "Um, I think you might want to get that one yourself" Koto chuckled.

"What?"

"You have a leech on your ball, Mr Matt" Koto replied with a huge grin on his face.

Matt leapt from the platform, falling over as his right foot painfully hit the ground. He stood quickly, making hysterical sounds as he hopped around a few times until he realised the folly of it all.

"How do I get it out?" He walked over to Koto and turned around.

Koto reached over, put one hand back on his leg and with the other pinched the leech between his fingers and sharply pulled it out. "You'll know next time!" he laughed out loud. "Now you can practice on those little ones between your toes."

Matt shivered. He saw a drop of blood fall to the ground where the leech had been removed. "Aren't you supposed to use a cigarette or something?"

"I'll go to the shop and get some, then hold the lighted end to your ball. Is that what you want?"

Now Matt was laughing as well. He sat on the platform, raised his right foot and looked at it. The dirty specks were drops of blood. He had four tiny leeches embedded between his toes. The other foot was the same.

"You must regularly check for leeches. They live throughout the forest, not just in the river. Every few hours you must pull them out."

Koto soaked the dark green leaves in another can of water he had brought from the other side of the clearing while Matt quickly got the hang of removing leeches. Each wound itched a little once the black slimy creature had been pulled out, but compared to the thorns in his hand and foot and the multiple lacerations on his body, the sensation was little more than an irritant. At Koto's instruction, Matt picked a soggy dark green leaf from the can and put it, now black, in his mouth and chewed. It was horribly bitter as he tasted the juice run down his throat.

When he was clear of leeches he asked if he could help Koto remove leeches from his body. Koto turned to look at him and smiled widely. "I'm done, thanks. But we must get these big leaves on the roof of the shelter."

They worked together for about half an hour, carefully wedging the new green leaves under the established brown roofing to prevent them from being blown free. The largest leaves were to be used as blankets and Koto had already laid them out in the last sun of the day. Matt finished the mango while Koto cracked some nuts on the ground with a small rock.

"Time for bed!" announced Koto cheerfully.

Matt sat up on the platform and swung around to face Koto. He was beginning to build real confidence in his friend and his Dayak knowledge. He smiled and said "despite nasty assassins, assault rifles, the biggest crocodile ever, no clothes, cigarettes or food, we're still alive." He looked directly at Koto's dirty smiling face and said "Thank you."

"Just another day in the jungle, Mr Matt."

They lay down on the wooden planks next to each other and rested some huge leaves over them. It was quite warm and not yet dark, but Matt closed his eyes and passed out almost immediately. Koto could hear his breathing, indicating he was going into a deep sleep. The leaves he had chewed would probably knock him out all night. Koto had decided this was preferable to him feeling the mosquitoes feeding on his body, buzzing in his ear, mercilessly gorging themselves on these unexpected but welcome naked mammals.

He gently rolled out from under the leaves and dropped onto the ground. If they were going to survive, they were going to have to rest here for a few days while Matt's foot healed and they foraged for food and other necessities. Koto was too worried to sleep; he had to know what else they had to work with.

He carefully made his way along the path they had taken from the river, marking the ground with broken leaves; it would be almost dark when he returned and he was aware of the dangers of getting lost. When the path opened up at the tree trunk river crossing, a hornbill was disturbed and its large black wings beat slowly as it took off and flew upriver, as if it was upset at being bothered with flying. A second followed lazily in the same direction, its large bill so distinct and its wing beat so slow that it was unmistakeably the partner of the first.

Koto crouched low, his eyes following the departing birds. "Please help me, my ancestors" he whispered.

The first hornbill beat harder, flew above the tree canopy turning slowly to make a full circle around to the lake where Koto and Matt had been thrown to the crocodile. The second bird turned more rapidly, coming back along the river towards the tree trunk across the river. The first, having swung over the lake came in from the opposite direction and they both landed simultaneously on the small branch, that a few hours earlier, had been home to a small green and yellow snake. Koto smiled, yet tears were pouring from his eyes so fast that his face was already glistening in the fading evening light. He breathed deeply and cried out as he had on *Bukit Tiga* on the journey up the Sekonyer River. Unlike the small birds that had fled on that occasion, the hornbills hardly moved, just turned and faced the opposite bank.

His chest was so expanded that when Koto spoke, it came more as an exhaled, eerily distorted gasp. "I don't know enough to survive. I don't belong in the forest. What can I do?" He punctuated his speech with violent sobbing. "Grandfather, grandmother, father. Am I to die with the forest?"

The hornbills had settled in for the night, watching over the river.

When the light had gone, he returned to the camp empty handed and crept under the leaves next to Matt. His English friend was sleeping soundly. Koto, more scared than he had ever been before, put an arm around Matt and cuddled up close to his back until he was breathing in his rhythm.

"You are right" he whispered to an unconscious Matt. "We don't stand a chance."

CHAPTER THIRTY TWO
Singapore

"He's really mad" warned Michelle as Hazim stepped into the *Regency* penthouse from the lift. "Go carefully; he's with his wife, in the sunset lounge."

Hazim, breathing deeply and focusing his dark eyes on her, hardly disguised his own fury at being "summoned" to Singapore, when he had far more important business in Jakarta. Widodo had called him for a meeting, but he had left before finding out what was going on. He had also been unable to pay off the policeman who arrested Mohammed Widodo; there was little doubt that if he didn't receive his money soon, the lad would be permanently absorbed by the Indonesian justice system. He needed to keep control of these matters; his father had no idea of how much he really did for him, yet was jeopardising millions of dollars of investment in the Vietnamese ships by insisting he join him at short notice.

He stopped, took a very deep breath, and calmly walked along the corridor to the west wing.

"Father" he called out as he saw Aziz sitting in the white leather sofa next to his wife. "Ma'am."

"Ah, there you are." His father stood and walked towards him stating quietly "she's just going back to the house." He turned, "that was lovely darling, and of course we'll have this charity event for the American school now that the American Ambassador will come. You're so good at this."

Hazim was clinging on to a frozen smile with real difficulty.

"Good, then that's settled. We've only got two weeks to prepare, so please inform the senior staff so they can meet with the Embassy security people." She acknowledged Hazim with a smile, moved slowly past him before turning and saying "I hope you will be there Hazim, it would be good for you to learn some diplomacy."

Hazim nodded at her. "I would of course love to be there if my extremely heavy workload allows me, madam."

"Good. Call it work and put it in your schedule" she ordered as she walked away from them both without looking back.

The smile on Hazim's face fooled nobody. He was appalled at being spoken to like that about the family business, especially by this haughty bitch. She clearly believed she had gained some power in this family and it was extremely worrying. He turned back to his father who was already pouring two drinks at the bar.

"Come over here and explain to me why my good name is being defamed all over the world. Tell me what is going on" he demanded quietly, but firmly, motioning Hazim to sit in the white chair as he lounged on the sofa. Hazim had no illusions about this meeting and knew of the significance of being put in the white chair, a position preferred by his father for his adversaries.

They sat politely.

"Everything is under control" said Hazim curtly.

"Under control?" barked Aziz. "I'm being accused on the BBC and CNN of murdering an English tourist, running an international mafia network and single-handedly causing a cuddly, iconic orange monkey to become extinct. You call that under control?"

"I know it looks bad right now, but we will get the cargo on those boats released this week. The murder stories will fade when no bodies are found and the monkey stories are just for selling the story. I have Widodo on the ropes."

"And his son in jail" added Aziz. He paused and stared at Hazim, shaking his head slowly. "You think I don't know?"

"Then you know that our interests are being protected. Father, you entrusted me with your timber operations and I'm acting in our best interest."

"I knew that boy when he was eight years old" continued Aziz as if he wasn't listening to his son. "You won't remember because you were at school in Malaysia, but Aman Widodo and his wife visited your mother and me in Pangkalan Bun, and brought Mo with them. He was a good Muslim boy. Now he's been caught up in your drug addiction and used as a pawn. Poor boy has probably already been some criminal's plaything."

Hazim stood angrily and faced his father. "Poor boy?" he shouted. "That poor boy has been dealing drugs for months. He's a nasty piece of shit." He threw three large pictures on the coffee table and walked to the window, giving his father time to absorb the blow ups of Mohammed's hand pushing a young, anguished lad's mouth down on his erect penis, against his will.

"He's a fucking queer" announced Hazim with impeccable timing, knowing that homosexuality would disgust his pious father. "He likes young, post pubescent, teenage boys. He screwed this one the same night he was arrested. Get fucking real."

Abdullah Aziz rarely questioned his view of the world, perhaps because if he did his criminal activities would unravel his belief that he was a good Muslim. It is extraordinary that in so many devoutly Islamic parts of the world, corruption and crooked business are so common place they hardly seem to register as sins on the consciousness of those perpetrating them. It is true that similar observations can be made of Christianity, but, in Indonesia, it is as if the corrupt elite really cannot see any problem with their criminal actions clashing so directly with Islamic faith.

For Aziz, it was easier to fall back on the tried and tested "sins" such as homosexuality. The pictures showed Mohammed Widodo's abuse of a child and Aziz had never before seen such vile photographs. There was no need to discuss this issue again: Mohammed Widodo wasn't worthy of life.

Hazim felt an exciting throb in his trousers as he sensed his father's pain and simple conclusion. How easy it had been to discard this naïve young man and throw him to the hungry, sweaty, brutes in Jakarta's notoriously ugly prison. He would decide himself whether this best served his purpose.

"That may be so and in that case he deserves to have his sins beaten out of him" confirmed Aziz, "and you may be right about me being out of touch. But none of that changes the appalling international media coverage in which I am being blamed of things I have no knowledge of."

Hazim could sense an almost tangible change in mood, the hypocrisy and self-deceit were unforgivable. "So where do you think the orang-utans are going to live when we've chopped all the trees down and moved to Singapore, father?" he asked belligerently. He was on the attack. "And who are your international business contacts if not some kind of Asian Mafia?"

"I won't be spoken to like that" retaliated Aziz. "I built our family business up from nothing and now I'm being accused of being a murderer. I want to know what has happened to that Englishman and his guide. Have you got anything to do with this Hazim?"

Hazim sat down again, deciding it was time to make his father feel comfortable and trusting. "I have no idea who these people are, father. The stories are coming from a small organisation based in Jakarta which accuses you of destroying Tanjung Puting. They are closely connected to the Forestry Minister and one of their members is the sister of that Dayak murdered in Pangkalan Bun. This is all about revenge."

The sun had started to turn golden as it snuck down behind the tall buildings of the city centre, the dark shadow forming across Aziz's face added twenty years to his appearance. He sighed heavily, not wishing to pursue this line any further; afraid of finding out his son was behind this death as well. "Tell me your plan."

The figure sitting in front of Hazim hardly resembled the man he looked up to as his father. To him, this wizened old man was no longer capable of running an empire as broad and diverse as the family business. He was weak, both physically and mentally, his thoughts polluted by his wife, the socialite. Sure, it was useful to meet people like the American Ambassador, but it was also dangerous; the Americans had many enemies in the region and if you were seen too close, they could turn on you.

As he outlined how Widodo was going to get the navy to release the Vietnamese ships to the police, his discontent and pride subconsciously conspired to develop a new idea, one that his father would never expect. He smiled at Aziz, sitting quietly, sufficiently shocked into submission, but inside he could feel this exciting new plan emerge. He could see he didn't need his father anymore.

Jakarta

There was no sign of Widodo's wife at their family home in South Jakarta as Hazim pulled up in his black Mercedes later that same evening. He felt buoyant; somehow different. He wasn't quite sure what it was, but he would soon realise he had left in Singapore, at that moment when the sun turned red, dependence on his father. He would rationalise that he felt this to support his mother, deserted and left to rot in Pangkalan Bun in the house he had grown up in. But it was really all about power.

He walked into the house without waiting to be invited. Aman Widodo, looking broken, walked up to him and shook his hand. In the back of the house a dog was barking while another whimpered.

"I haven't much time" stated Hazim with an air of extreme petulance. "Just tell me when the timber will be released." He sat on the sofa.

Widodo had thought about this moment all day. He knew his life was at risk directly from this young, upstart child of Aziz, but even more important was the quick release of Mohammed, his son. He had decided to explain the situation as honestly as he could so that they could resolve the situation together. The Coordinating Minister may have him by the balls, but Hazim held his son's life in his hands.

"I need to talk this through with you" started Widodo, surprised that Hazim was looking at him quietly; waiting to hear what was on offer. He lit up a cigarette. "You have my son's life in your hands, I know that. What you don't know is that I spent last night in jail." Hazim looked at Widodo and smiled. "Santoso knows of my relationship with your father and is looking for a way to use me. He wants the logging to stop in the Park and he wants your father out of the business. I don't know what to do."

Hazim sat back and looked at this old man. It was so much easier than dealing with his father because his superiority had been clearly established. Yesterday he would have screamed and threatened, but today he was in a different position. It was worth thinking this through and looking after his own interests. "OK, let's think about this" he responded. "If you want to see your son happy again, you will only talk to me about this matter. Not my father. You must understand that I can work with you but only I have the power to help your son. Only me. My father has given up on him." He threw the photographs of Mohammed and the young boy on the table in front of Widodo.

The Secretary General reached down and looked at the pictures. He withheld any expression of emotion to prevent feeding

202

Hazim's obvious pleasure at the cruelty he was inflicting. Every part of him denied what was in front of him and every part of him hated Hazim more than he could have believed possible. He answered calmly "so I will only deal with you. But you want the timber, don't you? And I don't know how to deliver it to you."

"Tell me what Santoso said to you" interrupted Hazim.

"He wants to destroy your father."

"Interesting" said Hazim. "And how?"

"He seemed to think Imam Bakti may be a key" replied Widodo, confused as to how a famous religious figure could help.

Hazim was intrigued by the Coordinating Minister's perceptive comment. How quickly his world had changed and his alliances shifted. He stood abruptly, turned to leave. "Let me think how I can bring the good Imam into our negotiations" he said as he walked towards the door. "I'll meet you tomorrow with my orders."

Widodo accompanied him to the door. "I'll do what you ask, but you must get Mohammed out of jail tonight."

"Or what? We'll talk again tomorrow. Don't worry old man, he's probably enjoying himself."

Hazim was very pleased with the photographs of Mo; they had been useful with his father, and now Widodo. It had been his father who had bought him his first camera ten years earlier.

As he walked to his car, the dog had stopped barking, but the whimpering continued. He listened closer, wondering what terrible suffering a dog would go through to be making such a noise. Then he realised, with an increasing sense of pleasure and control that the sound came, not from a dog, but a woman.

The Widodo family was now totally in his control.

CHAPTER THIRTY THREE
Jakarta

Probo was unsure how to handle the current crisis. He could see the opportunities the international media offered, but at the same time he had to represent his government. It would be difficult for him if the press depicted Indonesia as a backward, useless, lawless nation, incapable of protecting its tourists. In cabinet this morning he had been warned by the Minister of Tourism to be very careful or he would blame the decline in tourists directly on him. Considering the failure of tourism, clearly due to incompetence, greedy visa restrictions, a failure to invest and a number of bomb attacks, Probo brushed aside such blatant attempts to absolve responsibility.

More importantly, he had spoken with Bambang Santoso who had offered him complete support. The plan was to use this incident to launch a huge enforcement operation in Tanjung Puting National Park coordinated by the Ministry of Forestry but including the army, the navy, the police and the Ministry of Trade and Commerce, which had jurisdiction for the sawmills. He was authorised to allow some media to accompany him as he oversaw the mission, which was codenamed, in his opinion rather frivolously, *Operation Johnson*, the name of the missing foreigner.

In the press room on the ground floor, the journalists were chatting and renewing acquaintances over the impressive array of spring rolls, pastries, biscuits and Indonesian coffee. The national media were overwhelmed by the international interest in this story. It seemed that most of the Asia-based journalists and television crews had arrived from their bases in Bangkok and Singapore, to cover the story. Only a decade earlier it would have been impossible to imagine such an occasion in Jakarta.

Watching the proceedings were others with an interest in the developments. Debi, Sam and Rita were hoping to make press contacts. Debi had already been assured by Probo that he would announce their presence and the fact that Sam and Rita had seen both Mr Johnson and Koto only a few days ago. Three journalists working for the Pangkalan Bun local media, feeling out of their depth, were smoking near the coffee. Two of them were on

Hazim's payroll with implicit instructions to get a list and photograph of everyone there, their contact details and purpose. Embassy officials, assorted ministry officials, and various donor agency representatives were mingling in the crowd awaiting the Minister's arrival.

Already sitting, Pauline was alone. Her local stringer contact had said he had another appointment so she had been left to fend for herself. Exhausted, jetlagged, and emotionally confused, despite having worked as a journalist for five years, she felt she had nothing in common with the vultures behind her. It had been less than three weeks since she had thrown Matt out of their flat in Brixton and now she was in a country she had never planned to visit, waiting to report on his death. Around her the rows of seats started to fill. The Minister was on his way.

In Kumai Bay, as the Minister walked out of his office in Manggala Wanabakti, three naval frigates blocked all water traffic to the sea. Simultaneously, a smaller frigate dropped its anchor off the Arut River, the seaward route from the Pangkalan Bun sawmills. Two mobile army units flew NBell 412 helicopters into a base just north of the town, blocking any road transport out towards the provincial capitol Palangkaraya. National police arrived at the local police station for the second time in as many weeks, taking over the operation from the locally, compromised force. To informed observers it was immediately obvious that "Operation Johnson" had very little to do with finding the missing tourist and his guide, but more to do with a full scale attack on the anarchy and corruption that had prevailed for the last ten years under the control of Abdullah Aziz. For many citizens in this remote part of the world it represented their first sense of hope. For others, it seemed as if the cookie jar had just been slammed shut.

"I would like to welcome the international media to the Ministry of Forestry" announced Probo to the hundred people in the audience. "I have just come from a cabinet meeting where we officially launched "Operation Johnson", a three pronged strategy. Our first objective is, of course, to find Mr Matt Johnson, a British tourist, and his Dayak guide, Mr Koto. Our second is to destroy all illegal camps within Tanjung Puting National Park, confiscate the timber and prosecute those responsible for illegal logging. The third immediate objective is to close down all illegal sawmills."

Probo continued by making promises to the gathered audience that all those responsible for the anarchy in Central Kalimantan Province where Tanjung Puting is located, would be brought to justice through the Indonesian courts. He outlined the agencies involved in the operation, gave timelines, showed maps and handed over to the army, police and navy representative to explain their tactics.

Pauline was impressed. Maybe there was a chance that Matt could be rescued. She listened intently as the plans were revealed, amazed that such action could be sparked by her ex getting into trouble, although Matt and trouble were something she had learned to expect. She recognised three of the British journalists from television and when they asked questions she forgot to concentrate on what they were asking, she was so star struck by their interest. Then an Indonesian woman stood to ask a question. Pauline recognised her as the one that she had seen on her monitor at work two days ago. She asked why anyone should believe the government when Abdullah Aziz had been allowed to grow increasingly powerful for so many years. What had changed?

Probo replied unsurprisingly with statistics and a "renewed determination to crack down on the timber mafia. But let me explain, not just to the news media present today" he said with a practised politician's smile, "but directly to Mr Matt Johnson's girlfriend, Ms Pauline Brand."

Pauline was horrified as she saw her publishing group's stringer, who had just entered the room, beckoning her to stand. Everyone was staring at her. A photograph of Matt and his guide was projected onto a screen at the front of the room and she was escorted towards it to stand with the Minister. The room was alive with the flashes that grabbed the front cover pictures of hundreds of newspapers around the world: the girlfriend looking for her lost, kidnapped lover, in the Borneo jungle. The television pictures of this moment would be broadcast to hundreds of millions of television sets. At last the story had a strong personal angle, the girlfriend hoping, perhaps against the odds, to be reunited with her handsome boyfriend.

Probo graciously lowered his head as Pauline approached, then he shook her hand and asked her to sit next to him. "Ms Brand. It is shocking that we meet under these circumstances" he spoke to her through the microphone. "Your partner's kidnap shames our country. Our President, just one hour ago, has ordered us to do everything" he paused, "everything in our power to bring Mr Johnson back to you. God willing." He went on to point out Rita and Sam as the people present who last saw Matt and announced that he was leaving for Borneo within the hour. "I would like to invite Ms Brand to accompany me personally to see the efforts we are making."

The press started to call out questions to Pauline but it was all a horrible blur. "Come with me" offered Rita kindly as she approached the podium where she was standing, "come and sit down and think about what is happening." Pauline obediently followed this kind looking woman, about the same age as herself. They left the room, shaking off most of the press who wanted to grab the Minister before he left Jakarta. A few British journalists followed them to a Chinese restaurant a little down the ministry corridor, but returned to the press conference when they had seen where they had gone. They would be back soon.

Sam was already seated at a table and he stood to pull out a chair for Pauline. "I'm Sam" he said simply, smiling kindly. "Rita and I met with Matt a few days ago in Tanjung Puting National Park. It was us that introduced him to Koto, his guide. We first met him in Bali" he realised that Pauline was calming as he spoke and, encouraged by her response, he glanced at Rita before adding "in a reggae bar."

Rita reached out to Sam and put her arm around him. "You don't have to talk. I just felt that you were lost in there" she offered.

Pauline, sensing their kindness, allowed a few tears to roll down her cheeks. She had no idea what she was feeling: jilted, angered, fake, lost? But she was aware that she had a professional role as a journalist to perform, although the antics of her supposed companion had broken any trust between them. Her control of her life had all unravelled the moment Matt's face had appeared on her monitor at the *Greater London Gazette* office in Brixton.

"I should get back in there" she stated weakly, "I'm working and have to get this story."

"We can give you that" replied Rita, still smiling. "We work with Debi for an environmental group. We were the last people present who saw Matt and Koto, Sam was the first contacted by the skipper of the boat they were kidnapped from. We have his personal belongings and film from his trip into the forest. You have the story here with us. Then you can go to Borneo with the Minister. He's alright."

Pauline pulled out a notepad and pen from her bag and sat back in her chair. "Before we start, can I ask you what you think has happened to Matt? Off the record."

Rita looked at Sam and sat down next to him. "May I ask you something first?" she said looking at Pauline directly.

"You know that we are no longer together, don't you?" replied Pauline.

"Yes, that was it" Rita nodded as she spoke. "But more important. Are you in love with Matt?"

It was now Pauline's turn to smile. "I think I probably hate him" she stated quietly. "But I'm told that means I love him. He hurt me in a way I cannot forgive, only a few weeks ago. Now I'm caught up in this awful nightmare with my editor throwing me to the press to boost his group's profits. I'm supposed to be looking for my lover when I'm really looking for my cheat."

Rita reached out for Pauline's hand which was given willingly. "Matt was caught up in a fight to stop the destruction of the national park he was travelling through."

Pauline's face drained. "Was?"

"I'm sorry" said Rita. "My English is not that great. We don't know whether he is dead or alive. He was kidnapped at gunpoint by the same thugs that recently murdered my brother-in-law. Whether they have the nerve to kill a foreigner, we don't know. If they are alive in the forest, then he's with Koto, who is a generous and kind man. He is Dayak, a local. He is in good hands."

"Do you think they are alive?" she asked again.

"Look" Rita replied. "They were kidnapped by killers. They had no protection and they were taken while swimming. They are naked. If they survived the guns then surviving the forest will be a huge challenge. Get out there and look for them as quickly as possible. Give me your hand phone number. We'll be in touch."

A posse of journalists appeared at the restaurant door. Sam rushed over to stop them from interfering.

"You should understand" added Rita, "if they are alive, I don't think they will want to be found. They won't trust anyone. My guess is that Koto will be heading for a Dayak village. But this is virgin forest, no trails, no camps. Even if you don't find them, it doesn't mean they are dead."

Pauline glanced at the journalists and photographers being held back by Sam and quickly scribbled her mobile number on a piece of paper, handing it to Rita. "One more thing. I have to know." She stopped for a moment staring into Rita's eyes. "Was this Koto, a good friend of Matt's?"

"He was his guide."

Pauline continued to stare at Rita.

"He was not his lover."

"Thanks" whispered Pauline.

She stood and went over to the media scrum by the door. Sam pointed out a man from the ministry beckoning her to follow him to meet with Probo. *"Might as well see where this takes me"* she thought as she strode past the impatient crowd. "Sorry guys, I've got my story to file" she shouted out with a confidence that belied the fear growing in her heart as she was led away to the Minister's waiting car. The journalists, seeing their quarry escape, turned and moved in on Rita and Sam.

Probo welcomed Pauline and ordered his new driver to drop Ms Brand at her hotel to pick up some clothes.

"This must be very difficult for you Ms Brand" he stated cautiously.

"Very" replied Pauline quietly, staring at the road ahead. Her mind was still on Rita's last words *"He was not his lover"*. *"There's that word again"* thought Pauline. *"Was."*

CHAPTER THIRTY FOUR
Borneo

The slim, sexy girl behind the bar was looking at him in the mirror as she punched the keyboard of the cash register. He returned her cheeky glance with his killer smile, taking a deep drag on his cigarette, blowing the smoke over towards her. He could see a curling wisp of smoke dive down below the bar and rise, confidently, under her skirt. He smiled again, this time lifting his cold pint of lager to his lips. She breathed in deeply as if she had felt a tickle from the smoke, lifting her breasts as she turned away from the mirror to face him.

"Matt."

It wasn't the girl's voice.

"Matt."

Pauline had arrived carrying a Habitat bag. "The tube was packed" she complained. "You're smoking, Matt. Put that out. You know how I hate cigarettes."

The girl behind the bar smiled at Pauline. "Can I get you a drink?" she asked professionally. But before any response was possible, a loud explosion ripped through the already darkened room and Matt could see the girl's skimpy skirt on fire as fluorescent reds, blues and greens battled the gloom. Within seconds the girl was completely naked, standing in front of him, pleading to him, reaching down to touch herself, desperately. As he watched he saw smoke, perhaps his smoke, bellowing from her vagina.

"Let's get out of here" stated Pauline in a very matter-of-fact voice as she grabbed his hand, dragging him onto the Brixton street. "You'll love the curtains" she tapped her bag, "they're just what we've been looking for."

They crossed over Acre Lane at the Town Hall, past the *Fridge* and up Brixton Hill towards their flat. Three red double-decker buses identified the London scene, but behind them they could hear sirens; an ambulance raced down the hill towards them as cars pulled over to let it past.

"What a din!" moaned Pauline raising her eye-brows. "Let's get inside and look at those curtains."

The flat was spotless, magazines piled neatly on a glass-topped coffee table in the lounge with a white leather sofa and two chairs. Matt did not recognise the place, although there was a familiar aroma; something that lifted his spirits. Its source seemed to be coming from the bedroom, but before he could check it out Pauline had rushed ahead of him.

He heard her scream and rushed in after her. Lying on the bed was a naked man provocatively writhing around with his cock in one hand and his camera phone in the other. It was Ardi. Before Matt could respond to the scene in front of him, Ardi had pounced from the bed and sunk his teeth into Pauline's neck; blood was pouring down her blouse and an ugly gurgling sound filled the room. The aroma Matt had recognised became even stronger as he looked down and saw Ardi ejaculating over Pauline's leg as she screamed and screamed.

His body jumped violently; enough to wake him and see the first light in the forest clearing. He lay still, trying to shake himself from the nightmare and take in his surroundings. A high pitched whining sound passed his ear and he gradually felt the wounds that had been inflicted on him yesterday by the forest and, overnight, by the mosquitoes. He would have leapt from the platform to escape the biting if it hadn't been for the comforting embrace of Koto. He could feel his arms around him, holding him close as if he was frightened that if he let go, he would disappear forever.

He listened to the sounds as he recognised the difference between night and day. The forest was much louder in darkness, the creatures crying out, he thought, for recognition when the sun had set. But perhaps the lack of light was less of a burden to most of the forest than it was to him. Other senses of smell and hearing were more important to dogs and cats than sight, so why not to crickets and frogs? He realised how little he knew about his own senses. As if to mock him, he heard Koto sniff sharply as he tightened his sleepy grip on his torso.

This was that moment when he first thought about cigarettes. He would roll over, feel for his packet without looking and, half awake, light it and take his first drag. Lying naked under leaves with his guide clinging on to him, the thought of a cigarette immediately felt absurd. Perhaps it was the trigger for wider

211

thoughts of their predicament. He remembered the guns and the crocodile. He opened his eyes, saw the trees and thick undergrowth just metres from their shelter, and smelt the damp chilly air. The mosquito bites were quite serious so he ran his right hand down his body, counting the number of attacks. He had reached twenty on his right side before running his fingers over his own buttocks where a particularly nasty bite was swelling, as if it was the most recent. His hand brushed against Koto's erection. He withdrew his arm immediately, holding it nervously in front of his chest, listened, trembling slightly, to Koto's rhythmic breathing: he was still asleep.

Why was he so afraid? Koto was a good looking young man with his own mind and thoughts. He should not feel responsible for anything other than his own actions, should he? But he was the client and Koto his guide. Didn't this put him in a position of power that he had to be careful not to abuse? Besides, sex was not the first thing on his mind: it was survival. In fact, although they had been naked together since yesterday morning, Matt realised this was the first time he had thought of sex since the kidnap and even now, he felt no arousal. His overwhelming emotion was fear. He was lost in a world known better to his companion and he was his best chance of finding their way out of the forest. He mustn't let anything get in the way of that.

Koto sniffed again, shifting his body slightly, releasing his hold on Matt but pushing his hard penis into his back. He groaned as Matt slid his body away, carefully trying not to wake him, rolling off the edge of the platform.

The pain was immediate. The thorn in his foot had infected his heel and part of the sole; he was unable to stand on it. His underarm was painful and sticky; he remembered the deep cut he had found the night before. He could smell his sweat and, looking over his body, he could see he was filthy. A stomach pain reminded him he was very hungry. But overwhelmingly, the greatest shock was the number of mosquito bites. He was covered from head to foot in reddened lumps indicating the bites. He scratched the one on his buttock, causing it to puff out and itch even more. Any thought of sex had already disappeared into the recesses of his mind and he only had three thoughts: to pee, to cry, and to silently plea for Koto to wake up.

He hopped over to the other side of the clearing, remembering from somewhere that you should never urinate too close to home. He held himself up by leaning against a tree as he pissed on it, feeling that familiar morning relief.

"No!" Koto was shouting at him. "Stop, please, Mr Matt!"

Matt, completely surprised that Koto was awake, but shocked at the desperate tone in his voice, tried to stop peeing and shook himself, very self consciously looking back at Koto over his shoulder. Somehow, being naked today was more difficult than yesterday.

Koto, still with his morning hard-on, was rushing towards him urgently. Matt couldn't help but look at this wild charging Dayak, his manhood slapping from side to side, with real concern. Now he didn't even want to face Koto, his embarrassment over-riding any realistic logic. Koto it appeared did not share his reticence.

"Please, you cannot pee without asking for permission" Koto gasped as he came to stand directly in front of Matt. "We need help from the forest and we must treat it with respect. You must not see peeing against a tree as a simple function. The tree is involved as well."

"Morning" responded Matt, still not wanting to face Koto, although relieved that there was an explanation for his charge.

"*Selamat pagi,* good morning" responded Koto with a grin growing on his face. "I am serious." Matt had inadvertently noticed that Koto's hard-on had already subsided. "Please Mr Matt. You must be serious too. Respect is what it is about. If you ask permission first, then you can pee in the forest. Look."

Koto, unabashed, spoke quietly to the same tree, bowed his head, and then reached down and peed.

It was hours before Matt was able to accept his nakedness in front of Koto. They went together to the river and washed, but Matt kept his distance, hopping behind him on the way back to the camp. Koto had found a pair of rubber flip-flops, abandoned by a logger, next to the river where he washed, and offered them to Matt. It was the first time Matt believed they had a chance of survival. Unknown to him, Koto was still feeling completely out of his depth.

Once back at the camp, Koto suggested Matt rest his foot and went off into the forest to look for food. While he was gone Matt hopped around the clearing, talking to the plants just to make sure he was not upsetting anyone. He accepted they needed all the help they could get. Near the tree he had leant on in the morning, he found a rusty green plastic lighter under a leaf he was ripping off a plant, with permission, to plug a hole in the roof of their shelter. He decided to dry the lighter out before seeing if it worked, although the fluid inside indicated he may have helped them leap millennia of evolution and discovered a simple way to make fire. He was quite proud of his foraging skills, which encouraged him to venture a little further.

The sun rose and the forest became increasingly hot. He marvelled at some of the plants hanging on to the side of trees, others growing out of a puddle. Brightly coloured fungi warned him to leave them alone. But the biggest surprise was the devastation caused by the loggers. He came across the stumps of old trees more than two metres across, but surrounding every large stump was an area of smaller trees ripped from the ground and left to rot. The removal of each giant caused a scar as huge as the influence of the tree during its hundreds of years of life.

Matt sat on one of the fallen entourage and examined his foot. The swelling was beginning to eject the thorn, but he thought it would be days before he would be able to pull it out. He found leeches between his toes, pulled them out as instructed by Koto yesterday. "Sorry" he added, unsure whether respect should be offered to these bloodsuckers as well as the trees. Better to be safe than sorry. The flip-flops had already made walking so much easier and he had great hopes for the lighter. He would share that moment with Koto. It is extraordinary, he thought, how from one day to another, such small things could become so significant in your life.

He stood, caught a light shining from the side of a living tree about twenty metres from him. Hopping over towards it, he recognised a ten litre jerry can as he approached the reflection. It must have been left by the loggers. He crouched down beside it, unscrewed the top and smelled petrol. There was less than half a litre inside, but coupled with the lighter he could already imagine a wild boar turning on a spit over a raging fire.

Then he felt the first sting. He looked down and saw large ants climbing up his legs. Standing immediately, he brushed the ants from his leg, but more were running up his shins, some having already reached his thighs. He hopped madly, slightly deranged by the severe pain the first bite had inflicted, feeling a second and third dig their fangs into his skin. By now he realised he had to move away quickly, the ground was alive with large red ants crawling onto his feet. He hopped clear and thrashed around, flicking them from his body as he cried out in pain.

Ten metres from the battle, he stopped, convinced he had brushed all the ants from his body. The jerry can stared at him, inviting him to return, but the pain was too stark. "Respect" he cried out. "Fuck you!"

He turned; ready to hop back to the clearing, but could not see which way he had come. He shouted out for Koto.

Along the river, Koto was pleased with what he had found. There were fruit trees that would provide them with mango and durian. He decided to search the river after finding the flip-flops in the morning. This was where the loggers would wash every morning, and he guessed they would fish as well. Sure enough, a little further up the river he found a fish trap discarded on the bank. This basket-like contraption was made from branches and leaves, wide at its mouth but narrowing, closed at the bottom. When placed in the river in an appropriate current, the fish would swim in, unable to swim back. Koto had been taught to use a similar trap by his father when he was a small boy.

He had just finished setting the trap in the river when he found a rusty red lighter near where the flip-flops had been in the morning. He flicked it, but the flint was too wet to spark. He decided to dry it out for later.

He could have sat by the river all day. For him, the river was more comforting than the loggers' camp, but he recognised how important the shelter was to them both. They had been lucky last night it had remained dry. The leaves they had placed in the roof were strong, but they would undoubtedly get soaked if heavy rain hit. He wondered if Matt would feel better after some food. He had been taking tourists into the park for years, but this was the first time he had been forced to rely on a foreigner.

In some ways Koto gained strength from Matt. It would have been impossible for Matt to understand at this moment, but Koto saw a man, strong, confident, thousands of kilometres from home. It seemed to him that Matt would find a way to survive. Whereas, he had been thrown back into the world of his Dayak ancestors, unsure whether he could live up to it.

He liked Matt. Some of his clients were arrogant and stupid, but Matt showed an open heart. It was understandable that being kidnapped and left for dead would be challenging for a foreigner and Matt's wounds were bad. He would search for some medicine plants this afternoon. He was intrigued by this strong Englishman who Sam had described to him a few days earlier as gay, as if this was a weakness. Koto, although educated by Christians, had not really understood the idea of separation from nature they preached and he had no time for unkind prejudice. His father had certainly loved his uncle; they often went hunting together for days. His mother asked his uncle for help when his father died of malaria and he remembered them crying together.

He chuckled as he thought of Matt hiding himself from him this morning, his obvious embarrassment when he had shown him how to pee! It was strange that a man described as gay would then be so ashamed of his nakedness in front of another man. His Dayak upbringing had no shame in nakedness, but it was something he had been familiar with in the missionary school. His people had no social definition of gay; it really did not seem important to him at all. Christians seemed to have so many things they were not allowed to do! Yet they seemed to reject all the wonderful support offered by nature and the forest spirits. He had never understood why they made everything so difficult.

He picked some fruit and headed back to the clearing. There was no sign of Matt so he stacked the fruit near the platform and collected some water. After a few minutes he started to worry, shouting out for Matt at the top of his voice. He heard a response almost immediately and made his way towards the sound.

By the time Koto arrived, Matt had swollen up badly where the ants had stung him and was feeling very vulnerable. "I'll get the can" Koto stated "and then we'll go back to the camp together. I'll find you some leaves to rub on those stings."

Koto had insisted that Matt rest. He disappeared a few times, returning with leaves and the roots of another plant. They ate the fruit and Koto explained that Matt had been attacked by fire ants. It was important to always keep a look out for these aggressive insects because they attacked without provocation. He applied a concoction made from the root, explaining it would help with the pain and the swelling.

In the afternoon Koto started a fire with his dry lighter and a small amount of petrol. Ten minutes later he had cooked a small fish caught in the fish trap. It was already obvious that they would be able to live off the forest for a few weeks if necessary, at least as long as the fruit was in season. They had decided to keep out of the way of everyone until they were both strong, and to achieve that they would stay in this camp. Then they would head east.

"You know" said Koto as he removed a fish bone from his teeth. "Yesterday I wondered if we had any chance together. Last night I cried." Matt was astonished. "But today, together, I think we have the strength to survive. Today we are friends, not guide and client."

"I had no idea you were so sad." said Matt.

"Not sad. Frightened" replied Koto. "But it is you. I held you all night and awoke stronger" replied Koto. "You know, I think this forest is our world. At least for the moment it respects us too. Both of us. Together."

"You think we'll make it?"

Koto flashed his widest smile and brushed his hair back behind his ears. "I don't know" he paused to look directly at Matt. "I think we need to feel the forest spirits in us as well as some of the worldliness you bring. But I also think we both belong."

CHAPTER THIRTY FIVE
Jakarta

It felt unreal returning to his office in the Ministry. In the last few days Aman Widodo's membership of the political elite had crumbled to a point where he had contemplated taking his own life. His wife had moved out of his house to stay with her sister and his youngest son … his beloved Mohammed, was still locked up with criminals. He had pleaded for permission to visit him, making repeated calls to the national police, but they kept referring him to the Attorney General's office. If convicted of drug dealing, his son would, most likely, they said, be executed by firing squad.

He had met with Hazim earlier in the day who had ordered him to set up a meeting with the Coordinating Minister, Bambang Santoso. Hazim would ensure Imam Bakti would attend and they could discuss how, mutually, they may achieve their "primary goals". Widodo was confused. The launch of "Operation Johnson" had been publicised on television all day, yet Hazim was not screaming and shouting in the way he usually did when his family's assets were threatened. There had been no mention of the ships. He had no idea what he was up to and, if he was honest, only one sentence from the conversation with Hazim really mattered to Widodo, even though it had been delivered with deliberate cruelty. "You get me this meeting, and if it goes well, you'll have your queer son back. Used, but alive."

Just a few moments earlier he had received a call from Abdullah Aziz in Singapore. He was very angry, demanding to know what Widodo was doing to prevent the closure of his sawmills and the return of the cargo from the two Vietnamese ships. He had been lost for words at first, resorting to "Hazim and I are working very hard on this issue." But in truth he had no idea what Hazim was playing at.

It was with huge relief he heard from Bambang Santoso's secretary that the Coordinating Minister was prepared to meet the good Imam and his friend at three this afternoon. Widodo was informed curtly that he should not attend.

*

Hazim spent the morning with Imam Bakti at a small mosque in South Jakarta. They spoke like student and teacher, never mentioning the militia of trained and equipped thugs that bound them more closely than Islam. It was an intriguing alliance between ruthless business and a hard line Muslim fanatic. Hazim needed some assurance that his sadistic nature was, at least understood, by a great religious teacher. Bakti, pushing pragmatism beyond most peoples' sensitivities, needed the money.

When Widodo called Hazim to confirm the meeting, Imam Bakti spoke kindly to Hazim, suggesting they go to Mecca on the Haj together next year. "Your father has robbed his people, Hazim. You must understand that I can no longer protect him. Maybe today we can find a new way forward and build on it together. You and me."

Hazim knew he had found a new ally, someone who appreciated his skills of business negotiation. But perhaps more important to him was the possibility of some redemption for all his ungodly thoughts and actions. Hazim understood his predeliction to power and the infliction of pain; it was also true that he enjoyed seeing his opponents suffer. But he was young, alone and isolated, driven by an inflated ego which he understood gave him good reason to fear himself.

"Teacher, I need your advice" Hazim admitted.

"God is listening."

"I have a troubled heart" Hazim continued. "My body has not always been strong."

The Imam nodded kindly.

"As a child I would cut my arms and legs, as if I was driven to it." He had never admitted this to anyone before, only his family knew of the physical self abuse. "I needed the pain."

Imam Bakri gently placed his hand on Hazim's right shoulder as the young man pulled up a sleave and revealed the scars.

"Please help me. I don't understand my weakness."

"Do you still harm yourself Hazim?" the Imam asked softly.

"No.Now I treat my body well."

"So are you troubled by the past" Bakti paused "or is there something else?"

"I still feel the same urge to inflict pain" Hazim replied, his voice cracking slightly, his head now bowing towards the floor. "But not on myself."

*

Bambang Santoso cleared all appointments in the afternoon to give him time between lunchtime prayers and the meeting with the Imam to think. He was certain this religious leader was behind attacks on property in the Jakarta area, such as night clubs and massage parlours. It seemed likely that men under his influence were acting as a private militia for Aziz, probably responsible for a number of deaths, including the grisly murder in Pangkalan Bun last week and likely to be behind the kidnap of this English tourist. It was good that he could talk with him privately, although the presence of Aziz's son troubled him deeply.

He stared at the photograph of his late wife on his desk with four framed pictures of his four daughters flanking her on both sides. "What do you think?" he asked softly. "Sometimes I find myself in unholy positions which come with my rank. Do I make a deal if I can get what I believe best for my President and my God? Or do I act honestly, piously, protecting my own soul before that of my President and his people?"

He realised he had already taken the first step by protecting Widodo, at least temporarily, in the belief that he could be useful to him. He thought of his daughters, especially the kindness of his youngest. She would tell him to be true to himself, not devious for the State. But she was young and idealistic, something which he no longer had the privilege to enjoy. His decisions had immediate consequences.

He turned and looked at the bookcase behind his desk. It contained his most treasured books, including a gold leafed copy of the Koran given to him by one of Indonesia's greatest Islamic scholars, a man who had long since died but whose influence he held close to him. He pulled it from the bookcase and opened it to the title page. Opposite the first print, the scholar had written *"Bambang, a true friend and servant of our prophet. A man of trust."* Could that still be said of him today?

He looked out over Jakarta from this vantage point and saw a jumble of colour and noise, new and old, overshadowed by thick thunder clouds rolling in from the Java Sea. This was no longer the land he remembered and had served for so long. The complications were vast, the internal civil unrest, the awful poverty, the crime and violence. Surely, if he could agree to stamp out some of this violence and corruption, freeing tens of thousands of people from fear, with simple measures, then that was a good thing, wasn't it? But he knew already that "simple measures" was a cowardly description of actions that condoned murder and violence. He could see his youngest daughter shaking her head.

Directly below, a limousine was pulling up outside the building with bodyguards surrounding the car. Hardly anyone noticed as the Imam and Hazim entered the building unannounced. On the twelfth floor the security arrangements were far more rigorous with professional military police officers searching their bags and their person. The bodyguards were refused entry.

Bambang's secretary informed him that his two guests were in the waiting area.

"I'll hear what they have to say" he whispered to his wife "before deciding how to play this. Stay close."

Hazim was dressed in a dark suit, keeping a respectful distance behind Imam Bakti as they entered the office of the Coordinating Minister for Politics and Security. They were greeted by Bambang who then led them to the four black leather sofas in the centre of the room. They each took a sofa, a gesture significant to any bystander, demonstrating their own inflated views of themselves. This was a meeting of men who were used to consequences and adept at manoeuvring situations to their own advantage. It was difficult to see how they could agree a mutual course of action.

"Welcome, gentlemen" offered Bambang.

"Minister" replied the Imam "it is a great honour to be welcome in your government office. Dialogue is free and often eludes great men. But with your foresight and leadership we may find we are closer than we all think."

Hazim smiled, aware that it would be best if he played a guiding, but more silent role.

221

"We almost certainly have more in common than not" reassured Bambang. Coffee arrived and was placed in front of him on the carved teak coffee table, for him to serve. "May I offer you coffee, sir?" he asked the Imam.

"Water, please."

Bambang smiled, ordered a glass of water, pouring two coffees for himself and Hazim.

"I would like to suggest that we view this as a private meeting and our discussion is kept between the three of us" Bambang stated as the water was brought into the room by his secretary. They were both nodding in agreement.

"I am deeply disturbed by the recent disappearance of an English tourist in Tanjung Puting National Park in Central Kalimantan." Bambang had decided to get his issues out on the table. "This incident has attracted the media from all over the world, especially from the UK and is a great embarrassment to our President and this country."

The Imam shifted in his seat and murmured agreement.

"I have ordered the Minister of Forestry to launch a full scale search in the Park and to seek out illegal camps and sawmills. The area has been run as a private fiefdom profiting on illegal timber for too long." Bambang stared uncompromisingly at Hazim who, to his surprise, was nodding.

"The people have been robbed" added the Imam helpfully.

Bambang glanced over at the photo of his wife which was facing him on his desk. She seemed noncommittal.

"Mr Aziz" Bambang addressed Hazim directly. "Your father has been running a timber mafia in Indonesia for too long and I need to know that he will back off. These two Vietnamese ships are evidence of the scale of the theft and you must know that you will never get that cargo returned. Already Widodo has tried, on your father's behalf, to bribe the armed forces. It has gone too far."

It was now Hazim's turn to surprise. "Minister" he started, "I understand your predicament. You must understand that I do not represent my father today in this private meeting." Imam Bakti smiled in agreement.

"Minister" butted in the Imam. "It is crucial that we act as responsible stewards of God's gifts. The destruction of the forest in Central Kalimantan must end. We are in agreement. But I doubt if Hazim's father would agree."

"What can be done about that?" asked Bambang before he had thought through the consequences of such a question.

"This meeting gives me great warmth" said the Imam. "You understand we have different views of the world but we have common needs. You are a religious man, Minister, I know that. I feel much more secure in the knowledge that you welcome dialogue. Hazim is my student and I am sure that between us we can ensure the forest in Borneo sings aloud in bountiful joy."

"That is all I ask" replied Bambang, increasingly concerned by the complete agreement in the room. "Let us do our work to support the people of Borneo. I would be most grateful and, I'm sure, so would our President. Your fight is not with Indonesia and its people and I ask that we may be left to find our way, like children growing into adults, taking their first steps into a perilous but exciting world."

"Yes, yes" dismissed the Imam. "Fine words. I only seek peace. My house is watched, my life is under constant scrutiny. I have no quarrel with you or Indonesia. You should have no quarrel with me."

It was clear to everyone in the room that a deal had been struck. Bambang would get the intelligence services to withdraw their surveillance of the Imam and he would, in return, orchestrate Adbullah Aziz's withdrawal from Central Kalimantan.

"And what of the English tourist?" asked Bambang, feeling he was on a roll.

"Let's hope he lives" replied Imam Bakti softly. "But I believe that is in God's hands, not ours." He stood to leave, thanking Bambang for his hospitality and dialogue. Hazim stood and followed like a good student.

When they had gone, Bambang Santoso looked out of his window and minutes later, watched these two vipers get into their limousine below, surrounded by bodyguards, and pull out into the Jakarta traffic. He walked over to his desk, sat back in his leather chair, leaned forward and picked up the photo of his wife. Something was wrong. It was too easy.

He could sense his wife shaking her head emphatically.

CHAPTER THIRTY SIX
Jakarta

It had been months since Abdullah Aziz stepped on Indonesian soil, but that, he thought, was the problem. He had left his timber interests in the hands of his son, Hazim, trusting him to act intelligently. The growth in the business in the last year had pleased him, but now he could see the chinks in the strategy. Hazim had upset too many people, used his power indiscriminately and, although it hurt his father to recognise it, played out his personal, violent fantasies, in the name of business.

He had not told his wife he was going to Jakarta, but that he would be home late because of meetings. Fortunately, she was preoccupied with next week's charity reception she was organising with the American Ambassador's wife and asked no questions.

He bought his own first class ticket at Singapore's Changi airport, flown on a commercial Singapore Airlines flight and arrived at Jakarta's Soekarno-Hatta International airport in time to meet his lawyer for lunch. He made his own way through the airport, booked a limousine at the "Bluebird" desk in arrivals and was driven to the Hilton International Hotel, surrounded by gardens, where he kept a suite. It was mid-day. None of his employees or family knew he had left Singapore; his business did not concern them.

*

Bambang Santoso felt troubled all morning. He attended a cabinet meeting and gave the latest report on the logging crackdown in Borneo. Minister Probowo was overseeing the operation personally and was unable to attend. A local newspaper report that morning claimed a tourist had seen a crocodile with bits of a shirt in its mouth. He had been in politics for years, but this was the first time he felt completely exasperated and increasingly depressed. At cabinet he challenged the Chief of Police over the Vietnamese ships only to be shouted at by the Minister of Maritime Affairs. He then challenged the Minister for De-Centralisation over the corruption in Central Kalimantan and was warned that the fate of the tourist was irrelevant. Were these really the best people Indonesia could come up with? The interests of each faction were well known, but he had clearly stirred up a hornet's nest.

As he was leaving the meeting, he was approached by a senior member of his party, who asked him to join him for coffee, before lunch-time prayers.

"Bambang, we've known each other for years" he said obviously. "I breakfasted with our party chairman, this morning. He is very worried by the assumption of guilt being thrown at Abdullah Aziz by the Minister of Forestry."

"Oh, is he?" Bambang replied angrily. "And is that because the party finances have been bolstered by stealing from Borneo and murdering tourists?"

His uncompromising response shocked his colleague. "Be careful Bambang" were his parting words.

He was not surprised by the warning, only by the particular colleague who delivered it. It was obvious to him that Aziz would fight back and call in his favours. At the moment the best protection he and Probo would gain was from the publicity. If the Borneo operation could be considered successful it would be very difficult for anyone else to damage him – at least, immediately. But as he knew, in Indonesia it was not always wise to believe a threat had passed. He had lost a few friends himself in suspicious car accidents, sometimes two years after they had poked their heads into areas best left alone.

More troubling was the deal he had wrapped up with Imam Bakti and Aziz's awful son. He had thought about it all night. If he took the outcome at face value, he could only imagine that Aziz and his son were fighting and it suited the son to get his father out of the business. But the Imam's involvement suggested a larger scheme, with consequences he really did not want to countenance. Had he, as a senior Government Minister, given the go-ahead to some kind of assassination?

*

226

The teak walls that shielded Abdullah Aziz's table from the other five star diners at the hotel gave him the privacy this trip required. His lawyer had already advised him on his next course of legal action regarding the newspaper accusations being thrown at him. But more important, he had also lined up a series of afternoon meetings, all to be held in this private corner of one of the oldest luxury hotels in Jakarta, conveniently situated next to the Parliament buildings. At least his political "friends" would not have too far to travel.

"*Pak* Aziz, how lovely to see you in Jakarta again" lied all his paid-off political contacts. The most senior, chair of the ruling party, had personally received twenty thousand dollars a month for two years and secured hundreds of thousands of dollars in donations to his party. Each payment had been recorded by Aziz, a fact that there was no need to explain to his beneficiary.

"It's Probowo, he's the problem" the seasoned politician offered. "Although Probowo couldn't do anything without Santoso" he stated unhelpfully.

"If he's the problem, then why haven't you dealt with him?" asked Aziz perfectly reasonably. These politicians were the trickiest and biggest thieves.

"I have made sure Santoso knows he's out of line on this one."

"Out of line?" fumed Aziz. "I don't care if you have to cut his fucking throat. You have twenty four hours to get him off my back. I want the cargo from those ships released within forty eight hours. And, just in case you think life goes on merrily without consequences, I want your government to issue a statement completely denying any investigation into my family and companies." He stared at his adversary, leaving no doubt as to the sincerity of his words.

"It may be very complicated" he dared respond. "The President is behind Probowo's mission."

Aziz leaned forward in a threatening manner. "Then kill the fucking President" he whispered conspiratorially. "If it all sounds a little distasteful to your delicate nature, then return all my money today and cut your own throat tomorrow."

The other meetings went no better. Aziz realised that, despite being a generous benefactor to countless individuals in Jakarta, these weasels were unprepared to use their power if it was at any personal risk. What a total waste of fucking money! The most depressing meeting had been with Widodo, who fell onto his knees and begged Aziz to get his faggot son released from prison. "Use some of the money I've given you for years to have him put down humanely" he had cruelly suggested.

By the end of the afternoon he welcomed Imam Bakti to his table, a last resort.

"My good Imam" Aziz spat, unable to hide his fury at the lack of support he felt in this godless city. "The time has come for me to ask directly for your urgent support."

The Imam smiled, uttered reassuring words, but failed to convince that he understood the gravity of the situation facing Aziz's empire.

"I need to see Probowo dead, tomorrow. I need everyone to realise they can't fuck with me. Can you do it?" asked Aziz bluntly.

"The Minister of Forestry may collapse if it is God's will" had been his pompous response. *Did this mean he would do it?* "Abdullah, you have been very generous to God's work and I'm sure you rank highly in God's thoughts. But the latest revelations and the growing anger against you, gives everyone time to ponder on your theft of God's gifts to the people of Borneo."

*

Bambang Santoso, after evening prayers, sat in his study at home and contemplated his future. This entire episode raised so many unsavoury issues he was increasingly unsure whether he could continue in this government. His love for his wife and daughters was clashing directly with his duty. He would have liked to talk with the President, but knew that his involvement in this mess was, to some degree, because of him. He now realised how naïve he had been at that Conference in Bali just over a week ago. Was it really only a week?

Probo called from Pangkalan Bun where he was staying in the local Governor's home surrounded by an army mobile brigade. He sounded scared. Over the last week Bambang had grown to see Probo as a brave and honest man, in fact if he thought about it right now, which he did, he was one of his closest, perhaps only, ally.

"It's extraordinary here" Probo had explained. "The national police have locked the local police in the police station, the navy have blocked the seaward escape, and thousands of local citizens have been offering our people rice and God's speed."

"You sound scared" observed Bambang.

"The local Governor has his own militia, and they are on the loose. He's being very obstructive. I'm staying in his home and expect to be visited by an assassin at any moment. It's scary, although I have the mobile brigade to protect me."

"Any sign of the English tourist?" asked Bambang thoughtfully. He was ashamed that an innocent tourist was caught up in such a mess.

"Not yet. We've flown over part of the Park, but because of tree cover I think we'll have to rely on the navy's inflatables. The scale of the timber theft is impossible to explain. The illegal sawmills are gigantic, processing timber to be loaded onto barges and out of the country. It is too early to guess the loss to the local people and the nation."

Bambang listened intently and when the call was finished, sat alone for over an hour. His daughter came in to see if he was alright. She gave him a very big hug which brought a tear to his eye, although he was careful to wipe it away before she had noticed.

*

Abdullah Aziz's last meeting of the day was held in the limousine on the way back to the airport before returning to Singapore. His lawyer had been summoned back for an emergency planning session. The day had gone far worse than Aziz could ever have imagined. He had not realised how out of touch he had become, or how successful his opponents had been at frightening his contacts. It was clear that some heads had to roll. His lawyer was to copy the ledgers used to pay all the people he had met today and send a copy to each of them. They would understand.

He also needed to see Wahid. At least he could be relied on.

When you paid him well, someone always died.

CHAPTER THIRTY SEVEN
Borneo

The only sound was the roar of the outboards on the three Zodiac inflatables as a naval team sped up the Sekonyer River. Pauline, on the last, felt as if she had been ripped from her mother's womb and battered in an uncompromising land. Only days earlier she had been trying to pull her life together in South London, without Matt. Now she was noisily racing upriver in Borneo with men in uniforms, searching for his corpse. Being in the last, their boat was hammered by the wake of the two ahead, a harder ride than she would have thought possible on water.

Unknown to Pauline, as the trees passed by on both banks of the river, she was being watched by proboscis monkeys, gharials and orang-utans. But the speed and noise, in which she was enveloped, passed them by without the slow wisdom of a guide like Koto. Their assault on the forest resembled that of the loggers' paymasters visiting the illegal camps, ensuring a return from the rain, wild animals and mosquitoes, by sunset.

She had filed her first story to her editor last night, who had surprised her, by calling back within ten minutes. He was very pleased. *"Girlfriend in tragic split wants jungle boy back."* She decided that if she was going to go through with this, she might as well make something out of it. Today's piece would, most likely, be something along the lines of *"Heartache in search for jungle boy."* She was accompanied by Troy, an Australian freelance photographer hired by the *Greater London Gazette*, on a day fee. This was an international scoop and the paper wanted to keep it under their control. Troy was in the second Zodiac rolling off shots of Pauline on her hopeless search. They had to keep a glimmer of hope in the story or it would die too quickly. Tomorrow she needed a clue to his whereabouts, or demise.

Other journalists had arrived at the *Sungai Arut Hotel*, where she was staying. The Minister had dropped her off last night and driven off with an army convoy. He had impressed her on the flight, with his openness and kindness. She had heard about the local timber baron Abdullah Aziz and his control over the area. This was why, he had explained, they had brought police, army and naval personnel with them from Jakarta. The local authorities were up to their necks in all local crime.

The naval officer in the first Zodiac ordered them to tie up at the orang-utan orphanage at Tanjung Harapan, where Rita had told her they had last seen Matt. She had seen the pictures of baby orang-utans, taken by Matt days earlier, now she was confronted with the babies hanging in a tree. Troy shot a load of cute photos of the babies. He asked the vet if Pauline could hold one of them, and after exchanging glances with the naval officer, she agreed.

A picture of Pauline holding a baby orang-utan against her chest would appear on the front page of newspapers from Indonesia to China, Japan, Argentina, Cuba, the USA and every European country. Masaii warriors would see it in Kenya, Saudi Princes in Riyadh. The modern media was immediate and truly world-wide. The newspaper group owning the *Greater London Gazette* and paying for Pauline and Troy had already hit the jackpot.

The picture, with Pauline's copy, would be sent out from Pangkalan Bun by email through a laptop, with a mobile phone internet connection, to London. With the time difference between Indonesia and London, there was plenty of time for the editor to work on the copy and make the syndication deals.

Realising her story would now focus on the loss of her lover, the loss of the chance to be a mother, to accompany the photos, Pauline decided it would be best to get back to Pangkalan Bun immediately and work on the copy. This was going to be difficult. She knew this naval team was there to help her file her stories, not find Matt. An aerial and water search was being carried out which had a better chance than her unusually handsome and photogenic, rugged naval team. She knew she was being used as part of a government public relations drive, just as they understood they were being used by the media. Mutual. At least her journalistic antennae were alert and functioning well!

*

Probo found the naval support helpful and cooperative in the search and rescue mission. But the army was less accommodating with the closure of sawmills. The two star General commanding the units had a long standing relationship with Borneo, having been stationed in East Kalimantan for seven years. Probo realised that any commanding officer in an area where timber was the biggest commodity, would already have a relationship with Aziz or one of his associates. So far, the army, with four hundred men, had only visited two sawmills owned by Koreans. To say they were dragging their feet would have been a huge understatement. Nonetheless, the naval blockade was preventing any timber leaving the area by sea.

The lack of cooperation from the General gave Probo little reason to feel secure. The local Governor had refused to meet with him even though he was staying in the VIP suite of the Governor's official residence. The Governor's militia was rumoured to be nearby, waiting for a moment to strike. The mobile army unit protecting him was under the command of the uncooperative General, although Probo doubted that he would dare let anything serious happen to a Government Minister. Then he remembered that, only last year, an ambassador from a European country had been shot at while bird-watching in the national park.

"I've asked the Admiral to get a small detachment to you within the hour" explained Bambang Santoso in one of his regular conversations with Probo. "I will feel happier if I know you are secure. Meanwhile I'm meeting with the Minister of Defence later today. I'll see what can be done about the General."

It was a great boost to know that the Coordinating Minister for Politics and Security was on his side. Probo had warmed to Bambang in a way that surprised him. He guessed it was because he trusted him and they shared knowledge of what they were up against.

His official car, with military police outriders, drove into Pangkalan Bun around midday, at about the same time that Pauline, having been photographed with the baby orang-utan, decided to get back to her hotel. He had been asked to attend a briefing at the police station by the national police commander. There had been some trouble with the journalists that had arrived in this backwater town.

The Minister of Forestry stepped from his car in front of the picket fence where less than two weeks ago a limb had been

232

thrown from a passing green Pajero. That same night he had received the macabre voicemail message announcing the murder of Murkha, the gentle Dayak schoolteacher who had decided to stand up against Aziz. These thoughts clouded his senses as he opened the white gate, stepping into a starkly inhospitable office, designed to intimidate.

"Minister" a national police officer stated, "please come through here with me."

They walked through two sparsely kitted out offices with local policemen sitting at their desks, staring at Probo as if he had come to reprimand them. Probo stopped, looked around, and decided these men needed to be told who was boss.

"Stand to attention" he ordered. The sorry group of local officers shuffled to their feet, more out of shock than respect. Fans turned on the ceiling, mocking the absence of any other energy in the room. Probo barked "I could have you imprisoned for gross insolence at the very least. Right now!" he shouted at them with more confidence than he actually felt. "I represent the President in my capacity as a Government Minister, yet you don't even stand when I enter the room."

They were standing to attention. "I want each of you to write down all your personal bank account numbers, including any abroad. I want you to swear and sign that you are telling the truth." The men were looking around the room at each other in disbelief. "Then I will send these details, today, to Jakarta to be processed by law through the anti-corruption commission. Anyone found receiving money as bribes or concealing information will be prosecuted. Maybe next time you will respect a Government Minister as more important than a local timber baron."

There was utter silence, only broken by the entrance of the national police commander sent to over-ride the local police. "Welcome Minister" he said politely. "I see you've met our local representatives." Probo followed him into a private room.

The commander outlined the problems he faced with the totally corrupt local police. "They're the private force of Abdullah Aziz" he remarked, without any real surprise. "The journalists that have arrived are having some serious problems with thugs hired by

Aziz's company. We've got more violence than I think we can handle."

"You need more officers?" asked Probo.

"Yes. But I think we're trying to do too much at the same time. This entire area is at risk of exploding. We all remember the Dayak beheadings a few years ago."

The rampage by Dayaks had caused over four hundred deaths and the government had neither anticipated it, nor known how to stop it. Only Dayak leaders had been able to do that.

"There has been one high profile assassination of the Dayak school teacher. Now a Dayak guide has disappeared with his English client. There is another Dayak man who, although badly injured, survived an attack by one of Aziz's thugs and his son. But his daughters were abducted and raped. He is the focus of renewed Dayak anger."

Probo felt out of his depth. He had always known that "forestry" involved crime and social issues, but to be the man dealing with police and army mutiny and, now, indigenous uprising, left him feeling inadequate.

"Thank you commander. I respect what you say" he said. "I will convey your concerns to Jakarta and come back to you later today."

He returned to his car and called Bambang immediately. After a difficult conversation where he suspected Bambang Santoso also felt inadequate, he called Debi. He needed to talk.

*

As soon as Pauline was back in Pangkalan Bun, within mobile phone reception, she received an SMS from Rita. *"Arrive today. Will call."* Before she had put her phone back in her bag, it rang. It was Rita.

"Sam's here with me" she explained. "We've come to ensure the story gets out." They arranged to meet for dinner.

The baby, its mouth cracking from the heat, pushed its tiny, five finger hand into my hair. It was an orphan, its family life destroyed by men with chainsaws. Its dark eyes stared into mine; pleading for something I wasn't sure I could offer.

This jungle is deeper than the trees that line the rivers, on which I've been travelling all day, looking for my Matt. My life, as if echoing the tiny pleas of a baby orang-utan, may have been destroyed by the same men with chainsaws. All around me in this awful town in Borneo, people tell me that Abdullah Aziz, the timber baron, runs this part of the world. If Matt is alive it is because Aziz says he can be. If he's dead …"

Today I've seen the harsh cruelty of the jungle, but I've also witnessed its beauty. If Matt is still out there I know he'll be living off its beauty, his generous heart mining the last rays of hope."

Pauline stopped typing on her laptop keyboard. She felt she was going too far. What if Matt was still alive? These words would be out there. Today, she really felt there was no chance he was still alive; the forest was too wild, too deep, and too dangerous. She tried to imagine herself, naked in the forest, left to survive. No chance. But this was her moment to enjoy international recognition in a profession that was more cut-throat than television phone-ins.

She stared at the keyboard and watched as her fingers tapped out her next sentence: *"The orang-utan reminded me of the baby Matt and I may never have."* There. She had said it. She had sold her soul.

There was a knock on her door. It was Troy asking whether the copy was ready. Together with five hundred words of background, Pauline thought it would be best to get this out as soon as possible. As Troy entered her room, for the first time she noticed his blond surfer's hair and build. *"Best not shag the photographer while searching for your long lost love in front of the international media"* she thought, smiling at Troy. God she was such a mess!

Dinner was a rowdy affair with fourteen journalists demanding different food from three young girls masquerading as waitresses. The frustration building in the fluorescent-lit basement dining area could have been enough to cause an international incident, if they had not all been so tired. Pauline was in a unique position, being given every support by the government and, being part of the story. The others, with angry editors on the end of the phone, were trying to find different angles or get to Pauline. So far she had cold shouldered them all on strict orders from her own editor. If you wanted her story, you bought it from her paper.

235

Rita and Sam gave interviews to some of the other journalists and pointed them in the direction of Abdullah Aziz. But most of the time they stayed with Pauline and her photographer, Troy.

"Tomorrow, we'll introduce you to the skipper of the boat they were kidnapped from. You can get some pictures on board the boat, the *Bukit Tiga*" offered Sam. We're going to introduce him to other journalists as well, that's our job, but you'll get the pictures of you on the boat first."

"How are you holding up?" enquired Rita, perceptively recognising that Pauline was even less stable than she had been in Jakarta.

*

In a small wooden shack, built over a pond just outside Pangkalan Bun, a proud Dayak father addressed a group of thirteen Dayak men. Together, they recounted the death of Murkha, the green Pajero and the religious dress of the men armed by Aziz. They talked about Koto, a popular Dayak, who had been educated with Murkha and helped tourists understand something about the Dayak way. But most of all they talked about Hazim Aziz and the tall man who had raped his two daughters. He described every part of the stranger's features and clothes to the men seated on his floor. They shared their knowledge of outsiders in their own areas, covering most of Central and part of South Kalimantan. Between them they built a picture of what had been happening to their Dayak brothers and sisters.

And between them they had a plan.

*

Probo was surprised to receive a call from Debi the next morning. "I'm in town" she said without any dramatic emphasis.

"This town?" replied Probo with utter surprise.

"I couldn't leave an old friend all on his own" she said. He was silent. "Well, are you going to tell these nice men that I'm not an assassin or leave me in my hot, smelly taxi? Outside."

236

He was excited and concerned. His work here was on behalf of his country and his President, which he understood was a different path to that of his activist friend. But he felt so inadequate that, even her voice, made him better. Once inside, Debi explained that Rita and Sam were also in town, staying at Rita's sister's house who was still in Jakarta. They were trying to nudge the press pack to question Aziz's power.

"But what about you?" asked Debi. "You sounded beaten on the phone."

He explained the problems that were brewing. Already, that morning, he had been told by the national police commander that a hired gang of mill workers was on its way to the hotel where the international media were staying.

"That'll give them great photos!" reasoned Debi.

"As long as no one gets hurt. We've got one missing tourist already" replied Probo "and after yesterday's reports and our park fly-over, I don't hold out much chance for him and his guide."

Debi sat at the table in the dining area of the VIP suite, picking at some watermelon left over from breakfast. She was surprised how comfortable she felt with her old friend, in his private quarters. She was disturbed at the tone in his voice yesterday, but after thinking about the responsibilities he was carrying, realised it was naïve to think that anyone could juggle the complicated political, legal and social issues, without the stress. Probo was an honest man, and he wanted to do his best. She picked up another piece of the pink fruit, playfully resting it on her tongue.

Relaxing with Debi, Probo realised it was a huge relief to know that he had a friend to confide in at this difficult time. The Coordinating Minister had insisted that Operation Johnson continued despite the concerns of the national police commander on the ground. "This is an opportunity" he had told Probo. Although he agreed, Probo was facing the reality of trying to work in the hornet's nest. He knew that most of the residents of the area despised Aziz and his henchmen, but the financial resources at Aziz's disposal far outreached the budget for this operation. So entrenched was his power in this area.

He looked at Debi, his old friend flying out to support him. He could drop all ministerial pretences with her – they would not work anyway! But, as he turned to look at her sitting at the table, it was with some alarm that he noticed the way she played with the watermelon on her tongue.

"I've been thinking about the oil palm plantation" he stated with a certainty that killed any other moment more effectively than spraying mosquitoes with neat deet. "When we've finished our search I intend to drop in and see what's going on with all that telecommunications equipment on the border of the park."

"Interesting you should be thinking of that" mused Debi. "I spoke to my friends in the human rights movement. They would agree that thousands of trained militia with a vision do not just disappear. They seem to think that many of them have been hired out for money, as a means to increase the funds available to promote their vision of an Islamic state. I would make sure you have some of your men in uniform with you if you plan to drop in on that plantation."

*

The *Bukit Tiga* was performing its racket for Pauline at the same jetty in Kumai that it had for Matt. Skipper welcomed her on board, and through Sam as interpreter, explained that Matt had been a wonderful client. He apologised for "losing him" and promised it was the first time such an incident had happened under his command. Matey watched from below, unable to talk about the kidnap. His face was badly bruised from the resistance he had put up when *Bukit* had been forced to leave Koto and Matt in the water on the Sekonyer *Kanan*. Skipper had pleaded him to stop fighting, but his youthful vigour had overridden his boss's orders. He hadn't spoken to Skipper since.

Skipper described the men that had forced him, at gunpoint, to leave his passengers in the water and the men in Arab headdresses that had taken the two swimmers. On a map, he described the exact position of *Bukit* that last night. After Troy took some photos of Pauline on the upper deck of the *klotok*, Sam suggested they join the naval team for another trip up the river, this time to the place where Matt was last seen alive. Rita stayed behind to work with other journalists on their stories.

The small flotilla of Zodiacs wound its way past the nipa palms, the Tanjung Harapan veterinary station and up the Sekonyer River, where they failed to notice the hornbills that flew over, to inform them that they had entered the forest. At the right fork in the river, Pauline could not understand what Sam, the kind young man in a blue baseball cap, was saying over the noise of the outboards. His explanation of the black water was lost.

They slowed and stopped at Camp Leakey. Pauline was enthralled by the "wild" orang-utans that came to greet her. Troy made certain he photographed her with the same mother, Julia, and her baby, that Matt had photographed on the rolls of film available through Sam and Rita. It was clear to him that at the weekend, news magazines would be crying out for full colour spreads of this touching, tragic story. His digital Nikon was in the right place, with the right person, at the right time. He could make his name off this.

They talked to the ranger who had met Matt before they had moved upriver for the night. A few minutes later, their speedy Zodiacs arrived at the jetty where Matt and Koto had spent their last night on *Bukit Tiga*.

Pauline sat in the inflatable dinghy, not wanting to get out. "What's the point?" she asked. He's not here. I know he's not here, I would feel if he was." That was a good quote for the story. She scribbled it down in her notebook.

"This is where they swam and were kidnapped by the men in Arab headdresses" explained Sam helpfully, despite being dismayed by Pauline's disinterest in the forest. "The speedboat headed upriver with them on board" he added pointing up the river.

"I want to go further upriver" demanded Pauline with petulance only excusable to a woman in grief.

Sam exchanged glances with the naval commander.

The three Zodiacs untied, pushing off from the jetty with Pauline in the last, Troy in the second, and the commander in the leading inflatable. They moved slowly as the river narrowed, the commander pointing out floating branches and weed that could catch in the outboard propellers. They edged forward, and as they slowly progressed, Pauline, for the first time, felt the forest. It was hot, wet and frightening. She would rather walk naked down Brixton High Street than take a single step into the unknown world of orang-utans and, she thought, snakes.

They travelled long enough for Pauline to feel she had left behind everything she understood, a sense of deep jungle; somewhere she had no reason to be. As the river widened into a small lake, they slowed and stopped. Troy eagerly pointed his camera at the opposite bank: a huge crocodile was lying on the mud.

"Oh my god!" exclaimed Pauline, with a slight shriek in her voice. Troy immediately turned his camera on her reaction. "You don't think?" she added without finishing. Troy's motor drive captured her realisation.

"It's always possible their bodies were fed to the crocodiles" replied Sam, he thought helpfully.

"Oh my god!" Pauline burst into tears, the entire river trip not only bashing her body around, but bringing unrecognised thoughts to the surface. "He's dead, isn't he?" she whispered. The motor drive intrusively fired five shots every second.

Sam looked at Pauline, paused and lowered his gaze. "I think so" he said quietly. "Koto too. But let's not give up; we can go a little further upriver before we have to turn back today."

The commander nodded in agreement, much more comfortable with the sound of the three outboards than the tears of the missing tourist's girlfriend. The Zodiacs spluttered, moving forward through the lake. As they passed the crocodile, it slipped into the water. Sam noticed that Pauline was looking in the other direction and decided not to point out the giant reptile's current trajectory.

The lake narrowed and they were on a small river again. Ahead, the commander could see a tree fallen over the river from which two large birds flew as the inflatable dinghies approached. They slowed and he signalled for everyone to lower their heads. The engines were killed, the propellers pulled out of the water to avoid the vegetation. With their forward momentum they floated silently under the tree.

Pauline was shaking her head, in a physically and emotionally uncomfortable world of her own. "It's a waste of time. They're not here" she said to no one in particular. "I feel so alone." Tears added to the sweat already dripping down her cheeks.

Sam ignored Pauline. He was very alert. He could not say why, but something had suddenly given him hope. It may have been the large birds, hornbills, two of them together on the fallen tree. But it was more than that. He removed his baseball cap and looked around in the silence. Something larger than he had ever imagined was unfolding and in his small way he knew he was a part of it. He breathed in deeply, expanding his chest, absorbing the damp heat of the day. The energy he felt in this place was different. Something was happening, something had been released, was unstoppable now. Everything was changing whether Koto and Matt were alive or not.

His emotions were charged from the last few romantic days with Rita and the horror of Murkha's demise. An image of the bare-chested, elderly Dayak man he had met near Murkha's house, just after his death, came to him. As he stared at the fallen tree he could see him sitting on the trunk, naked, drying his cheap blue trousers on a branch. The expression on his face was mischievous but unmistakably echoing his sentiment days earlier. "I told you so. Don't forget, please thank your friend for me."

Sam smiled gently. "I promise" he muttered as he looked around, scouring the forest for any sign of Koto and Matt.

The commander, uncomfortable with Pauline's tears, ordered his men to start up the engines on the three Zodiacs, blanking out any other sound.

The dinghies turned and drifted under the fallen tree before speeding up, heading back to the other world.

CHAPTER THIRTY EIGHT
Borneo

It seemed extraordinary how quickly they had set up home. Food was available within a few hundred metres of the camp, closer Matt mused than Tesco had been from his flat in Brixton. Admittedly, the choice was limited to fruit, some green leaves, an unnamed root vegetable and fresh fish. Koto had hinted at wild boar, but the hunting method had still not become clear.

On the second morning, Koto was up first. In the early light he crept down to the river and sat in the mud on the bank watching the flow of the water. A gibbon whooped its warning call; he kept completely still, waiting to see what the fuss was about. The morning forest odours created an inclusive sense of safety, but Koto knew the forest may be his friend, but it was not his protector.

On the opposite bank he sensed a movement, without raising his head looked up and for the first time in his life saw the forest's feline celebrity, so often talked about, but so rarely seen alive: a clouded leopard. It had always seemed to Koto that, the only reason he knew this magnificent cat inhabited this forest, was because of dead animals found in cruel traps and skins cut and ripped from their corpses, sold illegally in dirty, urban markets by unshaven men with unhappy eyes.

But here, surrounded by the sounds and smells of first light, he watched her, alive, breathing, slink down towards the water's edge to furtively drink. It was so quiet he could hear her lapping at the water; see her stopping and looking around before he could hear her lapping again. Her face, symmetrical patterns of dark grey and white, slightly orange in the early light, seemed too wonderful to be hidden. When she turned to the side, her fur contrasted with such beauty, that he remembered his father explaining that her patterns mimicked the python that shared, at its own risk, the trees they both lived in. Her long tail could have been a thick snake, but softer and kinder than the skin of a reptile, despite her being a fierce predator, capable of killing macaques, wild boar and deer.

When she stepped back into the undergrowth, her camouflage stripe and blotchy coat caused her to disappear as miraculously as a rabbit from a magician's hat. The gibbon called again, but it was obvious to all living creatures within hearing distance, that the moment had passed. The visit, although unplanned, had been as if someone very special had called by. Just the sight of her gave the forest a reassurance that it was, perhaps more dangerous, but at least complete.

Koto's sense of awe was compounded by thoughts of his father. *"You have to be a wild man of the forest to see a living clouded leopard"* he had told him. *"It's a privilege offered rarely by our ancestors."*

"Thank you father" Koto spoke aloud.

Matt had organised the camp. The leaf blanket was already drying in the sun, fruit had been peeled and a can of water was on the fire, boiling with aromatic leaves for morning tea. Koto threw fresh fish on the fire, already gutted by the river. Just two days before, neither of them would have believed the ease by which they now fed themselves, although both were aware that the fire would not always be there when both lighters failed to spark, and the petrol had run dry.

"*Selamat pagi*" Matt grinned at Koto.

"Morning" Koto replied quietly without looking at his friend.

They carried on with breakfast in silence, Koto solemnly staring at his food. When Matt had finished, he inspected his heel and his hand. The thorn was already visible in his foot, possibly ready for extraction in a few days, but the swelling was as large as it had been on the first day. His hand appeared a little better. Most worrying were the increasing number of mosquito bites. The concoction made from the root was reducing the inflammation and itching but much of the perception of pain was overridden by the agony in his foot.

The sun had greeted them for the second morning, giving the camp a vaguely mysterious feeling, with primary coloured butterflies flitting from one dry mud bowl to another, as if searching for water. Matt, enjoying the raw pleasure of the sun, beauty and survival, realised, without concern, that Koto had headed back to the river. He knew something was bothering his companion but, his own happiness, made it easier for him to give Koto the space he seemed to need.

Six hours later, he was battling between anger, concern and fear.

243

Not a word from Koto and during the day he suffered a severe headache and discovered their rain water supply was almost gone. He wanted to talk to Koto about these problems, but without any thought for him, Koto had wandered off. Maybe he was injured? Or was Koto angry with him about something? Had he been deserted? Was Koto not what he had first seemed? Kidnapped, survived crocodile attack, primal screaming, the convenience of finding a logging camp. Had he been lured into some game that only Koto and his accomplices could be expected to understand?

But despite some paranoia, his overwhelming emotion was concern. Koto had appeared depressed at breakfast and only uttered one word to him all day.

When he finally appeared, Koto was smiling and carrying four durian fruits. Matt, so relieved to see him, stood and started to run towards him, stopping when he realised how desperate he looked, limping at speed.

"I bring fruit. More fruit!" joked Koto, beaming at his friend, touched by his obvious desperation when he entered the clearing. He dropped the large durians on the ground. "Now, I bet you've never had durian."

Matt was incapable of speech. He was so pleased to see Koto that he was fighting his anger with joy. It showed on his face.

"I apologise for disappearing this morning" Koto said without further explanation. He stared at Matt and gave a reconciliation smile. When there was no response he lowered his gaze and added "I see from your tiny, shrivelled cock, you're angry!"

"You fucker!" screamed Matt, his anger definitely winning over. "There's no water, I've been sick."

"What's wrong?"

"I didn't know where you were. I've had horrible thoughts. Koto, please don't do that again."

"Sorry. I should have phoned." His humour wasn't helping.

"I have a headache."

"And I was washing my hair." Nothing was going to spoil his moment.

They stared at each other, for a little more than a moment, before Matt limped slowly up to Koto, put his arms around him and gave him a huge hug. "I was frightened" he admitted.

244

The four durian fruits lay near the fire, thorny dark green rugby balls slightly cracking. Matt had read about this, uniquely Southeast Asian delicacy, but this was the first time he had seen it. "It doesn't smell too bad" he commented. The guidebooks explained that many establishments such as hotels and restaurants banned durian because of its foul smell. He had seen official red warning signs of the fruit crossed out in public places. This "King of Fruits" was as complex as the repertoire of a celebrity chef, not surprising since it was the result of extraordinary biodiversity, so many species existing in the wild, especially Borneo; these four fruits had fallen from a tree over thirty five metres high.

"We have fish and vegetables for dinner. Then we get drunk with ripened durian" announced Koto. "We will enjoy a wonderful meal together."

Koto's cheerful mood disturbed Matt. He was too happy. He remembered the positive "born again" ranting of one of his closest friends in London who had sounded so good, but was clearly lost. Something had happened today and he wanted to understand what it was.

Koto had also brought leaves, which he told Matt to rub on his skin to repel insects. While his friend prepared the fish, Matt spent half an hour ensuring every part of his body was covered. If this was going to work he wanted to be sure he made the most of it. If it was useless, he wanted to be sure he had tried his best. It was a win-win, or lose-lose. But at least he would know.

Once opened, the smell of durian went some way to explaining the warning posters. The pale yellow flesh gave off an odour resembling a pair of sweaty nylon socks inflated by schoolboy farts. Koto's enthusiasm for the experience pushed Matt's olfactory prejudices aside for a moment, just long enough, to taste the slightly nutty, definitely naughty, caramel pulp.

"I saw a clouded leopard this morning" teased Koto deliberately.

"Wow. Where?"

"Drinking at the river. She helped me identify the good spirits in me."

They picked the last bits off the first durian as Koto cracked open the second.

"Good spirits?"

"Yes" explained Koto. "My father welcomed me to the forest."

Matt felt very warm as he thought how comforting it must be to have your father helping out. "Do you feel more confident?"

"No. But I know my spirit is in balance with the forest."

Matt, a little confused, but eager to understand, added "does that give me a better chance of survival?"

"You are part of my balance" stated Koto simply. "We depend on each other. We are spiritually bonded." He turned to look at his friend. "Don't you feel that?"

The night pushed them closer to the small fire. The third durian was opened to reveal a stronger stench than the first two, indicating it had ripened even further. They shared it out and moved around to sit next to each other on a dry plank they had positioned near the fire.

"I was very scared today" confided Matt. "I started to think you had schemed against me. I didn't know why. I thought you had other people who would use me in some way: maybe as a ransom. I don't know. But I lost it today because I didn't know where you were."

Koto pulled his hair back behind his ears with both hands, looked forward and crunched his face before reaching over to Matt and resting his left hand on his friend's shoulder. "I'm sorry" was all he said. There was a long pause while Matt's heart pumped his blood faster around his body, speeding up the healing process and enlivening his senses.

"Koto" he said "you overwhelm me."

"In my world, I live with my spirits. They control me" Koto responded ignoring Matt's confession. "They are part of my world, not just me. They are my parents and my grandparents. They are the logs I've burned to keep warm and the cows I've fed on. I have no way of separating myself from my world, I am part of it. It gives me energy and creates consequences." He turned his head to look directly into Matt's eyes, just a breath away. "You are part of my world."

Matt could feel the intoxicating chemicals from the durian taking hold as he took a deep breath, as if inhaling Koto. "And you are part of mine."

246

"Of course" added Koto dismissively. Matt was too drunk to recognise the same attributes in his companion, but Koto was on a roll as he cracked open the fourth durian.

"I don't know what is happening out there" said Koto. "But Sam and Rita know what has happened. They are in contact with the government. Murkha has been murdered. You, a foreigner, a *boleh*, are missing. I am missing, Murkha's friend, a Dayak son. The world is not as we last saw it. We are not as we were yesterday."

It was completely dark now. The sounds of the forest had heated up, the invisible animals were shouting out loud. The night had begun, louder than the day. Koto sat back, tightening his embrace of Matt with his left arm and pulling him closer. He took deep breaths, expanding his chest in a slow rhythm, increasing Matt's heartbeat as he felt Koto's warmth. There was a moment when the power of their touch burned, their fiery consent, screamed out across the darkness. At that moment the forest stopped. It lost its noise, its dark confidence; it gave way to Matt and Koto. It accepted their superior equilibrium: momentarily. And at last, they both felt it, in the silence, nagged by the honesty of nature itself.

In the morning it started to rain. They sat on the platform under the shelter and remained dry until a slow drip penetrated the leaves. Most of the day was spent thinking about the rain and the damp. They both wished they had stored fresh leaves and food under a shelter before the rain, inevitably, started. Walking around in light rain was easy and warm, but during the heavy downpours and thunder the raindrops could hurt as they hit naked flesh. For the first time, they spent all day with each other, Matt limping to the river to watch Koto check the fish trap and collect fruit, sheltering under a tree together when the skies opened and deluged the forest.

The next night was very difficult. The rain relentlessly tested their shelter until, at around two in the morning a break in the leaves woke them both with a torrent of water. It was cold and extremely uncomfortable. They shifted over to the edge of the shelter which was still dry and diverted the water from the other side of the platform so it fell on the ground. It was impossible for the two of them to stay dry in such a small space, so without

247

thinking, Koto crawled on top of Matt, lying face to face. Matt closed his arms protectively around his friend. They slept until daybreak, waking in the same position.

"It's still raining" whispered Koto, not sure if Matt was awake.

"Good" Matt replied gently.

"What? Why good?"

"If it was dry you would get up and leave. I'm very happy you are lying on top of me."

Koto giggled, but stopped suddenly.

"What is it?" asked Matt.

"My giggling made me think of my friend Murkha, he had an infectious laugh. Perhaps his spirit has entered me. It is a good spirit." He shifted his position slightly, giggling again, so that his body pressed hard on Matt's.

The rain stopped mid-morning and they took advantage of the dry period to collect five fish from the trap and store extra fruit and leaves under a small shelter near their own. After two hours they repaired the roof of their shelter, storing additional leaves alongside their leaf blanket.

"I think this thorn might come out tomorrow" commented Matt reluctantly. He knew that once he was fit, they would have to move out, which would be fraught with difficulty. He did not want to break the relationship that had developed with Koto.

Suddenly, they both stopped and stared in the direction of the river.

"Can you hear that?" asked Koto.

Moving cautiously towards the river, they saw a speedboat stop at the fallen tree. Three men were talking, but it was impossible to understand what they were saying with the outboard motor running.

They stayed hidden less than ten metres from the intruders, partly camouflaged by the mud on their bodies.

The speedboat killed its engine and for a couple of minutes there was only the sound of the forest. Then one of the passengers spoke in Indonesian. Matt looked as if he was about to call out. Koto shook his head, reached out and put his hand against Matt's chest as if holding him back. A few moments later the engine was fired up and the speedboat headed back in the direction of Kumai.

"They were looking for us" explained Koto. "More accurately, they were checking that we were dead."

Later in the day a helicopter could be heard passing over the river, but they remained hidden in the trees near their camp and only lit a fire after dark, fearful that the smoke would identify their presence.

It rained again most of the night, but the shelter remained dry. The next morning their food had been raided by macaques. Hungry, Koto led Matt across the river by the fallen tree, past the point where he had seen the clouded leopard and away from the river towards a tall durian tree. They shared some of the fruit.

"Do you see that track? Come with me and I'll show you what I was doing all day. The day you got frightened."

They moved cautiously around trees, keeping sight of an animal track that clearly passed through undergrowth, under fallen trees, and through swamp. Koto crouched, placing each foot deliberately in front of the other, watching for twigs that would crack, progressing slowly but smoothly. Matt limped less confidently, hearing every branch break as he accidentally trod on it, waiting to be scowled at by Koto. But every now and again, Koto would reach back and grab Matt's hand to gently guide him forward. Without warning, he stopped, turned to look at Matt, raising his right forefinger to his lips and crouched. Matt slunk down beside his hunter friend. They stayed in that position for two or three minutes, suddenly aware of more engine noise from the river. It sounded like a number of outboards and they were getting closer.

A pair of hornbills took flight, passing directly overhead at the same time as a commotion ahead in the undergrowth, accompanied by frantic squealing. The engines revved and were shut off. Koto and Matt crouched in the forest at least one hundred metres from the river, their senses aching to decipher the jumble of sound. A few moments later a woman's voice drifted through the heat, sounding despondent and final, but her exact words were impossible to understand. Koto sniffed the air like a hound, looking at Matt's reaction to the visitors. Unlike yesterday, Matt kept perfectly still, held Koto's hand tightly, crouching quietly.

They looked at each other confused, each of them unwilling to let go of the possibility that they might be rescued. Koto's eyes widened as he cocked his head to listen more intently. Matt shivered.

Before they were able to react, the engines started up and the three small boats noisily headed back the way they had come, towards Kumai.

"I'm glad they've gone" whispered Matt.

"I heard a woman" replied Koto shaking his head. "And I felt something very big, very disturbing. We must get that thorn out of your foot and move on as soon as we can. I think it is best the world believes we are dead."

"What was that noise ahead?"

"Wild pigs."

They stood and moved over towards the undergrowth from where the squealing sounds had come, but Koto stopped and started to pick up sticks from the ground. Matt could see a pit in front of him with something inside it. He peered over Koto's shoulder as he lifted the body of a tiny piglet that had been skewered by a sharpened stick.

"It's a pit trap. I dug it the other day. This baby pig fell through the camouflaged pit and died on this stake. Its mother and family must have been hanging around." As Koto lifted the piglet to show it to Matt, blood poured from the corpse over his chest and dark red drops fell to the ground, spattering his legs and crotch. Unperturbed, Koto lifted the tiny body to his face and kissed the piglet's head marking his nose with more blood. "Thank you."

Matt was impressed. By now he recognised the respect required in this world, Koto's world. For the first time he wondered if it might be his world too; at least, as long as he was with Koto. He looked at his friend, bloodied from the prey. This had, so quickly, become his normality. He felt scared.

It was time to move on.

CHAPTER THIRTY NINE
Borneo

Probo's naval protection unit cleared a way into the *Sungai Arut Hotel*. He had arrived as quickly as possible when he had heard of the violence. A group of at least a hundred men, almost certainly paid for by Abdullah Aziz, had surrounded the taxis of the journalists one by one. The first man to get out of his car, a photographer with a British tabloid newspaper, had been badly knifed across his face. The crowd of men had been shouting "Get out of town, we want our jobs" in Indonesian, so hardly any of the international media had any idea what was going on.

The other journalists had run to help and been punched and robbed in the scrum. Local police had stood back and, as one photograph published worldwide the next day testified, laughed. Three of the journalists had lost their cameras and one a tape recorder. If the thugs had wanted to frighten the press, they had succeeded. But the story had just got bigger.

Talking on his phone to Bambang Santoso, the Minister of Forestry, accompanied by the national police commander, walked through the naval cordon into reception. "I understand, sir, yes it will look terrible for our President."

He finished his call, frustrated by the lack of understanding in Jakarta of what he was up against. The obstructive General had been ordered back to barracks, but his replacement would not arrive until tomorrow. Had the army moved decisively against Aziz's sawmills, this violence could probably have been avoided. Now Probo had to face an angry press. He was ushered into a small conference room. There was a captive audience waiting to hear what he said before filing.

"Thank you for your patience" he started. There was an irreverent chuckle from some of the foreign media who hated being cooped up like this. "I would like to apologise on behalf of my government for the appalling treatment some of you have received today." He looked around and saw they were now hanging on his every word. Two television camera crews had arrived from Bangkok and Jakarta, just after the attack. They had filmed blood pouring from the gash on the photographer's face and interviewed witnesses to the attack. He saw Pauline Brand sitting in the back row.

"You have witnessed what we are up against in this part of our country, and what Matt Johnson most likely, probably unwittingly, faced."

There were a few shouts from the press "are you saying he is dead?"

Probo looked at Pauline and smiled kindly. "No I am not saying that. Our search and rescue mission continues, but so far we have found no sign of Mr Johnson and Mr Koto. I'm sorry Ms Brand."

He went on to describe the next stage of their mission: to close all illegal sawmills and break down logging camps in the park. A few of the journalists asked why this had not happened already. One in particular pressed the point.

"Our first priority" explained Probo "is to find our missing persons."

"Is it true that the army have been plotting against you?" asked the persistent journalist.

Probo laughed. "No, it is not true at all! Our naval support has been exemplary, although we have had some logistical problems with our mobile army brigade which will be resolved tomorrow. We have carried out a thorough aerial grid search across the park and in the next two days we expect to have covered all the main river systems. Operation Johnson will find Matt Johnson if he is still alive. Operation Johnson will also clear the park of all illegal camps."

Pauline raised her hand and asked if any action would be taken against Abdullah Aziz.

"Thank you, Ms Brand." Probo responded. "We will follow the letter of the law. If Mr Aziz is found to be involved in the violence, illegal logging or illegal sawmills, he will be prosecuted."

The national police commander stepped forward and was invited to the front by Probo. He explained he was there to root out local police officers in the pay of the timber baron. "May I add my regret to the Minister's for the way you have been treated" he stated.

Three different angles were written up in the hours that followed.

The first was a detailed description of the operation as described by Probo. This was the *factual angle*. He had answered additional questions on the logistics of the next two days. Three of the journalists had visited one of Aziz's sawmills and wanted to know why it had been so easy for them, yet the government was still prevaricating. *"Anarchy in the forest, Indonesia claims it will take control."*

The second focused on the crowd violence. This was the *sensational angle*. *"Violence in Borneo."*

The last came from Pauline. She was tired of her pretence and wanted to get out of this horrible town. Troy's pictures would be great for the weekend story which she would write up tomorrow. But she wanted to bring this sordid chapter to a close. *"I would feel him. I know that if he was around I would know. But everything in this damp, mosquito infested jungle, despite the oppressive heat, feels cold to me. The rivers go on for ever, the trees, home to orang-utans and snakes, give me no signs. Matt is gone. I know it in my heart. When I saw the huge crocodile today, [photo] just upriver from where Matt was last seen, I knew my search was over. This nightmare grew worse when hired thugs attacked my colleagues from the media. How could Matt have survived the people and the jungle?*

"I thought of my gentle, loving Matt as my speedboat raced back to this insignificant corner of our world. I only wish he could have been here for me." A picture of her in tears next to the crocodile would accompany the piece. *The personal / emotional angle.*

Tomorrow, she would write about the orang-utans and their fight for survival. She would talk to Rita and see if she could turn Matt into an eco-warrior in the weekend edition's longer feature.

*

The newly appointed General in charge of the army operation had received instructions directly from the President. After his arrival by helicopter, shortly after dawn, he had moved swiftly. By sunset all of Abdullah Aziz's sawmills had been closed, filmed and photographed, their managers taken into custody. He would question some of those detained before retiring. Tomorrow his troops would move into the other, smaller sawmills.

The naval assault on logging camps was also prioritised, albeit secretly so that a pretence of a viable search and rescue mission could be salvaged. Nobody realistically believed they were still alive. There were no loggers in the park, all having left the first day, but the camps had been left suddenly. The naval teams destroyed all structures, removed food and supplies and carried out an inventory on the logs floating in log ponds. At last, the enforcement operation was effective and in full flow.

Probo moved out of the local Governor's VIP quarters into the official residence, the Governor having been recalled to Jakarta and immediately placed under arrest. He was still protected by the naval unit, even though he calculated that the army, police and Governor's militia had been neutralised as a personal threat. Everything seemed to be moving forward at last. He had even received a small group of professional locals who thanked him for his decisive actions and offered their help to rebuild their community. They requested financial support and ideas to help the local economy grow without the timber baron.

His biggest problem was international relations. The newspaper and television reports had embarrassed Indonesia in ways it could do without. Lawlessness and incompetence were huge turn-offs to investors; the Minister of Finance had made that very clear to him in a phone conversation at six in the morning: suggestions that parts of the country were out of the control of central government frightened off lenders, international companies and tourists. He was half expecting the Minister of Tourism to blame him for a collapse in air traffic to Bali.

His greatest fan was Debi. He was so happy that she offered him support, because at this time, he felt so alone. His wife, although always there for him, had no idea what he was up against. Debi was staying with her colleagues from YHB who had successfully focused some of the media on Abdullah Aziz. The enforcement operations carried out today had gone some way to showing the government was sincere in stamping out lawlessness. It was only now, at the end of the day, he realised he should have invited the press along for the story.

*

254

"So, what do you think?" asked Sam as he stroked Rita's hair. His question was not aimed at Rita, but at Debi who had moved in with them.

"They could be alive" she said with warmth in her voice that Sam had rarely heard.

"I agree" he responded, "I felt something upriver that gave me a strong sense they were out there. It may have been wishful thinking, but it seemed too strong for that." He leant down and kissed Rita on the mouth. They all knew that his overtly romantic actions were deliberately establishing his right to love Rita in front of Debi.

"But they've given up" Debi said sadly. "The Minister was losing the media battle as long as the thugs maintained control. He had to put all his efforts into destroying the camps and attacking Aziz's empire. If Koto and Mr Johnson are injured and need help, the media attention may have killed them."

"Perhaps we should mount our own search" suggested Rita, now lying in Sam's lap.

Debi smiled and moved over to her two colleagues. Something was different. They were on the front line together. Probo was their ally and the world's media were camping out on their issue. This was her moment and she, unexpectedly, enjoyed sharing it with Rita and Sam. For the first time she saw YHB beyond her own lifetime. She saw Rita and Sam lunching with ministers and working the media. They were good at what they did and their obvious love for each other warmed her frosty heart. "What do you think of Pauline?" she asked.

There was a short silence.

"Come on" insisted Debi. "I know it's difficult since she's lost her boyfriend, but I don't think she's genuine. What do you think?"

Sam leant back as Rita pulled herself out of his lap and shifted alongside him on the floor, leaning against the wall of Murkha and Setin's living room.

"She's trying to make something out of it" commented Sam. "It's definitely been difficult for her. She has no feeling for the forest. But she's got stories to write. And Matt had left her."

Rita joined in. "She's written a long piece about the park. How Matt would be proud to know that the operation in his name had cleared the loggers. But she has given up on him, she's certain he's dead. I think she needs him to be dead, he had already given up on her."

"Your idea isn't crazy" said Sam to Rita referring to her suggestion to launch a search. "Why don't we mount a search asking local Dayaks to help?"

They thought about it for a while without speaking, feeling they had to do something if everyone else had given up.

"It's a good idea, I'll talk to Probo in the morning" offered Debi. "We'll see if he can pay locals to carry on the search."

*

Pauline was woken by her phone at four on Sunday morning. She shifted uneasily in the bed, wondering what could possibly be so urgent. Her feature length story had been filed ten hours earlier.

"Um, Pauline?" her editor asked unnecessarily.

"What is it?"

"I want your reaction to allegations we are publishing tomorrow. A young man in Bali claims he is Matt's lover. What do you have to say to that?"

Pauline was suddenly wide awake.

"What young man? What do you mean?" she stumbled with her response.

"Did you know Matt is gay?"

"You can't publish that!" she screamed down the phone, choking back tears.

"Did you know Matt is gay?" he repeated.

"Of course I know!" she replied, throwing her mobile across the hotel room, keener to get out of this godforsaken place than ever before.

It had been five restless hours before she had been able to download the full story on her laptop. Five hours to realise that her charade had cost her a great deal of personal anguish, despite it gaining her professional respect. Now she just wanted to hide. Just escape.

There was a knock on her door.

Facing her on the laptop a headline stopped her dead.

Missing Matt: Gay Sex Shocker – the pictures Pauline won't want to see.

Under the headline, front page text spelled out the story Pauline dreaded.

Lost jungle hunk Matt Johnson was dramatically exposed last night as a two-time love rat. First: he abandoned raven-haired journalist Pauline Brand when he flew to the tropical paradise island of Bali. Then: he ditched local MAN Ardi to disappear into the jungle with his male guide.

Last night Balinese beach boy Ardi, 23, sobbed as he described how blond-haired Matt Johnson plied him with drugs and alcohol before seducing him.

"He told me he loved me and wanted to spend his life with me. Pauline wasn't important to him. He realised he was gay."

She clicked on the highlighted italic word *pictures*.

There was Matt naked in a Bali bathroom, his genitals covered by a star. In the mirror behind him a naked young man pointed the camera. Under the picture was a caption *"What has our Pauline to say about this?"*

There was another knock on the door.

*

It had taken all morning for Debi to get hold of Probo. He had been coordinating with the naval and army chiefs and talking with Bambang Santoso on the phone. The latest "gay" revelation about Matt Johnson was extremely problematic for the government. They had no less of a reason to find him, but to have named their enforcement operation after a gay man whose body was exposed all over the world's newspapers, was causing considerable concern: only weeks ago parliament had been debating new legislation to prohibit kissing in public! Now their armed forces were racing around Borneo on, what the television stations were naming, *Operation Gay Boleh (foreigner)*. Already, in the local press, the man from Bali, Ardi, had made additional accusations of Matt "plotting" with environmentalists.

"Sorry to be so late" apologised Probo when he saw Debi walking towards his official car carrying a small cardboard folder.

"Let's take a walk. I've got to get back to do an interview for two Indonesian TV channels."

He looked shattered; the responsibilities had taken their toll over the last few days.

"Did you know Johnson was homosexual?" asked Probo, slightly concerned about what else may have been kept from him.

"No, I didn't" she answered truthfully. "Although my colleagues did, but could not see why it was relevant." She looked at Probo straight in the eyes "and I agree."

Debi realised that the operation had become a huge embarrassment for Probo but advised he held firm. Mr Johnson's sexuality was irrelevant to the operation. "Focus on the park, the murders and the mob violence" she said. "You need some local people to stand up and thank the government for what you've done here."

"Some came to me yesterday. But it's not easy for me to arrange" responded Probo as they walked slowly down the tree clad road, not far from the *Sungai Arut Hotel*. It was hot and clammy, threatening rain.

"I've brought some names of local Dayaks that could help launch a search for Koto and Mr Johnson" explained Debi. "It would be great if the government could provide some money for the boats and their time. They could also probably offer support to Operation Johnson." She lifted the folder to reach inside but it slipped from her hand and fell on the road.

"Let me get that for you" offered Probo as he bent over to pick it up.

A loud crack came, just as he bent double, his first thought being that he had done something to his back. But as he looked up he saw Debi thrown back, blood bursting from her forehead. He reached out to catch his friend, but it felt like the world had slipped into slow motion despite her being propelled across the road so fast he had no chance to prevent her crashing into the dirt.. His naval protection unit surrounded him with their bodies, forcing him back to the ground. He tried to look over to see if Debi was alright, but a naval officer was already shaking his head next to Debi Sudarto's crumpled body.

*

Escape. It had been her only thought when she had read the gay story. She immediately packed, checked-out and headed for the airport. She waited all morning to get the flight, but at last she was in the air over the Java Sea heading back towards Jakarta away from the press pack. And then London. She would have to quit work; she could never work with her editor again.

The man sitting next to Pauline on the afternoon flight out of Pangkalan Bun had good reason to want to escape as well. This was the first time in twenty years he had failed Abdullah Aziz. He could not understand what had gone wrong.

Wahid never missed.

CHAPTER FORTY
Singapore

The Singapore television channels picked up on the international story of logging, murder and, now, assassination in Borneo. *The Straits Times*, Singapore's leading English language newspaper, ran Pauline's feature alongside the gay allegations; more disturbing to Abdullah Aziz were the box insert about his logging interests. The editorial linked his residence in the island state to political negotiations on an extradition treaty between Singapore and Indonesia: the implication being that he was a wealthy crook who should be sent home to face the music.

His wife, seeing his distress, advised him to distance himself from the affairs of Borneo. "You are a reputable businessman and luxury hotel owner. Let me surround and protect you with Singaporean social support" she confidently offered.

"She might be right" he thought. The reception for the charity event with the American Ambassador would give him additional clout in Singapore. But would the Ambassador still come to an event patronised by a man accused of theft and murder? If anyone could get him there, it was his wife, bless her.

He leaned back in the comfort of the white leather sofa in the penthouse west wing, looking across the Singapore skyline. "Gin and tonic" he waved to his regular "boy" in a colonial manner Singaporeans had once become accustomed to. The handsome Indonesian waiter smiled, poured the drink and placed it gently on a gold coaster on the glass topped coffee table, and invisibly withdrew.

"She was definitely right" he thought, feeling lonelier than he had for years. He could not talk about the possible involvement of Hazim in the disappearance of the Englishman to his wife or any work colleagues. His son had not only made him lonely, but also extremely vulnerable. He was at a loss to know how to fight back with his sawmill closures. This enforcement operation had the backing of the President. His contacts in Jakarta had weighed the risks and decided to defy him. He would start to hear them squealing when they received the information about his payments to their accounts. But at this moment his was an idle threat: he

could not afford to be further embroiled in bribery and blackmail accusations. Even Wahid had let him down, killing that wretched Sudarto woman. The best thing to do was to let his lawyer fight the Indonesian government while he, conspicuously, socialised with the great and the good, brushing aside any idea that he was taking the allegations seriously.

"Sir" the waiter announced, "your guests have arrived."

Abdullah Aziz sighed wearily, but stood and turned to see Colin and Mary Grady being shown into the room.

"Ah Colin, this must be your wonderful wife" he gushed on autopilot. "She is even more beautiful than you described" he flattered as he moved forward and kissed Mary's hand.

She was taken back by the grandeur of the *Regency* and now this elegant gentleman had invited her into his inner sanctum, the penthouse suite. She could immediately see how hasty she had been to admonish Colin last week when this ugly story in Borneo had first broken.

"Mr Aziz, your hotel is most splendid" Mary responded in a way that suggested she may also be caught in the colonial era.

"How good to see you again" Colin Grady added with a huge smile. He gave no indication of his growing concern over emerging details from Borneo. Two of his clients had called him today, a Sunday, to ask some difficult questions. He knew he could not ask Aziz to explain the media frenzy in front of Mary.

"It is a wonderful pleasure to have you both here at this time" Aziz continued. "I explained to Colin last time we met, that we try to mix business with friendship. It means a great deal to me to meet you, Mary. If I may call you that?"

Mary blushed. They were offered a drink while Aziz explained some of the history of the hotel. She was enthralled by the opulence, asking all the right questions.

"Now you must forgive me" announced Aziz. "My wife needs me at home this evening. I know she wants to meet you as soon as possible. You will find her quite stressed at the moment because she's organising a huge charity event for Wednesday in our famous *Regency* atrium. The American Ambassador and other Singaporean dignitaries will be here. You will of course be our guests. It will give you a chance to talk with Hazim, Colin. He arrives on Tuesday in time for the gala."

With the Gradys dismissed, he called Hazim and ordered him to fly in on Tuesday. It was time for them to be seen as a family.

"Of course. I wouldn't miss it" Hazim had replied cheerfully.

*

One day of shopping in Singapore removed any nagging doubts Mary Grady had over the reputation of her host. Fortunately, being on holiday, she was not reading the papers or watching television news. Had she, in a bored moment, turned on any news channel, it might have reignited initial suspicions: Abdullah Aziz's name was associated with an assassination attempt against an Indonesian government minister.

Aziz's wife faced a string of questions from the Ambassador's wife, but it still seemed likely he would attend Wednesday's gala in aid of the American school. Her social circle dismissed the media claims as attempts by business competitors to tarnish her husband's name. Abdullah Aziz was an extremely rich successful businessman; of course he would be put through difficult times through jealousy and opponent's greed. It came with his power and influence and it was the duty of those he favoured to dismiss such gossip.

On Tuesday morning Colin received a call from Hazim and they agreed to meet in an apartment Hazim kept near Orchard Road. He was surprised that Hazim did not stay in the hotel, but was glad to get away from the *Regency* and his wife for a couple of hours.

The third floor, two-bedroom apartment, although clean, did not seem to fit Hazim as Colin Grady saw him. The entrance, off a tiny landing, did not announce this son of a multi millionaire. Inside, the small lounge was furnished with a green leather sofa facing a flat screen television mounted on the wall with a wooden chair next to it. There was light from a small window in the open plan kitchenette at the back of the lounge, but this had a shutter closed over it. A sound system had been installed and tall floor-standing speakers dominated two corners, somewhat

262

overwhelming the space. Uninteresting prints decorated the magnolia painted walls and ceiling lights created a stark mood.

"I've just moved in" explained Hazim as he ushered Colin into his living room. "There comes a time when a son has to fly the nest" he added with a grin on his face.

Colin smiled and sat in the chair.

"Now, let's get down to business shall we?" suggested Hazim. "I trust your clients are happy and you will make a great deal of money!"

"Yes, thank you" replied Colin, feeling slightly uneasy in this small space. Hazim had not sat down as he had expected, but towered over him, turning a remote control over in his hand. He thought he heard the sound of someone coughing in one of the bedrooms and asked nervously if they were alone.

"I have some friends staying" replied Hazim.

Colin knew he had to ask about the news stories. All his clients would have heard about the accusations by now and six of them had so far threatened to cancel orders. He needed to get some answers that would satisfy them but he was feeling increasingly scared of Hazim in this cramped space.

"So, you've come to place new orders?" asked Hazim, looking Colin in the eyes.

Colin shifted uncomfortably in his seat. "I need to know a few things first."

Hazim put the remote control on the arm of the sofa, walked over to the kitchenette and pulled a soda from the fridge without offering one to Colin. "You want to know about the news reports?" he suggested helpfully.

Colin nodded.

"Well, I think it is almost certainly true that the English tourist is dead. And his Dayak guide. I wouldn't be at all surprised if they were eaten by a huge crocodile." Hazim moved back into the room, sat down on the sofa and leaned back, stretching his arms in a manner that gave him a relaxed advantage. "I can't be certain he was queer."

It was an act of arrogance which gave Colin a sick feeling in his stomach. He tried to compose himself, knowing that if he gave away how scared he was, Hazim would have gained even more of an advantage. "Actually, it was your sawmills I was most concerned about" he said with an even voice.

"Closed" replied Hazim bluntly, offering nothing more.

"So" said Colin slowly "where does that leave you as a supplier?"

"Nothing has changed. We'll probably get the mills operating again soon. If we don't, you'll have to buy different species from my other operation. I can supply you with unlimited merbau, for example. Great for flooring."

"My clients need assurances that I'm supplying them legal, sustainable timber from a reputable supplier" replied Colin too pompously.

There was a laugh from one of the bedrooms momentarily diverting Colin's attention.

Hazim smiled mischievously, turning his head towards the bedroom door. "Two friends" he teased, without elaborating. "So, what is your problem Colin? Give them the assurances they need. We give you the paperwork you want. I'll get my timber endorsed by the fucking United Nations if that will make you happy." He paused and said directly "you will place another larger order. You know that, don't you?"

It was as clear that Hazim was enjoying the menace as it was clear that Colin was scared, but he had to speak up. "Is there any truth in the allegations that your father was behind the kidnapping of that English tourist and the assassination attempt on the Indonesian minister?"

"Ah" retorted Hazim, still refusing to rise to the bait. He was in control, in his own space, with his friends in the room next door. And best of all, he had the remote control! He hit the TV button and called for his friends to join them. Two young powerful men came into the living room, both dressed in jeans and tight t-shirts, one taller than the other. Colin recognised the tall one as the man in Islamic dress who had driven the other car in Pangkalan Bun, the night the two young girls had been dragged from their home.

"Colin, you know one of my friends already. Please say hello."

The men joined Hazim on the sofa and stared at the flat screen as if they had come around to watch the football. The taller young man nodded recognition at Colin who forced a smile back.

"Colin wants to know about the gruesome murders in Borneo" Hazim said to the other two sitting either side of him on the sofa. "All in good time, Colin" said Hazim, laughing out loud as he spoke "but let's watch a movie first" and he pressed a second button on the remote.

A woman spoke from the floor-standing speakers, so clearly it was as if she was in the room. Colin knew it was Michelle and looking at the television could see her beautiful body, even more wonderful than his fantasies of the last weeks, lowering onto his erect penis. "You're beautiful Colin, please, please" she coaxed as he entered her. He groaned so loud that the sound distorted and the three men on the sofa laughed in chorus. His flabby old body was pounding so hard on the screen that his face shone in bright orange, resembling the head of a stiff old pig on a roasting spit.

The three Indonesians were in hysterics, buckled over, laughing so loud they, thankfully, drowned out some of Colin's distorted moaning. Hazim, ignoring Colin, joked with his friends "there's a great bit I edited out in a moment, watch." The scene changed and Colin, lying naked on his back, softly lit by the bedside lamps, had a damp hard-on having just withdrawn from Michelle. His face was contorted by his panting; Michelle had turned away from him and was looking straight at the camera. "Oh, that was wonderful Colin" she muttered as she grimaced and let her tongue hang out of her mouth in disgust for the camera.

The tall Indonesian started to choke on his laughing so Hazim slapped his back. All three of them turned in unison to Colin, sitting quietly in shock. "You disgusting, filthy, flabby old man" said Hazim, encouraging another round of laughter.

Colin's face was ashen.

"Now, how about the murders?" he faced the tall young man. "Colin really wants to know. Did the English queer get swallowed whole by the crocodile or was he eaten in handy bite-size bits?"

CHAPTER FORTY ONE
Borneo

Koto, his body still blood-splashed, had, rather disrespectfully Matt thought, skewered the piglet back at the clearing. They had taken turns in spit roasting the animal over a fire while the other collected fruit, fish and water to prepare for leaving their camp early the next day. Little was said as they busied themselves, they were so absorbed they could almost hear each other thinking.

Finally, Koto broke the silence. "It won't be as hard as it was that first day" he offered helpfully. "You are part of this forest now. We are part of this forest." Seeing his friend ignoring his attempts to comfort him, he added, he thought helpfully, "you have flip flops."

Matt stopped peeling a mango, smiled weakly and looked up at his friend. "I know" was all he said before pulling more skin from the green fruit.

The piglet's blood on Koto's face had darkened as it dried, temporarily removing his bright demeanour, replacing it with a face of doom. He moved around the clearing as if carrying a great weight, taking twice as long to collect water, nuts or leaves. He crouched on his haunches and stared at Matt as he turned the roasting meat. "What is happening?" he asked sadly. Just three metres from him Matt was also crouching, but facing the other way. He could see the red swellings on his back and buttocks from the mosquito bites but he could not see his expression. The back of his head was moving slightly, but almost without purpose. "Please, Matt. Tell me. What is happening?"

Matt slowly turned towards Koto, showed his tear-stained face but tried to smile. Pushing himself up he limped over to Koto, reached out, holding Koto's head between his hands and lowered himself beside him. "I can't tell you what is happening to you my friend, but my heart is breaking in two." He wiped his face with the back of his hand, smearing the tears and dirt. "Part of it is pumping my blood so forcefully to overcome my fear, but the rest of it is crying out its love for you."

Koto surrendered the weight of his body to Matt, both of them sitting back on the ground holding each other.

266

"We've grown safe in the last few days" Matt continued. "The forest has been good to us. The idea of moving on brings the outside world into our lives again with all that it entails. Yes, I'm frightened of the cuts and bruises and the snakes that threaten us as we walk out of this forest. But I'm more frightened of what we walk into. And what we are giving up."

Koto looked into Matt's blue eyes as he straightened his back and felt some of his doom lift. "So, the weight I feel is not a burden, it is not a test" he whispered to Matt. "It is a part of me that I have found but not recognised." He pushed himself up, standing next to Matt smiling. "I had no idea that love could be so heavy. I must learn to use it to push myself along rather than weigh me down."

They hugged each other, neither daring to be the first to let go. But they were naked, in a rainforest, and a mosquito biting Matt's neck broke the moment.

Within minutes they were walking around finishing their chores, preparing for the next day's long trek. They were moving on without exploring what they had started, back into a world that thought them dead.

When first light came to their clearing, the rain started falling. They hardly spoke as they gathered their food wrapped in leaves. Along with the two lighters and the flip flops on Matt's feet, it was all they had: chunks of roast pig and enough fruit for a first meal. Koto had insisted they left the jerry can even though a little petrol remained.

"We'll head east, avoiding the river" he explained. "The walking will be much easier if we keep away from the river. The rain makes it easier for us to collect water. If all goes well I think we'll find a friendly village in three or four days."

Matt's mood was low but he tried to appear ready for the trip, although he needed help to extract the thorn. Koto cradled his foot in his lap and picked at the wound in his friend's heal. In minutes, the two centimetre thorn had been removed to the sound of a satisfied sigh from Koto. Across the clearing, just out of their sight and unknown to them, a group of macaques sat quietly in pairs, removing ticks and fleas from each other, soothing each others wounds. The cool mornings and evenings provided the best time for grooming, even in the rain.

The first day travelling was hard for them both. Koto's feet were torn badly by unexpected roots and sharp spines fallen from plants he failed to avoid. Matt moved more easily, his flip flops protecting his feet and the relief of the thorn removal reminding him of a time without pain. His bites still hurt, at times the mosquitoes seemed to swarm around him, but his greatest suffering was seeing Koto's pain.

As evening approached they heard rustling in the canopy above them and both crouched instinctively, resting on each other for better balance. High above there was an orang-utan sitting on a branch looking down on them. It was still raining and she was holding a huge leaf over her in the same way as the big male at Camp Leakey, like an umbrella to keep her head dry. After a few minutes they noticed another movement and saw a younger orang-utan picking fruit high in the same tree.

"They'll build a nest near here in the canopy" said Koto, speaking softly. "We must think of doing the same. It is too dangerous on the ground."

They ate fresh fruit from a nearby tree and as much of the piglet they could manage, knowing it would be rotten by the next day. Little survived the heat and damp, the forest devouring everything soon after death. By nightfall they found a suitable tree with a huge fork five metres from the ground, wedged themselves in, facing each other, their legs dangling either side of a large branch, in the belief that they could sleep without falling. It stopped raining soon after dark but neither of them slept, their bodies weary and aching from the day, their minds racing in a way that they had not felt in the safety of their camp.

At first light they clambered down and searched for fresh fruit for their morning meal, but Koto encountered a snake at the base of the tree so they moved on without nourishment, stopping only to drink fresh rainwater captured on leaves. They spoke very little, Koto always out front, heading east. The undergrowth was sometimes impenetrable causing them to detour, wade through a swamp, or climb a tree to decide on their next step. Koto was cut badly across his back from a nasty fall from a tree he was climbing to get a bearing. Matt offered to wash the wound but was told they could not afford to waste any time.

The second night was worse. Already exhausted by the terrain and the loss of one night's sleep, they left it too late to find a suitable place of relative safety in a tree, spending the night sitting, not even trying to sleep, listening to the sounds of the forest. The only tiny consolation was that it remained dry.

"We should rest tomorrow in daylight" suggested Matt.

"No" responded Koto too quickly. "We must move on."

"But why? What's the hurry?"

Koto sighed and looked at the ground. "I want to feel safe again." He looked up at Matt, a sad expression on his face. "I want it to be alright." They had hugged awkwardly, Koto concealing the pain he felt from his wounds.

In the morning they moved on without speaking, following the light from the rising sun. Neither of them really appreciated how close each other was to collapsing, their determination the only strength keeping them going.

Soon after midday, with no food in their stomachs, the forest becoming denser yet offering less food, they stepped up onto a pathway made from long thin logs two abreast, a metre apart, crossed with shorter planks, cutting through the forest. It headed south, not east, but neither of them really cared anymore. Balancing on the logs they travelled twice as fast, over the wet swamp, avoiding sharp roots that ripped the feet. Matt had seen such pathways in Central America on a holiday with Pauline when they had spent one day in the "jungle" on an organised *overnight safari*. But he had not realised their purpose, here in the thick of this forest.

"It's a log-rail" Koto said matter-of-factly, looking slightly removed from their predicament.

"But what is it for? asked Matt.

Koto turned back to look at him. He stood, slightly stooping, keeping his weight from his left leg, his hair matted across his face. Fresh blood dripped from his left nipple which had been pierced cruelly by a dozen tiny razor hairs as he brushed past the plant they were designed to protect. He looked beaten. As if seeing himself in Matt's eyes, he fell to his knees, holding his head in his hands. Matt stepped forward to comfort him, crouching down and wiping Koto's hair from his face.

"We'll be OK" he said unconvincingly, only just realising how badly Koto was injured by the forest. As the one out front, he had endured the worst of the undergrowth lashings, stepped on the sharpest roots before warning his companion to avoid them. Two sleepless nights, little food for the last twenty four hours, had crushed his pride and undermined his determination to protect them both. He had forgotten that they had grown in strength in their camp together, not alone, and again tried to take the role of lonely guide. And Matt had let him.

As he felt the warmth of Matt's hands on his face he looked up. "It's for moving logs. We must be near a big logging camp."

A kilometre further along the rail they came across a camp: blue canvas hung over tent frames, clothes hung on lines between the tents. They staggered into the camp, realising that they could not afford to be alone anymore. The loggers probably worked for the people who threw them to a crocodile, but they were still their best chance. Maybe they would be Dayak. Maybe they would be isolated enough to know nothing of Matt and Koto, maybe they had food and water, maybe …

Nothing. It was deserted. There was nobody to be found, although there were signs that the camp had been left suddenly, without prior warning. A coffee pot still stood over a fireplace, long doused by the rain, loose tent flaps waved in occasional gusts of wind, men's shorts and t-shirts dripped on the drying lines from recent downpours, the warming sun encouraging steam to rise all around the camp.

"It's a big logging camp" observed Koto. "But for some reason it's been evacuated at very short notice. Look over there by the coffee pot."

Matt glanced over and saw a red packet of Marlboros near the steaming fireplace.

"Nobody leaves their cigarettes unless they're in a hurry" observed Koto.

While his friend rested in the sun Matt checked out the camp, pleased with what he found. One of the tents contained food supplies including rice, onions, chillies and dried noodles. There was coffee in a small sack, sugar and four full cartons of cigarettes. At the back of the food tent were three cages, made from rattan, containing dead chickens, left in such a hurry that no one had fed or watered them. It was extraordinary that no wild animals had eaten them, but Matt guessed the camp was a forbidding environment for nature, its entire purpose to destroy it.

Inside the sleeping tents he found bedrolls, mosquito nets, dry clothes, flip flops and torches. Judging by the number of bedrolls it seemed the camp had been the home for thirty or forty people. A number of paths led from a big blue tent on the edge of the camp into the forest. Inside this tent were chainsaws, jerry cans full of petrol, tools and an old, partly dismantled outboard motor.

Returning to where Koto rested, Matt listed everything he had found. "There's enough here for us to live on for months" he enthused.

But Koto was less excited. "We can't stay. It's too dangerous. The usual reason for such a quick evacuation is that they have been told the authorities are carrying out an enforcement operation. They'll be back as soon as the men in uniform have gone home."

"But we can rest tonight and enjoy some good food and some pleasures" insisted Matt unwrapping the cellophane from a dry packet of cigarettes and placing one between Koto's lips before lighting his own.

They ate well, cleaned up and chose some dry clothes to protect themselves from the insects. Matt found it impossible to find anything that really fit him. All the t-shirts were so tight he had to cut the arms to prevent them pinching. He found one pair of green shorts that must have belonged to an unusually large Indonesian. "Probably the boss" noted Koto wryly as he chose some multi-coloured Hawaiian shorts, beginning to warm to their good fortune.

They slept dry in a tent under mosquito nets, so long that neither woke at dawn, resting well into mid-morning. It was Matt who first saw the sun outside the tent, but he was preoccupied with a weird feeling in his legs, a mild throbbing that acted more as a warning than a direct symptom of anything wrong. But by midday he was feeling nauseous and drained.

Koto, well rested but very sore from his cuts, busied around the camp, checking out every tent, brewing coffee and cooking rice. He wore his colourful shorts, brown t-shirt and flip flops, resembling a young camper on summer school with his long dark hair falling across his face in an expression of *"whatever".* But under his clothes his body had been seriously slashed, inside his head, his thoughts raced, confused and concerned.

By the afternoon Matt started to complain of the cold. Koto's eyes revealed informed fear, but he tried to be calm in front of his shivering friend. "It's just a fever, it'll pass" he whispered, hardly believing himself as he spoke. As darkness fell on them again, Matt started to shake uncontrollably, his face so white that its ghostly appearance added a macabre numbness to the atmosphere. Koto left his side to collect cold water, pulling his t-shirt off as he returned, soaking it and gently applying it to Matt's forehead.

Matt was slightly delirious, the fever heating his blood, working itself up from that first distress in his legs, to his head, his temple. It was as if something was thrashing at the insides of his veins, fighting to escape, pounding against his skull. He sensed the cooling as Koto's wet t-shirt pressed on his skin. His head throbbed, his eyes aching in a way that suggested they no longer belonged, but as he opened them to see Koto leaning so close, his heart weeping tears to add to the soaking t-shirt, he cried as well, big sobbing tears that mixed with Koto's; they could face anything, he knew it, together.

The fever broke. Sweat burst from his pumping face, his own t-shirt drenched as fast as in a tropical storm. The parasites lost their grip on his blood, Matt's first malaria fever would soon pass, but Koto knew it would be less than two days before his next.

"Lie back, I'll find you another shirt" Koto said, taking control. "We're in this together. Remember that."

By the time he returned with a new shirt, Matt was already asleep. He lit an oil lamp and stared at this battered, sick Englishman he had grown to care for as he did his own family. No, it was different to that. Why did he find it so difficult to place his own emotions? Matt would call it love. He smiled and reached over, gently pulling Matt up to remove his wet t-shirt, careful not to wake him, he wiped him down with a towel. Then, without even thinking, he stripped off, lying down next to his friend, pulling a blanket over to keep them both safe.

CHAPTER FORTY TWO
Jakarta

The family dog, muddy from the afternoon rain, had pushed her luck over the last two days, but it had paid off. Firstly, the house had always been off limits when the old man was at home, but today he had even called her into the lounge, for comfort. Secondly, she had not been up on the sofa since she was a puppy when the kind young daughter had made her feel at home. Now she was curled up on the sofa while the old man lay back in the armchair opposite her! Although feeling very comfortable, there was something disturbing about the time he now spent in that chair. He had changed since the old woman had walked out and the boy had disappeared.

Widodo did not even notice the dog on the sofa; he was so self-absorbed and depressed. It was three days since he had been in the office and three days since he had showered. His wife had left to stay at her sister's, his youngest son, in jail, was in a hideous video and his two other children had not even phoned to see if he was alright, having heard the sorry story from their mother. All his attempts to visit Mohammed had been rejected.

His anger at Hazim's video had been towards Hazim, but now it was with himself. The image of that boy being pushed down on Mo's swollen penis would not leave him. This was his son. He had no idea. Every time he thought about Mo in jail he feared for his life. A young man in jail ... he had heard the stories. But then, his mind wandered and he thought the unthinkable. Maybe Mo would like the attention of those criminals, maybe he should be left in there, maybe other peoples' children would be safer. He was so angry at himself for these thoughts. Mohammed was his son, his flesh and blood.

Outside, the sounds of his leafy corner of Jakarta seemed so normal. It was like any other day. He noticed the dog on the sofa, licking her muddy feet. "Hey, down!" He murmured. She looked up, unafraid of the tone of his voice and returned to her grooming. Even the dog didn't care about him anymore. His boss had not asked him to do anything since the meeting with Hazim and the Imam. He knew he had failed to keep abreast of the issues and alliances. Only days earlier he was balancing his boss and Hazim, but now neither of them seemed to be bothered by him at all. Even Abdullah Aziz had stopped calling.

He had lost his sense of time, dozing in the chair until after dark when he was woken by a taxi pulling up outside the house. A moment later the dog bounced off the sofa, running excitedly to the front of the house. *'Friend or foe?'* wondered a mildly disinterested Widodo, sitting up in his chair, suddenly conscious of his sweaty, dishevelled appearance and the overflowing ashtray, packed with Kent dogends. He could not be bothered to meet the visitor, if they wanted to see him they would have to come another day.

The dog came scampering, excitedly, into the lounge, skidded on the wooden floor as she turned to run outside again to greet the new arrival.

As Widodo looked towards the open door, he saw Mohammed standing in its frame, naked to the waist, barefoot, his blue jeans filthy and torn. His head was bowed as he shuffled towards his father, the dog expressing more energy than father and son together.

"Father, I'm sorry" whispered Mohammed, unable to look up, "I don't understand what happened."

Aman Widodo's mobile phone announced an SMS and he was relieved to have an excuse to look away from his son, that disgusting image all he could really see. He picked up the phone and read the message. "Now you both owe me. Enjoy ur son, heard everyone else has."

Widodo looked up at his broken Mohammed realising he had to say something. He was confused. There was a bark. The dog was barking at him, telling him to welcome his son.

He pushed himself to his feet, smiled with tears in his eyes. "Come here son. Don't worry. I know what happened." He could see it now, it was so clear. How could he have questioned his beautiful Mo? How could he have dragged his family into his corruption and lies?

"It wasn't you. It was me."

Mohammed moved towards his father, shocked by his appearance and the tears.

"I know what happened, Mo" he added, using Mohammed's nickname for the first time. "It was Hazim, using you to get to me."

*

Aman Widodo had not been forgotten. Not only had Hazim Aziz decided he might still be useful to him, but across Jakarta, Bambang Santoso was attempting to unravel the horrible mess he had been introduced to by Widodo. He sat in his office surrounded by the photos of his girls and wife, still disturbed by his meeting with Imam Bakti and Hazim Aziz, wondering whether it had anything to do with the assassination attempt on Minister Probowo and the tragic death of Debi Sudarto.

His mobile phone rang, it was his daughter, she was coming up and they were travelling home together. He loved it when she had time for him in these small, manageable ways. She knew he was far too busy to be around much, so she tried to grab time when he was in his car, or at the end of the day. She reminded him so much of his wonderful late wife.

"Father" she exclaimed as she beamed into his cavernous office. "What is my favourite man doing tonight?"

They hugged warmly before she confronted him with a question he had probably, subconsciously, wanted to be asked by her all week. "What's getting you so down, father?"

"It's a matter of state, my dear" he dodged, but wishing he could share his concerns with her more than ever before.

"You're depressed. That's a family matter. What is it?" she persisted. "I'm not giving up. You can talk now or be questioned by me all night."

He smiled in a way reserved for his girls. He was incredibly proud of them all and knew that he trusted them with his life. Why not share his thoughts?

"Sit down, my girl" he joked. "Yes, you're right. I need your advice."

She walked over to one of the huge sofas in the centre of his office, sat and patted the leather next to her. "Come on dad."

He sat beside her, explained what was happening in the forests of Central Kalimantan, his warmth towards the Minister of Forestry, the two assassination attempts and the awful murders of Murkha, Matt Johnson, Koto and Debi Sudarto. She asked the questions of an enquiring mind, questioned his reasoning and pressed him further.

"Abdullah Aziz represents the rape of Indonesia. His son is his trained rapist. I think they've become serial killers, but the authorities that should investigate the crimes are on their payroll."

His daughter put her hand on his. "That's not it, dad. We all know that. What's the real problem?"

He smiled again. She was right, he was not even being honest with himself. "I met the trained rapist and he brought his Imam with him. Bakti."

She sighed. Imam Bakti was known in the papers as an extremist, violent religious fanatic. "How did you come to meet them?"

He explained the ships and the timber. Then he told her about his Secretary General.

"And is he in jail?" she asked simply.

In a way, this is what he expected, but had not even realised it himself. The murders, kidnaps, stripped forests; they were all issues with simple reactions. But Widodo's corruption had allowed the rise of people like Aziz, his traitorous use of his public position spat in the face of his employers, every Indonesian citizen.

Bambang Santoso shuffled in his seat.

"He's not in jail, is he?" she asked.

"It's not as simple as it seems" Bambang explained. "He may be useful. He's already set up the meeting with Aziz's son and Bakti."

"And that's a good thing?" His daughter laughed, removed her hand from his, stood and walked around the three sofas, taking control of the discussion in a way that reminded Bambang of his wife.

"You've done something bad, haven't you?"

"I compromised your mother's ideals, our ideals, yes. But I'm a Government Minister, it's not …"

She cut him dead. "I know, it's not easy being honest in government. That's plainly obvious to every voter in the world! We carry the burden of corruption, the tool of government with Suharto. But not you, dad, you don't have to be like everyone else."

Bambang looked up at his daughter like a scolded child. He knew she was right. "But I'm not sure what I've done" he said rather cryptically. "You're right, I'm using Widodo rather than holding him to account. That's wrong. I must put that right. But my meeting with the Imam and Aziz's son was very cordial. We agreed on almost everything. That's why I'm concerned."

*

It seemed, to Imam Bakti, that the events of the next two days would set him on a new alliance, one that promised to be more definitive than the loose relationship he had experienced with Abdullah Aziz. Clearly, Hazim was a violent psychopath, addicted to power, but so full of energy! Focussed productively, his enormous wealth could be exactly what his vision of an Islamic state, needed. The meeting with Indonesia's Coordinating Minister for Politics and Security had been a minor coup.

He walked from the large living area, in a devout friend's home he had borrowed in South Jakarta, to the garden. He was alone, having made it clear to his entourage that he had important business tonight. It was hot and balmy, so it was with sweaty palms that he reached into his pocket for a mobile phone an aide had given him an hour earlier. Its new prepaid SIM card allowed him to make the two urgent calls without fear of the nosy Indonesian intelligence agency listening in. He would drop the phone in a canal on his way to the airport.

"Brother" he stated when the first number answered on the second ring. "It's an orange. Meet me when you can at P7, after the clean up." That was it, nothing more to say. The voice at the other end of the line acknowledged the instructions and they ended the call.

The second call was to Singapore. "My son" he started, recognising Hazim. "I'm quite surprised to hear you tonight. You must be busy helping your mother with the charity event." The phone was passed to another man who answered with the reverence the Imam expected.

"You are blessed" assured Bakti. "Both of you are blessed."

"We are privileged" came the prepared reply.

"I just want to say how proud your brothers and sisters are at the devotion you both have to our Almighty God. You are truly blessed as martyrs. Go well, God willing" the Imam promised as he ended the short call; no need to take unnecessary risks, the Singaporeans were in league with the Americans and had a sophisticated listening apparatus.

*

Less than an hour after Mohammed Widodo had returned home, their dog was barking again at the vehicles that had driven up to the front of the house. The military police that stormed into the house were astonished at the scene that greeted them. Aman and Mohammed Widodo, father and son, were stretched out on a sofa embracing each other. The father stank of old sweat but came with them quietly, almost willingly, cheerily waving goodbye to his bare-chested son who was wearing nothing more than a new pair of soiled and ripped blue jeans.

CHAPTER FORTY THREE
Borneo

From the flight deck of the navy's Westland Wasp helicopter, Minister Probowo peered out over the dense, leafy forest canopy of Tanjung Puting, in vain hope that Mr Johnson and Mr Koto were still alive. Clouds hugged much of the southern part of the Park, but it was relatively clear ahead. He travelled with two Indonesian newspaper journalists, the foreign press having lost interest in the search after the gay allegations, some of them moving on to Bali to interview the "boy lover". The two men seemed shocked by the huge rust coloured scars below, where earth turned to mud and dust alternately, its cohesion lost as the trees were felled and dragged away. The curse of commercial illegal logging now filled his every waking moment, but for them it was still a new "story".

The pilot banked the vintage helicopter to starboard, heading towards an area known to be heavily logged in the east of the Park. Probo was lost in thought. Just days earlier his old friend had come to his assistance - now, she was dead, a bullet lodged in her brain, her head blown open by a hired assassin. A bullet meant for him. He realised that Debi had been partly responsible for the depth of feeling he had for Indonesia's dwindling forests. She had, unknowingly, given him the understanding that, without its forests, Indonesia lost its soul. The nationalist mantra of keeping Indonesia together, from Papua to Sumatra, his government's and every political party's public policy, meant nothing if its diversity had already been pillaged by Indonesian criminals, the military and corrupt officials. He remembered an angry discussion with her, many years earlier, when she had suggested Indonesia's claim to East Timor had been futile, when the Timorese people, butchered and tortured by the Indonesian military, screamed hate with their last breaths.

Debi's young friend, Sam, had come to him, the evening after news of Debi's murder had broken. This young Batak man from Sumatra, his cropped dark hair giving an air of menace, had fallen on his knees and pleaded with Probo to reopen the search for Mr Johnson and Koto. "It's what she would want" Sam had insisted.

"Please Minister. In Debi's honour, find our friends." He had come with a beautiful, stylishly dressed Dayak woman named Rita, explaining that she had lobbied Bambang Santoso in Bali. As the sister-in-law of the murdered schoolteacher, she had suffered the loss of two friends in as many weeks and two others lost in the forest, but was still prepared to fight for her ancestors.

Probo had asked Sam to get off his knees and take a seat. "You are welcome here, young man. As is Rita." To the surprise of his two guests, Probo had wiped away tears, feeling able to express his grief for the first time with Debi's friends. They had talked for three hours, Probo telling stories about Debi in happier times, when her husband was still alive. He had described the fear that he and other acquaintances of Debi had felt when they had learned of the disappearance of her husband and child. "It was fear that kept us all quiet" he whispered, "fear is a powerful weapon used widely by governments all over the world. Debi's husband and child were two of many thousands of people that disappeared. Debi was never the same again." He had looked kindly at the two young activists listening to his confession. "It was as if her light had gone out."

Sam had explained his feelings on the speedboat with Pauline Brand. "She dismissed what seemed so clear to me" he murmured sadly. "I don't think she ever wanted to find Matt. He had hurt her too badly." He looked at the Minister's attentive face, reached out to hold Rita's hand, and added "they're still alive out there. Somewhere. I know it, I feel it. I have no doubt. Upriver, we came close to their spirits, joined. Alive and strong."

"But I don't think they want to be found" added Rita, as equally certain.

"Minister" crackled the voice of the pilot in his headphones, bringing Probo back from his thoughts. "I can see smoke ahead. I'm going to pass over, very low, please look out for any sign of life."

Below, the impenetrable canopy rushed towards them as the pilot lost altitude. A waft of smoke was drifting out of a clearing about a kilometre ahead. Probo caught a glimpse of a blue tent. "It's a logging camp" he confirmed shouting into his helmet's microphone, nodding at the pilot. They seemed to be overhead almost immediately, hovering above a large camp of tents. A fire was burning and a man wearing brightly coloured Hawaiian shorts was running into the trees.

"Probably a logger" shouted the pilot keeping the helicopter at an altitude of 100 metres.

"Keep hovering" Probo ordered. The journalists took a few photographs, but Probo just stared at the tents, one by one. "Can you land?" he asked.

"Far too risky, there's not enough room, sir. Tree cover is at forty metres. One gust and we're down."

There was something about the man in Hawaiian shorts, Probo just *knew* he was not a logger and he *knew* he was not alone. As if on command, a tent flap opened and Probo saw a man. A blond man. A *boleh*. The figure quickly retreated into the tent after glancing up at the military helicopter. On top of the tent, drying, was a pair of large green shorts and a t-shirt ripped at the arms.

"It's them" announced Probo to the pilot.

"Are you sure sir?"

The journalists looked quizzically at the Minister.

"It's them, I tell you. I just know it's them. I saw Mr Johnson. That was Mr Koto running away. Are you sure we can't get down there?" Probo was sounding a little hysterical and the journalists pulled out notepads to make a few notes.

"I will radio for ground support, sir. I'll send the coordinates."

"No!" shouted Probo, suddenly realising that he could not completely trust the military - understanding why Koto and Johnson were hiding. He looked at the journalists and said calmly "I have my search team already prepared. Just get me back to Pangkalan Bun."

*

The helicopter had surprised Koto. He had been up early searching for a small tree his father had said relieved malaria. He had found it, scraped off some bark and just returned to camp, singing a Bob Dylan song very badly and loudly, hardly pronouncing the words, to avoid admitting he had forgotten the lyrics. His vocal rendering woke Matt who, although still weak, had enough energy to shout out his objections.

The clattering noise at first confused Koto. Then he looked up and saw the metal bird, four wheels descending, missile tubes on either side.

Without thinking, he ran.

Making his way through the forest he sneaked up behind their tent, shouting at Matt to stay inside. He was not sure if Matt could hear him over the sound of the helicopter, but he could see a man wearing a helmet looking down on them from the sky. Koto was very scared. In his short life the military had threatened his community, extorting food and, on occasion, taking girls away to their camps. He had no reason to see the military helicopter as anything other than a deadly threat.

Before he decided on a course of action, the noise of the rotor blades faded as the aircraft ascended from the canopy and headed west. He ran out into the clearing, scanning the sky for signs of any other unwanted guests before running to the tent. Matt opened the flap as he leapt inside.

"We must go!" he shouted, not looking at Matt, but grabbing clothes and cigarettes. "They'll be back."

"But, maybe they want to rescue us" suggested Matt, tenderly staring at the cuts in Koto's flesh. "We're both in need of medical attention."

"That was a military helicopter. They saw me."

"Me too" said Matt, thinking he was being helpful.

Koto stopped and stared at Matt's tired face framed by his long matted blond hair. He reached out and touched the tangled locks. "Then they know we're alive" he stated quietly, adding rather unnecessarily "you're the only white man with yellow hair hiding out in this forest."

In less than half an hour they filled bags with food and cigarettes and walked into the forest on a track near the big blue tent, still heading east. Koto had told Matt of his hatred of the military and Aziz's links with all the local commands. Despite their ill health, he reluctantly agreed that seeking out a friendly Dayak village was less risky. The tree bark remedy for malaria would have to wait. It was still early and they hoped to find a village by nightfall.

Wearing clothes and flip flops, they both moved faster than on the previous days. The path led to a huge desolate clearing, at least a kilometre across. The wind blew as if attracted to horror: the land was beaten, unable to breathe, its pores clogged by caked mud and brown, rotting undergrowth. In the distance they could see the forest separated from them by despair. As they stepped into the battlefield, the ground was littered with cigarette ends, plastic water bottles, spilled rice with ants already clearing it up, running so fast they seemed to sense danger as they rushed back under the forest cover.

They smelt the stench before they saw the corpse. Matt, following the overwhelming decay, put his hand to his mouth and gasped. A wooden stake in the ground, a chain and a putrid mass of orange fur covering an orang-utan skeleton, added to a growing hopelessness. The hapless creature had probably starved when the loggers deserted the camp.

"It's too big to be captured for a pet" commented Koto. "It was probably only being kept for meat. At least it's in the forest." He dropped to his knees by the rotting carcass, disturbing hundreds of flies gorging on the flesh, removed the chain from the putrid arm and pulled the stake from the ground. Carrying the shackles he walked twenty metres and threw them in the bush. He returned to the remains of the orang-utan, knelt again, closed his eyes and smiled. A minute later he stood. "We had better keep moving."

The disfigured, scorching landscape assaulted their tired bodies and by the time they reached the edge of the forest they were sweating profusely, covered in dust by the hot, gusting wind. Matt's face was brown, his hair encrusted in wind-dried filthy moisture. Koto's eyes appeared to stare out of their sockets, whiter than before, surrounded by his dark, dusty skin.

It was midday, the sun, as always so close to the equator, directly above them, casting hard dark shadows under felled trees and burned undergrowth. Once in the forest again, the temperature plummeted but they were soaked by their perspiration, dehydrated by their exposure in the clearing. They stopped, sat next to each other on a log and pulled out a bottle of

284

water from a pack and the Marlboros. Within a minute, mosquitoes were gathering under their legs, searching for the soft skin behind their knees. Matt hardly noticed, days spent naked in the forest acclimatising him to the regular discomforts of biting insects. Now, with clothes, he had little concern.

Koto blew some smoke under his legs. "That'll keep them off" he remarked.

The next four hours were spent weaving their way between trees, picking up small paths and passing through small deserted logging camps. Ditches had been dug to transport logs to small tributaries and in some locations they found log ponds – collecting points for thousands of stolen trees representing, in some cases, a million dollars worth of timber to a trader. It seemed obvious to them that they were nearing the edge of the Park.

Then, without warning, the forest cover just stopped. The dampness of the forest gave way to hard baked soil sparsely covered by grass. Four hundred metres ahead of them they could see a line of palm trees but in front were row after row of black plastic bags full of soil with a small palm growing out of each.

They sat on the hard ground feeling the sun on their faces.

"Oil palm" explained Koto.

They finished their cigarettes before Matt asked the obvious question. "Are we near a village?"

But Koto shook his head and looked serious. "Not close. This will be owned by one of the big companies. We're still in the Park but this land has been logged and converted to an oil palm plantation. This is how many timber bosses launder their money. After raping the forest they plant these palms and sell the oil from their seeds. It's very big business."

They walked across the nursery area, down the rows of black plastic bags and entered the main plantation. It was easy walking, the area was devoid of undergrowth and the palms spaced evenly about four metres apart. Their thick green fronds pushed out of the ground into a lush explosion of growth, the sky broken by the dark green palm leaves neatly displaying symmetrical uniformity. And then another. Emerging from the forest, the plantation was as alien as the scorched earth they had witnessed hours earlier.

"Be careful" warned Koto. "It may look as if nothing else lives here, but I've heard these plantations are infested with rats and snakes. But not much else."

No one was around. They walked for twenty minutes before finding a small shelter, used by plantation workers during harvest. It was empty but they decided to stay. It would provide some protection for them through the night. Inside, a rattan mat lay on the ground, but nothing else. They ate, drank and smoked, while Koto told Matt what he knew about oil palm plantations.

Palm oil, extracted from the fruit of oil palms, is the biggest cash crop of Southeast Asia. Unlike tea and coffee, both well known to the main consumers in Europe and America, palm oil is used daily by most of the same western consumers without even realising. It is in food products, soap, cereal and bio-diesel. In fact, ironically, western politicians are focusing on vegetable oil such as palm oil, to counter the carbon emissions caused by petrol and diesel contributing to climate change. Yet here, virgin forest is being cut to make way for oil palms, increasing emissions.

"Most local workers are paid below the minimum wage, communities have lost their livelihoods with the destruction of the forest, and the criminal elite increase their profits and power" explained Koto as he picked leaches from between his toes. "In some parts of the world vital food crops are being replaced with bio-fuel crops, causing not just increased poverty, but starvation."

"Enough" Matt sighed. "Please. My world has already been turned inside out in Borneo. The forest stripped bare, the military threat and militant kidnappers with guns. Now you say that driving my car on bio-fuels causes starvation and fails to combat climate change. Let's just stick to normal things." He squashed a leach under his big toe on his left foot. "There. That's normal" he said, smiling at Koto, holding the parasite between his thumb and finger, his own blood oozing from the now familiar black smudge.

They slept under a sarong brought from the logging camp, both exhausted from the day. Before first light Matt started to shiver, waking Koto, who, lying alongside him could feel the heat from his friend. The fever came on faster and fiercer than the first, and by daylight Matt was shaking and holding his head which felt as if it was exploding.

Koto had found an irrigation pipe and traced it back to a tap in the dark. Soaking his t-shirt he tried desperately to cool Matt's forehead, but the shaking grew worse. He kept rushing out to get fresh cool water but each time he returned, Matt grabbed him and pulled him closer.

"Please don't leave me" he begged, his face soaked by the water but his eyes screwed up in pain. His headache surpassed anything he thought he could bear and the walls of the inside of the hut blurred and darkened as his blood temperature rose. Koto lay beside him placing his head against Matt's, wishing he could share the heat to relieve Matt's suffering.

"I must get more cold water."

Koto ran outside, his t-shirt in his hand, and bumped into a young, well dressed man, who was about to open the door.

Neither of them spoke but the man looked inside at Matt shaking under the sarong.

"Its malaria" explained Koto. "I'm just going to get water, please sit with him, he's very frightened."

Matt was becoming delirious and reaching out. The man gave him his hand. "Koto. Where's Koto?" asked Matt, realising with horror that he could not see anything but a hot black space. "Koto" he screamed.

The man replied in Indonesian.

When Koto returned he placed the cold, wet t-shirt on Matt's head and stroked his hair. "It's going to be alright."

"I can't see. Who is that man?" murmured Matt, adding "I missed you."

The man told Koto he would get help, leaving them alone. As soon as he was gone Koto lay down again beside his friend, holding him close, reassuring him that everything would be alright "as long as we stick together." The dark blindness frightened Matt to silence as his friend held his shivering body close and it was Koto who noticed the fever break when he felt Matt's sweat on his own face and chest as he pressed against him.

Neither of them heard the vehicle draw up outside and when three men came in through the door, they were in a close embrace on the rattan mat. They were helped up, led outside into a metallic green Mitsubishi Pajero 4x4 and driven four kilometres to a group of buildings. Koto became aware of a strange silence between the men and when he stepped out of the vehicle was surprised by the huge antennae and three parabolic dishes mounted high on a radio mast.

Then he became scared.

"Come this way" ordered one of the young men. When Koto did not move, two men came either side of him and led him into the closest building. Matt, hardly conscious, was helped by the third man through the door.

Inside, boxes of papers, computers and other equipment were stacked. It looked as if they were moving out. But one man sat at a table with a simple radio telephone.

"You were right to call" a voice crackled in Indonesian over a tinny sounding speaker. "Have you completed the clean up?"

"Affirmative. P7 in two days."

"And you're sure it's them?"

"Affirmative."

"Brother." The connection crackled to make his next words unintelligible.

"Again please."

"The sword" came an irritated reply. "You put me at great risk, brother. They must not be found. Wield the sword."

"We must get one of these" Mary Grady enthused as she lay back in the sunken Jacuzzi. "Come on, get in with me. It's romantic."

Colin Grady was not in a romantic mood. Tonight's charity event had the potential to wreck his marriage and his business – the time spent with Hazim and his spooky friends the day before had left him in no doubt about that.

The two young men with Hazim had freaked him out more than the psychopath son of Abdullah, and that was really saying something. The taller of the two, the one he had seen in Borneo, seemed supremely confident. A few comments he had made gave the impression he believed he could do anything he liked because nobody on earth had a right to judge him. "That's God's will" he and his more nervous side-kick had chanted at regular intervals. It was as if they need not take any responsibility for any of their actions.

The threats from Hazim had been real enough, but the cold-blooded comments from the twenty-something Muslim freak had left him stunned.

"Why do you want this fornicator's business?" he had asked, continuing before Hazim had a chance to answer "I would happily cut his balls off and send them to his poor wife with the video. I'll do it now for you, brother. If it is God's will."

"If it's God's will" his partner repeated.

"Or I could just slice his throat. Wield my sword."

"God's will."

Hazim had laughed, put an arm around Colin and shaken his head gently. "Colin knows what I want" he said quietly, turning his head to face him, smiling.

So upset by the video and threats, he had returned to the third floor apartment that morning to try and talk with Hazim. The tape of him with Michelle had to be destroyed, but when he stepped out of the lift he could see the door to the small hallway wide open. On closer inspection the entire space was empty: no sign of beds, sofas, or a flat screen television. It was as if his awful meeting with Hazim had never taken place.

289

"Come on Colin" shouted out Mary impatiently. "Try to get work out of your head for a moment and enjoy some time with me in this foam." He turned and saw her emerging from the Jacuzzi, her large breasts red from the heat, sagging under their weight, beckoning him to join her. He fought to rid his mind of an image of the beautiful siren, Michelle - her betrayal ridiculing his new sense of himself.

"Can't you see I'm not interested" he snapped. "You have no idea what I'm going through!"

Hurt and humiliated, Mary retreated to the foam, ensuring her body was completely covered by bubbles, newly ashamed of her nakedness. Colin had become arrogant and tetchy since they arrived in Singapore, showing no interest in her whatsoever. But he was not going to ruin her holiday; her mind turned to the charity gala and the new gown she had bought. *'If he's not interested, the dress may just attract someone who is"* she thought, recovering quickly from self doubt. Nothing was going to spoil her night.

*

"There you are Hazim" shouted out Abdullah's wife as she swept him up in her rush towards the atrium. "I'm so glad you came, your father will be so pleased. Now, don't just stand there. Introduce me to your friends."

The two young men had entered the hotel with Hazim, whisked from their limousine into the private inner sanctum of the hotel. Their large suitcases had been placed in a private dayroom on the ground floor behind the atrium waterfall. Dressed in chinos and tight Armani shirts, they each cut a convincing complement to Hazim's muscular style.

"Just two acquaintances to add some colour" he explained seriously. "Jo and Mo."

His stepmother looked the men up and down, grinning appreciatively. "Pleased to meet you both" she cooed, slightly too obviously, although she could have sworn the shorter of the two had touched himself as she spoke.

"Now, your father wants to see you in the penthouse" she instructed moving between Hazim and the others. "Why don't you leave your friends with me? I could do with some help with these American flags."

The bridges over the artificial streams had already been decorated with buntings made up of tiny stars and stripes but three full size flags lay on the floor.

"One of these must be hung between the date palms" she explained "and the other two will hang over the balcony of the fourth floor above the waterfall. Let's find someone who can do it for us, you don't want to get those shirts dirty."

*

Abdullah Aziz was watching television news on a huge plasma flat-screen in the west wing lounge. The sun was high, the cityscape hidden by white silk blinds providing plenty of natural light, only softer.

The Indonesian Chief of Police was holding a press conference in Jakarta, carried live with simultaneous translation on Singapore's twenty four hour news channel.

"He looks stressed" commented Abdullah to his son as he entered the room. "I must invite him to another golfing weekend when everything settles."

The news commentator was giving a background to the live statements. "Apparently the assassination attempt on the Minister of Forestry, Mohammed Probowo, was the second attempt on his life in the last few weeks. His driver was killed in an appalling car crash caused by a bullet in the front tyre of his official vehicle. Probowo was not in the car at the time." The commentator put her hand to her ear "we're going over to Jakarta, live."

The police chief in full uniform appeared on the screen. His flabby face wobbled as he spoke, his laughter lines extinguished many years earlier by his unsightly race for money. He was so clearly uncomfortable that it would have been credible to believe he had fired the bullets at the Minister himself. As Chief of Police, he was hugely feared, but rarely believed.

"Our investigations suggest the attempts on the Minister's life were orchestrated from abroad" he read from a pre-prepared statement. "This attack on a Republic of Indonesia cabinet member is part of a carefully organised plan by foreign forces to destabilise the democratically elected government."

He offered no evidence or explanation and walked briskly from the podium. The press shouted out questions, but he had gone.

"That's a hundred thousand dollars well spent" stated Abdullah Aziz calmly.

In an unexpected rush of pride Hazim nodded approval and sat next to his father, avoiding the white chair. "Impressive. The weasel came through."

"I'm not finished yet" noted Abdullah confidently shaking his son's hand. "I'm pleased you came, it is very important that we show the strength of our family at this time."

The two men exchanged family pleasantries as if to convince each other the conflict between them was an aberration. Family is family. But Abdullah sensed a shift. His secret visit to Jakarta had convinced him of the foolishness of trusting Hazim to run the Borneo timber business. Years of goodwill, contacts and nurturing political connections, had been destroyed by impatience and violence. Indonesia's elite held on to their power with money, corruption providing one shaky pillar, developed during dictator Suharto's era, on which Indonesia stood. But there were still limits and his son had arrogantly stepped over the mark with his public use of violence.

For his part, Hazim sensed the old businessman had regrouped and strategized his future without his input. This father-son routine was orchestrated as deliberately as the assassination attempt on Probowo. And just as that had failed, so this family solidarity was empty, but in classic counter strategy, he would play along.

"I would like to apologise for failing to secure the Vietnamese ships, father" Hazim bowed his head, suitably contrite. "I was wrong. We are up against political forces supported by the President."

Abdullah laid his hand on his son's, enjoying the apology, much more comfortable with his dominant role: this was going more easily than he had expected. Since his last meeting with his son, there had been a nagging fear they were too far apart, but this apology had been difficult for Hazim ...

"I don't really care about the ships" he offered in conciliation. "It's a huge financial loss, but in real terms only two or three per cent of this year's profit. I don't want us to fight over money." He stood and walked over to the bar. "I don't know about you, but I need a drink."

They stood together, glasses in hand, the television on mute, the silk blinds open, Singapore stretching out towards the horizon, father and son, playing each other ruthlessly.

"I want you to come to Singapore and work with me here" confided Abdullah at the appropriate moment. "I want you to learn the business with me by your side."

Hazim smiled warmly. "I see my home here, father."

Abdullah was surprised how easy and warm this discussion had been. Maybe his son genuinely recognised the errors of his ways. The charity event tonight now seemed bearable – a reminder to Singapore's social elite that this island city state was built by family entrepreneurs.

"Yes, this is *my* home" repeated Hazim, his emphasis more selfish than noticed by his father. "I see that now."

CHAPTER FORTY FIVE
Borneo

Thirty men stared at a clutch of buildings, looking at a green Pajero parked outside the largest wooden structure. They had come from all parts of the Province, representative of their Dayak communities. Their leader, proudly wearing a headdress of feathers with a clean Nike t-shirt was brandishing a deadly Dayak ceremonial *parang*, its half metre blade fashioned from iron, its wooden handle proudly carved and painted. He had watched his daughters dragged from his stilted house weeks earlier, been left for dead in the marsh under his hut, his wife screaming. His companions, a rag tag group of Dayak sons and fathers, some in traditional dress, others in t-shirts and shorts, were equally determined, angry and armed.

Over the last week since some of them had met in Pangkalan Bun, grieving the loss of Dayak brothers, they had pieced together information on Aziz's Islamic henchmen. A phone call from the town of Sampit had confirmed their target was hiding out in this baking hot oil palm plantation just inside Tanjung Puting National Park's eastern border, known locally as "satellite plantation" because of its sophisticated dishes and antennae.

There was no discussion, their spirits already joined by tradition, their adrenalin close to boiling.

Three ran across the large clearing, positioned themselves behind the main building, and waited. Two others climbed into the Pajero, smiling as they removed the keys from the ignition. Three groups of four men checked out the three other buildings: each of them empty.

The rest moved silently to the sides of the main building, their *parang* drawn.

Ready for revenge.

*

Matt and Koto had been ordered to remove their clothes and wrap sarongs around their bodies. Koto resisted but an AK47 was raised and pointed at his head. Once changed, the man who had found them struck him brutally with the handle of the Kalashnikov, causing him to fall unconscious to the floor, his head bleeding through a gash above his left ear. Matt, hardly able to move, his body exhausted from the malaria, fell next to him and shielded his friend's head with his hands, smearing the blood.

"Get this stuff into the car" ordered the radio operator, "we have to clear out of here." The two others opened the door and lifted a box each, kicking the door shut behind them.

"Once the room's clear you take them out" he ordered the man with the AK47. "Take them to the forest. There must be no trace."

In the corner of the room Matt, unable to understand the words but clear about their intentions, lay on the floor hugging Koto's broken body. His mind was sharpening, overcoming the fever, aware of the need for urgent action to save them both from these killers. "You can't escape the military" he mumbled in English, remembering the naval helicopter.

The two men looked over at his sad face, lying next to the bleeding Dayak, and laughed.

"Now the military is your friend?" the radio operator mocked in English. "I don't think so. You don't have enough money!"

"On their way" whispered Matt. "They'll catch up with you. Let us go."

"Too late, Englishman. Kiss your friend before you die, there will be no mercy for the depraved." He shook his head, looked at the door and back to the other man. "What is keeping those two?"

"Shall I go and see?"

"Take the Englishman, I'll drag the Dayak."

He grabbed Koto's feet, dragging him towards the door, a line of blood from his head staining the floor, while his companion pressed the Kalashnikov into Matt's back. "Up" he ordered.

"What's taking you two so long?" shouted the radio operator as he opened the door, turned and dragged Koto, moving backwards towards the Pajero.

There was no reply.

Lifting Matt, the last man placed his gun on the desk and peered towards the open door. At one moment, the radio operator was grimacing at the Dayak, flexing his muscles as he pulled Koto's dead weight across the baked earth, the next his torso seemed to fall in slow motion, highly oxygenated, backlit crimson blood spouting from his neck, his head tumbling towards the ground, the eyes failing to express the gravity of the moment. Behind him, two men came into view, each holding, recognisably, the head of one of his two other companions. In the eerie silence that preceded the slushy, blood spattering thump, as the radio operator's head hit the ground, he thought he could hear singing.

*

It had taken twenty fours hours for Probo to return to search for Mr Johnson and Mr Koto, but the army NBell 412 helicopters had been deployed in the capital Palangkaraya. A call to Bambang Santoso had secured three, with a full complement of Special Forces, to head towards the logging camp and then the oil palm plantation he had spoken to Debi about the day before her death.

Sam and Rita accompanied him and the pilot on the flight deck of the lead helicopter, ten highly trained soldiers with their kit behind. Each of the other two fighting machines contained a pilot and twelve soldiers. The government were unsure what to expect, but Probo had convinced Bambang there could be armed resistance.

The plantation had been at the back of his mind since talking with Debi weeks ago in Jakarta. His concern about the trained, violent *Laksar Jihad* fanatics providing some explanation for the independent power Aziz had gained in the area. The excessive telecommunications equipment and shareholding by an American intelligence official in one of his Singaporean companies were fairly strong evidence that the plantation was not just producing oil. Tracing Johnson and Koto's known whereabouts from kidnap to yesterday's logging camp; this plantation seemed to be their next port of call.

Rita stared down at the forest, quiet and pensive, thinking of Murkha and Koto, remembering their easy friendship. She missed them both so much. Now she had Sam, her strong Sumatran warrior, with his cropped hair and square jawed face, not out of place in this military helicopter packed with sweat and muscle. And guns. Except, of course, that Sam wept at injustice and was no armed soldier. He held her tight, always wanting to protect her.

Sam looked at her hopeful eyes, her beautiful face framed by her short silky dark hair. *How had he been so lucky to meet and fall in love with Rita?* He placed his hand on her lap, a gesture noticed by Probowo with a reassuring smile. For the Minister, young love was a powerful counter to the horror of the last few weeks.

They could see the logging camp ahead and their helicopter passed by, very low, giving them a fleeting glance of the blue canvas tents. No smoke. No fire. The second aircraft came in behind them, hovering over the clearing, whipping up dust from the ground as a rope was lowered from the side door. Three soldiers descended to the camp in seconds, hitting the ground running. They checked every tent, ran around the camp perimeter, kicked the ash in the fire, and consulted each other before reporting back through their helmet microphones that the camp was empty. Five minutes after their descent they were being winched back onto their helicopter and the NBell 412s were flying towards the plantation.

"Wow" shouted Sam, shaking his head in disbelief and admiration. "Did you see how fast they were?"

Probo and Rita both smiled.

They passed over a large deforested clearing, barren and dusty, a trail of churned earth flying behind them. Then more forest canopy before it was replaced by the monotonous rows of oil palms.

"This is it" announced the pilot. The helicopters lined up alongside each other and moved slowly forward. As soon as they saw the buildings, their two escorts separated, one flying beyond the clearing, the other slowing to a hover. The lead helicopter with the Minister lowered its rope and eight soldiers descended before it gained altitude, safely away from any possible danger, two soldiers remaining on board for protection.

From the lead helicopter, now hovering at five hundred meters, they could see the soldiers descending from the other two, and moving in on the clearing from all sides. Men rushed towards a green 4x4, others flanked each building before kicking in each door. Eight men stood outside the largest, surrounding something not far from the vehicle. Another group stood to attention around the 4x4.

"Secure, sir. You may descend."

Their helicopter gently lost altitude as they prepared to land at the edge of the large clearing in front of the buildings. Grabbing for cameras, Rita and Sam did not watch the ground as it reached up closer to their craft. So it was with ignorance, more than innocence that they stepped onto the warm dry soil of "satellite plantation." Probowo was already prepared, having read the message from the sky.

Four headless torsos lay near the main building, slashed with arbitrary relentless cuts. A soldier led the three civilians past the gory scene towards the Pajero. Inside, a human head had been placed on each of the four seats.

Rita gasped. "Their souls have been separated from their bodies. They are no longer." Sam and Probo turned to her for an explanation. "They're not Koto or Matt. It's Dayak revenge for the war on the forest and our spirits."

The soldier looked at Probo and nodded towards the clearing. Although better viewed from the air, the message was clear from where they now stood. Four letters, each three metres high, had been dug in the ground. Each filled with blood and severed limbs, no longer red from life, but blackening in death.

"Sir" called a soldier coming out of the main building. "I think you should see this."

They walked around the Pajero into the building. A line of blood was smeared across the floor from the back of the room to the door. Radio equipment was still connected on a desk.

"Over here sir" beckoned the soldier. "I think this fits your description."

In the corner, two pairs of shorts, one large and green, the other brightly coloured Hawaiian, had been discarded. A t-shirt, its arms ripped, drenched in pungent sweat lay nearby.

"They were here" confirmed Probo. "Mr Johnson and Mr Koto were definitely here."

Sam and Rita stood behind Probo, staring at the scene, piecing together the information when the radio phone started to ring. Sam stepped forward and pressed the lighted button. "Hello?"

There was a pause. Then an older voice spoke through the tinny speaker. "Brother?"

"Brother" repeated Sam.

"The sword. No trace. Are you finished?"

Three soldiers rushed in and took the phone from Sam. Two of them plugged miniature equipment into the receiver and set up a search before nodding at Sam eagerly.

"We are finished, brother."

"P7."

The soldiers were shaking their heads.

"What brother?" asked Sam.

The line went dead.

Outside, the army had already set up a tent for their command. Soldiers were photographing the scene, gathering together evidence and rummaging through boxes, connecting computers. The units chosen for this mission had been trained in telecommunications counter espionage. They moved effortlessly, cataloguing their gruesome findings, working efficiently through a chain of command.

"They're not here I'm afraid" said Probo to Rita and Sam. "I'm sorry you saw this. It's grotesque."

Rita smiled, her Dayak ancestry sensing some balance.

"I think we should return. The soldiers will resume a search from here. At least we know they were here. But, what happened, I don't know."

They walked slowly across the clearing to the helicopter. As they took off, looking down on the letters, the message of the ritual slaughter was clear. The four letters spelled out by sixteen severed limbs and dried, blackened human blood, took on an absolute clarity: "AZIZ".

CHAPTER FORTY SIX
Singapore

It was an important night for the *Regency*. Laser cannons were trained on the outside of the building, arching and dipping electric blue patterns on the upper floors. Besides looking stylish, it informed Singaporeans that tonight, the *Regency* was the place to be. The entrance was under the control of US Embassy security, only room for one car to pull up at a time, and only after it had been checked by a private security company, always hired by the Americans.

Within the security cordon, a full team of cheerleaders energetically, but silently, went through their prepared routine, each waving a coloured pompon: red, white and blue. Some of the regular staff, dressed in black suits and sunglasses, were themed to look like "Men in Black". At first, the Embassy representative had complained that it would confuse their own security, who suffered an uncanny resemblance to their movie counterparts, but when it became clear that the genuine Americans were all at least thirty centimetres taller, they relented.

The atrium was magnificent in its overstatement. The flags had been positioned so as to deny any guests the pretence of being in Singapore. A jazz band had been flown in from New Orleans and they played from an island stage in the pool with the waterfall as backdrop. The water, falling thirty metres, had been divided into three separate cascades for this special occasion, ecological dyes – so as to cause no harm to the valuable carp - coloured each red, white and blue. Waitresses, adorned in Donna Karen gowns, would move effortlessly among the guests, offering cocktails such as whisky sour, Manhattan, Tom Collins, and, in a small recognition to the city island state, Singapore Sling.

"Tonight" Abdullah's wife had insisted, "is for the Americans."

*

Unsure whether to attend the charity event, Colin Grady paced the balcony in his room on the twentieth floor. Mary had been in the bedroom getting ready for over an hour and he knew she would

300

find it difficult to forgive him if he backed out now. His reasoning was clouded by fear, but at good moments he realised that if he played along with Hazim he could be safe and rich. At other, perhaps more rational moments, he felt out of his depth. The truth was though, if he wanted to admit it, that without Aziz his business was finished. His current shipment would net him a small fortune and, if he could waylay his clients' fears, the next would set him up for comfortable retirement.

The bedroom door opened and Mary Grady walked boldly towards him. She was wearing a shapely turquoise dress, cut low, revealing more of her breasts than Colin had seen her display for years. Her hair was cut short, her eyes sparkling through matching turquoise contacts. But he saw, for the first time in months, the woman he had married *until death do us part*. He liked what he saw: the mother of his children, his confidant and friend. What had happened to them these last few months? The answer, he knew, was "Michelle" who he now knew to be a scheming bitch. How pathetic he had been.

"Wow!" he exclaimed as she shimmered past him, smiling confidently. "You look stunning." And he meant it.

"Oh? The business mogul has finally noticed his wife!" she teased kindly.

They embraced, although Mary warned him to be careful not to mess her up – it had taken a lot of time and money for her to look this good.

He poured an expensive bottle of *Bollinger RD 1996* he had kept on ice; they raised their glasses as he toasted "my gorgeous wife, our wonderful children and the fun we're going to have for years to come."

Mary, slightly taken aback by his romance, gently dabbed her eyes with the back of her hand "now look what you've made me do" she chided. "I'll have to go and tidy up before we go downstairs."

They looked at each other in a way they seemed to have lost and silently mouthed "love you" in the same way they used to across the living room, when their kids were preoccupied with television or their Nintendo.

The west wing lounge in the penthouse was for family only tonight. Abdullah, his wife and Hazim were all on their best behaviour. Hazim had even complemented his step mother on her organisation of the charity night. The American Ambassador's wife had called and confirmed that her husband was coming.

"Apparently, he said that if he avoided parties thrown by people accused of crimes by the media, he'd hardly go out!" she proudly recounted to the two men.

"I have to admit" congratulated Hazim "I never thought you would get him. You women certainly know how to control your husbands" he teased.

"That's enough of that" his father cut in. "I always knew he couldn't turn you down. Thank you for tonight my dear. We have a lot to learn from you" he said with admiration, smiling at Hazim, so happy they were being civilised to each other. "This charity gala puts the Aziz family back on the map in Singapore and we will all be safer because of it."

They could see their guests arriving on the huge flat screen television, CCTV beaming images of the entrance hall and the atrium, giving them the opportunity to perfectly judge the best moment for their entrance. Two famous Singaporean soap opera actors, dressed in tuxedos, walked through the security cordon smiling at the cameras, always at work. The head master from the American school stood by security with his wife, welcoming the guests. The roll call was impressive: chief executives of three foreign banks, two mining companies, every local television network, designers, artists, politicians, musicians and bureau chiefs from all the foreign media.

"Should we go down?" asked Abdullah.

"Yes, I think we should mingle a little before the Ambassador arrives" advised his wife.

"I'll join you in a minute" said Hazim, "I've got a couple of things to attend to. I promise I won't be long. I know this is important."

His father smiled appreciatively, believing that, at last, his son might be recognising the value of friends in business. Not enemies. It was a good start.

But of course he was wrong.

When they had gone, Hazim moved over to the window to look at the cityscape, its lights twinkling reliably. He took a sip from his glass before turning and surveying the room as he walked towards the bar where he cut a huge line of cocaine and expertly snorted it up a solid silver straw. Holding a finger over his right nostril, then his left, sniffing loudly to ensure there were no traces, he sauntered over to the white sofa. At first he sat on the comfortable leather, running his left hand over the texture, and then he lay back, feeling the coke rush, boosting his already extreme confidence.

Smiling widely, he laughed out loud.

*

At least three hundred people were already enjoying cocktails, picking at various hors d'oeuvres selected from the *Regency* restaurants. As Abdullah Aziz and his wife walked under the American flag, hanging between the date palms into the atrium, a pre-planned ripple of applause broke out, which escalated into a full-scale appreciative reception as guests put their hands together, despite most being unaware of why they were clapping. Abdullah was genuinely humbled by the spontaneity of the praise and his hand tightened its grip on his wife. She was less surprised, simply happy that everything was going so well.

It would have been difficult for the event to go badly with the A-list Singaporean guests and the venue. The atrium was designed for parties, its winding walkways, bridges, carved wooden benches and magnificent vegetation. The waterfall provided an extraordinary backdrop, the eco dyes plummeting into the pool, spotlights turning every coloured droplet into a magical sparkle. The jazz band presented the perfect mood for a charity event, raising the temperature enough for generosity and, when the saxophonist took the lead, giving the largely older audience a sexy feel: always good for extracting money.

The themed staff moved effortlessly among the guests, providing only the best, reinforcing the *Regency's* reputation for service. Cards were exchanged, opportunities opened and old acquaintances reunited. By the time the American Ambassador arrived the party was in full swing, only the band playing "the star spangled banner" diverting the guests' attention from their own networking.

Abdullah was ushered by his wife to the Ambassador who graciously thanked him for his kind invitation as cameras flashed to record the moment. Hazim appeared in a tuxedo alongside his step-mother and was introduced, first to the Ambassador and then to his wife. "It's a great honour to welcome you to the *Regency*" he stated, receiving a slightly disapproving glance from his father who thought it should have been his line.

Mary Grady was already feeling quite drunk. She had noticed a few men looking at her breasts, a recognition she had not experienced for years. Colin had put his work behind him tonight and seemed to be enjoying himself at last. The evening was everything she had hoped it would be; Colin's rekindled warmth, the best she could have dreamed for.

The music stopped, the chattering quietened as the Ambassador climbed onto a podium with a microphone. "Ladies and Gentlemen. I have been asked by our generous hosts to announce that our target for tonight has just been doubled because we've already raised half a million Singapore dollars." There was a collective gasp followed by applause. "So, please give generously to help make it a million."

"More money well spent" thought Aziz as he put an arm around his wife.

Colin and Mary approached Aziz to congratulate him on such a wonderful evening. The Ambassador's wife was introduced to them and they were soon hearing about the work of the American school. Hazim edged closer to Colin, glancing down at his watch.

"I need to talk to you urgently."

Despite his fear of Hazim, Colin had reconciled the idea of placing another order and pictures of this prestigious night would certainly help assuage the concerns of most of his clients. Besides, he considered this particular moment rather opportune. The

Ambassador's wife seemed to be working through the rather long history of the school and, if he had to talk to Hazim tonight, it might as well be now. He touched Mary's shoulder affectionately. "I'll be back in a minute darling." They moved off together passing the date palms where they saw the Ambassador talking with his chief of security in the hotel lobby.

Two men, one taller than the other, emerged from behind the waterfall dressed in rather large "Men in Black" suits. The taller of the two walked towards the date palms, out of sight of his companion, passed the Ambassador and out into the warm oppressive heat of equatorial Singapore. Colin saw him get into a taxi and drive away.

The other, believing his companion was headed for the Ambassador, unaware of his flight, walked over towards the Ambassador's wife who was still talking at her socially captive audience. Seeing an opportunity to break the flow, Abdullah's wife moved to introduce the approaching young man who seemed to be sweating rather profusely in a very badly fitting suit.

"My dear, I just must introduce you to this fine young friend of Hazim's. I'm sorry, is it Jo or Mo?" she asked feeling slightly embarrassed at the appalling appearance of this youth, now regretting her intervention.

The Ambassador's wife cut off from her monologue and broke into a practised smile, nodding at Abdullah Aziz, his wife and Mary Grady, holding her hand out to welcome the young man. He had started to shake.

"Are you alright, dear?" asked Mary Grady.

But to everyone's discomfort he failed to respond to both women, but instead put both his arms in the air, revealing unsightly underarm sweat marks, pressed a button and detonated the five kilogramme TNT bomb he had strapped around his waist.

CHAPTER FORTY SEVEN
Jakarta

The metal tree sculpture still welcomed visitors to the Ministry of Forestry, perhaps a little more proudly since Mohamed Probowo had taken on the timber baron in Central Kalimantan. Reports suggested that Tanjung Puting National Park had been better protected, logging camps dismantled and some illegal sawmills closed. Local residents had praised the government but asked for financial assistance to rebuild their community. In the absence of any tangible support so far, the praise had already started to turn to hostility and everyone knew, from experience, that it would take very little, maybe just the removal of the Minister, to signal the return of the loggers. In every directorate at least one senior official waited impatiently for the Minister to go and the money to flow into their bank account again.

The horrific death of Abdullah Aziz, his wife, the American Ambassador to Singapore's wife and thirteen other guests in the *Regency* hotel had sent shock waves through the Singaporean and Indonesian political establishments. Rumours were rife. Was this the actions of Islamic extremists or of the Indonesian Intelligence Agency? Singaporean investigators, aided by the Americans, had focused, at least publicly, on an unlikely conspiracy between the two. Imam Bakti, not seen since the day of the suicide bomb, was under suspicion. A meeting between the Imam and the Coordinating Minister for Politics and Security had been questioned in the media, implying his prior knowledge of the attack. Bambang Santoso had denied any involvement stating that the meeting had been an attempt to open dialogue with the Imam in the interests of the Indonesian people. His resignation weeks later "for family reasons" had, however, fuelled the speculation.

"I don't know what to think" explained Probo to Sam and Rita, sitting in his office in the Ministry. "I miss his support, but the media coverage of his meeting with the Imam has been very damaging to this government."

Sam and Rita had received enormous support for YHB since the tragic death of Debi and the internationally publicised Dayak beheadings of Islamic extremists holding Matt and Koto. Their experience that day, shared with Probo, followed by the news that same evening of the suicide bombing in Singapore, had brought them closer to the Minister.

"You know" confided Probo, "I haven't said this to anyone." He paused. "But that voice."

"On the radio telephone?" asked Sam.

"Yes. I can't help thinking it was Imam Bakti. I can feel it was him."

"But what was he talking about?" added Rita.

"Intelligence has come up with a theory" he replied "but they are keeping quiet since the revelations that Bambang Santoso had met with Bakti. They believe the reference to the sword is consistent with the Imam's promotion of violent jihad. And they have told me that the jihad training camps in Mindanao in the southern Philippines are known by numbers. They think P7 is Philippine camp 7."

"Wow!" gasped Sam, still amazed he was privy to such information.

"But, why they would target Abdullah Aziz is a mystery, except of course that he was hosting a charity event for the American school with the American Ambassador present."

"Surely that's not enough?" Rita questioned sensing there was more to this than Probo was telling.

"Well, there is another interesting but embarrassing fact emerging which confuses all these theories" he confided, trusting Sam and Rita as he had Debi. "It seems that at the meeting between Bambang Santoso and the Imam, Aziz's son was present."

They fell silent.

Rita was the first to change the subject. "We have decided to trust you, Minister, in the way that you have shown your trust in us. We have two pieces of information for you."

Probo looked at Rita warmly. How much she reminded him of the young Debi, bursting with courage. Then he smiled at her partner, Sam, looking less fierce since his hair had started to grow out. *"Rita's influence"* he thought.

"Koto and Matt are alive."

307

"I had decided not to ask" he replied. "But I thought so. Thank you. I look forward to welcoming them to my home when they are ready."

Sam looked at Rita who nodded gently. "We have information on factories in China processing logs illegally exported from West Papua" he said.

Papua

The city of Sorong, on the north western tip of West Papua, provided Hazim Aziz with a useful hide-out for the moment. He was happy to wait for his rightful inheritance, still held up by investigations into the events of that night when his father and step mother had been blown to pieces, their body parts making such a mess he had been forced to order the atrium closed for refurbishment.

Three thousand kilometres east of Jakarta, Sorong offered opportunities to anyone armed with money. The military were more in control in this backwater than in Borneo, so business was going well. Grady, despite the death of his wife, had been so scared he had come up with a large order of merbau timber flooring, just in time for Hazim's new flooring factory on the eastern Indonesian island of Flores to fulfil. Apparently, the Europeans still had an insatiable demand for cheap wood.

The sweeping harbour and wide horizon, popular for young lovers walking its length at sunset, were of little interest to Hazim and his tall young Islamic bodyguard. Inside one of the numerous "discos", a local euphemism for "brothel", they sat in the dark, fuelled by expensive malt whisky, bellowing orders to three naked girls.

"Shit" Hazim complained to the manager. "I told you I wanted *young* girls, not hags like these three."

"They're on their way, sir."

Half an hour later, if anyone had been watching, if anyone had cared, they would have seen two scared teenage girls led out under garish flashing coloured lights and pushed into the back of a metallic green Mitsubishi Pajero.

At first, life in a Dayak longhouse had been difficult for Matt. Twenty three families living in one very long wooden building failed to provide the privacy he felt he needed. Koto's home village was very traditional, the main longhouse where they lived at the centre, running along the river, fishponds and crops all around. A platform ran its length, providing outside access to each door. Each door represented a family.

When the Dayak warriors had recognised Koto and his *buleh* companion at "satellite plantation" they had immediately removed them from the macabre scene of the beheadings. Koto had regained consciousness and peered up at these Dayak men, their bodies taut, blood spattered testament to the ultimate Dayak revenge. He had reached over to Matt who was crouching over him, visibly trembling, unsure whether it was malaria fever or raw fear.

"These men are our friends" reassured Koto, certain of the horrors seen by Matt, despite being unconscious himself. The men around him were staring at Matt still holding their *parang,* each blade smeared with blood. "It is Dayak justice. The forest is fighting back."

The warriors had left Koto and Matt alone for a few minutes to reassure the Englishman he was no longer in danger. They had returned eager to leave the plantation, kindly offering them support to move on. Each of the warriors had passed through a spiritual moment of ruthless frenzy to unbridled, unexpected excitement in the rescue of Koto, their brother believed dead.

They had quietly walked out of the plantation to a small river where seven dug-out canoes were lined up on the muddy riverbank. As this small flotilla silently slipped into the water the men looked up into the sky without speaking. Not far away at "satellite plantation", the unmistakable sound of helicopter blades indicated that their revenge would soon be known by outsiders.

The lead canoe had separated from the others, guided by Koto to the larger Seruyan River, south to his mother's village. The two Dayak warriors dropped them off without speaking to the villagers, paddling back to their daily lives, sworn to secrecy. The

Dayak rescue and day of revenge would be talked about for generations, but the identity of the warriors would never be known.

Koto's mother took them in, nursing them both back to health. Koto's wounds had been superficial, easily healed by the care of his mother and sisters. Traditional malaria medicine had, at least for now, defeated the malaria parasites in Matt's blood.

Once the fevers subsided, and the children of the village stopped staring Matt was able to absorb the peaceful nature of living comfortably in the forest. The river provided the community with irrigation for their crops and water to drink and to bathe in. But its quality was deteriorating rapidly and already some children had fallen sick, blamed on pollution.

Around the village, ponds had been dug and filled with water from the river. Fish were bred, providing necessary protein and oils for the community. Growing high around the fishponds, crops of rattan provided material for furniture, baskets and blinds, hand-made by the community and sold to buyers who visited the village monthly.

"This is how my people survive" explained Koto, beaming with Dayak pride. "But the elders fear the expansion of the oil palm plantations will pollute the river even more than the loggers have in the last few years."

Matt felt such relief at their rescue, he was unsure if his joy was from this, or from being with Koto and his family. But when his friend suggested they continue to hide from the outside world a little longer, he understood that Koto was his source of happiness.

"I agree we should assess the risk of returning to our lives" echoed Matt.

Someone had tried to kill them and they did not know if that risk still existed. Dayaks returning from Sampit gave them news of the search and media interest. But it was still not clear.

At least that's what they told each other.

Koto contacted Skipper who arrived with Matt's camera, some film and huge apologies for "losing" them. He seemed so happy to have found them, smiling in a way neither of them would have believed he was capable of. He brought news of Abdullah Aziz's death and the Singapore bomb attack. They asked him to inform

Sam and Rita they were alive, but beyond that their survival was a secret.

"I think you should contact your family" advised Koto.

A week after his recovery from malaria, Matt was taken by canoe to a point on the river where a mobile phone signal was strong. Using an elder's phone he called his mother, listened to her emotional response, and begged her to keep his survival a secret. "Lives depend on it, mum" he pleaded.

She honoured his wishes and although he felt bad for his friends and family in the UK, he believed his temporary disappearance and planned reappearance would, in the long run, protect Koto.

He moved easily through the village day and night, given a unique opportunity to photograph other villagers.

Matt found the sociable, tactile nature of the community extraordinary and unbelievably welcoming. The first night, after the fever had left his body, he removed his t-shirt and stretched out on a hard large floor mat under a thin blanket. He listened to Koto talking with his mother, animatedly exchanging words he could not understand, but leaving respectful space between each others' responses. He heard them caring for each other without needing to understand the words. Then Koto left his mother and walked around the flimsy rattan partition to where he laid.

He pulled his t-shirt over his head, shook his long, jet black hair as the garment fell to the floor, as if he had been freed from its shackles. He breathed in very deeply, expanded his bare chest and looked down at Matt's blue eyes staring up. Then he removed his shorts as deliberately as anyone had ever stripped before and joined Matt under the blanket.

Together they were strong.